EVERYMAN,

I WILL GO WITH THEE,

AND BE THY GUIDE,

IN THY MOST NEED

TO GO BY THY SIDE

SAKI

SELECTED
STORIES

EDITED BY DIANA SECKER TESDELL

EVERYMAN'S POCKET CLASSICS
Alfred A. Knopf New York London Toronto

THIS IS A BORZOI BOOK
PUBLISHED BY ALFRED A. KNOPF

This selection by Diana Secker Tesdell first published in
Everyman's Library, 2017
Copyright © 2017 by Everyman's Library

www.randomhouse.com/everymans
www.everymanslibrary.co.uk

ISBN: 978-1-101-90794-8 (US)
978-1-84159-624-2 (UK)

A CIP catalogue reference for this book is available from the
British Library

Library of Congress Cataloging-in-Publication Data

Names: Saki, 1870–1916, author.
Title: Selected stories / Saki.
Description: New York: Everyman's Library, [2017] | Series:
Everyman's Library pocket classics
Identifiers: LCCN 2017016820 | ISBN 9781101907948 (hardcover: acid-
free paper)
Subjects: | BISAC: FICTION / Humorous. | FICTION / Short Stories
(single author). | FICTION / Classics.
Classification: LCC PR6025.U675 A6 2017 | DDC 823/.914–dc23
LC record available at https://lccn.loc.gov/2017016820

Typography by Peter B. Willberg

Typeset in the UK by Input Data Services Ltd, Somerset

Printed and bound in Germany by GGP Media GmbH, Pössneck

Contents

FROM

REGINALD (1904)

Reginald's Choir Treat

'NEVER,' WROTE REGINALD to his most darling friend, 'be a pioneer. It's the Early Christian that gets the fattest lion.'

Reginald, in his way, was a pioneer.

None of the rest of his family had anything approaching Titian hair or a sense of humour, and they used primroses as a table decoration.

It follows that they never understood Reginald, who came down late to breakfast, and nibbled toast, and said disrespectful things about the universe. The family ate porridge, and believed in everything, even the weather forecast.

Therefore the family was relieved when the vicar's daughter undertook the reformation of Reginald. Her name was Amabel; it was the vicar's one extravagance. Amabel was accounted a beauty and intellectually gifted; she never played tennis, and was reputed to have read Maeterlinck's *Life of the Bee*. If you abstain from tennis *and* read Maeterlinck in a small country village, you are of necessity intellectual. Also she had been twice to Fécamp to pick up a good French accent from the Americans staying there; consequently she had a knowledge of the world which might be considered useful in dealings with a worldling.

Hence the congratulations in the family when Amabel undertook the reformation of its wayward member.

Amabel commenced operations by asking her unsuspecting pupil to tea in the vicarage garden; she believed in the healthy influence of natural surroundings, never having been in Sicily, where things are different.

And like every woman who has ever preached repentance to unregenerate youth, she dwelt on the sin of an empty life, which always seems so much more scandalous in the country, where people rise early to see if a new strawberry has happened during the night.

Reginald recalled the lilies of the field, 'which simply sat and looked beautiful, and defied competition'.

'But that is not an example for us to follow,' gasped Amabel.

'Unfortunately, we can't afford to. You don't know what a world of trouble I take in trying to rival the lilies in their artistic simplicity.'

'You are really indecently vain of your appearance. A good life is infinitely preferable to good looks.'

'You agree with me that the two are incompatible. I always say beauty is only sin deep.'

Amabel began to realize that the battle is not always to the strong-minded. With the immemorial resource of her sex, she abandoned the frontal attack and laid stress on her unassisted labours in parish work, her mental loneliness, her discouragements – and at the right moment she produced strawberries and cream. Reginald was obviously affected by the latter, and when his preceptress suggested that he might begin the strenuous life by helping her to supervise the annual outing of the bucolic infants who composed the local choir, his eyes shone with the dangerous enthusiasm of a convert.

Reginald entered on the strenuous life alone, as far as Amabel was concerned. The most virtuous women are not proof against damp grass, and Amabel kept her bed with a cold. Reginald called it a dispensation; it had been the dream of his life to stage-manage a choir outing. With strategic insight, he led his shy, bullet-headed charges to the nearest woodland stream and allowed them to bathe; then he seated himself on their discarded garments and discoursed on their immediate future, which, he decreed, was to embrace a Bacchanalian procession through the village. Forethought had provided the occasion with a supply of tin whistles, but the introduction of a he-goat from a neighbouring orchard was a brilliant afterthought. Properly, Reginald explained, there should have been an outfit of panther skins; as it was, those who had spotted handkerchiefs were allowed to wear them, which they did with thankfulness. Reginald recognized the impossibility, in the time at his disposal, of teaching his shivering neophytes a chant in honour of Bacchus, so he started them off with a more familiar, if less appropriate, temperance hymn. After all, he said, it is the spirit of the thing that counts. Following the etiquette of dramatic authors on first nights, he remained discreetly in the background while the procession, with extreme diffidence and the goat, wound its way lugubriously towards the village. The singing had died down long before the main street was reached, but the miserable wailing of pipes brought the inhabitants to their doors. Reginald said he had seen something like it in pictures; the villagers had seen nothing like it in their lives, and remarked as much freely.

Reginald's family never forgave him. They had no sense of humour.

Reginald on Besetting Sins

THERE WAS ONCE (said Reginald) a woman who told the truth. Not all at once, of course, but the habit grew upon her gradually, like lichen on an apparently healthy tree. She had no children – otherwise it might have been different. It began with little things, for no particular reason except that her life was a rather empty one, and it is so easy to slip into the habit of telling the truth in little matters. And then it became difficult to draw the line at more important things, until at last she took to telling the truth about her age; she said she was forty-two and five months – by that time, you see, she was veracious even to months. It may have been pleasing to the angels, but her elder sister was not gratified. On the Woman's birthday, instead of the opera-tickets which she had hoped for, her sister gave her a view of Jerusalem from the Mount of Olives, which is not quite the same thing. The revenge of an elder sister may be long in coming, but, like a South-Eastern express, it arrives in its own good time.

The friends of the Woman tried to dissuade her from over-indulgence in the practice, but she said she was wedded to the truth; whereupon it was remarked that it was scarcely logical to be so much together in public. (No really provident woman lunches regularly with her husband if she wishes to burst upon him as a revelation at dinner. He must have time to forget; an afternoon is not enough.) And after a while her friends began to thin out in patches. Her passion for the truth was not compatible with a large visiting-list. For instance, she told Miriam

Klopstock *exactly* how she looked at the Ilexes' ball. Certainly Miriam had asked for her candid opinion, but the Woman prayed in church every Sunday for peace in our time, and it was not consistent.

It was unfortunate, every one agreed, that she had no family; with a child or two in the house, there is an unconscious check upon too free an indulgence in the truth. Children are given us to discourage our better emotions. That is why the stage, with all its efforts, can never be as artificial as life; even in an Ibsen drama one must reveal to the audience things that one would suppress before the children or servants.

Fate may have ordained the truth-telling from the commencement and should justly bear some of the blame; but in having no children the Woman was guilty, at least, of contributory negligence.

Little by little she felt she was becoming a slave to what had once been merely an idle propensity; and one day she knew. Every woman tells ninety per cent of the truth to her dressmaker; the other ten per cent is the irreducible minimum of deception beyond which no self-respecting client trespasses. Madame Draga's establishment was a meeting-ground for naked truths and overdressed fictions, and it was here, the Woman felt, that she might make a final effort to recall the artless mendacity of past days. Madame herself was in an inspiring mood, with the air of a sphinx who knew all things and preferred to forget most of them. As a War Minister she might have been celebrated, but she was content to be merely rich.

'If I take it in here, and – Miss Howard, one moment, if you please – and there, and round like this – so – I really think you will find it quite easy.'

The Woman hesitated; it seemed to require such a small

effort to simply acquiesce in Madame's views. But habit had become too strong. 'I'm afraid,' she faltered, 'it's just the least little bit in the world too –'

And by that least little bit she measured the deeps and eternities of her thraldom to fact. Madame was not best pleased at being contradicted on a professional matter, and when Madame lost her temper you usually found it afterwards in the bill.

And at last the dreadful thing came, as the Woman had foreseen all along that it must; it was one of those paltry little truths with which she harried her waking hours. On a raw Wednesday morning, in a few ill-chosen words, she told the cook that she drank. She remembered the scene afterwards as vividly as though it had been painted in her mind by Abbey. The cook was a good cook, as cooks go; and as cooks go she went.

Miriam Klopstock came to lunch the next day. Women and elephants never forget an injury.

Reginald's Christmas Revel

THEY SAY (SAID REGINALD) that there's nothing sadder than victory except defeat. If you've ever stayed with dull people during what is alleged to be the festive season, you can probably revise that saying. I shall never forget putting in a Christmas at the Babwolds'. Mrs Babwold is some relation of my father's – a sort of to-be-left-till-called-for cousin – and that was considered sufficient reason for my having to accept her invitation at about the sixth time of asking; though why the sins of the father should be visited by the children – you won't find any notepaper in that drawer; that's where I keep old menus and first-night programmes.

Mrs Babwold wears a rather solemn personality, and has never been known to smile, even when saying disagreeable things to her friends or making out the Stores list. She takes her pleasures sadly. A state elephant at a Durbar gives one a very similar impression. Her husband gardens in all weathers. When a man goes out in the pouring rain to brush caterpillars off rose trees, I generally imagine his life indoors leaves something to be desired; anyway, it must be very unsettling for the caterpillars.

Of course there were other people there. There was a Major Somebody who had shot things in Lapland, or somewhere of that sort; I forget what they were, but it wasn't for want of reminding. We had them cold with every meal almost, and he was continually giving us details of what they measured from tip to tip, as though he thought we were going to make them warm under-things for the winter. I used to listen to him with a rapt attention that I thought rather suited me, and then one day I quite modestly gave the dimensions of an okapi I had shot in the Lincolnshire fens. The Major turned a beautiful Tyrian scarlet (I remember thinking at the time that I should like my bathroom hung in that colour), and I think that at that moment he almost found it in his heart to dislike me. Mrs Babwold put on a first-aid-to-the-injured expression, and asked him why he didn't publish a book of his sporting reminiscences; it would be *so* interesting. She didn't remember till afterwards that he had given her two fat volumes on the subject, with his portrait and autograph as a frontispiece and an appendix on the habits of the Arctic mussel.

It was in the evening that we cast aside the cares and distractions of the day and really lived. Cards were thought to be too frivolous and empty a way of passing the time, so most of them played what they called a book game. You went out into the hall – to get an inspiration, I suppose – then you came in again with a muffler tied round your neck and looked silly, and the others were supposed to guess that you were *Wee MacGreegor.* I held out against the inanity as long as I decently could, but at last, in a lapse of good-nature, I consented to masquerade as a book, only I warned them that it would take some time to carry out. They waited for the best part of forty minutes while I went and played wineglass skittles with the pageboy in the pantry; you play it with a champagne cork, you know, and the one who knocks down the most glasses without breaking them wins. I won, with four unbroken out of seven; I think William suffered from over-anxiousness. They were rather mad in the drawing-room at my not having come back, and they weren't a bit pacified when I told them afterwards that I was *At the end of the passage.*

'I never did like Kipling,' was Mrs Babwold's comment, when the situation dawned upon her. 'I couldn't see anything clever in *Earthworms out of Tuscany* – or is that by Darwin?'

Of course these games are very educational, but, personally, I prefer bridge.

On Christmas evening we were supposed to be specially festive in the Old English fashion. The hall was horribly draughty, but it seemed to be the proper place to revel in, and it was decorated with Japanese fans and Chinese lanterns, which gave it a very Old English effect. A young lady with a confidential voice favoured us with a long recitation about a little girl who died or did something equally hackneyed, and then the Major gave us a graphic account of a struggle he had with a wounded bear. I privately wished that the bears would win sometimes on these occasions; at least they wouldn't go vapouring about it afterwards. Before we had time to recover our spirits, we were indulged with some thought-reading by a young man whom one knew instinctively had a good mother and an indifferent tailor – the sort of young man who talks unflaggingly through the thickest soup, and smooths his hair dubiously as though he thought it might hit back. The thought-reading was rather a success; he announced that the hostess was thinking about poetry, and she admitted that her mind was dwelling on one of Austin's odes. Which was near enough. I fancy she had been really wondering whether a scrag-end of mutton and some cold plum-pudding would do for the kitchen dinner next day. As a crowning dissipation, they all sat down to play progressive halma, with milk-chocolate for prizes. I've been carefully brought up, and I don't like to play games of skill for milk-chocolate, so I invented a headache and retired from the scene. I had been preceded a few minutes earlier by Miss Langshan-Smith, a rather formidable lady, who always got up at some uncomfortable hour in the morning, and gave you the impression that she had been in communication with most of the European Governments before breakfast. There was a paper pinned on her door with a signed request that she might be called particularly early on the morrow. Such an opportunity does not come twice in a lifetime. I covered up everything except the signature with another notice, to the effect that before these words should meet the eye she would have ended a misspent life, was sorry for the trouble she was giving, and would like a military funeral. A few minutes later I violently exploded an air-filled paper bag on the landing, and gave a stage moan that could have been heard in the cellars. Then I pursued my original intention and went to bed. The noise those people made in forcing open the good lady's door was positively indecorous; she resisted gallantly, but I believe they searched her for bullets for about a quarter of an hour, as if she had been a historic battlefield.

I hate travelling on Boxing Day, but one must occasionally do things that one dislikes.

FROM

REGINALD IN
RUSSIA (1910)

The Reticence of Lady Anne

EGBERT CAME INTO the large, dimly lit drawing-room with the air of a man who is not certain whether he is entering a dovecote or a bomb factory, and is prepared for either eventuality. The little domestic quarrel over the luncheon-table had not been fought to a definite finish, and the question was how far Lady Anne was in a mood to renew or forgo hostilities. Her pose in the arm-chair by the tea-table was rather elaborately rigid; in the gloom of a December afternoon Egbert's pince-nez did not materially help him to discern the expression of her face.

By way of breaking whatever ice might be floating on the surface he made a remark about a dim religious light. He or Lady Anne were accustomed to make that remark between 4.30 and 6 on winter and late autumn evenings; it was a part of their married life. There was no recognized rejoinder to it, and Lady Anne made none.

Don Tarquinio lay astretch on the Persian rug, basking in the firelight with superb indifference to the possible ill-humour of Lady Anne. His pedigree was as flawlessly Persian as the rug, and his ruff was coming into the glory of its second winter. The page-boy, who had Renaissance tendencies, had christened him Don Tarquinio. Left to themselves, Egbert and Lady Anne would unfailingly have called him Fluff, but they were not obstinate.

Egbert poured himself out some tea. As the silence gave no sign of breaking on Lady Anne's initiative, he braced himself for another Yermak effort.

'My remark at lunch had a purely academic application,' he announced; 'you seem to put an unnecessarily personal significance into it.'

Lady Anne maintained her defensive barrier of silence. The bullfinch lazily filled in the interval with an air from *Iphigénie en Tauride*. Egbert recognized it immediately, because it was the only air the bullfinch whistled, and he had come to them with the reputation for whistling it. Both Egbert and Lady Anne would have preferred something from *The Yeoman of the Guard*, which was their favourite opera. In matters artistic they had a similarity of taste. They leaned towards the honest and explicit in art, a picture, for instance, that told its own story, with generous assistance from its title. A riderless warhorse with harness in obvious disarray, staggering into a courtyard full of pale swooning women, and marginally noted 'Bad News', suggested to their minds a distinct interpretation of some military catastrophe. They could see what it was meant to convey, and explain it to friends of duller intelligence.

The silence continued. As a rule Lady Anne's displeasure became articulate and markedly voluble after four minutes of introductory muteness. Egbert seized the milk-jug and poured some of its contents into Don Tarquinio's saucer; as the saucer was already full to the brim an unsightly overflow was the result. Don Tarquinio looked on with a surprised interest that evanesced into elaborate unconsciousness when he was appealed to by Egbert to come and drink up some of the spilt matter. Don Tarquinio was prepared to play many rôles in life, but a vacuum carpet-cleaner was not one of them.

'Don't you think we're being rather foolish?' said Egbert cheerfully.

If Lady Anne thought so she didn't say so.

'I daresay the fault has been partly on my side,' continued Egbert, with evaporating cheerfulness. 'After all,

I'm only human, you know. You seem to forget that I'm only human.'

He insisted on the point, as if there had been unfounded suggestions that he was built on Satyr lines, with goat continuations where the human left off.

The bullfinch recommenced its air from *Iphigénie en Tauride*. Egbert began to feel depressed. Lady Anne was not drinking her tea. Perhaps she was feeling unwell. But when Lady Anne felt unwell she was not wont to be reticent on the subject. 'No one knows what I suffer from indigestion' was one of her favourite statements; but the lack of knowledge can only have been caused by defective listening; the amount of information available on the subject would have supplied material for a monograph.

Evidently Lady Anne was not feeling unwell.

Egbert began to think he was being unreasonably dealt with; naturally he began to make concessions.

'I daresay,' he observed, taking as central a position on the hearth-rug as Don Tarquinio could be persuaded to concede him, 'I may have been to blame. I am willing, if I can thereby restore things to a happier standpoint, to undertake to lead a better life.'

He wondered vaguely how it would be possible. Temptations came to him, in middle age, tentatively and without insistence, like a neglected butcher-boy who asks for a Christmas box in February for no more hopeful reason than that he didn't get one in December. He had no more idea of succumbing to them than he had of purchasing the fish-knives and fur boas that ladies are impelled to sacrifice through the medium of advertisement columns during twelve months of the year. Still, there was something impressive in this unasked-for renunciation of possibly latent enormities.

25

Lady Anne showed no sign of being impressed.

Egbert looked at her nervously through his glasses. To get the worst of an argument with her was no new experience. To get the worst of a monologue was a humiliating novelty.

'I shall go and dress for dinner,' he announced in a voice into which he intended some shade of sternness to creep.

At the door a final access of weakness impelled him to make a further appeal.

'Aren't we being very silly?'

'A fool,' was Don Tarquinio's mental comment as the door closed on Egbert's retreat. Then he lifted his velvet forepaws in the air and leapt lightly on to a bookshelf immediately under the bullfinch's cage. It was the first time he had seemed to notice the bird's existence, but he was carrying out a long-formed theory of action with the precision of mature deliberation. The bullfinch, who had fancied himself something of a despot, depressed himself of a sudden into a third of his normal displacement; then he fell to a helpless wing-beating and shrill cheeping. He had cost twenty-seven shillings without the cage, but Lady Anne made no sign of interfering. She had been dead for two hours.

The Lost Sanjak

THE PRISON CHAPLAIN entered the condemned's cell for the last time, to give such consolation as he might.

'The only consolation I crave for,' said the condemned, 'is to tell my story in its entirety to some one who will at least give it a respectful hearing.'

'We must not be too long over it,' said the Chaplain, looking at his watch.

The condemned repressed a shiver and commenced.

'Most people will be of opinion that I am paying the penalty of my own violent deeds. In reality I am a victim to a lack of specialization in my education and character.'

'Lack of specialization!' said the Chaplain.

'Yes. If I had been known as one of the few men in England familiar with the fauna of the Outer Hebrides, or able to repeat stanzas of Camoëns' poetry in the original, I should have had no difficulty in proving my identity in the crisis when my identity became a matter of life and death for me. But my education was merely a moderately good one, and my temperament was of the general order that avoids specialization. I know a little in a general way about gardening and history and old masters, but I could never tell you off-hand whether "Stella van der Loopen" was a chrysanthemum or a heroine of the American War of Independence, or something by Romney in the Louvre.'

The Chaplain shifted uneasily in his seat. Now that the alternatives had been suggested they all seemed dreadfully possible.

'I fell in love, or thought I did, with the local doctor's

27

wife,' continued the condemned. 'Why I should have done so, I cannot say, for I do not remember that she possessed any particular attractions of mind or body. On looking back at past events it seems to me that she must have been distinctly ordinary, but I suppose the doctor had fallen in love with her once, and what man has done man can do. She appeared to be pleased with the attentions which I paid her, and to that extent I suppose I might say she encouraged me, but I think she was honestly unaware that I meant anything more than a little neighbourly interest. When one is face to face with Death one wishes to be just.'

The Chaplain murmured approval. 'At any rate, she was genuinely horrified when I took advantage of the doctor's absence one evening to declare what I believed to be my passion. She begged me to pass out of her life and I could scarcely do otherwise than agree, though I hadn't the dimmest idea of how it was to be done. In novels and plays I knew it was a regular occurrence, and if you mistook a lady's sentiments or intentions you went off to India and did things on the frontier as a matter of course. As I stumbled along the doctor's carriage-drive I had no very clear idea as to what my line of action was to be, but I had a vague feeling that I must look at the *Times* Atlas before going to bed. Then, on the dark and lonely highway, I came suddenly on a dead body.'

The Chaplain's interest in the story visibly quickened.

'Judging by the clothes it wore the corpse was that of a Salvation Army captain. Some shocking accident seemed to have struck him down, and the head was crushed and battered out of all human semblance. Probably, I thought, a motor-car fatality; and then, with a sudden overmastering insistence, came another thought, that here was a remarkable opportunity for losing my identity and passing out of the life of the doctor's wife for ever. No tiresome and risky voyage to distant lands, but a mere exchange of clothes and identity with the unknown victim of an unwitnessed accident. With considerable difficulty I undressed the corpse, and clothed it anew in my own garments. Any one who has valeted a dead Salvation Army captain in an uncertain light will appreciate the difficulty. With the idea, presumably, of inducing the doctor's wife to leave her husband's roof-tree for some habitation which would be run at my expense, I had crammed my pockets with a store of banknotes, which represented a good deal of my immediate worldly wealth. When, therefore, I stole away into the world in the guise of a nameless Salvationist, I was not without resources which would easily support so humble a rôle for a considerable period. I tramped to a neighbouring market-town, and, late as the hour was, the production of a few shillings procured me supper and a night's lodging in a cheap coffee-house. The next day I started forth on an aimless course of wandering from one small town to another. I was already somewhat digusted with the upshot of my sudden freak; in a few hours' time I was considerably more so. In the contents-bill of a local news sheet I read the announcement of my own murder at the hands of some person unknown; on buying a copy of the paper for a detailed account of the tragedy, which at first had aroused in me a certain grim amusement, I found that the deed was ascribed to a wandering Salvationist of doubtful antecedents, who had been seen lurking in the roadway near the scene of the crime. I was no longer amused. The matter promised to be embarrassing. What I had mistaken for a motor accident was evidently a case of savage assault and murder, and, until the real culprit was found, I should have much difficulty in explaining my intrusion into the affair. Of course I could establish my own identity; but how, without disagreeably involving the doctor's wife, could I give any adequate reason for changing clothes with the murdered man? While my brain worked feverishly at this problem, I subconsciously obeyed a secondary instinct – to get as far away as possible from the scene of the crime, and to get rid at all costs of my incriminating uniform. There I found a difficulty. I tried two or three obscure clothes shops, but my entrance invariably aroused an attitude of hostile suspicion in the proprietors, and on one excuse or another they avoided serving me with the now ardently desired change of clothing. The uniform that I had so thoughtlessly donned seemed as difficult to get out of as the fatal shirt of – You know, I forget the creature's name.'

'Yes, yes,' said the Chaplain hurriedly. 'Go on with your story.'

'Somehow, until I could get out of those compromising garments, I felt it would not be safe to surrender myself to the police. The thing that puzzled me was why no attempt was made to arrest me, since there was no question as to the suspicion which followed me, like an inseparable shadow, wherever I went. Stares, nudgings, whisperings, and even loud-spoken remarks of "that's 'im" greeted my every appearance, and the meanest and most deserted eating-house that I patronized soon became filled with a crowd of furtively watching customers. I began to sympathize with the feelings of Royal personages trying to do a little private shopping under the unsparing scrutiny of an irrepressible public. And still, with all this inarticulate shadowing, which weighed on my nerves almost worse than open hostility would have done, no attempt was made to interfere with my liberty. Later on I discovered the reason. At the time of the murder on the lonely highway a series of important bloodhound trials had been taking place in the near neighbourhood, and some dozen and a half couples of trained animals had been put on the track of the supposed murderer – on my track. One of our most public-spirited London dailies had offered a princely prize to the owner of the pair that should first track me down, and betting on the chances of the respective competitors became rife throughout the land. The dogs ranged far and wide over about thirteen counties, and though my own movements had become by this time perfectly well known to police and public alike, the sporting instincts of the nation stepped in to prevent my premature arrest. "Give the dogs a chance," was the prevailing sentiment, whenever some ambitious local constable wished to put an end to my drawn-out evasion of justice. My final capture by the winning pair was not a very dramatic episode, in fact, I'm not sure that they would have taken any notice of me if I hadn't spoken to them and patted them, but the event gave rise to an extraordinary amount of partisan excitement. The owner of the pair who were next nearest up at the finish was an American, and he lodged a protest on the ground that an otterhound had married into the family of the winning pair six generations ago, and that the prize had been offered to the first pair of bloodhounds to capture the murderer, and that a dog that had one sixty-fourth part of otterhound blood in it couldn't technically be considered a bloodhound. I forget how the matter was ultimately settled, but it aroused a tremendous amount of acrimonious discussion on both sides of the Atlantic. My own contribution to the controversy consisted in pointing out that the whole dispute was beside the mark, as the actual murderer had not yet been captured; but I soon discovered that on this point there was not the least divergence of public or expert opinion. I had looked forward apprehensively to the proving of my identity and the establishment of my motives as a disagreeable necessity; I speedily found out that the most disagreeable part of the business was that it couldn't be done. When I saw in the glass the haggard and hunted expression which the experiences of the past few weeks had stamped on my erstwhile placid countenance, I could scarcely feel surprised that the few friends and relations I possessed refused to recognize me in my altered guise, and persisted in their obstinate but widely shared belief that it was I who had been done to death on the highway. To make matters worse, infinitely worse, an aunt of the really murdered man, an appalling female of an obviously low order of intelligence, identified me as her nephew, and gave the authorities a lurid account of my depraved youth and of her laudable but unavailing efforts to spank me into a better way. I believe it was even proposed to search me for finger-prints.'

'But,' said the Chaplain, 'surely your educational attainments –'

'That was just the crucial point,' said the condemned; 'that was where my lack of specialization told so fatally against me. The dead Salvationist, whose identity I had so lightly and so disastrously adopted, had possessed a veneer of cheap modern education. It should have been easy to demonstrate that my learning was on altogether another plane to his, but in my nervousness I bungled miserably over test after test that was put to me. The little French I had ever known deserted me; I could not render a simple phrase about the gooseberry of the gardener into

32

that language, because I had forgotten the French for gooseberry.'

The Chaplain again wriggled uneasily in his seat. 'And then,' resumed the condemned, 'came the final discomfiture. In our village we had a modest little debating club, and I remembered having promised, chiefly, I suppose, to please and impress the doctor's wife, to give a sketchy kind of lecture on the Balkan Crisis. I had relied on being able to get up my facts from one or two standard works, and the back-numbers of certain periodicals. The prosecution had made a careful note of the circumstance that the man whom I claimed to be – and actually was – had posed locally as some sort of second-hand authority on Balkan affairs, and, in the midst of a string of questions on indifferent topics, the examining counsel asked me with a diabolical suddenness if I could tell the Court the whereabouts of Novibazar. I felt the question to be a crucial one; something told me that the answer was St Petersburg or Baker Street. I hesitated, looked helplessly round at the sea of tensely expectant faces, pulled myself together, and chose Baker Street. And then I knew that everything was lost. The prosecution had no difficulty in demonstrating that an individual, even moderately versed in the affairs of the Near East, could never have so unceremoniously dislocated Novibazar from its accustomed corner of the map. It was an answer which the Salvation Army captain might conceivably have made – and I had made it. The circumstantial evidence connecting the Salvationist with the crime was overwhelmingly convincing, and I had inextricably identified myself with the Salvationist. And thus it comes to pass that in ten minutes' time I shall be hanged by the neck until I am dead in expiation of the murder of myself, which murder never took place, and of which, in any case, I am necessarily innocent.'

When the Chaplain returned to his quarters, some fifteen minutes later, the black flag was floating over the prison tower. Breakfast was waiting for him in the dining-room, but he first passed into his library, and, taking up the *Times* Atlas, consulted a map of the Balkan Peninsula. 'A thing like that,' he observed, closing the volume with a snap, 'might happen to any one.'

Gabriel-Ernest

'THERE IS A wild beast in your woods,' said the artist Cunningham, as he was being driven to the station. It was the only remark he had made during the drive, but as Van Cheele had talked incessantly his companion's silence had not been noticeable.

'A stray fox or two and some resident weasels. Nothing more formidable,' said Van Cheele. The artist said nothing.

'What did you mean about a wild beast?' said Van Cheele later, when they were on the platform.

'Nothing. My imagination. Here is the train,' said Cunningham.

That afternoon Van Cheele went for one of his frequent rambles through his woodland property. He had a stuffed bittern in his study, and knew the names of quite a number of wild flowers, so his aunt had possibly some justification in describing him as a great naturalist. At any rate, he was a great walker. It was his custom to take mental notes of everything he saw during his walks, not so much for the purpose of assisting contemporary science as to provide topics for conversation afterwards. When the bluebells began to show themselves in flower he made a point of informing every one of the fact; the season of the year might have warned his hearers of the likelihood of such an occurrence, but at least they felt that he was being absolutely frank with them.

What Van Cheele saw on this particular afternoon was, however, something far removed from his ordinary range of experience. On a shelf of smooth stone overhanging a deep pool in the hollow of an oak coppice a boy of about sixteen lay asprawl, drying his wet brown limbs luxuriously in the sun. His wet hair, parted by a recent dive, lay close to his head, and his light-brown eyes, so light that there was an almost tigerish gleam in them, were turned towards Van Cheele with a certain lazy watchfulness. It was an unexpected apparition, and Van Cheele found himself engaged in the novel process of thinking before he spoke. Where on earth could this wild-looking boy hail from? The miller's wife had lost a child some two months ago, supposed to have been swept away by the mill-race, but that had been a mere baby, not a half-grown lad.

'What are you doing there?' he demanded.

'Obviously, sunning myself,' replied the boy.

'Where do you live?'

'Here, in these woods.'

'You can't live in the woods,' said Van Cheele.

'They are very nice woods,' said the boy, with a touch of patronage in his voice.

'But where do you sleep at night?'

'I don't sleep at night; that's my busiest time.'

Van Cheele began to have an irritated feeling that he was grappling with a problem that was eluding him.

'What do you feed on?' he asked.

'Flesh,' said the boy, and he pronounced the word with slow relish, as though he were tasting it.

'Flesh! What flesh?'

'Since it interests you, rabbits, wild-fowl, hares, poultry, lambs in their season, children when I can get any; they're usually too well locked in at night, when I do most of my hunting. It's quite two months since I tasted child-flesh.'

Ignoring the chaffing nature of the last remark Van

Cheele tried to draw the boy on the subject of possible poaching operations.

'You're talking rather through your hat when you speak of feeding on hares.' (Considering the nature of the boy's toilet the simile was hardly an apt one.) 'Our hillside hares aren't easily caught.'

'At night I hunt on four feet,' was the somewhat cryptic response.

'I suppose you mean that you hunt with a dog?' hazarded Van Cheele.

The boy rolled slowly over on to his back, and laughed a weird low laugh, that was pleasantly like a chuckle and disagreeably like a snarl.

'I don't fancy any dog would be very anxious for my company, especially at night.'

Van Cheele began to feel that there was something positively uncanny about the strange-eyed, strange-tongued youngster.

'I can't have you staying in these woods,' he declared authoritatively.

'I fancy you'd rather have me here than in your house,' said the boy.

The prospect of this wild, nude animal in Van Cheele's primly ordered house was certainly an alarming one.

'If you don't go I shall have to make you,' said Van Cheele.

The boy turned like a flash, plunged into the pool, and in a moment had flung his wet and glistening body halfway up the bank where Van Cheele was standing. In an otter the movement would not have been remarkable; in a boy Van Cheele found it sufficiently startling. His foot slipped as he made an involuntary backward movement, and he found himself almost prostrate on the slippery weed-grown bank, with those tigerish yellow eyes not very far from his own. Almost instinctively he half raised his hand to his throat. The boy laughed again, a laugh in which the snarl had nearly driven out the chuckle, and then, with another of his astonishing lightning movements, plunged out of view into a yielding tangle of weed and fern.

'What an extraordinary wild animal!' said Van Cheele as he picked himself up. And then he recalled Cunningham's remark, 'There is a wild beast in your woods.'

Walking slowly homeward, Van Cheele began to turn over in his mind various local occurrences which might be traceable to the existence of this astonishing young savage.

Something had been thinning the game in the woods lately, poultry had been missing from the farms, hares were growing unaccountably scarcer, and complaints had reached him of lambs being carried off bodily from the hills. Was it possible that this wild boy was really hunting the countryside in company with some clever poacher dog? He had spoken of hunting 'four-footed' by night, but then, again, he had hinted strangely at no dog caring to come near him, 'especially at night'. It was certainly puzzling. And then, as Van Cheele ran his mind over the various depredations that had been committed during the last month or two, he came suddenly to a dead stop, alike in his walk and his speculations. The child missing from the mill two months ago – the accepted theory was that it had tumbled into the mill-race and been swept away; but the mother had always declared she had heard a shriek on the hill side of the house, in the opposite direction from the water. It was unthinkable, of course, but he wished that the boy had not made that uncanny remark about child-flesh eaten two months ago. Such dreadful things should not be said even in fun.

Van Cheele, contrary to his usual wont, did not feel disposed to be communicative about his discovery in the wood. His position as a parish councillor and justice of the peace seemed somehow compromised by the fact that he was harbouring a personality of such doubtful repute on his property; there was even a possibility that a heavy bill of damages for raided lambs and poultry might be laid at his door. At dinner that night he was quite unusually silent.

'Where's your voice gone to?' said his aunt. 'One would think you had seen a wolf.'

Van Cheele, who was not familiar with the old saying, thought the remark rather foolish; if he *had* seen a wolf on his property his tongue would have been extraordinarily busy with the subject.

At breakfast next morning Van Cheele was conscious that his feeling of uneasiness regarding yesterday's episode had not wholly disappeared, and he resolved to go by train to the neighbouring cathedral town, hunt up Cunningham, and learn from him what he had really seen that had prompted the remark about a wild beast in the woods. With this resolution taken, his usual cheerfulness partially returned, and he hummed a bright little melody as he sauntered to the morning-room for his customary cigarette. As he entered the room the melody made way abruptly for a pious invocation. Gracefully asprawl on the ottoman, in an attitude of almost exaggerated repose, was the boy of the woods. He was drier than when Van Cheele had last seen him, but no other alteration was noticeable in his toilet.

'How dare you come here?' asked Van Cheele furiously.

'You told me I was not to stay in the woods,' said the boy calmly.

'But not to come here. Supposing my aunt should see you!'

And with a view to minimizing that catastrophe Van Cheele hastily obscured as much of his unwelcome guest as possible under the folds of a *Morning Post*. At that moment his aunt entered the room.

'This is a poor boy who has lost his way – and lost his memory. He doesn't know who he is or where he comes from,' explained Van Cheele desperately, glancing apprehensively at the waif's face to see whether he was going to add inconvenient candour to his other savage propensities.

Miss Van Cheele was enormously interested.

'Perhaps his underlinen is marked,' she suggested.

'He seems to have lost most of that, too,' said Van Cheele, making frantic little grabs at the *Morning Post* to keep it in its place.

A naked homeless child appealed to Miss Van Cheele as warmly as a stray kitten or derelict puppy would have done.

'We must do all we can for him,' she decided, and in a very short time a messenger, dispatched to the rectory, where a page-boy was kept, had returned with a suit of pantry clothes, and the necessary accessories of shirt, shoes, collar, etc. Clothed, clean, and groomed, the boy lost none of his uncanniness in Van Cheek's eyes, but his aunt found him sweet.

'We must call him something till we know who he really is,' she said. 'Gabriel-Ernest, I think; those are nice suitable names.'

Van Cheele agreed, but he privately doubted whether

they were being grafted on to a nice suitable child. His misgivings were not diminished by the fact that his staid and elderly spaniel had bolted out of the house at the first incoming of the boy, and now obstinately remained shivering and yapping at the farther end of the orchard, while the canary, usually as vocally industrious as Van Cheele himself, had put itself on an allowance of frightened cheeps. More than ever he was resolved to consult Cunningham without loss of time.

As he drove off to the station his aunt was arranging that Gabriel-Ernest should help her to entertain the infant members of her Sunday-school class at tea that afternoon.

Cunningham was not at first disposed to be communicative.

'My mother died of some brain trouble,' he explained, 'so you will understand why I am averse to dwelling on anything of an impossibly fantastic nature that I may see or think that I have seen.'

'But what *did* you see?' persisted Van Cheele.

'What I thought I saw was something so extraordinary that no really sane man could dignify it with the credit of having actually happened. I was standing, the last evening I was with you, half-hidden in the hedgegrowth by the orchard gate, watching the dying glow of the sunset. Suddenly I became aware of a naked boy, a bather from some neighbouring pool, I took him to be, who was standing out on the bare hillside also watching the sunset. His pose was so suggestive of some wild faun of Pagan myth that I instantly wanted to engage him as a model, and in another moment I think I should have hailed him. But just then the sun dipped out of view, and all the orange and pink slid out of the landscape, leaving it cold and grey.

And at the same moment an astounding thing happened – the boy vanished too!'

'What! vanished away into nothing?' asked Van Cheele excitedly.

'No; that is the dreadful part of it,' answered the artist; 'on the open hillside where the boy had been standing a second ago, stood a large wolf, blackish in colour, with gleaming fangs and cruel, yellow eyes. You may think –'

But Van Cheele did not stop for anything as futile as thought. Already he was tearing at top speed towards the station. He dismissed the idea of a telegram. 'Gabriel-Ernest is a werewolf' was a hopelessly inadequate effort at conveying the situation, and his aunt would think it was a code message to which he had omitted to give her the key. His one hope was that he might reach home before sundown. The cab which he chartered at the other end of the railway journey bore him with what seemed exasperating slowness along the country roads, which were pink and mauve with the flush of the sinking sun. His aunt was putting away some unfinished jams and cake when he arrived.

'Where is Gabriel-Ernest?' he almost screamed.

'He is taking the little Toop child home,' said his aunt. 'It was getting so late, I thought it wasn't safe to let it go back alone. What a lovely sunset, isn't it?'

But Van Cheele, although not oblivious of the glow in the western sky, did not stay to discuss its beauties. At a speed for which he was scarcely geared he raced along the narrow lane that led to the home of the Toops. On one side ran the swift current of the mill-stream, on the other rose the stretch of bare hillside. A dwindling rim of red sun showed still on the skyline, and the next turning must bring him in view of the ill-assorted couple he was pursuing. Then the colour went suddenly out of things, and a grey light settled itself with a quick shiver over the landscape. Van Cheele heard a shrill wail of fear, and stopped running.

Nothing was ever seen again of the Toop child or Gabriel-Ernest, but the latter's discarded garments were found lying in the road, so it was assumed that the child had fallen into the water, and that the boy had stripped and jumped in, in a vain endeavour to save it. Van Cheele and some workmen who were near by at the time testified to having heard a child scream loudly just near the spot where the clothes were found. Mrs Toop, who had eleven other children, was decently resigned to her bereavement, but Miss Van Cheele sincerely mourned her lost foundling. It was on her initiative that a memorial brass was put up in the parish church to 'Gabriel-Ernest, an unknown boy, who bravely sacrificed his life for another'.

Van Cheele gave way to his aunt in most things, but he flatly refused to subscribe to the Gabriel-Ernest memorial.

The Soul of Laploshka

LAPLOSHKA WAS ONE of the meanest men I have ever met, and quite one of the most entertaining. He said horrid things about other people in such a charming way that one forgave him for the equally horrid things he said about oneself behind one's back. Hating anything in the way of ill-natured gossip ourselves, we are always grateful to those who do it for us and do it well. And Laploshka did it really well.

Naturally Laploshka had a large circle of acquaintances, and as he exercised some care in their selection it followed that an appreciable proportion were men whose bank balances enabled them to acquiesce indulgently in his rather one-sided views on hospitality. Thus, although possessed of only moderate means, he was able to live comfortably within his income, and still more comfortably within those of various tolerantly disposed associates.

But towards the poor or to those of the same limited resources as himself his attitude was one of watchful anxiety; he seemed to be haunted by a besetting fear lest some fraction of a shilling or franc, or whatever the prevailing coinage might be, should be diverted from his pocket or service into that of a hard-up companion. A two-franc cigar would be cheerfully offered to a wealthy patron, on the principle of doing evil that good may come, but I have known him indulge in agonies of perjury rather than admit the incriminating possession of a copper coin when change was needed to tip a waiter. The coin would have been duly returned at the earliest opportunity – he would have taken means to ensure against forgetfulness on the part of the borrower – but accidents might happen, and

44

even the temporary estrangement from his penny or sou was a calamity to be avoided.

The knowledge of this amiable weakness offered a perpetual temptation to play upon Laploshka's fears of involuntary generosity. To offer him a lift in a cab and pretend not to have enough money to pay the fare, to fluster him with a request for a sixpence when his hand was full of silver just received in change, these were a few of the petty torments that ingenuity prompted as occasion afforded. To do justice to Laploshka's resourcefulness it must be admitted that he always emerged somehow or other from the most embarrassing dilemma without in any way compromising his reputation for saying 'No.' But the gods send opportunities at some time to most men, and mine came one evening when Laploshka and I were supping together in a cheap boulevard restaurant. (Except when he was the bidden guest of some one with an irreproachable income, Laploshka was wont to curb his appetite for high living; on such fortunate occasions he let it go on an easy snaffle.) At the conclusion of the meal a somewhat urgent message called me away, and without heeding my companion's agitated protest, I called back cruelly, 'Pay my share; I'll settle with you tomorrow.' Early on the morrow Laploshka hunted me down by instinct as I walked along a side street that I hardly ever frequented. He had the air of a man who had not slept.

'You owe me two francs from last night,' was his breathless greeting.

I spoke evasively of the situation in Portugal, where more trouble seemed brewing. But Laploshka listened with the abstraction of the deaf adder, and quickly returned to the subject of the two francs.

'I'm afraid I must owe it to you,' I said lightly and

brutally. 'I haven't a sou in the world,' and I added mendaciously, 'I'm going away for six months or perhaps longer.'

Laploshka said nothing, but his eyes bulged a little and his cheeks took on the mottled hues of an ethnographical map of the Balkan Peninsula. That same day, at sundown, he died. 'Failure of the heart's action' was the doctor's verdict; but I, who knew better, knew that he had died of grief.

There arose the problem of what to do with his two francs. To have killed Laploshka was one thing; to have kept his beloved money would have argued a callousness of feeling of which I am not capable. The ordinary solution, of giving it to the poor, would by no means fit the present situation, for nothing would have distressed the dead man more than such a misuse of his property. On the other hand, the bestowal of two francs on the rich was an operation which called for some tact. An easy way out of the difficulty seemed, however, to present itself the following Sunday, as I was wedged into the cosmopolitan crowd which filled the side-aisle of one of the most popular Paris churches. A collecting-bag, for 'the poor of Monsieur le Curé', was buffeting its tortuous way across the seemingly impenetrable human sea, and a German in front of me, who evidently did not wish his appreciation of the magnificent music to be marred by a suggestion of payment, made audible criticisms to his companion on the claims of the said charity.

'They do not want money,' he said; 'they have too much money. They have no poor. They are all pampered.'

If that were really the case my way seemed clear. I dropped Laploshka's two francs into the bag with a murmured blessing on the rich of Monsieur le Curé.

46

Some three weeks later chance had taken me to Vienna, and I sat one evening regaling myself in a humble but excellent little Gasthaus up in the Währinger quarter. The appointments were primitive, but the Schnitzel, the beer, and the cheese could not have been improved on. Good cheer brought good custom, and with the exception of one small table near the door every place was occupied. Half-way through my meal I happened to glance in the direction of that empty seat, and saw that it was no longer empty. Poring over the bill of fare with the absorbed scrutiny of one who seeks the cheapest among the cheap was Laploshka. Once he looked across at me, with a com-prehensive glance at my repast, as though to say, 'It is my two francs you are eating,' and then looked swiftly away. Evidently the poor of Monsieur le Curé had been genuine poor. The Schnitzel turned to leather in my mouth, the beer seemed tepid; I left the Emmenthaler untasted. My one idea was to get away from the room, away from the table where *that* was seated; and as I fled I felt Laploshka's reproachful eyes watching the amount that I gave to the piccolo – out of his two francs. I lunched next day at an expensive restaurant which I felt sure that the living Laploshka would never have entered on his own account, and I hoped that the dead Laploshka would observe the same barriers. I was not mistaken, but as I came out I found him miserably studying the bill of fare stuck up on the portals. Then he slowly made his way over to a milk-hall. For the first time in my experience I missed the charm and gaiety of Vienna life.

After that, in Paris or London or wherever I happened to be, I continued to see a good deal of Laploshka. If I had a seat in a box at a theatre I was always conscious of his eyes furtively watching me from the dim recesses of the

47

gallery. As I turned into my club on a rainy afternoon I would see him taking inadequate shelter in a doorway opposite. Even if I indulged in the modest luxury of a penny chair in the Park he generally confronted me from one of the free benches, never staring at me, but always elaborately conscious of my presence. My friends began to comment on my changed looks, and advised me to leave off heaps of things. I should have liked to have left off Laploshka.

On a certain Sunday – it was probably Easter, for the crush was worse than ever – I was again wedged into the crowd listening to the music in the fashionable Paris church, and again the collection-bag was buffeting its way across the human sea. An English lady behind me was making ineffectual efforts to convey a coin into the still distant bag, so I took the money at her request and helped it forward to its destination. It was a two-franc piece. A swift inspiration came to me, and I merely dropped my own sou into the bag and slid the silver coin into my pocket. I had withdrawn Laploshka's two francs from the poor, who should never have had that legacy. As I backed away from the crowd I heard a woman's voice say, 'I don't believe he put my money in the bag. There are swarms of people in Paris like that!' But my mind was lighter than it had been for a long time.

The delicate mission of bestowing the retrieved sum on the deserving rich still confronted me. Again I trusted to the inspiration of accident, and again fortune favoured me. A shower drove me, two days later, into one of the historic churches on the left bank of the Seine, and there I found, peering at the old wood-carvings, the Baron R., one of the wealthiest and most shabbily dressed men in Paris. It was now or never. Putting a strong American inflection into the French which I usually talked with an unmistakable British accent, I catechized the Baron as to the date of the church's building, its dimensions, and other details which an American tourist would be certain to want to know. Having acquired such information as the Baron was able to impart on short notice, I solemnly placed the two-franc piece in his hand, with the hearty assurance that it was 'pour vous', and turned to go. The Baron was slightly taken aback, but accepted the situation with a good grace. Walking over to a small box fixed in the wall, he dropped Laploshka's two francs into the slot. Over the box was the inscription, 'Pour les pauvres de M. le Curé'.

That evening, at the crowded corner by the Café de la Paix, I caught a fleeting glimpse of Laploshka. He smiled, slightly raised his hat, and vanished. I never saw him again. After all, the money had been *given* to the deserving rich, and the soul of Laploshka was at peace.

The Bag

'THE MAJOR IS coming in to tea,' said Mrs Hoopington to her niece. 'He's just gone round to the stables with his horse. Be as bright and lively as you can; the poor man's got a fit of the glooms.'

Major Pallaby was a victim of circumstances, over which he had no control, and of his temper, over which he had very little. He had taken on the Mastership of the Pexdale Hounds in succession to a highly popular man who had fallen foul of his committee, and the Major found himself confronted with the overt hostility of at least half the hunt, while his lack of tact and amiability had done much to alienate the remainder. Hence subscriptions were beginning to fall off, foxes grew provokingly scarcer, and wire obtruded itself with increasing frequency. The Major could plead reasonable excuse for his fit of the glooms.

In ranging herself as a partisan on the side of Major Pallaby Mrs Hoopington had been largely influenced by the fact that she had made up her mind to marry him at an early date. Against his notorious bad temper she set his three thousand a year, and his prospective succession to a baronetcy gave a casting vote in his favour. The Major's plans on the subject of matrimony were not at present in such an advanced stage as Mrs Hoopington's, but he was beginning to find his way over to Hoopington Hall with a frequency that was already being commented on.

'He had a wretchedly thin field out again yesterday,' said Mrs Hoopington. 'Why you didn't bring one or two hunting men down with you, instead of that stupid Russian boy, I can't think.'

'Vladimir isn't stupid,' protested her niece; 'he's one of the most amusing boys I ever met. Just compare him for a moment with some of your heavy hunting men –'

'Anyhow, my dear Norah, he can't ride.'

'Russians never can; but he shoots.'

'Yes; and what does he shoot? Yesterday he brought home a woodpecker in his game-bag.'

'But he'd shot three pheasants and some rabbits as well.'

'That's no excuse for including a woodpecker in his game-bag.'

'Foreigners go in for mixed bags more than we do. A Grand Duke pots a vulture just as seriously as we should stalk a bustard. Anyhow, I've explained to Vladimir that certain birds are beneath his dignity as a sportsman. And as he's only nineteen, of course, his dignity is a sure thing to appeal to.'

Mrs Hoopington sniffed. Most people with whom Vladimir came in contact found his high spirits infectious, but his present hostess was guaranteed immune against infection of that sort.

'I hear him coming in now,' she observed. 'I shall go and get ready for tea. We're going to have it here in the hall. Entertain the Major if he comes in before I'm down, and, above all, be bright.'

Norah was dependent on her aunt's good graces for many little things that made life worth living, and she was conscious of a feeling of discomfiture because the Russian youth whom she had brought down as a welcome element of change in the country-house routine was not making a good impression. That young gentleman, however, was supremely unconscious of any shortcomings, and burst into the hall, tired, and less sprucely groomed than usual, but distinctly radiant. His game-bag looked comfortably full.

'Guess what I have shot,' he demanded.

'Pheasants, wood-pigeons, rabbits,' hazarded Norah.

'No; a large beast; I don't know what you call it in English. Brown, with a darkish tail.' Norah changed colour.

'Does it live in a tree and eat nuts?' she asked, hoping that the use of the adjective 'large' might be an exaggeration.

Vladimir laughed.

'Oh, no; not a *biyelka*.'

'Does it swim and eat fish?' asked Norah, with a fervent prayer in her heart that it might turn out to be an otter.

'No,' said Vladimir, busy with the straps of his game-bag; 'it lives in the woods, and eats rabbits and chickens.'

Norah sat down suddenly, and hid her face in her hands.

'Merciful Heaven!' she wailed; 'he's shot a fox!'

Vladimir looked up at her in consternation. In a torrent of agitated words she tried to explain the horror of the situation. The boy understood nothing, but was thoroughly alarmed.

'Hide it, hide it!' said Norah frantically, pointing to the still unopened bag. 'My aunt and the Major will be here in a moment. Throw it on the top of that chest; they won't see it there.'

Vladimir swung the bag with fair aim; but the strap caught in its flight on the outstanding point of an antler fixed in the wall, and the bag, with its terrible burden, remained suspended just above the alcove where tea would presently be laid. At that moment Mrs Hoopington and the Major entered the hall.

'The Major is going to draw our covers tomorrow,' announced the lady, with a certain heavy satisfaction. 'Smithers is confident that we'll be able to show him some sport; he swears he's seen a fox in the nut copse three times this week.'

'I'm sure I hope so; I hope so,' said the Major moodily. 'I must break this sequence of blank days. One hears so often that a fox has settled down as a tenant for life in certain covers, and then when you go to turn him out there isn't a trace of him. I'm certain a fox was shot or trapped in Lady Widden's woods the very day before we drew them.'

'Major, if any one tried that game on in my woods they'd get short shrift,' said Mrs Hoopington.

Norah found her way mechanically to the tea-table and made her fingers frantically busy in rearranging the parsley round the sandwich dish. On one side of her loomed the morose countenance of the Major, on the other she was conscious of the scared, miserable eyes of Vladimir. And above it all hung *that*. She dared not raise her eyes above the level of the tea-table, and she almost expected to see a spot of accusing vulpine blood drip down and stain the whiteness of the cloth. Her aunt's manner signalled to her the repeated message to 'be bright'; for the present she was fully occupied in keeping her teeth from chattering.

'What did you shoot today?' asked Mrs Hoopington suddenly of the unusually silent Vladimir.

'Nothing – nothing worth speaking of,' said the boy.

Norah's heart, which had stood still for a space, made up for lost time with a most disturbing bound.

'I wish you'd find something that was worth speaking about,' said the hostess; 'every one seems to have lost their tongues.'

'When did Smithers last see that fox?' said the Major.

'Yesterday morning; a fine dog-fox, with a dark brush,' confided Mrs Hoopington.

'Aha, we'll have a good gallop after that brush tomorrow,' said the Major, with a transient gleam of good humour. And then gloomy silence settled again round the tea-table, a silence broken only by despondent munchings and the occasional feverish rattle of a teaspoon in its saucer. A diversion was at last afforded by Mrs Hoopington's fox-terrier, which had jumped on to a vacant chair, the better to survey the delicacies of the table, and was now sniffing in an upward direction at something apparently more interesting than cold tea-cake.

'What is exciting him?' asked his mistress, as the dog suddenly broke into short, angry barks, with a running accompaniment of tremulous whines.

'Why,' she continued, 'it's your game-bag, Vladimir! What *have* you got in it?'

'By Gad,' said the Major, who was now standing up; 'there's a pretty warm scent!'

And then a simultaneous idea flashed on himself and Mrs Hoopington. Their faces flushed to distinct but harmonious tones of purple, and with one accusing voice they screamed, 'You've shot the fox!'

Norah tried hastily to palliate Vladimir's misdeed in their eyes, but it is doubtful whether they heard her. The Major's fury clothed and reclothed itself in words as frantically as a woman up in town for one day's shopping tries on a succession of garments. He reviled and railed at fate and the general scheme of things, he pitied himself with a strong, deep pity too poignant for tears, he condemned every one with whom he had ever come in contact to endless and abnormal punishments. In fact, he conveyed the

54

impression that if a destroying angel had been lent to him for a week it would have had very little time for private study. In the lulls of his outcry could be heard the querulous monotone of Mrs Hoopington and the sharp staccato barking of the fox-terrier. Vladimir, who did not understand a tithe of what was being said, sat fondling a cigarette and repeating under his breath from time to time a vigorous English adjective which he had long ago taken affectionately into his vocabulary. His mind strayed back to the youth in the old Russian folk-tale who shot an enchanted bird with dramatic results. Meanwhile, the Major, roaming round the hall like an imprisoned cyclone, had caught sight of and joyfully pounced on the telephone apparatus, and lost no time in ringing up the hunt secretary and announcing his resignation of the Mastership. A servant had by this time brought his horse round to the door, and in a few seconds Mrs Hoopington's shrill monotone had the field to itself. But after the Major's display her best efforts at vocal violence missed their full effect; it was as though one had come straight out from a Wagner opera into a rather tame thunderstorm. Realizing, perhaps, that her tirades were something of an anticlimax, Mrs Hoopington broke suddenly into some rather necessary tears and marched out of the room, leaving behind her a silence almost as terrible as the turmoil which had preceded it.

'What shall I do with – *that*?' asked Vladimir at last.

'Bury it,' said Norah.

'Just plain burial?' said Vladimir, rather relieved. He had almost expected that some of the local clergy would have insisted on being present, or that a salute might have to be fired over the grave.

And thus it came to pass that in the dusk of a November

evening the Russian boy, murmuring a few of the prayers of his Church for luck, gave hasty but decent burial to a large polecat under the lilac trees at Hoopington.

The Baker's Dozen

CHARACTERS
Major Richard Dumbarton
Mrs Carewe
Mrs Paly-Paget

SCENE Deck of eastward-bound steamer. Major Dumbarton seated on deck-chair, another chair by his side, with the name 'Mrs Carewe' painted on it, a third near by.

(*Enter, R., Mrs Carewe, seats herself leisurely in her deck-chair, the Major affecting to ignore her presence.*)

Major (*turning suddenly*): Emily! After all these years! This is fate!

Em.: Fate! Nothing of the sort; it's only me. You men are always such fatalists. I deferred my departure three whole weeks, in order to come out in the same boat that I saw you were travelling by. I bribed the steward to put our chairs side by side in an unfrequented corner, and I took enormous pains to be looking particularly attractive this morning, and then you say, 'This is fate.' I *am* looking particularly attractive, am I not?

Maj.: More than ever. Time has only added a ripeness to your charms.

Em.: I knew you'd put it exactly in those words. The phraseology of love-making is awfully limited, isn't it? After all, the chief charm is in the fact of being made love to. You *are* making love to me, aren't you?

Maj.: Emily dearest, I had already begun making advances, even before you sat down here. I also bribed the steward to put our seats together in a secluded corner. 'You may consider it done, sir,' was his reply. That was immediately after breakfast.

Em.: How like a man to have his breakfast first. I attended to the seat business as soon as I left my cabin.

Maj.: Don't be unreasonable. It was only at breakfast that I discovered your blessed presence on the boat. I paid violent and unusual attention to a flapper all through the meal in order to make you jealous. She's probably in her cabin writing reams about me to a fellow-flapper at this very moment.

Em.: You needn't have taken all that trouble to make me jealous, Dickie. You did that years ago, when you married another woman.

Maj.: Well, you had gone and married another man – a widower, too, at that.

Em.: Well, there's no particular harm in marrying a widower, I suppose. I'm ready to do it again, if I meet a really nice one.

Maj.: Look here, Emily, it's not fair to go at that rate. You're a lap ahead of me the whole time. It's my place to propose to you; all you've got to do is to say 'Yes.'

Em.: Well, I've practically said it already, so we needn't dawdle over that part.

Maj.: Oh, well –

(*They look at each other, then suddenly embrace with considerable energy.*)

Maj.: We dead-heated it that time. (*Suddenly jumping to his feet.*) Oh, d— I'd forgotten!

Em.: Forgotten what?

Maj.: The children. I ought to have told you. Do you mind children?

Em.: Not in moderate quantities. How many have you got?

Maj. (*counting hurriedly on his fingers*): Five.

Em.: Five!

Maj. (*anxiously*): Is that too many?

Em.: It's rather a number. The worst of it is, I've some myself.

Maj.: Many?

Em.: Eight.

Maj.: Eight in six years! Oh, Emily!

Em.: Only four were my own. The other four were by my husband's first marriage. Still, that practically makes eight.

Maj.: And eight and five make thirteen. We can't start our married life with thirteen children; it would be most unlucky. (*Walks up and down in agitation.*) Some way must be found out of this. If we could only bring them down to twelve. Thirteen is so horribly unlucky.

Em.: Isn't there some way by which we could part with one or two? Don't the French want more children? I've often seen articles about it in the *Figaro*.

Maj.: I fancy they want French children. Mine don't even speak French.

Em.: There's always a chance that one of them might turn out depraved and vicious, and then you could disown him. I've heard of that being done.

Maj.: But, good gracious, you've got to educate him first. You can't expect a boy to be vicious till he's been to a good school.

Em.: Why couldn't he be naturally depraved? Lots of boys are.

Maj.: Only when they inherit it from depraved parents. You don't suppose there's any depravity in me, do you?

Em.: It sometimes skips a generation, you know. Weren't any of your family bad?

Maj.: There was an aunt who was never spoken of.

Em.: There you are!

Maj.: But one can't build too much on that. In mid-Victorian days they labelled all sorts of things as unspeakable that we should speak about quite tolerantly. I daresay this particular aunt had only married a Unitarian, or rode to hounds on both sides of her horse, or something of that sort. Anyhow, we can't wait indefinitely for one of the children to take after a doubtfully depraved great aunt. Something else must be thought of.

Em.: Don't people ever adopt children from other families?

Maj.: I've heard of it being done by childless couples, and those sort of people –

Em.: Hush! Some one's coming. Who is it?

Maj.: Mrs Paly-Paget.

Em.: The very person!

Maj.: What, to adopt a child? Hasn't she got any?

Em.: Only one miserable hen-baby.

Maj.: Let's sound her on the subject.

(*Enter Mrs Paley-Paget, R.*)

Ah, good morning, Mrs Paly-Paget. I was just wondering at breakfast where did we meet last?

Mrs P.-P.: At the Criterion, wasn't it? (*Drops into vacant chair.*)

Maj.: At the Criterion, of course.

Mrs P.-P.: I was dining with Lord and Lady Slugford. Charming people, but so mean. They took us afterwards to the Velodrome, to see some dancer interpreting Mendelssohn's 'songs without clothes'. We were all packed up in a little box near the roof, and you may imagine how hot it was. It was like a Turkish bath. And, of course, one couldn't see anything.

Maj.: Then it was not like a Turkish bath.

Mrs P.-P.: Major!

Em.: We were just talking of you when you joined us.

Mrs P.-P.: Really! Nothing very dreadful, I hope.

Em.: Oh, dear, no! It's too early on the voyage for that sort of thing. We were feeling rather sorry for you.

Mrs P.-P.: Sorry for me? Whatever for?

Maj.: Your childless hearth and all that, you know. No little pattering feet.

Mrs P.-P.: Major! How dare you? I've got my little girl, I suppose you know. Her feet can patter as well as other children's.

Maj.: Only one pair of feet.

Mrs P.-P.: Certainly. My child isn't a centipede. Considering the way they move us about in those horrid jungle stations, without a decent bungalow to set one's foot in, I consider I've got a heartless child, rather than a childless hearth. Thank you for your sympathy all the same. I daresay it was well meant. Impertinence often is.

Em.: Dear Mrs Paly-Paget, we were only feeling sorry for your sweet little girl when she grows older, you know. No little brothers and sisters to play with.

Mrs P.-P.: Mrs Carewe, this conversation strikes me as being indelicate, to say the least of it. I've only been married two and a half years, and my family is naturally a small one.

Maj.: Isn't it rather an exaggeration to talk of one little female child as a family? A family suggests numbers.

Mrs P.-P.: Really, Major, your language is extraordinary. I daresay I've only got a little female child, as you call it, at present –

Maj.: Oh, it won't change into a boy later on, if that's what you're counting on. Take our word for it; we've had so much more experience in these affairs than you have. Once a female, always a female. Nature is not infallible, but she always abides by her mistakes.

Mrs P.-P. (*rising*): Major Dumbarton, these boats are uncomfortably small, but I trust we shall find ample accommodation for avoiding each other's society during the rest of the voyage. The same wish applies to you, Mrs Carewe.

(*Exit Mrs Paly-Paget, L.*)

Maj.: What an unnatural mother! (*Sinks into chair.*)

Em.: I wouldn't trust a child with any one who had a temper like hers. Oh, Dickie, why did you go and have such a large family? You always said you wanted me to be the mother of your children.

Maj.: I wasn't going to wait while you were founding and fostering dynasties in other directions. Why you couldn't be content to have children of your own, without collecting them like batches of postage stamps I can't think. The idea of marrying a man with four children!

Em.: Well, you're asking me to marry one with five.

Maj.: Five! (*Springing to his feet.*) Did I say five?

Em.: You certainly said five.

Maj.: Oh, Emily, supposing I've miscounted them! Listen now, keep count with me. Richard – that's after me, of course.

Em.: One.

Maj.: Albert-Victor – that must have been in Coronation year.

Em.: Two!

Maj.: Maud. She's called after –

Em.: Never mind who she's called after. Three!

Maj.: And Gerald.

Em.: Four!

Maj.: That's the lot.

Em.: Are you sure?

Maj.: I swear that's the lot. I must have counted Albert-
Victor as two.

Em.: Richard!

Maj.: Emily!

(*They embrace.*)

FROM

THE CHRONICLES
OF CLOVIS (1911)

The Match-Maker

THE GRILL-ROOM CLOCK struck eleven with the respectful unobtrusiveness of one whose mission in life is to be ignored. When the flight of time should really have rendered abstinence and migration imperative the lighting apparatus would signal the fact in the usual way.

Six minutes later Clovis approached the supper-table, in the blessed expectancy of one who has dined sketchily and long ago.

'I'm starving,' he announced, making an effort to sit down gracefully and read the menu at the same time.

'So I gathered,' said his host, 'from the fact that you were nearly punctual. I ought to have told you that I'm a Food Reformer. I've ordered two bowls of bread-and-milk and some health biscuits. I hope you don't mind.'

Clovis pretended afterwards that he didn't go white above the collar-line for the fraction of a second.

'All the same,' he said, 'you ought not to joke about such things. There really are such people. I've known people who've met them. To think of all the adorable things there are to eat in the world, and then to go through life munching sawdust and being proud of it.'

'They're like the Flagellants of the Middle Ages, who went about mortifying themselves.'

'They had some excuse,' said Clovis. 'They did it to save their immortal souls, didn't they? You needn't tell me that a man who doesn't love oysters and asparagus and good wines has got a soul, or a stomach either. He's simply got the instinct for being unhappy highly developed.'

Clovis relapsed for a few golden moments into tender

intimacies with a succession of rapidly disappearing oysters.

'I think oysters are more beautiful than any religion,' he resumed presently. 'They not only forgive our unkindness to them; they justify it, they incite us to go on being perfectly horrid to them. Once they arrive at the supper-table they seem to enter thoroughly into the spirit of the thing. There's nothing in Christianity or Buddhism that quite matches the sympathetic unselfishness of an oyster. Do you like my new waistcoat? I'm wearing it for the first time tonight.'

'It looks like a great many others you've had lately, only worse. New dinner waistcoats are becoming a habit with you.'

'They say one always pays for the excesses of one's youth; mercifully that isn't true about one's clothes. My mother is thinking of getting married.'

'Again!'

'It's the first time.'

'Of course, you ought to know. I was under the impression that she'd been married once or twice at least.'

'Three times, to be mathematically exact. I meant that it was the first time she'd thought about getting married; the other times she did it without thinking. As a matter of fact, it's really I who am doing the thinking for her in this case. You see, it's quite two years since her last husband died.'

'You evidently think that brevity is the soul of widowhood.'

'Well, it struck me that she was getting moped, and beginning to settle down, which wouldn't suit her a bit. The first symptom that I noticed was when she began to complain that we were living beyond our income. All decent people live beyond their incomes nowadays, and those who aren't respectable live beyond other people's. A few gifted individuals manage to do both.'

'It's hardly so much a gift as an industry.'

'The crisis came,' returned Clovis, 'when she suddenly started the theory that late hours were bad for one, and wanted me to be in by one o'clock every night. Imagine that sort of thing for me, who was eighteen on my last birthday.'

'On your last two birthdays, to be mathematically exact.'

'Oh, well, that's not my fault. I'm not going to arrive at nineteen as long as my mother remains at thirty-seven. One must have some regard for appearances.'

'Perhaps your mother would age a little in the process of settling down.'

'That's the last thing she'd think of. Feminine reformations always start in on the failings of other people. That's why I was so keen on the husband idea.'

'Did you go as far as to select the gentleman, or did you merely throw out a general idea, and trust to the force of suggestion?'

'If one wants a thing done in a hurry one must see to it oneself. I found a military Johnny hanging round on a loose end at the club, and took him home to lunch once or twice. He'd spent most of his life on the Indian frontier, building roads, and relieving famines and minimizing earthquakes, and all that sort of thing that one does do on frontiers. He could talk sense to a peevish cobra in fifteen native languages, and probably knew what to do if you found a rogue elephant on your croquet-lawn; but he was shy and diffident with women. I told my mother privately that he was an absolute woman-hater; so, of course, she laid herself out to flirt all she knew, which isn't a little.'

'And was the gentleman responsive?'

'I hear he told some one at the club that he was looking out for a Colonial job, with plenty of hard work, for a young friend of his, so I gather that he has some idea of marrying into the family.'

'You seem destined to be the victim of the reformation, after all.'

Clovis wiped the trace of Turkish coffee and the beginnings of a smile from his lips, and slowly lowered his dexter eyelid. Which, being interpreted, probably meant, 'I *don't* think!'

Tobermory

IT WAS A CHILL, rain-washed afternoon of a late August day, that indefinite season when partridges are still in security or cold storage, and there is nothing to hunt – unless one is bounded on the north by the Bristol Channel, in which case one may lawfully gallop after fat red stags. Lady Blemley's house-party was not bounded on the north by the Bristol Channel, hence there was a full gathering of her guests round the tea-table on this particular afternoon. And, in spite of the blankness of the season and the triteness of the occasion, there was no trace in the company of that fatigued restlessness which means a dread of the pianola and a subdued hankering for auction bridge. The undisguised open-mouthed attention of the entire party was fixed on the homely negative personality of Mr Cornelius Appin. Of all her guests, he was the one who had come to Lady Blemley with the vaguest reputation. Some one had said he was 'clever', and he had got his invitation in the moderate expectation, on the part of his hostess, that some portion at least of his cleverness would be contributed to the general entertainment. Until tea-time that day she had been unable to discover in what direction, if any, his cleverness lay. He was neither a wit nor a croquet champion, a hypnotic force nor a begetter of amateur theatricals. Neither did his exterior suggest the sort of man in whom women are willing to pardon a generous measure of mental deficiency. He had subsided into mere Mr Appin, and the Cornelius seemed a piece of transparent baptismal bluff. And now he was claiming to have launched on the world a discovery beside which the invention of gunpowder, of the printing-press, and of steam locomotion were inconsiderable trifles. Science had made bewildering strides in many directions during recent decades, but this thing seemed to belong to the domain of miracle rather than to scientific achievement.

'And do you really ask us to believe,' Sir Wilfrid was saying, 'that you have discovered a means for instructing animals in the art of human speech, and that dear old Tobermory has proved your first successful pupil?'

'It is a problem at which I have worked for the last seventeen years,' said Mr Appin, 'but only during the last eight or nine months have I been rewarded with glimmerings of success. Of course I have experimented with thousands of animals, but latterly only with cats, those wonderful creatures which have assimilated themselves so marvellously with our civilization while retaining all their highly developed feral instincts. Here and there among cats one comes across an outstanding superior intellect, just as one does among the ruck of human beings, and when I made the acquaintance of Tobermory a week ago I saw at once that I was in contact with a "Beyond-cat" of extraordinary intelligence. I had gone far along the road to success in recent experiments; with Tobermory, as you call him, I have reached the goal.'

Mr Appin concluded his remarkable statement in a voice which he strove to divest of a triumphant inflection. No one said 'Rats,' though Clovis's lips moved in a monosyllabic contortion which probably invoked those rodents of disbelief.

'And do you mean to say,' asked Miss Resker, after a slight pause, 'that you have taught Tobermory to say and understand easy sentences of one syllable?'

'My dear Miss Resker,' said the wonder-worker patiently, 'one teaches little children and savages and backward adults in that piecemeal fashion; when one has once solved the problem of making a beginning with an animal of highly developed intelligence one has no need for those halting methods. Tobermory can speak our language with perfect correctness.'

This time Clovis very distinctly said, 'Beyond-rats!' Sir Wilfrid was more polite, but equally sceptical.

'Hadn't we better have the cat in and judge for ourselves?' suggested Lady Blemley.

Sir Wilfrid went in search of the animal, and the company settled themselves down to the languid expectation of witnessing some more or less adroit drawing-room ventriloquism.

In a minute Six Wilfrid was back in the room, his face white beneath its tan and his eyes dilated with excitement.

'By Gad, it's true!'

His agitation was unmistakably genuine, and his hearers started forward in a thrill of awakened interest.

Collapsing into an armchair he continued breathlessly: 'I found him dozing in the smoking-room and called out to him to come for his tea. He blinked at me in his usual way, and I said, "Come on, Toby; don't keep us waiting"; and, by Gad! he drawled out in a most horribly natural voice that he'd come when he dashed well pleased! I nearly jumped out of my skin!'

Appin had preached to absolutely incredulous hearers; Sir Wilfrid's statement carried instant conviction. A Babel-like chorus of startled exclamation arose, amid which the scientist sat mutely enjoying the first fruit of his stupendous discovery.

In the midst of the clamour Tobermory entered the room and made his way with velvet tread and studied unconcern across to the group seated round the tea-table.

A sudden hush of awkwardness and constraint fell on the company. Somehow there seemed an element of embarrassment in addressing on equal terms a domestic cat of acknowledged dental ability.

'Will you have some milk, Tobermory?' asked Lady Blemley in a rather strained voice.

'I don't mind if I do,' was the response, couched in a tone of even indifference. A shiver of suppressed excitement went through the listeners, and Lady Blemley might be excused for pouring out the saucerful of milk rather unsteadily.

'I'm afraid I've spilt a good deal of it,' she said apologetically.

'After all, it's not my Axminster,' was Tobermory's rejoinder.

Another silence fell on the group, and then Miss Resker, in her best district-visitor manner, asked if the human language had been difficult to learn. Tobermory looked squarely at her for a moment and then fixed his gaze serenely on the middle distance. It was obvious that boring questions lay outside his scheme of life.

'What do you think of human intelligence?' asked Mavis Pellington lamely.

'Of whose intelligence in particular?' asked Tobermory coldly.

'Oh, well, mine for instance,' said Mavis, with a feeble laugh.

'You put me in an embarrassing position,' said Tobermory, whose tone and attitude certainly did not suggest a shred of embarrassment. 'When your inclusion in this house-party was suggested Sir Wilfrid protested that you were the most brainless woman of his acquaintance, and that there was a wide distinction between hospitality and the care of the feeble-minded. Lady Blemley replied that your lack of brain-power was the precise quality which had earned you your invitation, as you were the only person she could think of who might be idiotic enough to buy their old car. You know, the one they call "The Envy of Sisyphus", because it goes quite nicely up-hill if you push it.'

Lady Blemley's protestations would have had greater effect if she had not casually suggested to Mavis only that morning that the car in question would be just the thing for her down at her Devonshire home.

Major Barfield plunged in heavily to effect a diversion.

'How about your carryings-on with the tortoise-shell puss up at the stables, eh?'

The moment he had said it every one realized the blunder.

'One does not usually discuss these matters in public,' said Tobermory frigidly. 'From a slight observation of your ways since you've been in this house I should imagine you'd find it inconvenient if I were to shift the conversation on to your own little affairs.'

The panic which ensued was not confined to the Major.

'Would you like to go and see if cook has got your dinner ready?' suggested Lady Blemley hurriedly, affecting to ignore the fact that it wanted at least two hours to Tobermory's dinner-time.

'Thanks,' said Tobermory, 'not quite so soon after my tea. I don't want to die of indigestion.'

'Cats have nine lives, you know,' said Sir Wilfrid heartily.

'Possibly,' answered Tobermory; 'but only one liver.'

'Adelaide!' said Mrs Cornett, 'do you mean to

encourage that cat to go out and gossip about us in the servants' hall?'

The panic had indeed become general. A narrow ornamental balustrade ran in front of most of the bedroom windows at the Towers, and it was recalled with dismay that this had formed a favourite promenade for Tobermory at all hours, whence he could watch the pigeons – and heaven knew what else besides. If he intended to become reminiscent in his present outspoken strain the effect would be something more than disconcerting. Mrs Cornett, who spent much time at her toilet table, and whose complexion was reputed to be of a nomadic though punctual disposition, looked as ill at ease as the Major. Miss Scrawen, who wrote fiercely sensuous poetry and led a blameless life, merely displayed irritation; if you are methodical and virtuous in private you don't necessarily want every one to know it. Bertie van Tahn, who was so depraved at seventeen that he had long ago given up trying to be any worse, turned a dull shade of gardenia white, but he did not commit the error of dashing out of the room like Odo Finsberry, a young gentleman who was understood to be reading for the Church and who was possibly disturbed at the thought of scandals he might hear concerning other people. Clovis had the presence of mind to maintain a composed exterior; privately he was calculating how long it would take to procure a box of fancy mice through the agency of the *Exchange and Mart* as a species of hush-money.

Even in a delicate situation like the present, Agnes Resker could not endure to remain too long in the background.

'Why did I ever come down here?' she asked dramatically.

76

Tobermory immediately accepted the opening.

'Judging by what you said to Mrs Cornett on the croquet-lawn yesterday, you were out for food. You described the Blemleys as the dullest people to stay with that you knew, but said they were clever enough to employ a first-rate cook; otherwise they'd find it difficult to get any one to come down a second time.'

'There's not a word of truth in it! I appeal to Mrs Cornett –' exclaimed the discomfited Agnes.

'Mrs Cornett repeated your remark afterwards to Bertie van Tahn,' continued Tobermory, 'and said, "That woman is a regular Hunger Marcher; she'd go anywhere for four square meals a day," and Bertie van Tahn said –'

At this point the chronicle mercifully ceased. Tobermory had caught a glimpse of the big yellow Tom from the Rectory working his way through the shrubbery towards the stable wing. In a flash he had vanished through the open French window.

With the disappearance of his too brilliant pupil Cornelius Appin found himself beset by a hurricane of bitter upbraiding, anxious inquiry, and frightened entreaty. The responsibility for the situation lay with him, and he must prevent matters from becoming worse. Could Tobermory impart his dangerous gift to other cats? was the first question he had to answer. It was possible, he replied, that he might have initiated his intimate friend the stable puss into his new accomplishment, but it was unlikely that his teaching could have taken a wider range as yet.

'Then,' said Mrs Cornett, 'Tobermory may be a valuable cat and a great pet; but I'm sure you'll agree, Adelaide, that both he and the stable cat must be done away with without delay.'

'You don't suppose I've enjoyed the last quarter of an

hour, do you?' said Lady Blemley bitterly. 'My husband and I are very fond of Tobermory – at least, we were before this horrible accomplishment was infused into him; but now, of course, the only thing is to have him destroyed as soon as possible.'

'We can put some strychnine in the scraps he always gets at dinner-time,' said Sir Wilfrid, 'and I will go and drown the stable cat myself. The coachman will be very sore at losing his pet, but I'll say a very catching form of mange has broken out in both cats and we're afraid of its spreading to the kennels.'

'But my great discovery!' expostulated Mr Appin; 'after all my years of research and experiment –'

'You can go and experiment on the short-horns at the farm, who are under proper control,' said Mrs Cornett, 'or the elephants at the Zoological Gardens. They're said to be highly intelligent, and they have this recommendation, that they don't come creeping about our bedrooms and under chairs, and so forth.'

An archangel ecstatically proclaiming the Millennium, and then finding that it clashed unpardonably with Henley and would have to be indefinitely postponed, could hardly have felt more crestfallen than Cornelius Appin at the reception of his wonderful achievement. Public opinion, however, was against him – in fact, had the general voice been consulted on the subject it is probable that a strong minority vote would have been in favour of including him in the strychnine diet.

Defective train arrangements and a nervous desire to see matters brought to a finish prevented an immediate dispersal of the party, but dinner that evening was not a social success. Sir Wilfrid had had rather a trying time with the stable cat and subsequently with the coachman.

Agnes Resker ostentatiously limited her repast to a morsel of dry toast, which she bit as though it were a personal enemy; while Mavis Pellington maintained a vindictive silence throughout the meal. Lady Blemley kept up a flow of what she hoped was conversation, but her attention was fixed on the doorway. A plateful of carefully dosed fish scraps was in readiness on the sideboard, but sweets and savoury and dessert went their way, and no Tobermory appeared either in the dining-room or kitchen.

The sepulchral dinner was cheerful compared with the subsequent vigil in the smoking-room. Eating and drinking had at least supplied a distraction and cloak to the prevailing embarrassment. Bridge was out of the question in the general tension of nerves and tempers, and after Odo Finsberry had given a lugubrious rendering of 'Mélisande in the Wood' to a frigid audience, music was tacitly avoided. At eleven the servants went to bed, announcing that the small window in the pantry had been left open as usual for Tobermory's private use. The guests read steadily through the current batch of magazines, and fell back gradually on the 'Badminton Library' and bound volumes of *Punch*. Lady Blemley made periodic visits to the pantry, returning each time with an expression of listless depression which forestalled questioning.

At two o'clock Clovis broke the dominating silence.

'He won't turn up tonight. He's probably in the local newspaper office at the present moment, dictating the first instalment of his reminiscences. Lady What's-her-name's book won't be in it. It will be the event of the day.'

Having made this contribution to the general cheerfulness, Clovis went to bed. At long intervals the various members of the house-party followed his example.

The servants taking round the early tea made a

uniform announcement in reply to a uniform question. Tobermory had not returned.

Breakfast was, if anything, a more unpleasant function than dinner had been, but before its conclusion the situation was relieved. Tobermory's corpse was brought in from the shrubbery, where a gardener had just discovered it. From the bites on his throat and the yellow fur which coated his claws it was evident that he had fallen in unequal combat with the big Tom from the Rectory.

By midday most of the guests had quitted the Towers, and after lunch Lady Blemley had sufficiently recovered her spirits to write an extremely nasty letter to the Rectory about the loss of her valuable pet.

Tobermory had been Appin's one successful pupil, and he was destined to have no successor. A few weeks later an elephant in the Dresden Zoological Garden, which had shown no previous signs of irritability, broke loose and killed an Englishman who had apparently been teasing it. The victim's name was variously reported in the papers as Oppin and Eppelin, but his front name was faithfully rendered Cornelius.

'If he was trying German irregular verbs on the poor beast,' said Clovis, 'he deserved all he got.'

Mrs Packletide's Tiger

IT WAS Mrs Packletide's pleasure and intention that she should shoot a tiger. Not that the lust to kill had suddenly descended on her, or that she felt that she would leave India safer and more wholesome than she had found it, with one fraction less of wild beast per million of inhabitants. The compelling motive for her sudden deviation towards the footsteps of Nimrod was the fact that Loona Bimberton had recently been carried eleven miles in an aeroplane by an Algerian aviator, and talked of nothing else; only a personally procured tiger-skin and a heavy harvest of Press photographs could successfully counter that sort of thing. Mrs Packletide had already arranged in her mind the lunch she would give at her house in Curzon Street, ostensibly in Loona Bimberton's honour, with a tiger-skin rug occupying most of the foreground and all of the conversation. She had also already designed in her mind the tiger-claw brooch that she was going to give Loona Bimberton on her next birthday. In a world that is supposed to be chiefly swayed by hunger and by love Mrs Packletide was an exception; her movements and motives were largely governed by dislike of Loona Bimberton.

Circumstances proved propitious. Mrs Packletide had offered a thousand rupees for the opportunity of shooting a tiger without overmuch risk or exertion, and it so happened that a neighbouring village could boast of being the favoured rendezvous of an animal of respectable antecedents, which had been driven by the increasing infirmities of age to abandon game-killing and confine its appetite to the smaller domestic animals. The prospect of earning the thousand rupees had stimulated the sporting and commercial instinct of the villagers; children were posted night and day on the outskirts of the local jungle to head the tiger back in the unlikely event of his attempting to roam away to fresh hunting-grounds, and the cheaper kinds of goats were left about with elaborate carelessness to keep him satisfied with his present quarters. The one great anxiety was lest he should die of old age before the date appointed for the memsahib's shoot. Mothers carrying their babies home through the jungle after the day's work in the fields hushed their singing lest they might curtail the restful sleep of the venerable herd-robber.

The great night duly arrived, moonlit and cloudless. A platform had been constructed in a comfortable and conveniently placed tree, and thereon crouched Mrs Packletide and her paid companion, Miss Mebbin. A goat, gifted with a particularly persistent bleat, such as even a partially deaf tiger might be reasonably expected to hear on a still night, was tethered at the correct distance. With an accurately sighted rifle and a thumb-nail pack of patience cards the sportswoman awaited the coming of the quarry.

'I suppose we are in some danger?' said Miss Mebbin.

She was not actually nervous about the wild beast, but she had a morbid dread of performing an atom more service than she had been paid for.

'Nonsense,' said Mrs Packletide; 'it's a very old tiger. It couldn't spring up here even if it wanted to.'

'If it's an old tiger I think you ought to get it cheaper. A thousand rupees is a lot of money.'

Louisa Mebbin adopted a protective elder-sister attitude towards money in general, irrespective of nationality or denomination. Her energetic intervention had saved many a rouble from dissipating itself in tips in some

Moscow hotel, and francs and centimes clung to her instinctively under circumstances which would have driven them headlong from less sympathetic hands. Her speculations as to the market depreciation of tiger remnants were cut short by the appearance on the scene of the animal itself. As soon as it caught sight of the tethered goat it lay flat on the earth, seemingly less from desire to take advantage of all available cover than for the purpose of snatching a short rest before commencing the grand attack.

'I believe it's ill,' said Louisa Mebbin, loudly in Hindustani, for the benefit of the village headman, who was in ambush in a neighbouring tree.

'Hush!' said Mrs Packletide, and at that moment the tiger commenced ambling towards his victim.

'Now, now!' urged Miss Mebbin with some excitement; 'if he doesn't touch the goat we needn't pay for it.' (The bait was an extra.)

The rifle flashed out with a loud report, and the great tawny beast sprang to one side and then rolled over in the stillness of death. In a moment a crowd of excited natives had swarmed on to the scene, and their shouting speedily carried the glad news to the village, where a thumping of tom-toms took up the chorus of triumph. And their triumph and rejoicing found a ready echo in the heart of Mrs Packletide; already that luncheon-party in Curzon Street seemed immeasurably nearer.

It was Louisa Mebbin who drew attention to the fact that the goat was in death-throes from a mortal bullet-wound, while no trace of the rifle's deadly work could be found on the tiger. Evidently the wrong animal had been hit, and the beast of prey had succumbed to heart-failure, caused by the sudden report of the rifle, accelerated by senile decay. Mrs Packletide was pardonably annoyed at the discovery; but, at any rate, she was the possessor of a dead tiger, and the villagers, anxious for their thousand rupees, gladly connived at the fiction that she had shot the beast. And Miss Mebbin was a paid companion. Therefore did Mrs Packletide face the cameras with a light heart, and her pictured fame reached from the pages of the *Texas Weekly Snapshot* to the illustrated Monday supplement of the *Novoe Vremya*. As for Loona Bimberton, she refused to look at an illustrated paper for weeks, and her letter of thanks for the gift of a tiger-claw brooch was a model of repressed emotions. The luncheon-party she declined; there are limits beyond which repressed emotions become dangerous.

From Curzon Street the tiger-skin rug travelled down to the Manor House, and was duly inspected and admired by the county, and it seemed a fitting and appropriate thing when Mrs Packletide went to the County Costume Ball in the character of Diana. She refused to fall in, however, with Clovis's tempting suggestion of a primeval dance party, at which every one should wear the skins of beasts they had recently slain. 'I should be in rather a Baby Bunting condition,' confessed Clovis, 'with a miserable rabbit-skin or two to wrap up in, but then,' he added, with a rather malicious glance at Diana's proportions, 'my figure is quite as good as that Russian dancing boy's.'

'How amused every one would be if they knew what really happened,' said Louisa Mebbin a few days after the ball.

'What do you mean?' asked Mrs Packletide quickly.

'How you shot the goat and frightened the tiger to death,' said Miss Mebbin, with her disagreeably pleasant laugh.

'No one would believe it,' said Mrs Packletide, her face changing colour as rapidly as though it were going through a book of patterns before post-time.

'Loona Bimberton would,' said Miss Mebbin. Mrs Packletide's face settled on an unbecoming shade of greenish white.

'You surely wouldn't give me away?' she asked.

'I've seen a week-end cottage near Dorking that I should rather like to buy,' said Miss Mebbin with seeming irrelevance. 'Six hundred and eighty, freehold. Quite a bargain, only I don't happen to have the money.'

Louisa Mebbin's pretty week-end cottage, christened by her 'Les Fauves', and gay in summer-time with its garden borders of tiger-lilies, is the wonder and admiration of her friends.

'It is a marvel how Louisa manages to do it,' is the general verdict.

Mrs Packletide indulges in no more big-game shooting.

'The incidental expenses are so heavy,' she confides to inquiring friends.

The Stampeding of Lady Bastable

'IT WOULD BE rather nice if you would put Clovis up for another six days while I go up north to the MacGregors',' said Mrs Sangrail sleepily across the breakfast-table. It was her invariable plan to speak in a sleepy, comfortable voice whenever she was unusually keen about anything; it put people off their guard, and they frequently fell in with her wishes before they had realized that she was really asking for anything. Lady Bastable, however, was not so easily taken unawares; possibly she knew that voice and what it betokened – at any rate, she knew Clovis.

She frowned at a piece of toast and ate it very slowly, as though she wished to convey the impression that the process hurt her more than it hurt the toast; but no extension of hospitality on Clovis's behalf rose to her lips.

'It would be a great convenience to me,' pursued Mrs Sangrail, abandoning the careless tone. 'I particularly don't want to take him to the MacGregors', and it will only be for six days.'

'It will seem longer,' said Lady Bastable dismally. 'The last time he stayed here for a week –'

'I know,' interrupted the other hastily, 'but that was nearly two years ago. He was younger then.'

'But he hasn't improved,' said her hostess; 'it's no use growing older if you only learn new ways of misbehaving yourself.'

Mrs Sangrail was unable to argue the point; since Clovis had reached the age of seventeen she had never ceased to bewail his irrepressible waywardness to all her circle of acquaintances, and a polite scepticism would have greeted the slightest hint at a prospective reformation. She discarded the fruitless effort at cajolery and resorted to undisguised bribery.

'If you'll have him here for these six days I'll cancel that outstanding bridge account.'

It was only for forty-nine shillings, but Lady Bastable loved shillings with a great, strong love. To lose money at bridge and not to have to pay it was one of those rare experiences which gave the card-table a glamour in her eyes which it could never otherwise have possessed. Mrs Sangrail was almost equally devoted to her card winnings, but the prospect of conveniently warehousing her offspring for six days, and incidentally saving his railway fare to the north, reconciled her to the sacrifice; when Clovis made a belated appearance at the breakfast-table the bargain had been struck.

'Just think,' said Mrs Sangrail sleepily; 'Lady Bastable has very kindly asked you to stay on here while I go to the MacGregors'.'

Clovis said suitable things in a highly unsuitable manner, and proceeded to make punitive expeditions among the breakfast dishes with a scowl on his face that would have driven the purr out of a peace conference. The arrangement that had been concluded behind his back was doubly distasteful to him. In the first place, he particularly wanted to teach the MacGregor boys, who could well afford the knowledge, how to play poker-patience; secondly, the Bastable catering was of the kind that is classified as a rude plenty, which Clovis translated as a plenty that gives rise to rude remarks. Watching him from behind ostentatiously sleepy lids, his mother realized, in the light of long experience, that any rejoicing over the success of her manœuvre would be distinctly premature. It was one thing to fit Clovis into a convenient niche of the domestic jigsaw puzzle; it was quite another matter to get him to stay there.

Lady Bastable was wont to retire in state to the morning-room immediately after breakfast and spend a quiet hour in skimming through the papers; they were there, so she might as well get their money's worth out of them. Politics did not greatly interest her, but she was obsessed with a favourite foreboding that one of these days there would be a great social upheaval, in which everybody would be killed by everybody else. 'It will come sooner than we think,' she would observe darkly; a mathematical expert of exceptionally high powers would have been puzzled to work out the approximate date from the slender and confusing groundwork which this assertion afforded.

On this particular morning the sight of Lady Bastable enthroned among her papers gave Clovis the hint towards which his mind had been groping all breakfast time. His mother had gone upstairs to supervise packing operations, and he was alone on the ground-floor with his hostess – and the servants. The latter were the key to the situation. Bursting wildly into the kitchen quarters, Clovis screamed a frantic though strictly non-committal summons: 'Poor Lady Bastable! In the morning-room! Oh, quick!' The next moment the butler, cook, page-boy, two or three maids, and a gardener who had happened to be in one of the outer kitchens were following in a hot scurry after Clovis as he headed back for the morning-room. Lady Bastable was roused from the world of newspaper lore by hearing a Japanese screen in the hall go down with a crash. Then the door leading from the hall flew open and her young guest tore madly through the room, shrieked at her in passing, 'The jacquerie! They're on us!' and dashed like an escaping hawk out through the French window. The scared mob of servants burst in on his heels, the gardener still clutching the sickle with which he had been trimming hedges, and the impetus of their headlong haste carried them, slipping and sliding, over the smooth parquet flooring towards the chair where their mistress sat in panic-stricken amazement. If she had had a moment granted her for reflection she would have behaved, as she afterwards explained, with considerable dignity. It was probably the sickle which decided her, but anyway she followed the lead that Clovis had given her through the French window, and ran well and far across the lawn before the eyes of her astonished retainers.

Lost dignity is not a possession which can be restored at a moment's notice, and both Lady Bastable and the butler found the process of returning to normal conditions almost as painful as a slow recovery from drowning. A jacquerie, even if carried out with the most respectful of intentions, cannot fail to leave some traces of embarrassment behind it. By lunch-time, however, decorum had reasserted itself with enhanced rigour as a natural rebound from its recent overthrow, and the meal was served in a frigid stateliness that might have been framed on a Byzantine model. Half-way through its duration Mrs Sangrail was solemnly presented with an envelope lying on a silver salver. It contained a cheque for forty-nine shillings.

The MacGregor boys learned how to play poker-patience; after all, they could afford to.

The Background

'THAT WOMAN'S ART-JARGON tires me,' said Clovis to his journalist friend. 'She's so fond of talking of certain pictures as "growing on one", as though they were a sort of fungus.'

'That reminds me,' said the journalist, 'of the story of Henri Deplis. Have I ever told it you?'

Clovis shook his head.

'Henri Deplis was by birth a native of the Grand Duchy of Luxemburg. On maturer reflection he became a commercial traveller. His business activities frequently took him beyond the limits of the Grand Duchy, and he was stopping in a small town of Northern Italy when news reached him from home that a legacy from a distant and deceased relative had fallen to his share.

'It was not a large legacy, even from the modest standpoint of Henri Deplis, but it impelled him towards some seemingly harmless extravagances. In particular it led him to patronize local art as represented by the tattoo-needles of Signor Andreas Pincini. Signor Pincini was, perhaps, the most brilliant master of tattoo craft that Italy had ever known, but his circumstances were decidedly impoverished, and for the sum of six hundred francs he gladly undertook to cover his client's back, from the collar-bone down to the waist-line, with a glowing representation of the Fall of Icarus. The design, when finally developed, was a slight disappointment to Monsieur Deplis, who had suspected Icarus of being a fortress taken by Wallenstein in the Thirty Years' War, but he was more than satisfied with the execution of the work, which was acclaimed by all who had the privilege of seeing it as Pincini's masterpiece.

'It was his greatest effort, and his last. Without even waiting to be paid, the illustrious craftsman departed this life, and was buried under an ornate tombstone, whose winged cherubs would have afforded singularly little scope for the exercise of his favourite art. There remained, however, the widow Pincini, to whom the six hundred francs were due. And thereupon arose the great crisis in the life of Henri Deplis, traveller of commerce. The legacy, under the stress of numerous little calls on its substance, had dwindled to very insignificant proportions, and when a pressing wine bill and sundry other current accounts had been paid, there remained little more than 430 francs to offer to the widow. The lady was properly indignant, not wholly, as she volubly explained, on account of the suggested writing-off of 170 francs, but also at the attempt to depreciate the value of her late husband's acknowledged masterpiece. In a week's time Deplis was obliged to reduce his offer to 405 francs, which circumstance fanned the widow's indignation into a fury. She cancelled the sale of the work of art, and a few days later Deplis learned with a sense of consternation that she had presented it to the municipality of Bergamo, which had gratefully accepted it. He left the neighbourhood as unobtrusively as possible, and was genuinely relieved when his business commands took him to Rome, where he hoped his identity and that of the famous picture might be lost sight of.

'But he bore on his back the burden of the dead man's genius. On presenting himself one day in the steaming corridor of a vapour bath, he was at once hustled back into his clothes by the proprietor, who was a North Italian, and who emphatically refused to allow the celebrated Fall of Icarus to be publicly on view without the permission of the municipality of Bergamo. Public interest and official vigilance increased as the matter became more widely known, and Deplis was unable to take a simple dip in the sea or river on the hottest afternoon unless clothed up to the collar-bone in a substantial bathing garment. Later on the authorities of Bergamo conceived the idea that salt water might be injurious to the masterpiece, and a perpetual injunction was obtained which debarred the muchly harassed commercial traveller from sea bathing under any circumstances. Altogether, he was fervently thankful when his firm of employers found him a new range of activities in the neighbourhood of Bordeaux. His thankfulness, however, ceased abruptly at the Franco-Italian frontier. An imposing array of official force barred his departure, and he was sternly reminded of the stringent law which forbids the exportation of Italian works of art.

'A diplomatic parley ensued between the Luxemburgian and Italian Governments, and at one time the European situation became overcast with the possibilities of trouble. But the Italian Government stood firm; it declined to concern itself in the least with the fortunes or even the existence of Henri Deplis, commercial traveller, but was immovable in its decision that the Fall of Icarus (by the late Pincini, Andreas) at present the property of the municipality of Bergamo, should not leave the country.

'The excitement died down in time, but the unfortunate Deplis, who was of a constitutionally retiring disposition, found himself a few months later once more the storm-centre of a furious controversy. A certain German art expert, who had obtained from the municipality of Bergamo permission to inspect the famous masterpiece, declared it to be a spurious Pincini, probably the work of some pupil whom he had employed in his declining years. The evidence of Deplis on the subject was obviously worthless, as he had been under the influence of the customary narcotics during the long process of pricking in the design. The editor of an Italian art journal refuted the contentions of the German expert and undertook to prove that his private life did not conform to any modern standard of decency. The whole of Italy and Germany were drawn into the dispute, and the rest of Europe was soon involved in the quarrel. There were stormy scenes in the Spanish Parliament, and the University of Copenhagen bestowed a gold medal on the German expert (afterwards sending a commission to examine his proofs on the spot), while two Polish schoolboys in Paris committed suicide to show what *they* thought of the matter.

'Meanwhile, the unhappy human background fared no better than before, and it was not surprising that he drifted into the ranks of Italian anarchists. Four times at least he was escorted to the frontier as a dangerous and undesirable foreigner, but he was always brought back as the Fall of Icarus (attributed to Pincini, Andreas, early Twentieth Century). And then one day, at an anarchist congress at Genoa, a fellow-worker, in the heat of debate, broke a phial full of corrosive liquid over his back. The red shirt that he was wearing mitigated the effects, but the Icarus was ruined beyond recognition. His assailant was severely reprimanded for assaulting a fellow-anarchist and received seven years' imprisonment for defacing a national art treasure. As soon as he was able to leave the hospital Henri Deplis was put across the frontier as an undesirable alien.

'In the quieter streets of Paris, especially in the neighbourhood of the Ministry of Fine Arts, you may sometimes meet a depressed, anxious-looking man, who, if you pass him the time of day, will answer you with a slight Luxemburgian accent. He nurses the illusion that he is one of the lost arms of the Venus de Milo, and hopes that the French Government may be persuaded to buy him. On all other subjects I believe he is tolerably sane.'

Sredni Vashtar

CONRADIN WAS TEN years old, and the doctor had pronounced his professional opinion that the boy would not
live another five years. The doctor was silky and effete,
and counted for little, but his opinion was endorsed by
Mrs De Ropp, who counted for nearly everything. Mrs
De Ropp was Conradin's cousin and guardian, and in his
eyes she represented those three-fifths of the world that
are necessary and disagreeable and real; the other two-
fifths, in perpetual antagonism to the foregoing, were
summed up in himself and his imagination. One of these
days Conradin supposed he would succumb to the mas-
tering pressure of wearisome necessary things – such as
illnesses and coddling restrictions and drawn-out dulness.
Without his imagination, which was rampant under the
spur of loneliness, he would have succumbed long ago.

Mrs De Ropp would never, in her honestest moments,
have confessed to herself that she disliked Conradin,
though she might have been dimly aware that thwarting
him 'for his good' was a duty which she did not find particularly irksome. Conradin hated her with a desperate
sincerity which he was perfectly able to mask. Such few
pleasures as he could contrive for himself gained an added
relish from the likelihood that they would be displeasing
to his guardian, and from the realm of his imagination she
was locked out – an unclean thing, which should find no
entrance.

In the dull, cheerless garden, overlooked by so many
windows that were ready to open with a message not to
do this or that, or a reminder that medicines were due,
he found little attraction. The few fruit-trees that it

contained were set jealously apart from his plucking, as though they were rare specimens of their kind blooming in an arid waste; it would probably have been difficult to find a market-gardener who would have offered ten shillings for their entire yearly produce. In a forgotten corner, however, almost hidden behind a dismal shrubbery, was a disused tool-shed of respectable proportions, and within its walls Conradin found a haven, something that took on the varying aspects of a playroom and a cathedral. He had peopled it with a legion of familiar phantoms, evoked partly from fragments of history and partly from his own brain, but it also boasted two inmates of flesh and blood. In one corner lived a ragged-plumaged Houdan hen, on which the boy lavished an affection that had scarcely another outlet. Further back in the gloom stood a large hutch, divided into two compartments, one of which was fronted with close iron bars. This was the abode of a large polecat-ferret, which a friendly butcher-boy had once smuggled, cage and all, into its present quarters, in exchange for a long-secreted hoard of small silver. Conradin was dreadfully afraid of the lithe, sharp-fanged beast, but it was his most treasured possession. Its very presence in the tool-shed was a secret and fearful joy, to be kept scrupulously from the knowledge of the Woman, as he privately dubbed his cousin. And one day, out of Heaven knows what material, he spun the beast a wonderful name, and from that moment it grew into a god and a religion. The Woman indulged in religion once a week at a church near by, and took Conradin with her, but to him the church service was an alien rite in the House of Rimmon. Every Thursday, in the dim and musty silence of the tool-shed, he worshipped with mystic and elaborate ceremonial before the wooden hutch where dwelt Sredni Vashtar, the great ferret. Red flowers in their season and scarlet berries in the winter-time were offered at his shrine, for he was a god who laid some special stress on the fierce impatient side of things, as opposed to the Woman's religion, which, as far as Conradin could observe, went to great lengths in the contrary direction. And on great festivals powdered nutmeg was strewn in front of his hutch, an important feature of the offering being that the nutmeg had to be stolen. These festivals were of irregular occurrence, and were chiefly appointed to celebrate some passing event. On one occasion, when Mrs De Ropp suffered from acute toothache for three days, Conradin kept up the festival during the entire three days, and almost succeeded in persuading himself that Sredni Vashtar was personally responsible for the toothache. If the malady had lasted for another day the supply of nutmeg would have given out.

The Houdan hen was never drawn into the cult of Sredni Vashtar. Conradin had long ago settled that she was an Anabaptist. He did not pretend to have the remotest knowledge as to what an Anabaptist was, but he privately hoped that it was dashing and not very respectable. Mrs De Ropp was the ground plan on which he based and detested all respectability.

After a while Conradin's absorption in the tool-shed began to attract the notice of his guardian. 'It is not good for him to be pottering down there in all weathers,' she promptly decided, and at breakfast one morning she announced that the Houdan hen had been sold and taken away overnight. With her short-sighted eyes she peered at Conradin, waiting for an outbreak of rage and sorrow, which she was ready to rebuke with a flow of excellent precepts and reasoning. But Conradin said nothing: there was nothing to be said. Something perhaps in his white set face gave her a momentary qualm, for at tea that afternoon there was toast on the table, a delicacy which she usually banned on the ground that it was bad for him; also because the making of it 'gave trouble', a deadly offence in the middle-class feminine eye.

'I thought you liked toast,' she exclaimed, with an injured air, observing that he did not touch it.

'Sometimes,' said Conradin.

In the shed that evening there was an innovation in the worship of the hutch-god. Conradin had been wont to chant his praises, tonight he asked a boon.

'Do one thing for me, Sredni Vashtar.'

The thing was not specified. As Sredni Vashtar was a god he must be supposed to know. And choking back a sob as he looked at that other empty corner, Conradin went back to the world he so hated.

And every night, in the welcome darkness of his bedroom, and every evening in the dusk of the tool-shed, Conradin's bitter litany went up: 'Do one thing for me, Sredni Vashtar.'

Mrs De Ropp noticed that the visits to the shed did not cease, and one day she made a further journey of inspection.

'What are you keeping in that locked hutch?' she asked. 'I believe it's guinea-pigs. I'll have them all cleared away.'

Conradin shut his lips tight, but the Woman ransacked his bedroom till she found the carefully hidden key, and forthwith marched down to the shed to complete her discovery. It was a cold afternoon, and Conradin had been bidden to keep to the house. From the furthest window of the dining-room the door of the shed could just be seen beyond the corner of the shrubbery, and there Conradin stationed himself. He saw the Woman enter, and then he imagined her opening the door of the sacred hutch and peering down with her short-sighted eyes into the thick straw bed where his god lay hidden. Perhaps she would prod at the straw in her clumsy impatience. And Conradin fervently breathed his prayer for the last time. But he knew as he prayed that he did not believe. He knew that the Woman would come out presently with that pursed smile he loathed so well on her face, and that in an hour or two the gardener would carry away his wonderful god, a god no longer, but a simple brown ferret in a hutch. And he knew that the Woman would triumph always as she triumphed now, and that he would grow ever more sickly under her pestering and domineering and superior wisdom, till one day nothing would matter much more with him, and the doctor would be proved right. And in the sting and misery of his defeat, he began to chant loudly and defiantly the hymn of his threatened idol:

Sredni Vashtar went forth,
His thoughts were red thoughts and his teeth
    were white.
His enemies called for peace, but he brought
    them death.
Sredni Vashtar the Beautiful.

And then of a sudden he stopped his chanting and drew closer to the window-pane. The door of the shed still stood ajar as it had been left, and the minutes were slipping by. They were long minutes, but they slipped by nevertheless. He watched the starlings running and flying in little parties across the lawn; he counted them over and over again, with one eye always on that swinging door. A sour-faced maid came in to lay the table for tea, and still Conradin stood and waited and watched. Hope had crept by inches into his heart, and now a look of triumph began to blaze in his eyes that had only known the wistful patience of defeat. Under his breath, with a furtive exultation, he began once again the pæan of victory and devastation. And presently his eyes were rewarded: out through that doorway came a long, low, yellow-and-brown beast, with eyes a-blink at the waning daylight, and dark wet stains around the fur of jaws and throat. Conradin dropped on his knees. The great polecat-ferret made its way down to a small brook at the foot of the garden, drank for a moment, then crossed a little plank bridge and was lost to sight in the bushes. Such was the passing of Sredni Vashtar.

'Tea is ready,' said the sour-faced maid; 'where is the mistress?'

'She went down to the shed some time ago,' said Conradin.

And while the maid went to summon her mistress to tea, Conradin fished a toasting-fork out of the sideboard drawer and proceeded to toast himself a piece of bread. And during the toasting of it and the buttering of it with much butter and the slow enjoyment of eating it, Conradin listened to the noises and silences which fell in quick spasms beyond the dining-room door. The loud foolish screaming of the maid, the answering chorus of wondering ejaculations from the kitchen region, the scuttering footsteps and hurried embassies for outside help, and then, after a lull, the scared sobbings and the shuffling tread of those who bore a heavy burden into the house.

'Whoever will break it to the poor child? I couldn't for the life of me!' exclaimed a shrill voice. And while they debated the matter among themselves, Conradin made himself another piece of toast.

Adrian

A CHAPTER IN ACCLIMATIZATION

HIS BAPTISMAL REGISTER spoke of him pessimistically as John Henry, but he had left that behind with the other maladies of infancy, and his friends knew him under the front-name of Adrian. His mother lived in Bethnal Green, which was not altogether his fault; one can discourage too much history in one's family, but one cannot always prevent geography. And, after all, the Bethnal Green habit has this virtue – that it is seldom transmitted to the next generation. Adrian lived in a roomlet which came under the auspicious constellation of W.

How he lived was to a great extent a mystery even to himself; his struggle for existence probably coincided in many material details with the rather dramatic accounts he gave of it to sympathetic acquaintances. All that is definitely known is that he now and then emerged from the struggle to dine at the Ritz or Carlton, correctly garbed and with a correctly critical appetite. On these occasions he was usually the guest of Lucas Croyden, an amiable worldling, who had three thousand a year and a taste for introducing impossible people to irreproachable cookery. Like most men who combine three thousand a year with an uncertain digestion, Lucas was a Socialist, and he argued that you cannot hope to elevate the masses until you have brought plovers' eggs into their lives and taught them to appreciate the difference between coupe Jacques and Macédoine de fruits. His friends pointed out that it was a doubtful kindness to initiate a boy from behind a drapery counter into the blessedness of the higher catering, to which Lucas invariably replied that all kindnesses were doubtful. Which was perhaps true.

It was after one of his Adrian evenings that Lucas met his aunt, Mrs Mebberley, at a fashionable teashop, where the lamp of family life is still kept burning and you meet relatives who might otherwise have slipped your memory.

'Who was that good-looking boy who was dining with you last night?' she asked. 'He looked much too nice to be thrown away upon you.'

Susan Mebberley was a charming woman, but she was also an aunt.

'Who are his people?' she continued, when the protégé's name (revised version) had been given her.

'His mother lives at Beth –'

Lucas checked himself on the threshold of what was perhaps a social indiscretion.

'Beth? Where is it? It sounds like Asia Minor. Is she mixed up with Consular people?'

'Oh, no. Her work lies among the poor.'

This was a side-slip into truth. The mother of Adrian was employed in a laundry.

'I see,' said Mrs Mebberley, 'mission work of some sort. And meanwhile the boy has no one to look after him. It's obviously my duty to see that he doesn't come to harm. Bring him to call on me.'

'My dear Aunt Susan,' expostulated Lucas, 'I really know very little about him. He may not be at all nice, you know, on further acquaintance.'

'He has delightful hair and a weak mouth. I shall take him with me to Homburg or Cairo.'

'It's the maddest thing I ever heard of,' said Lucas angrily.

'Well, there is a strong strain of madness in our family.

If you haven't noticed it yourself all your friends must have.'

'One is so dreadfully under everybody's eyes at Homburg. At least you might give him a preliminary trial at Etretat.'

'And be surrounded by Americans trying to talk French? No, thank you. I love Americans, but not when they try to talk French. What a blessing it is that they never try to talk English. Tomorrow at five you can bring your young friend to call on me.'

And Lucas, realizing that Susan Mebberley was a woman as well as an aunt, saw that she would have to be allowed to have her own way.

Adrian was duly carried abroad under the Mebberley wing; but as a reluctant concession to sanity Homburg and other inconveniently fashionable resorts were given a wide berth, and the Mebberley establishment planted itself down in the best hotel at Dohledorf, an Alpine townlet somewhere at the back of the Engadine. It was the usual kind of resort, with the usual type of visitors, that one finds over the greater part of Switzerland during the summer season, but to Adrian it was all unusual. The mountain air, the certainty of regular and abundant meals, and in particular the social atmosphere, affected him much as the indiscriminating fervour of a forcing-house might affect a weed that had strayed within its limits. He had been brought up in a world where breakages were regarded as crimes and expiated as such; it was something new and altogether exhilarating to find that you were considered rather amusing if you smashed things in the right manner and at the recognized hours. Susan Mebberley had expressed the intention of showing Adrian a bit of the world; the particular bit of the world represented by Dohledorf began to be shown a good deal of Adrian.

Lucas got occasional glimpses of the Alpine sojourn, not from his aunt or Adrian, but from the industrious pen of Clovis, who was also moving as a satellite in the Mebberley constellation.

'The entertainment which Susan got up last night ended in disaster. I thought it would. The Grobmayer child, a particularly loathsome five-year-old, had appeared as "Bubbles" during the early part of the evening, and been put to bed during the interval. Adrian watched his opportunity and kidnapped it when the nurse was downstairs, and introduced it during the second half of the entertainment, thinly disguised as a performing pig. It certainly *looked* very like a pig, and grunted and slobbered just like the real article; no one knew exactly what it was, but every one said it was awfully clever, especially the Grobmayers. At the third curtain Adrian pinched it too hard, and it yelled "Marmar"! I am supposed to be good at descriptions, but don't ask me to describe the sayings and doings of the Grobmayers at that moment; it was like one of the angrier Psalms set to Strauss's music. We have moved to an hotel higher up the valley.'

Clovis's next letter arrived five days later, and was written from the Hotel Steinbock.

'We left the Hotel Victoria this morning. It was fairly comfortable and quiet – at least there was an air of repose about it when we arrived. Before we had been in residence twenty-four hours most of the repose had vanished "like a dutiful bream", as Adrian expressed it. However, nothing unduly outrageous happened till last night, when Adrian had a fit of insomnia and amused himself by unscrewing and transposing all the bedroom numbers on his floor. He transferred the bathroom label to the adjoining bedroom door, which happened to be that of Frau Hofrath Schilling, and this morning from seven o'clock onwards the old lady had a stream of involuntary visitors; she was too horrified and scandalized it seems to get up and lock her door. The would-be bathers flew back in confusion to their rooms, and, of course, the change of numbers led them astray again, and the corridor gradually filled with panic-stricken, scantily robed humans, dashing wildly about like rabbits in a ferret-infested warren. It took nearly an hour before the guests were all sorted into their respective rooms, and the Frau Hofrath's condition was still causing some anxiety when we left. Susan is beginning to look a little worried. She can't very well turn the boy adrift, as he hasn't got any money, and she can't send him to his people as she doesn't know where they are. Adrian says his mother moves about a good deal and he's lost her address. Probably, if the truth were known, he's had a row at home. So many boys nowadays seem to think that quarrelling with one's family is a recognized occupation.'

Lucas's next communication from the travellers took the form of a telegram from Mrs Mebberley herself. It was sent 'reply prepaid', and consisted of a single sentence: 'In Heaven's name, where is Beth?'

The Music on the Hill

SYLVIA SELTOUN ATE her breakfast in the morning-room at Yessney with a pleasant sense of ultimate victory, such as a fervent Iron-side might have permitted himself on the morrow of Worcester fight. She was scarcely pugnacious by temperament, but belonged to that more successful class of fighters who are pugnacious by circumstance. Fate had willed that her life should be occupied with a series of small struggles, usually with the odds slightly against her, and usually she had just managed to come through winning. And now she felt that she had brought her hardest and certainly her most important struggle to a successful issue. To have married Mortimer Seltoun, 'Dead Mortimer' as his more intimate enemies called him, in the teeth of the cold hostility of his family, and in spite of his unaffected indifference to women, was indeed an achievement that had needed some determination and adroitness to carry through; yesterday she had brought her victory to its concluding stage by wrenching her husband away from Town and its group of satellite watering-places and 'settling him down', in the vocabulary of her kind, in this remote wood-girt manor farm which was his country house.

'You will never get Mortimer to go,' his mother had said carpingly, 'but if he once goes he'll stay; Yessney throws almost as much a spell over him as Town does. One can understand what holds him to Town, but Yessney –' and the dowager had shrugged her shoulders.

There was a sombre almost savage wildness about Yessney that was certainly not likely to appeal to town-bred tastes, and Sylvia, notwithstanding her name, was accustomed to nothing much more sylvan than 'leafy Kensington'. She looked on the country as something excellent and wholesome in its way, which was apt to become troublesome if you encouraged it overmuch. Distrust of town-life had been a new thing with her, born of her marriage with Mortimer, and she had watched with satisfaction the gradual fading of what she called 'the Jermyn-Street-look' in his eyes as the woods and heather of Yessney had closed in on them yesternight. Her willpower and strategy had prevailed; Mortimer would stay.

Outside the morning-room windows was a triangular slope of turf, which the indulgent might call a lawn, and beyond its low hedge of neglected fuchsia bushes a steeper slope of heather and bracken dropped down into cavernous combes overgrown with oak and yew. In its wild open savagery there seemed a stealthy linking of the joy of life with the terror of unseen things. Sylvia smiled complacently as she gazed with a School-of-Art appreciation at the landscape, and then of a sudden she almost shuddered.

'It is very wild,' she said to Mortimer, who had joined her; 'one could almost think that in such a place the worship of Pan had never quite died out.'

'The worship of Pan never has died out,' said Mortimer. 'Other newer gods have drawn aside his votaries from time to time, but he is the Nature-God to whom all must come back at last. He has been called the Father of all the Gods, but most of his children have been stillborn.'

Sylvia was religious in an honest, vaguely devotional kind of way, and did not like to hear her beliefs spoken of as mere after-growths, but it was at least something new and hopeful to hear Dead Mortimer speak with such energy and conviction on any subject.

'You don't really believe in Pan?' she asked incredulously.

'I've been a fool in most things,' said Mortimer quietly, 'but I'm not such a fool as not to believe in Pan when I'm down here. And if you're wise you won't disbelieve in him too boastfully while you're in his country.'

It was not till a week later, when Sylvia had exhausted the attractions of the woodland walks round Yessney, that she ventured on a tour of inspection of the farm buildings. A farmyard suggested in her mind a scene of cheerful bustle, with churns and flails and smiling dairymaids, and teams of horses drinking knee-deep in duck-crowded ponds. As she wandered among the gaunt grey buildings of Yessney manor farm her first impression was one of crushing stillness and desolation, as though she had happened on some lone deserted homestead long given over to owls and cobwebs; then came a sense of furtive watchful hostility, the same shadow of unseen things that seemed to lurk in the wooded combes and coppices. From behind heavy doors and shuttered windows came the restless stamp of hoof or rasp of chain halter, and at times a muffled bellow from some stalled beast. From a distant corner a shaggy dog watched her with intent unfriendly eyes; as she drew near it slipped quietly into its kennel, and slipped out again as noiselessly when she had passed by. A few hens, questing for food under a rick, stole away under a gate at her approach. Sylvia felt that if she had come across any human beings in this wilderness of barn and byre they would have fled wraith-like from her gaze. At last, turning a corner quickly, she came upon a living thing that did not fly from her. Astretch in a pool of mud was an enormous sow, gigantic beyond the town-woman's wildest computation of swine-flesh, and speedily alert to resent and if necessary repel the unwonted intrusion. It was Sylvia's turn to make an unobtrusive retreat. As she threaded her way past rickyards and cowsheds and long blank walls, she started suddenly at a strange sound – the echo of a boy's laughter, golden and equivocal. Jan, the only boy employed on the farm, a tow-headed, wizen-faced yokel, was visibly at work on a potato clearing half-way up the nearest hill-side, and Mortimer, when questioned, knew of no other probable or possible begetter of the hidden mockery that had ambushed Sylvia's retreat. The memory of that untraceable echo was added to her other impressions of a furtive sinister 'something' that hung around Yessney.

Of Mortimer she saw very little; farm and woods and trout-streams seemed to swallow him up from dawn till dusk. Once, following the direction she had seen him take in the morning, she came to an open space in a nut copse, further shut in by huge yew trees, in the centre of which stood a stone pedestal surmounted by a small bronze figure of a youthful Pan. It was a beautiful piece of workmanship, but her attention was chiefly held by the fact that a newly cut bunch of grapes had been placed as an offering at its feet. Grapes were none too plentiful at the manor house, and Sylvia snatched the bunch angrily from the pedestal. Contemptuous annoyance dominated her thoughts as she strolled slowly homeward, and then gave way to a sharp feeling of something that was very near fright; across a thick tangle of undergrowth a boy's face was scowling at her, brown and beautiful, with un-utterably evil eyes. It was a lonely pathway, all pathways round Yessney were lonely for the matter of that, and she sped forward without waiting to give a closer scrutiny to this sudden apparition. It was not till she had reached the house that she discovered that she had dropped the bunch of grapes in her flight.

'I saw a youth in the wood today,' she told Mortimer that evening, 'brown-faced and rather handsome, but a scoundrel to look at. A gipsy lad, I suppose.'

'A reasonable theory,' said Mortimer, 'only there aren't any gipsies in these parts at present.'

'Then who was he?' asked Sylvia, and as Mortimer appeared to have no theory of his own, she passed on to recount her finding of the votive offering.

'I suppose it was your doing,' she observed; 'it's a harmless piece of lunacy, but people would think you dreadfully silly if they knew of it.'

'Did you meddle with it in any way?' asked Mortimer.

'I – I threw the grapes away. It seemed so silly,' said Sylvia, watching Mortimer's impassive face for a sign of annoyance.

'I don't think you were wise to do that,' he said reflectively. 'I've heard it said that the Wood Gods are rather horrible to those who molest them.'

'Horrible perhaps to those that believe in them, but you see I don't,' retorted Sylvia.

'All the same,' said Mortimer in his even, dispassionate tone, 'I should avoid the woods and orchards if I were you, and give a wide berth to the horned beasts on the farm.'

It was all nonsense, of course, but in that lonely wood-girt spot nonsense seemed able to rear a bastard brood of uneasiness.

'Mortimer,' said Sylvia suddenly, 'I think we will go back to Town some time soon.'

Her victory had not been so complete as she had supposed; it had carried her on to ground that she was already anxious to quit.

'I don't think you will ever go back to Town,' said Mortimer. He seemed to be paraphrasing his mother's prediction as to himself.

Sylvia noted with dissatisfaction and some self-contempt that the course of her next afternoon's ramble took her instinctively clear of the network of woods. As to the horned cattle, Mortimer's warning was scarcely needed, for she had always regarded them as of doubtful neutrality at the best: her imagination unsexed the most matronly dairy cows and turned them into bulls liable to 'see red' at any moment. The ram who fed in the narrow paddock below the orchards she had adjudged, after ample and cautious probation, to be of docile temper; today, however, she decided to leave his docility untested, for the usually tranquil beast was roaming with every sign of restlessness from corner to corner of his meadow. A low, fitful piping, as of some reedy flute, was coming from the depth of a neighbouring copse, and there seemed to be some subtle connection between the animal's restless pacing and the wild music from the wood. Sylvia turned her steps in an upward direction and climbed the heather-clad slopes that stretched in rolling shoulders high above Yessney. She had left the piping notes behind her, but across the wooded combes at her feet the wind brought her another kind of music, the straining bay of hounds in full chase. Yessney was just on the outskirts of the Devon-and-Somerset country, and the hunted deer sometimes came that way. Sylvia could presently see a dark body, breasting hill after hill, and sinking again and again out of sight as he crossed the combes, while behind him steadily swelled that relentless chorus, and she grew tense with the excited sympathy that one feels for any hunted thing in whose capture one is not directly interested. And at last

III

he broke through the outermost line of oak scrub and fern and stood panting in the open, a fat September stag carrying a well-furnished head. His obvious course was to drop down to the brown pools of Undercombe, and thence make his way towards the red deer's favoured sanctuary, the sea. To Sylvia's surprise, however, he turned his head to the upland slope and came lumbering resolutely onward over the heather. 'It will be dreadful,' she thought, 'the hounds will pull him down under my very eyes.' But the music of the pack seemed to have died away for a moment, and in its place she heard again that wild piping, which rose now on this side, now on that, as though urging the failing stag to a final effort. Sylvia stood well aside from his path, half hidden in a thick growth of whortle bushes, and watched him swing stiffly upward, his flanks dark with sweat, the coarse hair on his neck showing light by contrast. The pipe music shrilled suddenly around her, seeming to come from the bushes at her very feet, and at the same moment the great beast slewed round and bore directly down upon her. In an instant her pity for the hunted animal was changed to wild terror at her own danger; the thick heather roots mocked her scrambling efforts at flight, and she looked frantically downward for a glimpse of oncoming hounds. The huge antler spikes were within a few yards of her, and in a flash of numbing fear she remembered Mortimer's warning, to beware of horned beasts on the farm. And then with a quick throb of joy she saw that she was not alone; a human figure stood a few paces aside, knee-deep in the whortle bushes.

'Drive it off!' she shrieked. But the figure made no answering movement.

The antlers drove straight at her breast, the acrid smell

of the hunted animal was in her nostrils, but her eyes were filled with the horror of something she saw other than her oncoming death. And in her ears rang the echo of a boy's laughter, golden and equivocal.

The Way to the Dairy

THE BARONESS AND Clovis sat in a much-frequented corner of the Park exchanging biographical confidences about the long succession of passers-by.

'Who are those depressed-looking young women who have just gone by?' asked the Baroness; 'they have the air of people who have bowed to destiny and are not quite sure whether the salute will be returned.'

'Those,' said Clovis, 'are the Brimley Bomefields. I dare say you would look depressed if you had been through their experiences.'

'I'm always having depressing experiences,' said the Baroness, 'but I never give them outward expression. It's as bad as looking one's age. Tell me about the Brimley Bomefields.'

'Well,' said Clovis, 'the beginning of their tragedy was that they found an aunt. The aunt had been there all the time, but they had very nearly forgotten her existence until a distant relative refreshed their memory by remembering her very distinctly in his will; it is wonderful what the force of example will accomplish. The aunt, who had been unobtrusively poor, became quite pleasantly rich, and the Brimley Bomefields grew suddenly concerned at the loneliness of her life and took her under their collective wings. She had as many wings around her at this time as one of those beast-things in Revelation.'

'So far I don't see any tragedy from the Brimley Bomefields' point of view,' said the Baroness.

'We haven't got to it yet,' said Clovis. 'The aunt had been used to living very simply, and had seen next to nothing of what we should consider life, and her nieces didn't encourage her to do much in the way of making a splash with her money. Quite a good deal of it would come to them at her death, and she was a fairly old woman, but there was one circumstance which cast a shadow of gloom over the satisfaction they felt in the discovery and acquisition of this desirable aunt: she openly acknowledged that a comfortable slice of her little fortune would go to a nephew on the other side of her family. He was rather a deplorable thing in rotters, and quite hopelessly top-hole in the way of getting through money, but he had been more or less decent to the old lady in her unremembered days, and she wouldn't hear anything against him. At least, she wouldn't pay any attention to what she did hear, but her nieces took care that she should have to listen to a good deal in that line. It seemed such a pity, they said among themselves, that good money should fall into such worthless hands. They habitually spoke of their aunt's money as 'good money', as though other people's aunts dabbled for the most part in spurious currency.

'Regularly after the Derby, St Leger, and other notable racing events they indulged in audible speculations as to how much money Roger had squandered in unfortunate betting transactions.

'"His travelling expenses must come to a big sum," said the eldest Brimley Bomefield one day; "they say he attends every race-meeting in England, besides others abroad. I shouldn't wonder if he went all the way to India to see the race for the Calcutta Sweepstake that one hears so much about."

'"Travel enlarges the mind, my dear Christine," said her aunt.

'"Yes, dear aunt, travel undertaken in the right spirit,"

agreed Christine; "but travel pursued merely as a means towards gambling and extravagant living is more likely to contract the purse than to enlarge the mind. However, as long as Roger enjoys himself, I suppose he doesn't care how fast or unprofitably the money goes, or where he is to find more. It seems a pity, that's all."

'The aunt by that time had begun to talk of something else, and it was doubtful if Christine's moralizing had been even accorded a hearing. It was her remark, however – the aunt's remark, I mean – about travel enlarging the mind, that gave the youngest Brimley Bomefield her great idea for the showing-up of Roger.

'"If aunt could only be taken somewhere to see him gambling and throwing away money," she said, "it would open her eyes to his character more effectually than anything we can say."

'"My dear Veronique," said her sisters, "we can't go following him to race-meetings."

'"Certainly not to race-meetings," said Veronique, "but we might go to some place where one can look on at gambling without taking part in it."

'"Do you mean Monte Carlo?" they asked her, beginning to jump rather at the idea.

'"Monte Carlo is a long way off, and has a dreadful reputation," said Veronique; "I shouldn't like to tell our friends that we were going to Monte Carlo. But I believe Roger usually goes to Dieppe about this time of year, and some quite respectable English people go there, and the journey wouldn't be expensive. If aunt could stand the Channel crossing the change of scene might do her a lot of good."

'And that was how the fateful idea came to the Brimley Bomefields.

'From the very first set-off disaster hung over the expedition, as they afterwards remembered. To begin with, all the Brimley Bomefields were extremely unwell during the crossing, while the aunt enjoyed the sea air and made friends with all manner of strange travelling companions. Then, although it was many years since she had been on the Continent, she had served a very practical apprenticeship there as a paid companion, and her knowledge of colloquial French beat theirs to a standstill. It became increasingly difficult to keep under their collective wings a person who knew what she wanted and was able to ask for it and to see that she got it. Also, as far as Roger was concerned, they drew Dieppe blank; it turned out that he was staying at Pourville, a little watering-place a mile or two further west. The Brimley Bomefields discovered that Dieppe was too crowded and frivolous, and persuaded the old lady to migrate to the comparative seclusion of Pourville.

'"You won't find it dull, you know," they assured her; "there is a little casino attached to the hotel, and you can watch the people dancing and throwing away their money at *petits chevaux*."

'It was just before *petits chevaux* had been supplanted by *boule*.

'Roger was not staying in the same hotel, but they knew that the casino would be certain of his patronage on most afternoons and evenings.

'On the first evening of their visit they wandered into the casino after a fairly early dinner, and hovered near the tables. Bertie van Tahn was staying there at the time, and he described the whole incident to me. The Brimley Bomefields kept a furtive watch on the doors as though they were expecting some one to turn up, and the aunt got more and more amused and interested watching the little horses whirl round and round the board.

'"Do you know, poor little number eight hasn't won for the last thirty-two times," she said to Christine; "I've been keeping count. I shall really have to put five francs on him to encourage him."

'"Come and watch the dancing, dear," said Christine nervously. It was scarcely a part of their strategy that Roger should come in and find the old lady backing her fancy at the *petits chevaux* table.

'"Just wait while I put five francs on number eight," said the aunt, and in another moment her money was lying on the table. The horses commenced to move round; it was a slow race this time, and number eight crept up at the finish like some crafty demon and placed his nose just a fraction in front of number three, who had seemed to be winning easily. Recourse had to be had to measurement, and the number eight was proclaimed the winner. The aunt picked up thirty-five francs. After that the Brimley Bomefields would have had to have used concerted force to get her away from the tables. When Roger appeared on the scene she was fifty-two francs to the good; her nieces were hovering forlornly in the background, like chickens that have been hatched out by a duck and are despairingly watching their parent disporting herself in a dangerous and uncongenial element. The supper-party which Roger insisted on standing that night in honour of his aunt and the three Miss Brimley Bomefields was remarkable for the unrestrained gaiety of two of the participants and the funereal mirthlessness of the remaining guests.

'"I do not think," Christine confided afterwards to a friend, who re-confided it to Bertie van Tahn, "that I shall ever be able to touch *pâté de foie gras* again. It would bring back memories of that awful evening."

'For the next two or three days the nieces made plans for returning to England or moving on to some other resort where there was no casino. The aunt was busy making a system for winning at *petits chevaux*. Number eight, her first love, had been running rather unkindly for her, and a series of plunges on number five had turned out even worse.

'"Do you know, I dropped over seven hundred francs at the tables this afternoon," she announced cheerfully at dinner on the fourth evening of their visit.

'"Aunt! Twenty-eight pounds! And you were losing last night too."

'"Oh, I shall get it all back," she said optimistically; "but not here. These silly little horses are no good. I shall go somewhere where one can play comfortably at roulette. You needn't look so shocked. I've always felt that, given the opportunity, I should be an inveterate gambler, and now you darlings have put the opportunity in my way. I must drink your very good healths. Waiter, a bottle of *Pontet Canet*. Ah, it's number seven on the wine list; I shall plunge on number seven tonight. It won four times running this afternoon when I was backing that silly number five."

'Number seven was not in a winning mood that evening. The Brimley Bomefields, tired of watching disaster from a distance, drew near to the table where their aunt was now an honoured habituée, and gazed mournfully at the successive victories of one and five and eight and four, which swept "good money" out of the purse of seven's obstinate backer. The day's losses totalled something very near two thousand francs.

'"You incorrigible gamblers," said Roger chaffingly to them, when he found them at the tables.

'"We are not gambling," said Christine freezingly; "we are looking on."

'"I *don't* think," said Roger knowingly; "of course you're a syndicate and aunt is putting the stakes on for all of you. Any one can tell by your looks when the wrong horse wins that you've got a stake on."

'Aunt and nephew had supper alone that night, or at least they would have if Bertie hadn't joined them; all the Brimley Bomefields had headaches.

'The aunt carried them all off to Dieppe the next day and set cheerily about the task of winning back some of her losses. Her luck was variable; in fact, she had some fair streaks of good fortune, just enough to keep her thoroughly amused with her new distraction; but on the whole she was a loser. The Brimley Bomefields had a collective attack of nervous prostration on the day when she sold out a quantity of shares in Argentine rails. "Nothing will ever bring that money back," they remarked lugubriously to one another.

'Veronique at last could bear it no longer, and went home; you see, it had been her idea to bring the aunt on this disastrous expedition, and though the others did not cast the fact verbally in her face, there was a certain lurking reproach in their eyes which was harder to meet than actual upbraidings. The other two remained behind, forlornly mounting guard over their aunt until such time as the waning of the Dieppe season should at last turn her in the direction of home and safety. They made anxious calculations as to how little "good money" might, with reasonable luck, be squandered in the meantime. Here, however, their reckoning went far astray; the close of the

Dieppe season merely turned their aunt's thoughts in search of some other convenient gambling resort. "Show a cat the way to the dairy –" I forget how the proverb goes on, but it summed up the situation as far as the Brimley Bomefields' aunt was concerned. She had been introduced to unexplored pleasures, and found them greatly to her liking, and she was in no hurry to forgo the fruits of her newly acquired knowledge. You see, for the first time in her life the old thing was thoroughly enjoying herself; she was losing money, but she had plenty of fun and excitement over the process, and she had enough left to do very comfortably on. Indeed, she was only just learning to understand the art of doing oneself well. She was a popular hostess, and in return her fellow-gamblers were always ready to entertain her to dinners and suppers when their luck was in. Her nieces, who still remained in attendance on her, with the pathetic unwillingness of a crew to leave a foundering treasure ship which might yet be steered into port, found little pleasure in these Bohemian festivities; to see "good money" lavished on good living for the entertainment of a nondescript circle of acquaintances who were not likely to be in any way socially useful to them, did not attune them to a spirit of revelry. They contrived, whenever possible, to excuse themselves from participation in their aunt's deplored gaieties; the Brimley Bomefield headaches became famous.

'And one day the nieces came to the conclusion that, as they would have expressed it, "no useful purpose would be served" by their continued attendance on a relative who had so thoroughly emancipated herself from the sheltering protection of their wings. The aunt bore the announcement of their departure with a cheerfulness that was almost disconcerting.

'"It's time you went home and had those headaches seen to by a specialist," was her comment on the situation.

'The homeward journey of the Brimley Bomefields was a veritable retreat from Moscow, and what made it the more bitter was the fact that the Moscow, in this case, was not overwhelmed with fire and ashes, but merely extravagantly over-illuminated.

'From mutual friends and acquaintances they sometimes get glimpses of their prodigal relative, who has settled down into a confirmed gambling maniac, living on such salvage of income as obliging moneylenders have left at her disposal.

'So you need not be surprised,' concluded Clovis, 'if they do wear a depressed look in public.'

'Which is Veronique?' asked the Baroness.

'The most depressed-looking of the three,' said Clovis.

The Talking-Out of Tarrington

'HEAVENS!' EXCLAIMED THE aunt of Clovis, 'here's some one I know bearing down on us. I can't remember his name, but he lunched with us once in Town. Tarrington – yes, that's it. He's heard of the picnic I'm giving for the Princess, and he'll cling to me like a life-belt till I give him an invitation; then he'll ask if he may bring all his wives and mothers and sisters with him. That's the worst of these small watering-places; one can't escape from anybody.'

'I'll fight a rearguard action for you if you like to do a bolt now,' volunteered Clovis; 'you've a clear ten yards start if you don't lose time.'

The aunt of Clovis responded gamely to the suggestion, and churned away like a Nile steamer, with a long brown ripple of Pekingese spaniel trailing in her wake.

'Pretend you don't know him,' was her parting advice, tinged with the reckless courage of the non-combatant.

The next moment the overtures of an affably disposed gentleman were being received by Clovis with a 'silent-upon-a-peak-in-Darien' stare which denoted an absence of all previous acquaintance with the object scrutinized.

'I expect you don't know me with my moustache,' said the new-comer; 'I've only grown it during the last two months.'

'On the contrary,' said Clovis, 'the moustache is the only thing about you that seemed familiar to me. I felt certain that I had met it somewhere before.'

'My name is Tarrington,' resumed the candidate for recognition.

'A very useful kind of name,' said Clovis; 'with a name

of that sort no one would blame you if you did nothing in particular heroic or remarkable, would they? And yet if you were to raise a troop of light horse in a moment of national emergency, "Tarrington's Light Horse" would sound quite appropriate and pulse-quickening; whereas if you were called Spoopin, for instance, the thing would be out of the question. No one, even in a moment of national emergency, could possibly belong to Spoopin's Horse.'

The new-comer smiled weakly, as one who is not to be put off by mere flippancy, and began again with patient persistence:

'I think you ought to remember my name –'

'I shall,' said Clovis, with an air of immense sincerity. 'My aunt was asking me only this morning to suggest names for four young owls she's just had sent her as pets. I shall call them all Tarrington; then if one or two of them die or fly away, or leave us in any of the ways that pet owls are prone to, there will be always one or two left to carry on your name. And my aunt won't *let* me forget it; she will always be asking "Have the Tarringtons had their mice?" and questions of that sort. She says if you keep wild creatures in captivity you ought to see after their wants, and of course she's quite right there.'

'I met you at luncheon at your aunt's house once –' broke in Mr Tarrington, pale but still resolute.

'My aunt never lunches,' said Clovis; 'she belongs to the National Anti-Luncheon League, which is doing quite a lot of good work in a quiet, unobtrusive way. A subscription of half a crown per quarter entitles you to go without ninety-two luncheons.'

'This must be something new,' exclaimed Tarrington.

'It's the same aunt that I've always had,' said Clovis coldly.

'I perfectly well remember meeting you at a luncheon-party given by your aunt,' persisted Tarrington, who was beginning to flush an unhealthy shade of mottled pink.

'What was there for lunch?' asked Clovis.

'Oh, well, I don't remember that –'

'How nice of you to remember my aunt when you can no longer recall the names of the things you ate. Now my memory works quite differently. I can remember a menu long after I've forgotten the hostess that accompanied it. When I was seven years old I recollect being given a peach at a garden-party by some Duchess or other; I can't remember a thing about her, except that I imagine our acquaintance must have been of the slightest, as she called me a "nice little boy", but I have unfading memories of that peach. It was one of those exuberant peaches that meet you halfway, so to speak, and are all over you in a moment. It was a beautiful unspoiled product of a hot-house, and yet it managed quite successfully to give itself the airs of a compote. You had to bite it and imbibe it at the same time. To me there has always been something charming and mystic in the thought of that delicate velvet globe of fruit, slowly ripening and warming to perfection through the long summer days and perfumed nights, and then coming suddenly athwart my life in the supreme moment of its existence. I can never forget it, even if I wished to. And when I had devoured all that was edible of it, there still remained the stone, which a heedless, thoughtless child would doubtless have thrown away; I put it down the neck of a young friend who was wearing a very *décolleté* sailor suit. I told him it was a scorpion, and from the way he wriggled and screamed he evidently believed it, though where the silly kid imagined I could procure a live scorpion at a garden-party I don't know.

Altogether, that peach is for me an unfading and happy memory –'

The defeated Tarrington had by this time retreated out of earshot, comforting himself as best he might with the reflection that a picnic which included the presence of Clovis might prove a doubtfully agreeable experience.

'I shall certainly go in for a Parliamentary career,' said Clovis to himself as he turned complacently to rejoin his aunt. 'As a talker-out of inconvenient bills I should be invaluable.'

The Hounds of Fate

IN THE FADING light of a close dull autumn afternoon Martin Stoner plodded his way along muddy lanes and rut-seamed cart tracks that led he knew not exactly whither. Somewhere in front of him, he fancied, lay the sea, and towards the sea his footsteps seemed persistently turning; why he was struggling wearily forward to that goal he could scarcely have explained, unless he was possessed by the same instinct that turns a hard-pressed stag cliffward in its last extremity. In his case the hounds of Fate were certainly pressing him with unrelenting insistence; hunger, fatigue, and despairing hopelessness had numbed his brain, and he could scarcely summon sufficient energy to wonder what underlying impulse was driving him onward. Stoner was one of those unfortunate individuals who seem to have tried everything; a natural slothfulness and improvidence had always intervened to blight any chance of even moderate success, and now he was at the end of his tether, and there was nothing more to try. Desperation had not awakened in him any dormant reserve of energy; on the contrary, a mental torpor grew up round the crisis of his fortunes. With the clothes he stood up in, a halfpenny in his pocket, and no single friend or acquaintance to turn to, with no prospect either of a bed for the night or a meal for the morrow, Martin Stoner trudged stolidly forward, between moist hedgerows and beneath dripping trees, his mind almost a blank, except that he was subconsciously aware that somewhere in front of him lay the sea. Another consciousness obtruded itself now and then – the knowledge that he was miserably hungry. Presently he came to a halt by an open gateway that led into a spacious and rather neglected farm-garden; there was little sign of life about, and the farm-house at the further end of the garden looked chill and inhospitable. A drizzling rain, however, was setting in, and Stoner thought that here perhaps he might obtain a few minutes' shelter and buy a glass of milk with his last remaining coin. He turned slowly and wearily into the garden and followed a narrow, flagged path up to a side door. Before he had time to knock the door opened and a bent, withered-looking old man stood aside in the doorway as though to let him pass in.

'Could I come in out of the rain?' Stoner began, but the old man interrupted him.

'Come in, Master Tom. I knew you would come back one of these days.'

Stoner lurched across the threshold and stood staring uncomprehendingly at the other.

'Sit down while I put you out a bit of supper,' said the old man with quavering eagerness. Stoner's legs gave way from very weariness, and he sank inertly into the arm-chair that had been pushed up to him. In another minute he was devouring the cold meat, cheese, and bread, that had been placed on the table at his side.

'You'm little changed these four years,' went on the old man, in a voice that sounded to Stoner as something in a dream, far away and inconsequent; 'but you'll find us a deal changed, you will. There's no one about the place same as when you left; nought but me and your old Aunt. I'll go and tell her that you'm come; she won't be seeing you, but she'll let you stay right enough. She always did say if you was to come back you should stay, but she'd never set eyes on you or speak to you again.'

The old man placed a mug of beer on the table in front

of Stoner and then hobbled away down a long passage. The drizzle of rain had changed to a furious lashing downpour, which beat violently against door and windows. The wanderer thought with a shudder of what the sea-shore must look like under this drenching rainfall, with night beating down on all sides. He finished the food and beer and sat numbly waiting for the return of his strange host. As the minutes ticked by on the grandfather clock in the corner a new hope began to flicker and grow in the young man's mind; it was merely the expansion of his former craving for food and a few minutes' rest into a longing to find a night's shelter under this seemingly hospitable roof. A clattering of footsteps down the passage heralded the old farm servant's return.

'The old Missus won't see you, Master Tom, but she says you are to stay. 'Tis right enough, seeing the farm will be yours when she be put under earth. I've had a fire lit in your room, Master Tom, and the maids has put fresh sheets on to the bed. You'll find nought changed up there. Maybe you'm tired and would like to go there now.'

Without a word Martin Stoner rose heavily to his feet and followed his ministering angel along a passage, up a short creaking stair, along another passage, and into a large room lit with a cheerfully blazing fire. There was but little furniture, plain, old-fashioned, and good of its kind; a stuffed squirrel in a case and a wall-calendar of four years ago were about the only symptoms of decoration. But Stoner had eyes for little else than the bed, and could scarce wait to tear his clothes off him before rolling in a luxury of weariness into its comfortable depths. The hounds of Fate seemed to have checked for a brief moment.

In the cold light of morning Stoner laughed mirthlessly

as he slowly realized the position in which he found him-self. Perhaps he might snatch a bit of breakfast on the strength of his likeness to this other missing ne'er-do-well, and get safely away before any one discovered the fraud that had been thrust on him. In the room downstairs he found the bent old man ready with a dish of bacon and fried eggs for 'Master Tom's' breakfast, while a hard-faced elderly maid brought in a teapot and poured him out a cup of tea. As he sat at the table a small spaniel came up and made friendly advances.

''Tis old Bowker's pup,' explained the old man, whom the hard-faced maid had addressed as George. 'She was main fond of you; never seemed the same after you went away to Australee. She died 'bout a year agone. 'Tis her pup.'

Stoner found it difficult to regret her decease; as a wit-ness for identification she would have left something to be desired.

'You'll go for a ride, Master Tom?' was the next startling proposition that came from the old man. 'We've a nice little roan cob that goes well in saddle. Old Biddy is get-ting a bit up in years, though 'er goes well still, but I'll have the little roan saddled and brought round to door.'

'I've got no riding things,' stammered the castaway, almost laughing as he looked down at his one suit of well-worn clothes.

'Master Tom,' said the old man earnestly, almost with an offended air, 'all your things is just as you left them. A bit of airing before the fire an' they'll be all right. 'Twill be a bit of a distraction like, a little riding and wild-fowling now and agen. You'll find the folk around here has hard and bitter minds towards you. They hasn't forgotten nor forgiven. No one'll come nigh you, so you'd best get what distraction you can with horse and dog. They'm good company, too.'

Old George hobbled away to give his orders, and Stoner, feeling more than ever like one in a dream, went upstairs to inspect 'Master Tom's' wardrobe. A ride was one of the pleasures dearest to his heart, and there was some protection against immediate discovery of his imposture in the thought that none of Tom's aforetime companions were likely to favour him with a close inspection. As the interloper thrust himself into some tolerably well-fitting riding cords he wondered vaguely what manner of misdeed the genuine Tom had committed to set the whole countryside against him. The thud of quick, eager hoofs on damp earth cut short his speculations. The roan cob had been brought up to the side door.

'Talk of beggars on horseback,' thought Stoner to himself, as he trotted rapidly along the muddy lanes where he had tramped yesterday as a down-at-heel outcast; and then he flung reflection indolently aside and gave himself up to the pleasure of a smart canter along the turf-grown side of a level stretch of road. At an open gateway he checked his pace to allow two carts to turn into a field. The lads driving the carts found time to give him a prolonged stare, and as he passed on he heard an excited voice call out, ''Tis Tom Prike! I knowed him at once; showing hisself here agen, is he?'

Evidently the likeness which had imposed at close quarters on a doddering old man was good enough to mislead younger eyes at a short distance.

In the course of his ride he met with ample evidence to confirm the statement that local folk had neither forgotten nor forgiven the bygone crime which had come to him as a legacy from the absent Tom. Scowling looks, mutterings, and nudgings greeted him whenever he chanced upon human beings; 'Bowker's pup', trotting placidly by his side, seemed the one element of friendliness in a hostile world.

As he dismounted at the side door he caught a fleeting glimpse of a gaunt, elderly woman peering at him from behind the curtain of an upper window. Evidently this was his aunt by adoption.

Over the ample midday meal that stood in readiness for him Stoner was able to review the possibilities of his extraordinary situation. The real Tom, after four years of absence, might suddenly turn up at the farm, or a letter might come from him at any moment. Again, in the character of heir to the farm, the false Tom might be called on to sign documents, which would be an embarrassing predicament. Or a relative might arrive who would not imitate the aunt's attitude of aloofness. All these things would mean ignominious exposure. On the other hand, the alternative was the open sky and the muddy lanes that led down to the sea. The farm offered him, at any rate, a temporary refuge from destitution; farming was one of the many things he had 'tried', and he would be able to do a certain amount of work in return for the hospitality to which he was so little entitled.

'Will you have cold pork for your supper,' asked the hard-faced maid, as she cleared the table, 'or will you have it hotted up?'

'Hot, with onions,' said Stoner. It was the only time in his life that he had made a rapid decision. And as he gave the order he knew that he meant to stay.

Stoner kept rigidly to those portions of the house which seemed to have been allotted to him by a tacit treaty of delimitation. When he took part in the farm-work it was as one who worked under orders and never initiated them. Old George, the roan cob, and Bowker's pup were his sole companions in a world that was otherwise frostily silent and hostile. Of the mistress of the farm he saw nothing. Once, when he knew she had gone forth to church, he made a furtive visit to the farm parlour in an endeavour to glean some fragmentary knowledge of the young man whose place he had usurped, and whose ill-repute he had fastened on himself. There were many photographs hung on the walls, or stuck in prim frames, but the likeness he sought for was not among them. At last, in an album thrust out of sight, he came across what he wanted. There was a whole series, labelled 'Tom', a podgy child of three, in a fantastic frock, an awkward boy of about twelve, holding a cricket bat as though he loathed it, a rather good-looking youth of eighteen with very smooth, evenly parted hair, and, finally, a young man with a somewhat surly dare-devil expression. At this last portrait Stoner looked with particular interest; the likeness to himself was unmistakable.

From the lips of old George, who was garrulous enough on most subjects, he tried again and again to learn something of the nature of the offence which shut him off as a creature to be shunned and hated by his fellow-men.

'What do the folk around here say about me?' he asked one day as they were walking home from an outlying field.

The old man shook his head.

'They be bitter agen you, mortal bitter. Ay, 'tis a sad business, a sad business.'

And never could he be got to say anything more enlightening.

On a clear frosty evening, a few days before the festival of Christmas, Stoner stood in a corner of the orchard which commanded a wide view of the countryside. Here and there he could see the twinkling dots of lamp or candle glow which told of human homes where the good-will and jollity of the season held their sway. Behind him lay the grim, silent farm-house, where no one ever laughed, where even a quarrel would have seemed cheerful. As he turned to look at the long grey front of the gloom-shadowed building, a door opened and old George came hurriedly forth. Stoner heard his adopted name called in a tone of strained anxiety. Instantly he knew that something un-toward had happened, and with a quick revulsion of out-look his sanctuary became in his eyes a place of peace and contentment, from which he dreaded to be driven.

'Master Tom,' said the old man in a hoarse whisper, 'you must slip away quiet from here for a few days. Michael Ley is back in the village, an' he swears to shoot you if he can come across you. He'll do it, too, there's mur-der in the look of him. Get away under cover of night, 'tis only for a week or so, he won't be here longer.'

'But where am I to go?' stammered Stoner, who had caught the infection of the old man's obvious terror.

'Go right away along the coast to Punchford and keep hid there. When Michael's safe gone I'll ride the roan over to the Green Dragon at Punchford; when you see the cob stabled at the Green Dragon 'tis a sign you may come back agen.'

'But –' began Stoner hesitatingly.

''Tis all right for money,' said the other; 'the old Missus agrees you'd best do as I say, and she's given me this.'

The old man produced three sovereigns and some odd silver.

Stoner felt more of a cheat than ever as he stole away that night from the back gate of the farm with the old woman's money in his pocket. Old George and Bowker's pup stood watching him a silent farewell from the yard. He could scarcely fancy that he would ever come back, and he felt a throb of compunction for those two humble friends who would wait wistfully for his return. Some day perhaps the real Tom would come back, and there would be wild wonderment among those simple farm folks as to the identity of the shadowy guest they had harboured under their roof. For his own fate he felt no immediate anxiety; three pounds goes but little way in the world when there is nothing behind it, but to a man who has counted his exchequer in pennies it seems a good starting-point. Fortune had done him a whimsically kind turn when last he trod these lanes as a hopeless adventurer, and there might yet be a chance of his finding some work and making a fresh start; as he got further from the farm his spirits rose higher. There was a sense of relief in regaining once more his lost identity and ceasing to be the uneasy ghost of another. He scarcely bothered to speculate about the implacable enemy who had dropped from nowhere into his life; since that life was now behind him one unreal item the more made little difference. For the first time for many months he began to hum a careless light-hearted refrain. Then there stepped out from the shadow of an overhanging oak tree a man with a gun. There was no need to wonder who he might be; the moonlight falling on his white set face revealed a glare of human hate such as Stoner in the ups and downs of his wanderings had never seen before. He sprang aside in a wild effort to break through the hedge that bordered the lane, but the tough branches held him fast. The hounds of Fate had waited for him in those narrow lanes, and this time they were not to be denied.

FROM

BEASTS AND
SUPER-BEASTS
(1914)

The She-Wolf

LEONARD BILSITER WAS one of those people who have failed to find this world attractive or interesting, and who have sought compensation in an 'unseen world' of their own experience or imagination – or invention. Children do that sort of thing successfully, but children are content to convince themselves, and do not vulgarize their beliefs by trying to convince other people. Leonard Bilsiter's beliefs were for 'the few', that is to say, any one who would listen to him.

His dabblings in the unseen might not have carried him beyond the customary platitudes of the drawing-room visionary if accident had not reinforced his stock-in-trade of mystical lore. In company with a friend, who was interested in a Ural mining concern, he had made a trip across Eastern Europe at a moment when the great Russian railway strike was developing from a threat to a reality; its outbreak caught him on the return journey, somewhere on the further side of Perm, and it was while waiting for a couple of days at a wayside station in a state of suspended locomotion that he made the acquaintance of a dealer in harness and metalware, who profitably wiled away the tedium of the long halt by initiating his English travelling companion in a fragmentary system of folklore that he had picked up from Trans-Baikal traders and natives. Leonard returned to his home circle garrulous about his Russian strike experiences, but oppressively reticent about certain dark mysteries, which he alluded to under the resounding title of Siberian Magic. The reticence wore off in a week or two under the influence of an entire lack of general curiosity, and Leonard began to make more detailed allusions to the enormous powers which this new esoteric force, to use his own description of it, conferred on the initiated few who knew how to wield it. His aunt, Cecilia Hoops, who loved sensation perhaps rather better than she loved the truth, gave him as clamorous an advertisement as any one could wish for by retailing an account of how he had turned a vegetable marrow into a wood-pigeon before her very eyes. As a manifestation of the possession of supernatural powers, the story was discounted in some quarters by the respect accorded to Mrs Hoops' powers of imagination.

However divided opinion might be on the question of Leonard's status as a wonder-worker or a charlatan, he certainly arrived at Mary Hampton's house-party with a reputation for pre-eminence in one or other of those professions, and he was not disposed to shun such publicity as might fall to his share. Esoteric forces and unusual powers figured largely in whatever conversation he or his aunt had a share in, and his own performances, past and potential, were the subject of mysterious hints and dark avowals.

'I wish you would turn me into a wolf, Mr Bilsiter,' said his hostess at luncheon the day after his arrival.

'My dear Mary,' said Colonel Hampton, 'I never knew you had a craving in that direction.'

'A she-wolf, of course,' continued Mrs Hampton; 'it would be too confusing to change one's sex as well as one's species at a moment's notice.'

'I don't think one should jest on these subjects,' said Leonard.

'I'm not jesting, I'm quite serious, I assure you. Only don't do it today; we have only eight available bridge players, and it would break up one of our tables.

140

Tomorrow we shall be a larger party. Tomorrow night, after dinner –'

'In our present imperfect understanding of these hidden forces I think one should approach them with humbleness rather than mockery,' observed Leonard, with such severity that the subject was forthwith dropped.

Clovis Sangrail had sat unusually silent during the discussion on the possibilities of Siberian magic; after lunch he side-tracked Lord Pabham into the comparative seclusion of the billiard-room and delivered himself of a searching question.

'Have you such a thing as a she-wolf in your collection of wild animals? A she-wolf of moderately good temper?'

Lord Pabham considered. 'There is Louisa,' he said, 'a rather fine specimen of the timber-wolf. I got her two years ago in exchange for some Arctic foxes. Most of my animals get to be fairly tame before they've been with me very long; I think I can say Louisa has an angelic temper, as she-wolves go. Why do you ask?'

'I was wondering whether you would lend her to me for tomorrow night,' said Clovis, with the careless solicitude of one who borrows a collar stud or a tennis racquet.

'Tomorrow night?'

'Yes, wolves are nocturnal animals, so the late hours won't hurt her,' said Clovis, with the air of one who has taken everything into consideration; 'one of your men could bring her over from Pabham Park after dusk, and with a little help he ought to be able to smuggle her into the conservatory at the same moment that Mary Hampton makes an unobtrusive exit.'

Lord Pabham stared at Clovis for a moment in pardonable bewilderment; then his face broke into a wrinkled network of laughter.

'Oh, that's your game, is it? You are going to do a little Siberian magic on your own account. And is Mrs Hampton willing to be a fellow-conspirator?'

'Mary is pledged to see me through with it, if you will guarantee Louisa's temper.'

'I'll answer for Louisa,' said Lord Pabham.

By the following day the house-party had swollen to larger proportions, and Bilsiter's instinct for self-advertisement expanded duly under the stimulant of an increased audience. At dinner that evening he held forth at length on the subject of unseen forces and untested powers, and his flow of impressive eloquence continued unabated while coffee was being served in the drawing-room preparatory to a general migration to the card-room. His aunt ensured a respectful hearing for his utterances, but her sensation-loving soul hankered after something more dramatic than mere vocal demonstration.

'Won't you do something to *convince* them of your powers, Leonard?' she pleaded. 'Change something into another shape. He can, you know, if he only chooses to,' she informed the company.

'Oh, do,' said Mavis Pellington earnestly, and her request was echoed by nearly every one present. Even those who were not open to conviction were perfectly willing to be entertained by an exhibition of amateur conjuring.

Leonard felt that something tangible was expected of him.

'Has any one present,' he asked, 'got a three-penny bit or some small object of no particular value –?'

'You're surely not going to make coins disappear, or something primitive of that sort?' said Clovis contemptuously.

'I think it very unkind of you not to carry out my suggestion of turning me into a wolf,' said Mary Hampton, as she crossed over to the conservatory to give her macaws their usual tribute from the dessert dishes.

'I have already warned you of the danger of treating these powers in a mocking spirit,' said Leonard solemnly.

'I don't believe you can do it,' laughed Mary provocatively from the conservatory; 'I dare you to do it if you can. I defy you to turn me into a wolf.'

As she said this she was lost to view behind a clump of azaleas.

'Mrs Hampton –' began Leonard with increased solemnity, but he got no further. A breath of chill air seemed to rush across the room, and at the same time the macaws broke forth into ear-splitting screams.

'What on earth is the matter with those confounded birds, Mary?' exclaimed Colonel Hampton; at the same moment an even more piercing scream from Mavis Pellington stampeded the entire company from their seats. In various attitudes of helpless horror or instinctive defence they confronted the evil-looking grey beast that was peering at them from amid a setting of fern and azalea.

Mrs Hoops was the first to recover from the general chaos of fright and bewilderment.

'Leonard!' she screamed shrilly to her nephew, 'turn it back into Mrs Hampton at once! It may fly at us at any moment. Turn it back!'

'I – I don't know how to,' faltered Leonard, who looked more scared and horrified than any one.

'What!' shouted Colonel Hampton, 'you've taken the abominable liberty of turning my wife into a wolf, and now you stand there calmly and say you can't turn her back again!'

To do strict justice to Leonard, calmness was not a distinguishing feature of his attitude at the moment.

'I assure you I didn't turn Mrs Hampton into a wolf; nothing was farther from my intentions,' he protested.

'Then where is she, and how came that animal into the conservatory?' demanded the Colonel.

'Of course we must accept your assurance that you didn't turn Mrs Hampton into a wolf,' said Clovis politely, 'but you will agree that appearances are against you.'

'Are we to have all these recriminations with that beast standing there ready to tear us to pieces?' wailed Mavis indignantly.

'Lord Pabham, you know a good deal about wild beasts –' suggested Colonel Hampton.

'The wild beasts that I have been accustomed to,' said Lord Pabham, 'have come with proper credentials from well-known dealers, or have been bred in my own menagerie. I've never before been confronted with an animal that walks unconcernedly out of an azalea bush, leaving a charming and popular hostess unaccounted for. As far as one can judge from *outward* characteristics,' he continued, 'it has the appearance of a well-grown female of the North American timber-wolf, a variety of the common species *canis lupus.*'

'Oh, never mind its Latin name,' screamed Mavis, as the beast came a step or two further into the room; 'can't you entice it away with food, and shut it up where it can't do any harm?'

'If it is really Mrs Hampton, who has just had a very good dinner, I don't suppose food will appeal to it very strongly,' said Clovis.

'Leonard,' beseeched Mrs Hoops tearfully, 'even if this *is* none of your doing can't you use your great powers to turn this dreadful beast into something harmless before it bites us all – a rabbit or something?'

'I don't suppose Colonel Hampton would care to have his wife turned into a succession of fancy animals as though we were playing a round game with her,' interposed Clovis.

'I absolutely forbid it,' thundered the Colonel.

'Most wolves that I've had anything to do with have been inordinately fond of sugar,' said Lord Pabham; 'if you like I'll try the effect on this one.'

He took a piece of sugar from the saucer of his coffee cup and flung it to the expectant Louisa, who snapped it in mid-air. There was a sigh of relief from the company; a wolf that ate sugar when it might at the least have been employed in tearing macaws to pieces had already shed some of its terrors. The sigh deepened to a gasp of thanksgiving when Lord Pabham decoyed the animal out of the room by a pretended largesse of further sugar. There was an instant rush to the vacated conservatory. There was no trace of Mrs Hampton except the plate containing the macaws' supper.

'The door is locked on the inside!' exclaimed Clovis, who had deftly turned the key as he affected to test it.

Every one turned towards Bilsiter.

'If you haven't turned my wife into a wolf,' said Colonel Hampton, 'will you kindly explain where she has disappeared to, since she obviously could not have gone through a locked door? I will not press you for an explanation of how a North American timber-wolf suddenly appeared in the conservatory, but I think I have some right to inquire what has become of Mrs Hampton.'

Bilsiter's reiterated disclaimer was met with a general murmur of impatient disbelief.

'I refuse to stay another hour under this roof,' declared Mavis Pellington.

'If our hostess has really vanished out of human form,' said Mrs Hoops, 'none of the ladies of the party can very well remain. I absolutely decline to be chaperoned by a wolf!'

'It's a she-wolf,' said Clovis soothingly.

The correct etiquette to be observed under the unusual circumstances received no further elucidation. The sudden entry of Mary Hampton deprived the discussion of its immediate interest.

'Some one has mesmerized me,' she exclaimed crossly; 'I found myself in the game larder, of all places, being fed with sugar by Lord Pabham. I hate being mesmerized, and the doctor has forbidden me to touch sugar.'

The situation was explained to her, as far as it permitted of anything that could be called explanation.

'Then you *really* did turn me into a wolf, Mr Bilsiter?' she exclaimed excitedly.

But Leonard had burned the boat in which he might now have embarked on a sea of glory. He could only shake his head feebly.

'It was I who took that liberty,' said Clovis; 'you see, I happen to have lived for a couple of years in Northeastern Russia, and I have more than a tourist's acquaintance with the magic craft of that region. One does not care to speak about these strange powers, but once in a way, when one hears a lot of nonsense being talked about them, one is tempted to show what Siberian magic can accomplish in the hands of some one who really understands it. I yielded to that temptation. May I have some brandy? the effort has left me rather faint.'

If Leonard Bilsiter could at that moment have

transformed Clovis into a cockroach and then have stepped on him he would gladly have performed both operations.

The Boar-Pig

'THERE IS A back way on to the lawn,' said Mrs Philidore Stossen to her daughter, 'through a small grass paddock and then through a walled fruit garden full of gooseberry bushes. I went all over the place last year when the family were away. There is a door that opens from the fruit garden into a shrubbery, and once we emerge from there we can mingle with the guests as if we had come in by the ordinary way. It's much safer than going in by the front entrance and running the risk of coming bang up against the hostess; that would be so awkward when she doesn't happen to have invited us.'

'Isn't it a lot of trouble to take for getting admittance to a garden party?'

'To a garden party, yes; to *the* garden party of the season, certainly not. Every one of any consequence in the county, with the exception of ourselves, has been asked to meet the Princess, and it would be far more troublesome to invent explanations as to why we weren't there than to get in by a roundabout way. I stopped Mrs Cuvering in the road yesterday and talked very pointedly about the Princess. If she didn't choose to take the hint and send me an invitation it's not my fault, is it? Here we are: we just cut across the grass and through that little gate into the garden.'

Mrs Stossen and her daughter, suitably arrayed for a county garden party function with an infusion of Almanack de Gotha, sailed through the narrow grass paddock and the ensuing gooseberry garden with the air of state barges making an unofficial progress along a rural trout stream. There was a certain amount of furtive haste mingled with the stateliness of their advance as though hostile searchlights might be turned on them at any moment; and, as a matter of fact, they were not unobserved. Matilda Cuvering, with the alert eyes of thirteen years and the added advantage of an exalted position in the branches of a medlar tree, had enjoyed a good view of the Stossen flanking movement and had foreseen exactly where it would break down in execution.

'They'll find the door locked, and they'll jolly well have to go back the way they came,' she remarked to herself. 'Serves them right for not coming in by the proper entrance. What a pity Tarquin Superbus isn't loose in the paddock. After all, as every one else is enjoying themselves, I don't see why Tarquin shouldn't have an afternoon out.'

Matilda was of an age when thought is action; she slid down from the branches of the medlar tree, and when she clambered back again, Tarquin, the huge white Yorkshire boar-pig, had exchanged the narrow limits of his sty for the wider range of the grass paddock. The discomfited Stossen expedition, returning in recriminatory but otherwise orderly retreat from the unyielding obstacle of the locked door, came to a sudden halt at the gate dividing the paddock from the gooseberry garden.

'What a villainous-looking animal,' exclaimed Mrs Stossen; 'it wasn't there when we came in.'

'It's there now, anyhow,' said her daughter. 'What on earth are we to do? I wish we had never come.'

The boar-pig had drawn nearer to the gate for a closer inspection of the human intruders, and stood champing his jaws and blinking his small red eyes in a manner that was doubtless intended to be disconcerting, and, as far as the Stossens were concerned, thoroughly achieved that result.

'Shoo! Hish! Hish! Shoo!' cried the ladies in chorus.

'If they think they're going to drive him away by reciting lists of the kings of Israel and Judah they're laying themselves out for disappointment,' observed Matilda from her seat in the medlar tree. As she made the observation aloud Mrs Stossen became for the first time aware of her presence. A moment or two earlier she would have been anything but pleased at the discovery that the garden was not as deserted as it looked, but now she hailed the fact of the child's presence on the scene with absolute relief.

'Little girl, can you find some one to drive away –' she began hopefully.

'*Comment? Comprends pas,*' was the response.

'Oh, are you French? *Êtes vous française?*'

'*Pas de tous. 'Suis anglaise.*'

'Then why not talk English? I want to know if –'

'*Permettez-moi expliquer.* You see, I'm rather under a cloud,' said Matilda. 'I'm staying with my aunt, and I was told I must behave particularly well today, as lots of people were coming for a garden party, and I was told to imitate Claude, that's my young cousin, who never does anything wrong except by accident, and then is always apologetic about it. It seems they thought I ate too much raspberry trifle at lunch, and they said Claude never eats too much raspberry trifle. Well, Claude always goes to sleep for half an hour after lunch, because he's told to, and I waited till he was asleep, and tied his hands and started forcible feeding with a whole bucketful of raspberry trifle that they were keeping for the garden party. Lots of it went on to his sailor-suit and some of it on to the bed, but a good deal went down Claude's throat, and they can't say again that he has never been known to eat too much raspberry trifle. That is why I am not allowed to go to the party, and as an additional punishment I must speak French all the afternoon. I've had to tell you all this in English, as there were words like "forcible feeding" that I didn't know the French for; of course I could have invented them, but if I had said *nourriture obligatoire* you wouldn't have had the least idea what I was talking about. *Mais maintenant, nous parlons français.*'

'Oh, very well, *très bien*,' said Mrs Stossen reluctantly; in moments of flurry such French as she knew was not under very good control. '*Là, à l'autre côté de la porte, est un cochon –*'

'*Un cochon? Ah, le petit charmant!*' exclaimed Matilda with enthusiasm.

'*Mais non, pas du tout petit, et pas du tout charmant; un bête féroce –*'

'*Une bête*,' corrected Matilda, 'a pig is masculine as long as you call it a pig, but if you lose your temper with it and call it a ferocious beast it becomes one of us at once. French is a dreadfully unsexing language.'

'For goodness' sake let us talk English then,' said Mrs Stossen. 'Is there any way out of this garden except through the paddock where the pig is?'

'I always go over the wall, by way of the plum tree,' said Matilda.

'Dressed as we are we could hardly do that,' said Mrs Stossen; it was difficult to imagine her doing it in any costume.

'Do you think you could go and get some one who would drive the pig away?' asked Miss Stossen.

'I promised my aunt I would stay here till five o'clock; it's not four yet.'

'I am sure, under the circumstances, your aunt would permit –'

'My conscience would not permit,' said Matilda with cold dignity.

'We can't stay here till five o'clock,' exclaimed Mrs Stossen with growing exasperation.

'Shall I recite to you to make the time pass quicker?' asked Matilda obligingly. '"Belinda, the little Bread-winner", is considered my best piece, or, perhaps, it ought to be something in French. Henri Quatre's address to his soldiers is the only thing I really know in that language.'

'If you will go and fetch some one to drive that animal away I will give you something to buy yourself a nice present,' said Mrs Stossen.

Matilda came several inches lower down the medlar tree.

'That is the most practical suggestion you have made yet for getting out of the garden,' she remarked cheerfully; 'Claude and I are collecting money for the Children's Fresh Air Fund, and we are seeing which of us can collect the biggest sum.'

'I shall be very glad to contribute half a crown, very glad indeed,' said Mrs Stossen, digging that coin out of the depths of a receptacle which formed a detached out-work of her toilet.

'Claude is a long way ahead of me at present,' continued Matilda, taking no notice of the suggested offering; 'you see, he's only eleven, and has golden hair, and those are enormous advantages when you're on the collecting job. Only the other day a Russian lady gave him ten shillings. Russians understand the art of giving far better than we do. I expect Claude will net quite twenty-five shillings this afternoon; he'll have the field to himself, and he'll be able to do the pale, fragile, not-long-for-this-world business to perfection after his raspberry trifle experience. Yes, he'll be *quite* two pounds ahead of me by now.'

With much probing and plucking and many regretful murmurs the beleaguered ladies managed to produce seven-and-sixpence between them.

'I am afraid this is all we've got,' said Mrs Stossen.

Matilda showed no sign of coming down either to the earth or to their figure.

'I could not do violence to my conscience for anything less than ten shillings,' she announced stiffly.

Mother and daughter muttered certain remarks under their breath, in which the word 'beast' was prominent, and probably had no reference to Tarquin.

'I find I *have* got another half-crown,' said Mrs Stossen in a shaking voice; 'here you are. Now please fetch some one quickly.'

Matilda slipped down from the tree, took possession of the donation, and proceeded to pick up a handful of over-ripe medlars from the grass at her feet. Then she climbed over the gate and addressed herself affectionately to the boar-pig.

'Come, Tarquin, dear old boy; you know you can't resist medlars when they're rotten and squashy.'

Tarquin couldn't. By dint of throwing the fruit in front of him at judicious intervals Matilda decoyed him back to his sty, while the delivered captives hurried across the paddock.

'Well, I never! The little minx!' exclaimed Mrs Stossen when she was safely on the high road. 'The animal wasn't savage at all, and as for the ten shillings, I don't believe the Fresh Air Fund will see a penny of it!'

There she was unwarrantably harsh in her judgement. If you examine the books of the fund you will find the acknowledgement: 'Collected by Miss Matilda Cuvering, 2s. 6d.'

The Brogue

THE HUNTING SEASON had come to an end, and the Mullets had not succeeded in selling the Brogue. There had been a kind of tradition in the family for the past three or four years, a sort of fatalistic hope, that the Brogue would find a purchaser before the hunting was over; but seasons came and went without anything happening to justify such ill-founded optimism. The animal had been named Berserker in the earlier stages of its career; it had been rechristened the Brogue later on, in recognition of the fact that, once acquired, it was extremely difficult to get rid of. The unkinder wits of the neighbourhood had been known to suggest that the first letter of its name was superfluous. The Brogue had been variously described in sale catalogues as a light-weight hunter, a lady's hack, and, more simply, but still with a touch of imagination, as a useful brown gelding, standing 15.1. Toby Mullet had ridden him for four seasons with the West Wessex; you can ride almost any sort of horse with the West Wessex as long as it is an animal that knows the country. The Brogue knew the country intimately, having personally created most of the gaps that were to be met with in banks and hedges for many miles round. His manners and characteristics were not ideal in the hunting field, but he was probably rather safer to ride to hounds than he was as a hack on country roads. According to the Mullet family, he was not really road-shy, but there were one or two objects of dislike that brought on sudden attacks of what Toby called swerving sickness. Motors and cycles he treated with tolerant disregard, but pigs, wheelbarrows, piles of stones by the roadside, perambulators in a village street, gates painted too aggressively white, and sometimes, but not always, the newer kind of beehives, turned him aside from his tracks in vivid imitation of the zigzag course of forked lightning. If a pheasant rose noisily from the other side of a hedgerow the Brogue would spring into the air at the same moment, but this may have been due to a desire to be companionable. The Mullet family contradicted the widely prevalent report that the horse was a confirmed crib-biter.

It was about the third week in May that Mrs Mullet, relict of the late Sylvester Mullet, and mother of Toby and a bunch of daughters, assailed Clovis Sangrail on the outskirts of the village with a breathless catalogue of local happenings.

'You know our new neighbour, Mr Penricarde?' she vociferated; 'awfully rich, owns tin mines in Cornwall, middle-aged and rather quiet. He's taken the Red House on a long lease and spent a lot of money on alterations and improvements. Well, Toby's sold him the Brogue!'

Clovis spent a moment or two in assimilating the astonishing news; then he broke out into unstinted congratulation. If he had belonged to a more emotional race he would probably have kissed Mrs Mullet.

'How wonderful lucky to have pulled it off at last! Now you can buy a decent animal. I've always said that Toby was clever. Ever so many congratulations.'

'Don't congratulate me. It's the most unfortunate thing that could have happened!' said Mrs Mullet dramatically.

Clovis stared at her in amazement.

'Mr Penricarde,' said Mrs Mullet, sinking her voice to what she imagined to be an impressive whisper, though it rather resembled a hoarse, excited squeak, 'Mr Penricarde has just begun to pay attentions to Jessie. Slight at first, but now unmistakable. I was a fool not to have seen it sooner. Yesterday, at the Rectory garden party, he asked her what her favourite flowers were, and she told him carnations, and today a whole stack of carnations has arrived, clove and malmaison and lovely dark red ones, regular exhibition blooms, and a box of chocolates that he must have got on purpose from London. And he's asked her to go round the links with him tomorrow. And now, just at this critical moment, Toby has sold him that animal. It's a calamity!'

'But you've been trying to get the horse off your hands for years,' said Clovis.

'I've got a houseful of daughters,' said Mrs Mullet, 'and I've been trying – well, not to get them off my hands, of course, but a husband or two wouldn't be amiss among the lot of them; there are six of them, you know.'

'I don't know,' said Clovis, 'I've never counted, but I expect you're right as to the number; mothers generally know these things.'

'And now,' continued Mrs Mullet, in her tragic whisper, 'when there's a rich husband-in-prospect imminent on the horizon Toby goes and sells him that miserable animal. It will probably kill him if he tries to ride it; anyway it will kill any affection he might have felt towards any member of our family. What is to be done? We can't very well ask to have the horse back; you see, we praised it up like anything when we thought there was a chance of his buying it, and said it was just the animal to suit him.'

'Couldn't you steal it out of his stable and send it to grass at some farm miles away?' suggested Clovis. 'Write "Votes for Women" on the stable door, and the thing would pass for a Suffragette outrage. No one who knew the horse could possibly suspect you of wanting to get it back again.'

'Every newspaper in the country would ring with the affair,' said Mrs Mullet; 'can't you imagine the headline, "Valuable Hunter Stolen by Suffragettes"? The police would scour the countryside till they found the animal.'

'Well, Jessie must try and get it back from Penricarde on the plea that it's an old favourite. She can say it was only sold because the stable had to be pulled down under the terms of an old repairing lease, and that now it has been arranged that the stable is to stand for a couple of years longer.'

'It sounds a queer proceeding to ask for a horse back when you've just sold him,' said Mrs Mullet, 'but something must be done, and done at once. The man is not used to horses, and I believe I told him it was as quiet as a lamb. After all, lambs go kicking and twisting about as if they were demented, don't they?'

'The lamb has an entirely unmerited character for sedateness,' agreed Clovis.

Jessie came back from the golf links next day in a state of mingled elation and concern.

'It's all right about the proposal,' she announced, 'he came out with it at the sixth hole. I said I must have time to think it over. I accepted him at the seventh.'

'My dear,' said her mother, 'I think a little more maidenly reserve and hesitation would have been advisable, as you've known him so short a time. You might have waited till the ninth hole.'

'The seventh is a very long hole,' said Jessie; 'besides, the tension was putting us both off our game. By the time we'd got to the ninth hole we'd settled lots of things. The honeymoon is to be spent in Corsica, with perhaps a flying visit to Naples if we feel like it, and a week in London to wind up with. Two of his nieces are to be asked to be bridesmaids, so with our lot there will be seven, which is rather a lucky number. You are to wear your pearl grey, with any amount of Honiton lace jabbed into it. By the way, he's coming over this evening to ask your consent to the whole affair. So far all's well, but about the Brogue it's a different matter. I told him the legend about the stable, and how keen we were about buying the horse back, but he seems equally keen on keeping it. He said he must have horse exercise now that he's living in the country, and he's going to start riding tomorrow. He's ridden a few times in the Row on an animal that was accustomed to carry octogenarians and people undergoing rest cures, and that's about all his experience in the saddle – oh, and he rode a pony once in Norfolk, when he was fifteen and the pony twenty-four; and tomorrow he's going to ride the Brogue! I shall be a widow before I'm married, and I do so want to see what Corsica's like; it looks so silly on the map.'

Clovis was sent for in haste, and the developments of the situation put before him.

'Nobody can ride that animal with any safety,' said Mrs Mullet, 'except Toby, and he knows by long experience what it is going to shy at, and manages to swerve at the same time.'

'I did hint to Mr Penricarde – to Vincent, I should say – that the Brogue didn't like white gates,' said Jessie.

'White gates!' exclaimed Mrs Mullet; 'did you mention what effect a pig has on him? He'll have to go past Locky-er's farm to get to the high road, and there's sure to be a pig or two grunting about in the lane.'

'He's taken rather a dislike to turkeys lately,' said Toby.

'It's obvious that Penricarde mustn't be allowed to go out on that animal,' said Clovis, 'at least not till Jessie has married him, and tired of him. I tell you what: ask him to a picnic tomorrow, starting at an early hour; he's not the sort to go out for a ride before breakfast. The day after I'll get the rector to drive him over to Crowleigh before lunch, to see the new cottage hospital they're building there. The Brogue will be standing idle in the stable and Toby can offer to exercise it; then it can pick up a stone or something of the sort and go conveniently lame. If you hurry on the wedding a bit the lameness fiction can be kept up till the ceremony is safely over.'

Mrs Mullet belonged to an emotional race, and she kissed Clovis.

It was nobody's fault that the rain came down in torrents the next morning, making a picnic a fantastic impossibility. It was also nobody's fault, but sheer ill-luck, that the weather cleared up sufficiently in the afternoon to tempt Mr Penricarde to make his first essay with the Brogue. They did not get as far as the pigs at Lockyer's farm; the rectory gate was painted a dull unobtrusive green, but it had been white a year or two ago, and the Brogue never forgot that he had been in the habit of making a violent curtsey, a back-pedal and a swerve at this particular point of the road. Subsequently, there being apparently no further call on his services, he broke his way into the rectory orchard, where he found a hen turkey in a coop; later visitors to the orchard found the coop almost intact, but very little left of the turkey.

Mr Penricarde, a little stunned and shaken, and suffering from a bruised knee and some minor damages, good-naturedly ascribed the accident to his own inexperience with horses and country roads, and allowed Jessie to nurse him back into complete recovery and golf-fitness within something less than a week.

In the list of wedding presents which the local newspaper published a fortnight or so later appeared the following item:

'Brown saddle-horse, "The Brogue", bridegroom's gift to bride.'

'Which shows,' said Toby Mullet, 'that he knew nothing.'

'Or else,' said Clovis, 'that he has a very pleasing wit.'

The Hen

'DORA BITTHOLZ IS coming on Thursday,' said Mrs Sangrail.

'This next Thursday?' asked Clovis.

His mother nodded.

'You've rather done it, haven't you?' he chuckled. 'Jane Martlet has only been here five days, and she never stays less than a fortnight, even when she's asked definitely for a week. You'll never get her out of the house by Thursday.'

'Why should I?' asked Mrs Sangrail. 'She and Dora are good friends, aren't they? They used to be, as far as I remember.'

'They used to be; that's what makes them all the more bitter now. Each feels that she has nursed a viper in her bosom. Nothing fans the flame of human resentment so much as the discovery that one's bosom has been utilized as a snake sanatorium.'

'But what has happened? Has some one been making mischief?'

'Not exactly,' said Clovis; 'a hen came between them.'

'A hen? What hen?'

'It was a bronze Leghorn or some such exotic breed, and Dora sold it to Jane at a rather exotic price. They both go in for prize poultry, you know, and Jane thought she was going to get her money back in a large family of pedigree chickens. The bird turned out to be an abstainer from the egg habit, and I'm told that the letters which passed between the two women were a revelation as to how much invective could be got on to a sheet of notepaper.'

'How ridiculous!' said Mrs Sangrail. 'Couldn't some of their friends compose the quarrel?'

'People tried,' said Clovis, 'but it must have been rather like composing the storm music of the "Fliegende Holländer". Jane was willing to take back some of her most libellous remarks if Dora would take back the hen, but Dora said that would be owning herself in the wrong, and you know she'd as soon think of owning slum property in Whitechapel as do that.'

'It's a most awkward situation,' said Mrs Sangrail. 'Do you suppose they won't speak to one another?'

'On the contrary, the difficulty will be to get them to leave off. Their remarks on each other's conduct and character have hitherto been governed by the fact that only four ounces of plain speaking can be sent through the post for a penny.'

'I can't put Dora off,' said Mrs Sangrail. 'I've already postponed her visit once, and nothing short of a miracle would make Jane leave before her self-allotted fortnight is over.'

'Miracles are rather in my line,' said Clovis. 'I don't pretend to be very hopeful in this case, but I'll do my best.'

'As long as you don't drag me into it –' stipulated his mother.

'Servants are a bit of a nuisance,' muttered Clovis, as he sat in the smoking-room after lunch, talking fitfully to Jane Martlet in the intervals of putting together the materials of a cocktail, which he had irreverently patented under the name of an Ella Wheeler Wilcox. It was partly compounded of old brandy and partly of curaçao; there were other ingredients, but they were never indiscriminately revealed.

'Servants a nuisance!' exclaimed Jane, bounding into the topic with the exuberant plunge of a hunter when it leaves the high road and feels turf under its hoofs; 'I should think they were! The trouble I've had in getting suited this year you would hardly believe. But I don't see what you have to complain of – your mother is so wonderfully lucky in her servants. Sturridge, for instance – he's been with you for years, and I'm sure he's a paragon as butlers go.'

'That's just the trouble,' said Clovis. 'It's when servants have been with you for years that they become a really serious nuisance. The "here today and gone tomorrow" sort don't matter – you've simply got to replace them; it's the stayers and the paragons that are the real worry.'

'But if they give satisfaction –'

'That doesn't prevent them from giving trouble. Now, you've mentioned Sturridge – it was Sturridge I was particularly thinking of when I made the observation about servants being a nuisance.'

'The excellent Sturridge a nuisance! I can't believe it.'

'I know he's excellent, and we just couldn't get along without him; he's the one reliable element in this rather haphazard household. But his very orderliness has had an effect on him. Have you ever considered what it must be like to go on unceasingly doing the correct thing in the correct manner in the same surroundings for the greater part of a lifetime? To know and ordain and superintend exactly what silver and glass and table linen shall be used and set out on what occasions, to have cellar and pantry and plate-cupboard under a minutely devised and undeviating administration, to be noiseless, impalpable, omnipresent, and, as far as your own department is concerned, omniscient?'

'I should go mad,' said Jane with conviction.

'Exactly,' said Clovis thoughtfully, swallowing his completed Ella Wheeler Wilcox.

'But Sturridge hasn't gone mad,' said Jane with a flutter of inquiry in her voice.

'On most points he's thoroughly sane and reliable,' said Clovis, 'but at times he is subject to the most obstinate delusions, and on those occasions he becomes not merely a nuisance but a decided embarrassment.'

'What sort of delusions?'

'Unfortunately they usually centre round one of the guests of the house party, and that is where the awkwardness comes in. For instance, he took it into his head that Matilda Sheringham was the Prophet Elijah, and as all that he remembered about Elijah's history was the episode of the ravens in the wilderness he absolutely declined to interfere with what he imagined to be Matilda's private catering arrangements, wouldn't allow any tea to be sent up to her in the morning, and if he was waiting at table he passed her over altogether in handing round the dishes.'

'How very unpleasant. Whatever did you do about it?'

'Oh, Matilda got fed, after a fashion, but it was judged to be best for her to cut her visit short. It was really the only thing to be done,' said Clovis with some emphasis.

'I shouldn't have done that,' said Jane, 'I should have humoured him in some way. I certainly shouldn't have gone away.'

Clovis frowned.

'It is not always wise to humour people when they get these ideas into their heads. There's no knowing to what lengths they may go if you encourage them.'

'You don't mean to say he might be dangerous, do you?' asked Jane with some anxiety.

'One can never be certain,' said Clovis; 'now and then

he gets some idea about a guest which *might* take an unfortunate turn. That is precisely what is worrying me at the present moment.'

'What, has he taken a fancy about some one here now?' asked Jane excitedly. 'How thrilling! Do tell me who it is.'

'You,' said Clovis briefly.

'Me?'

Clovis nodded.

'Who on earth does he think I am?'

'Queen Anne,' was the unexpected answer.

'Queen Anne! What an idea. But, anyhow, there's nothing dangerous about her; she's such a colourless personality.'

'What does posterity chiefly say about Queen Anne?' asked Clovis rather sternly.

'The only thing that I can remember about her,' said Jane, 'is the saying "Queen Anne's dead."'

'Exactly,' said Clovis, staring at the glass that had held the Ella Wheeler Wilcox, 'dead.'

'Do you mean he takes me for the ghost of Queen Anne?' asked Jane.

'Ghost? Dear no. No one ever heard of a ghost that came down to breakfast and ate kidneys and toast and honey with a healthy appetite. No, it's the fact of you being so very much alive and flourishing that perplexes and annoys him. All his life he has been accustomed to look on Queen Anne as the personification of everything that is dead and done with, "as dead as Queen Anne", you know; and now he has to fill your glass at lunch and dinner and listen to your accounts of the gay time you had at the Dublin Horse Show, and naturally he feels that something's very wrong with you.'

'But he wouldn't be downright hostile to me on that account, would he?' Jane asked anxiously.

'I didn't get really alarmed about it till lunch today,' said Clovis; 'I caught him glowering at you with a very sinister look and muttering: "Ought to be dead long ago, she ought, and some one should see to it." That's why I mentioned the matter to you.'

'This is awful,' said Jane; 'your mother must be told about it at once.'

'My mother mustn't hear a word about it,' said Clovis earnestly; 'it would upset her dreadfully. She relies on Sturridge for everything.'

'But he might kill me at any moment,' protested Jane.

'Not at any moment; he's busy with the silver all the afternoon.'

'You'll have to keep a sharp look-out all the time and be on your guard to frustrate any murderous attack,' said Jane, adding in a tone of weak obstinacy: 'It's a dreadful situation to be in, with a mad butler dangling over you like the sword of What's-his-name, but I'm certainly not going to cut my visit short.'

Clovis swore horribly under his breath; the miracle was an obvious misfire.

It was in the hall the next morning after a late breakfast that Clovis had his final inspiration as he stood engaged in coaxing rust spots from an old putter.

'Where is Miss Martlet?' he asked the butler, who was at that moment crossing the hall.

'Writing letters in the morning-room, sir,' said Sturridge, announcing a fact of which his questioner was already aware.

'She wants to copy the inscription on that old basket-hilted sabre,' said Clovis, pointing to a venerable weapon

167

hanging on the wall. 'I wish you'd take it to her; my hands are all over oil. Take it without the sheath, it will be less trouble.'

The butler drew the blade, still keen and bright in its well-cared-for old age, and carried it into the morning-room. There was a door near the writing-table leading to a back stairway; Jane vanished through it with such lightning rapidity that the butler doubted whether she had seen him come in. Half an hour later Clovis was driving her and her hastily packed luggage to the station.

'Mother will be awfully vexed when she comes back from her ride and finds you have gone,' he observed to the departing guest, 'but I'll make up some story about an urgent wire having called you away. It wouldn't do, to alarm her unnecessarily about Sturridge.'

Jane sniffed slightly at Clovis' ideas of unnecessary alarm, and was almost rude to the young man who came round with thoughtful inquiries as to luncheon-baskets.

The miracle lost some of its usefulness from the fact that Dora wrote the same day postponing the date of her visit, but, at any rate, Clovis holds the record as the only human being who ever hustled Jane Martlet out of the time-table of her migrations.

The Open Window

'MY AUNT WILL be down presently, Mr Nuttel,' said a very self-possessed young lady of fifteen; 'in the meantime you must try and put up with me.'

Framton Nuttel endeavoured to say the correct something which should duly flatter the niece of the moment without unduly discounting the aunt that was to come. Privately he doubted more than ever whether these formal visits on a succession of total strangers would do much towards helping the nerve cure which he was supposed to be undergoing.

'I know how it will be,' his sister had said when he was preparing to migrate to this rural retreat; 'you will bury yourself down there and not speak to a living soul, and your nerves will be worse than ever from moping. I shall just give you letters of introduction to all the people I know there. Some of them, as far as I can remember, were quite nice.'

Framton wondered whether Mrs Sappleton, the lady to whom he was presenting one of the letters of introduction, came into the nice division.

'Do you know many of the people round here?' asked the niece, when she judged that they had had sufficient silent communion.

'Hardly a soul,' said Framton. 'My sister was staying here, at the rectory, you know, some four years ago, and she gave me letters of introduction to some of the people here.'

He made the last statement in a tone of distinct regret.

'Then you know practically nothing about my aunt?' pursued the self-possessed young lady.

'Only her name and address,' admitted the caller. He was wondering whether Mrs Sappleton was in the married or widowed state. An undefinable something about the room seemed to suggest masculine habitation.

'Her great tragedy happened just three years ago,' said the child; 'that would be since your sister's time.'

'Her tragedy?' asked Framton; somehow in this restful country spot tragedies seemed out of place.

'You may wonder why we keep that window wide open on an October afternoon,' said the niece, indicating a large French window that opened on to a lawn.

'It is quite warm for the time of the year,' said Framton; 'but has that window got anything to do with the tragedy?'

'Out through that window, three years ago to a day, her husband and her two young brothers went off for their day's shooting. They never came back. In crossing the moor to their favourite snipe-shooting ground they were all three engulfed in a treacherous piece of bog. It had been that dreadful wet summer, you know, and places that were safe in other years gave way suddenly without warning. Their bodies were never recovered. That was the dreadful part of it.' Here the child's voice lost its self-possessed note and became falteringly human. 'Poor aunt always thinks that they will come back some day, they and the little brown spaniel that was lost with them, and walk in at that window just as they used to do. That is why the window is kept open every evening till it is quite dusk. Poor dear aunt, she has often told me how they went out, her husband with his white waterproof coat over his arm, and Ronnie, her youngest brother, singing, "Bertie, why do you bound?" as he always did to tease her, because she said it got on her nerves. Do you know, sometimes on still, quiet evenings like this, I almost get a creepy feeling that they will all walk in through that window –'

She broke off with a little shudder. It was a relief to Framton when the aunt bustled into the room with a whirl of apologies for being late in making her appearance.

'I hope Vera has been amusing you?' she said.

'She has been very interesting,' said Framton.

'I hope you don't mind the open window,' said Mrs Sappleton briskly; 'my husband and brothers will be home directly from shooting, and they always come in this way. They've been out for snipe in the marshes today, so they'll make a fine mess over my poor carpets. So like you menfolk, isn't it?'

She rattled on cheerfully about the shooting and the scarcity of birds, and the prospects for duck in the winter. To Framton, it was all purely horrible. He made a desperate but only partially successful effort to turn the talk on to a less ghastly topic; he was conscious that his hostess was giving him only a fragment of her attention, and her eyes were constantly straying past him to the open window and the lawn beyond. It was certainly an unfortunate coincidence that he should have paid his visit on this tragic anniversary.

'The doctors agree in ordering me complete rest, an absence of mental excitement, and avoidance of anything in the nature of violent physical exercise,' announced Framton, who laboured under the tolerably wide-spread delusion that total strangers and chance acquaintances are hungry for the least detail of one's ailments and infirmities, their cause and cure. 'On the matter of diet they are not so much in agreement,' he continued.

'No?' said Mrs Sappleton, in a voice which only replaced a yawn at the last moment. Then she suddenly brightened into alert attention – but not to what Framton was saying.

'Here they are at last!' she cried. 'Just in time for tea, and don't they look as if they were muddy up to the eyes!'

Framton shivered slightly and turned towards the niece with a look intended to convey sympathetic comprehension. The child was staring out through the open window with dazed horror in her eyes. In a chill shock of nameless fear Framton swung round in his seat and looked in the same direction.

In the deepening twilight three figures were walking across the lawn towards the window; they all carried guns under their arms, and one of them was additionally burdened with a white coat hung over his shoulders. A tired brown spaniel kept close at their heels. Noiselessly they neared the house, and then a hoarse young voice chanted out of the dusk: 'I said, Bertie, why do you bound?'

Framton grabbed wildly at his stick and hat; the halldoor, the gravel-drive, and the front gate were dimly noted stages in his headlong retreat. A cyclist coming along the road had to run into the hedge to avoid imminent collision.

'Here we are, my dear,' said the bearer of the white mackintosh, coming in through the window; 'fairly muddy, but most of it's dry. Who was that who bolted out as we came up?'

'A most extraordinary man, a Mr Nuttel,' said Mrs Sappleton; 'could only talk about his illnesses, and dashed off without a word of good-bye or apology when you arrived. One would think he had seen a ghost.'

'I expect it was the spaniel,' said the niece calmly; 'he told me he had a horror of dogs. He was once hunted into a cemetery somewhere on the banks of the Ganges by a pack of pariah dogs, and had to spend the night in a newly dug grave with the creatures snarling and grinning and foaming just above him. Enough to make any one lose their nerve.'

Romance at short notice was her speciality.

The Treasure-Ship

THE GREAT GALLEON lay in semi-retirement under the sand, weed and water of the northern bay where the fortune of war and weather had long ago ensconced it. Three and a quarter centuries had passed since the day when it had taken to the high seas as an important unit of a fighting squadron – precisely which squadron the learned were not agreed. The galleon had brought nothing into the world, but it had, according to tradition and report, taken much out of it. But how much? There again the learned were in disagreement. Some were as generous in their estimate as an income-tax assessor, others applied a species of higher criticism to the submerged treasure chests, and debased their contents to the currency of goblin gold. Of the former school was Lulu, Duchess of Dulverton.

The Duchess was not only a believer in the existence of a sunken treasure of alluring proportions; she also believed that she knew of a method by which the said treasure might be precisely located and cheaply disembedded. An aunt on her mother's side of the family had been Maid of Honour at the Court of Monaco, and had taken a respectful interest in the deep-sea researches in which the Throne of that country, impatient perhaps of its terrestrial restrictions, was wont to immerse itself. It was through the instrumentality of this relative that the Duchess learned of an invention, perfected and very nearly patented by a Monegaskan savant, by means of which the home-life of the Mediterranean sardine might be studied at a depth of many fathoms in a cold white light of more than ballroom brilliancy. Implicated in this invention (and, in the Duchess's eyes, the most attractive part of it) was an electric suction dredge, specially designed for dragging to the surface such objects of interest and value as might be found in the more accessible levels of the ocean-bed. The rights of the invention were to be acquired for a matter of eighteen hundred francs, and the apparatus for a few thousand more. The Duchess of Dulverton was rich, as the world counted wealth; she nursed the hope of being one day rich at her own computation. Companies had been formed and efforts had been made again and again during the course of three centuries to probe for the alleged treasures of the interesting galleon; with the aid of this invention she considered that she might go to work on the wreck privately and independently. After all, one of her ancestors on her mother's side was descended from Medina Sidonia, so she was of opinion that she had as much right to the treasure as any one. She acquired the invention and bought the apparatus.

Among other family ties and encumbrances, Lulu possessed a nephew, Vasco Honiton, a young gentleman who was blessed with a small income and a large circle of relatives, and lived impartially and precariously on both. The name Vasco had been given him possibly in the hope that he might live up to its adventurous tradition, but he limited himself strictly to the home industry of adventurer, preferring to exploit the assured rather than to explore the unknown. Lulu's intercourse with him had been restricted of recent years to the negative processes of being out of town when he called on her, and short of money when he wrote to her. Now, however, she bethought herself of his eminent suitability for the direction of a treasure-seeking experiment; if any one could extract gold from an unpromising situation it would certainly be Vasco – of course, under the necessary safeguards

175

in the way of supervision. Where money was in question Vasco's conscience was liable to fits of obstinate silence.

Somewhere on the west coast of Ireland the Dulverton property included a few acres of shingle, rock, and heather, too barren to support even an agrarian outrage, but embracing a small and fairly deep bay where the lobster yield was good in most seasons. There was a bleak little house on the property, and for those who liked lobsters and solitude, and were able to accept an Irish cook's ideas as to what might be perpetrated in the name of mayonnaise, Innisgluther was a tolerable exile during the summer months. Lulu seldom went there herself, but she lent the house lavishly to friends and relations. She put it now at Vasco's disposal.

'It will be the very place to practise and experiment with the salvage apparatus,' she said; 'the bay is quite deep in places, and you will be able to test everything thoroughly before starting on the treasure hunt.'

In less than three weeks Vasco turned up in town to report progress.

'The apparatus works beautifully,' he informed his aunt; 'the deeper one got the clearer everything grew. We found something in the way of a sunken wreck to operate on, too!'

'A wreck in Innisgluther Bay!' exclaimed Lulu.

'A submerged motor-boat, the *Sub-Rosa*,' said Vasco.

'No! really?' said Lulu; 'poor Billy Yuttley's boat. I remember, it went down somewhere off that coast some three years ago. His body was washed ashore at the Point. People said at the time that the boat was capsized intentionally – a case of suicide, you know. People always say that sort of thing when anything tragic happens.'

'In this case, they were right,' said Vasco.

'What do you mean?' asked the Duchess hurriedly. 'What makes you think so?'

'I know,' said Vasco simply.

'Know? How can you know? How can any one know? The thing happened three years ago.'

'In a locker of the *Sub-Rosa* I found a water-tight strong-box. It contained papers.' Vasco paused with dramatic effect and searched for a moment in the inner breast-pocket of his coat. He drew out a folded slip of paper. The Duchess snatched at it in almost indecent haste and moved appreciably nearer the fireplace.

'Was this in the *Sub-Rosa's* strong-box?' she asked.

'Oh, no,' said Vasco carelessly, 'that is a list of the well-known people who would be involved in a very disagreeable scandal if the *Sub-Rosa's* papers were made public. I've put you at the head of it, otherwise it follows alphabetical order.'

The Duchess gazed helplessly at the string of names, which seemed for the moment to include nearly every one she knew. As a matter of fact, her own name at the head of the list exercised an almost paralysing effect on her thinking faculties.

'Of course you have destroyed the papers?' she asked, when she had somewhat recovered herself. She was conscious that she made the remark with an entire lack of conviction.

Vasco shook his head.

'But you should have,' said Lulu angrily; 'if, as you say, they are highly compromising –'

'Oh, they are, I assure you of that,' interposed the young man.

'Then you should put them out of harm's way at once. Supposing anything should leak out, think of all these poor, unfortunate people who would be involved in the disclosures,' and Lulu tapped the list with an agitated gesture.

'Unfortunate, perhaps, but not poor,' corrected Vasco; 'if you read the list carefully you'll notice that I haven't troubled to include any one whose financial standing isn't above question.'

Lulu glared at her nephew for some moments in silence. Then she asked hoarsely: "What are you going to do?'

'Nothing – for the remainder of my life,' he answered meaningly. 'A little hunting, perhaps,' he continued, 'and I shall have a villa at Florence. The Villa Sub-Rosa would sound rather quaint and picturesque, don't you think, and quite a lot of people would be able to attach a meaning to the name. And I suppose I must have a hobby; I shall probably collect Raeburns.'

Lulu's relative, who lived at the Court of Monaco, got quite a snappish answer when she wrote recommending some further invention in the realm of marine research.

The Lull

'I'VE ASKED LATIMER Springfield to spend Sunday with us and stop the night,' announced Mrs Durmot at the breakfast-table.

'I thought he was in the throes of an election,' remarked her husband.

'Exactly; the poll is on Wednesday, and the poor man will have worked himself to a shadow by that time. Imagine what electioneering must be like in this awful soaking rain, going along slushy country roads and speaking to damp audiences in draughty schoolrooms, day after day for a fortnight. He'll have to put in an appearance at some place of worship on Sunday morning, and he can come to us immediately afterwards and have a thorough respite from everything connected with politics. I won't let him even think of them. I've had the picture of Cromwell dissolving the Long Parliament taken down from the staircase, and even the portrait of Lord Rosebery's "Ladas" removed from the smoking-room. And, Vera,' added Mrs Durmot, turning to her sixteen-year-old niece, 'be careful what colour ribbon you wear in your hair; not blue or yellow on any account; those are the rival party colours, and emerald green or orange would be almost as bad, with this Home Rule business to the fore.'

'On state occasions I always wear a black ribbon in my hair,' said Vera with crushing dignity.

Latimer Springfield was a rather cheerless, oldish young man, who went into politics somewhat in the spirit in which other people might go into half mourning. Without being an enthusiast, however, he was a fairly strenuous plodder, and Mrs Durmot had been reasonably near the mark in asserting that he was working at high pressure over this election. The restful lull which his hostess enforced on him was decidedly welcome, and yet the nervous excitement of the contest had too great a hold on him to be totally banished.

'I know he's going to sit up half the night working up points for his final speeches,' said Mrs Durmot regretfully; 'however, we've kept politics at arm's length all the afternoon and evening. More than that we cannot do.'

'That remains to be seen,' said Vera, but she said it to herself.

Latimer had scarcely shut his bedroom door before he was immersed in a sheaf of notes and pamphlets, while a fountain-pen and pocket-book were brought into play for the due marshalling of useful facts and discreet fictions. He had been at work for perhaps thirty-five minutes, and the house was seemingly consecrated to the healthy slumber of country life, when a stifled squealing and scuffling in the passage was followed by a loud tap at his door. Before he had time to answer, a much-encumbered Vera burst into the room with the question: 'I say, can I leave these here?'

'These' were a small black pig and a lusty specimen of black-red gamecock.

Latimer was moderately fond of animals, and particularly interested in small livestock rearing from the economic point of view; in fact, one of the pamphlets on which he was at that moment engaged warmly advocated the further development of the pig and poultry industry in our rural districts; but he was pardonably unwilling to share even a commodious bedroom with samples of hen-roost and sty products.

'Wouldn't they be happier somewhere outside?' he

asked, tactfully expressing his own preference in the matter in an apparent solicitude for theirs.

'There is no outside,' said Vera impressively, 'nothing but a waste of dark, swirling waters. The reservoir at Brinkley has burst.'

'I didn't know there was a reservoir at Brinkley,' said Latimer.

'Well, there isn't now, it's jolly well all over the place, and as we stand particularly low we're the centre of an inland sea just at present. You see the river has overflowed its banks as well.'

'Good gracious! Have any lives been lost?'

'Heaps, I should say. The second housemaid has already identified three bodies that have floated past the billiard-room window as being the young man she's engaged to. Either she's engaged to a large assortment of the population round here or else she's very careless at identification. Of course it may be the same body coming round again and again in a swirl; I hadn't thought of that.'

'But we ought to go out and do rescue work, oughtn't we?' said Latimer, with the instinct of a Parliamentary candidate for getting into the local limelight.

'We can't,' said Vera decidedly, 'we haven't any boats and we're cut off by a raging torrent from any human habitation. My aunt particularly hoped you would keep to your room and not add to the confusion, but she thought it would be so kind of you if you would take in Hartlepool's Wonder, the gamecock, you know, for the night. You see, there are eight other gamecocks, and they fight like furies if they get together, so we're putting one in each bedroom. The fowl-houses are all flooded out, you know. And then I thought perhaps you wouldn't mind taking in this wee piggie; he's rather a little love, but he has a vile temper. He gets that from his mother – not that I like to say things against her when she's lying dead and drowned in her sty, poor thing. What he really wants is a man's firm hand to keep him in order. I'd try and grapple with him myself, only I've got my chow in my room, you know, and he goes for pigs wherever he finds them.'

'Couldn't the pig go in the bathroom?' asked Latimer faintly, wishing that he had taken up as determined a stand on the subject of bedroom swine as the chow had.

'The bathroom?' Vera laughed shrilly. 'It'll be full of Boy Scouts till morning if the hot water holds out.'

'Boy Scouts?'

'Yes, thirty of them came to rescue us while the water was only waist-high; then it rose another three feet or so and we had to rescue them. We're giving them hot baths in batches and drying their clothes in the hot-air cupboard, but, of course, drenched clothes don't dry in a minute, and the corridor and staircase are beginning to look like a bit of coast scenery by Tuke. Two of the boys are wearing your Melton overcoat; I hope you don't mind.'

'It's a new overcoat,' said Latimer, with every indication of minding dreadfully.

'You'll take every care of Hartlepool's Wonder, won't you?' said Vera. 'His mother took three firsts at Birmingham, and he was second in the cockerel class last year at Gloucester. He'll probably roost on the rail at the bottom of your bed. I wonder if he'd feel more at home if some of his wives were up here with him? The hens are all in the pantry, and I think I could pick out Hartlepool Helen; she's his favourite.'

Latimer showed a belated firmness on the subject of Hartlepool Helen, and Vera withdrew without pressing the point, having first settled the gamecock on his extemporized perch and taken an affectionate farewell of the pigling. Latimer undressed and got into bed with all due speed, judging that the pig would abate its inquisitorial restlessness once the light was turned out. As a substitute for a cosy, straw-bedded sty the room offered, at first inspection, few attractions, but the disconsolate animal suddenly discovered an appliance in which the most luxuriously contrived piggeries were notably deficient. The sharp edge of the underneath part of the bed was pitched at exactly the right elevation to permit the pigling to scrape himself ecstatically backwards and forwards, with an artistic humping of the back at the crucial moment and an accompanying gurgle of long-drawn delight. The gamecock, who may have fancied that he was being rocked in the branches of a pine-tree, bore the motion with greater fortitude than Latimer was able to command. A series of slaps directed at the pig's body were accepted more as an additional and pleasing irritant than as a criticism of conduct or a hint to desist; evidently something more than a man's firm hand was needed to deal with the case. Latimer slipped out of bed in search of a weapon of dissuasion. There was sufficient light in the room to enable the pig to detect this manœuvre, and the vile temper, inherited from the drowned mother, found full play. Latimer bounded back into bed, and his conqueror, after a few threatening snorts and champings of its jaws, resumed its massage operations with renewed zeal. During the long wakeful hours which ensued Latimer tried to distract his mind from his own immediate troubles by dwelling with decent sympathy on the second housemaid's bereavement, but he found himself more often wondering how many Boy Scouts were sharing his

Melton overcoat. The rôle of Saint Martin *malgré lui* was not one which appealed to him.

Towards dawn the pigling fell into a happy slumber, and Latimer might have followed its example, but at about the same time Stupor Hartlepooli gave a rousing crow, clattered down to the floor and forthwith commenced a spirited combat with his reflection in the wardrobe mirror. Remembering that the bird was more or less under his care Latimer performed Hague Tribunal offices by draping a bath-towel over the provocative mirror, but the ensuing peace was local and short-lived. The deflected energies of the gamecock found new outlet in a sudden and sustained attack on the sleeping and temporarily inoffensive pigling, and the duel which followed was desperate and embittered beyond any possibility of effective intervention. The feathered combatant had the advantage of being able, when hard pressed, to take refuge on the bed, and freely availed himself of this circumstance; the pigling never quite succeeded in hurling himself on to the same eminence, but it was not from want of trying.

Neither side could claim any decisive success, and the struggle had been practically fought to a standstill by the time that the maid appeared with the early morning tea.

'Lor, sir,' she exclaimed in undisguised astonishment, 'do you want those animals in your room?'

Want!

The pigling, as though aware that it might have outstayed its welcome, dashed out at the door, and the gamecock followed it at a more dignified pace.

'If Miss Vera's dog sees that pig – !' exclaimed the maid, and hurried off to avert such a catastrophe.

A cold suspicion was stealing over Latimer's mind; he went to the window and drew up the blind. A light, drizzling rain was falling, but there was not the faintest trace of any inundation.

Some half-hour later he met Vera on the way to the breakfast-room.

'I should not like to think of you as a deliberate liar,' he observed coldly, 'but one occasionally has to do things one does not like.'

'At any rate I kept your mind from dwelling on politics all the night,' said Vera.

Which was, of course, perfectly true.

The Romancers

IT WAS AUTUMN in London, that blessed season between the harshness of winter and the insincerities of summer; a trustful season when one buys bulbs and sees to the registration of one's vote, believing perpetually in spring and a change of Government.

Morton Crosby sat on a bench in a secluded corner of Hyde Park, lazily enjoying a cigarette and watching the slow grazing promenade of a pair of snow-geese, the male looking rather like an albino edition of the russet-hued female. Out of the corner of his eye Crosby also noted with some interest the hesitating hoverings of a human figure, which had passed and repassed his seat two or three times at shortening intervals, like a wary crow about to alight near some possibly edible morsel. Inevitably the figure came to an anchorage on the bench, within easy talking distance of its original occupant. The uncared-for clothes, the aggressive, grizzled beard, and the furtive, evasive eye of the new-comer bespoke the professional cadger, the man who would undergo hours of humiliating tale-spinning and rebuff rather than adventure on half a day's decent work.

For a while the new-comer fixed his eyes straight in front of him in a strenuous, unseeing gaze; then his voice broke out with the insinuating inflection of one who has a story to retail well worth any loiterer's while to listen to.

'It's a strange world,' he said.

As the statement met with no response he altered it to the form of a question.

'I dare say you've found it to be a strange world, mister?'

'As far as I am concerned,' said Crosby, 'the strangeness has worn off in the course of thirty-six years.'

'Ah,' said the greybeard, 'I could tell you things that you'd hardly believe. Marvellous things that have really happened to me.'

'Nowadays there is no demand for marvellous things that have really happened,' said Crosby discouragingly; 'the professional writers of fiction turn these things out so much better. For instance, my neighbours tell me wonderful, incredible things that their Aberdeens and chows and borzois have done; I never listen to them. On the other hand, I have read *The Hound of the Baskervilles* three times.'

The greybeard moved uneasily in his seat; then he opened up new country.

'I take it that you are a professing Christian,' he observed.

'I am a prominent and I think I may say an influential member of the Mussulman community of Eastern Persia,' said Crosby, making an excursion himself into the realms of fiction.

The greybeard was obviously disconcerted at this new check of introductory conversation, but the defeat was only momentary.

'Persia. I should never have taken you for a Persian,' he remarked, with a somewhat aggrieved air.

'I am not,' said Crosby; 'my father was an Afghan.'

'An Afghan!' said the other, smitten into bewildered silence for a moment. Then he recovered himself and renewed his attack.

'Afghanistan. Ah! We've had some wars with that country; now, I dare say, instead of fighting it we might have learned something from it. A very wealthy country, I believe. No real poverty there.'

He raised his voice on the word 'poverty' with a

suggestion of intense feeling. Crosby saw the opening and avoided it.

'It possesses, nevertheless, a number of highly talented and ingenious beggars,' he said; 'if I had not spoken so disparagingly of marvellous things that have really happened I would tell you the story of Ibrahim and the eleven camel-loads of blotting-paper. Also I have forgotten exactly how it ended.'

'My own life-story is a curious one,' said the stranger, apparently stifling all desire to hear the history of Ibrahim; 'I was not always as you see me now.'

'We are supposed to undergo complete change in the course of every seven years,' said Crosby, as an explanation of the foregoing announcement.

'I mean I was not always in such distressing circumstances as I am at present,' pursued the stranger doggedly.

'That sounds rather rude,' said Crosby stiffly, 'considering that you are at present talking to a man reputed to be one of the most gifted conversationalists of the Afghan border.'

'I don't mean in that way,' said the greybeard hastily; 'I've been very much interested in your conversation. I was alluding to my unfortunate financial situation. You mayn't hardly believe it, but at the present moment I am absolutely without a farthing. Don't see any prospect of getting any money, either, for the next few days. I don't suppose you've ever found yourself in such a position,' he added.

'In the town of Yom,' said Crosby, 'which is in Southern Afghanistan, and which also happens to be my birthplace, there was a Chinese philosopher who used to say that one of the three chiefest human blessings was to be absolutely without money. I forget what the other two were.'

'Ah, I dare say,' said the stranger, in a tone that betrayed no enthusiasm for the philosopher's memory; 'and did he practise what he preached? That's the test.'

'He lived happily with very little money or resources,' said Crosby.

'Then I expect he had friends who would help him liberally whenever he was in difficulties, such as I am in at present.'

'In Yom,' said Crosby, 'it is not necessary to have friends in order to obtain help. Any citizen of Yom would help a stranger as a matter of course.'

The greybeard was now genuinely interested. The conversation had at last taken a favourable turn.

'If some one, like me, for instance, who was in undeserved difficulties, asked a citizen of that town you speak of for a small loan to tide over a few days' impecuniosity – five shillings, or perhaps a rather larger sum – would it be given to him as a matter of course?'

'There would be a certain preliminary,' said Crosby; 'one would take him to a wine-shop and treat him to a measure of wine, and then, after a little high-flown conversation, one would put the desired sum in his hand and wish him good-day. It is a roundabout way of performing a simple transaction, but in the East all ways are roundabout.'

The listener's eyes were glittering.

'Ah,' he exclaimed, with a thin sneer ringing meaningly through his words, 'I suppose you've given up all those generous customs since you left your town. Don't practise them now, I expect.'

'No one who has lived in Yom,' said Crosby fervently, 'and remembers its green hills covered with apricot and almond trees, and the cold water that rushes down like a caress from the upland snows and dashes under the little wooden bridges, no one who remembers these things and treasures the memory of them would ever give up a single one of its unwritten laws and customs. To me they are as binding as though I still lived in that hallowed home of my youth.'

'Then if I was to ask you for a small loan –' began the greybeard fawningly, edging nearer on the seat and hurriedly wondering how large he might safely make his request, 'if I was to ask you for, say –'

'At any other time, certainly,' said Crosby; 'in the months of November and December, however, it is absolutely forbidden for any one of our race to give or receive loans or gifts; in fact, one does not willingly speak of them. It is considered unlucky. We will therefore close this discussion.'

'But it is still October!' exclaimed the adventurer with an eager, angry whine, as Crosby rose from his seat; 'wants eight days to the end of the month!'

'The Afghan November began yesterday,' said Crosby severely, and in another moment he was striding across the Park, leaving his recent companion scowling and muttering furiously on the seat.

'I don't believe a word of his story,' he chattered to himself; 'pack of nasty lies from beginning to end. Wish I'd told him so to his face. Calling himself an Afghan!'

The snorts and snarls that escaped from him for the next quarter of an hour went far to support the truth of the old saying that two of a trade never agree.

The Schartz-Metterklume Method

LADY CARLOTTA STEPPED out on to the platform of the small wayside station and took a turn or two up and down its uninteresting length, to kill time till the train should be pleased to proceed on its way. Then, in the roadway beyond, she saw a horse struggling with a more than ample load, and a carter of the sort that seems to bear a sullen hatred against the animal that helps him to earn a living. Lady Carlotta promptly betook her to the roadway, and put rather a different complexion on the struggle. Certain of her acquaintances were wont to give her plentiful admonition as to the undesirability of interfering on behalf of a distressed animal, such interference being 'none of her business'. Only once had she put the doctrine of non-interference into practice, when one of its most eloquent exponents had been besieged for nearly three hours in a small and extremely uncomfortable may-tree by an angry boar-pig, while Lady Carlotta, on the other side of the fence, had proceeded with the water-colour sketch she was engaged on, and refused to interfere between the boar and his prisoner. It is to be feared that she lost the friendship of the ultimately rescued lady. On this occasion she merely lost the train, which gave way to the first sign of impatience it had shown throughout the journey, and steamed off without her. She bore the desertion with philosophical indifference; her friends and relations were thoroughly well used to the fact of her luggage arriving without her. She wired a vague non-committal message to her destination to say that she was coming on 'by another train'. Before she had time to think what her next move might be she was confronted by an imposingly attired lady, who seemed to be taking a prolonged mental inventory of her clothes and looks.

'You must be Miss Hope, the governess I've come to meet,' said the apparition, in a tone that admitted of very little argument.

'Very well, if I must I must,' said Lady Carlotta to herself with dangerous meekness.

'I am Mrs Quabarl,' continued the lady; 'and where, pray, is your luggage?'

'It's gone astray,' said the alleged governess, falling in with the excellent rule of life that the absent are always to blame; the luggage had, in point of fact, behaved with perfect correctitude. 'I've just telegraphed about it,' she added, with a nearer approach to truth.

'How provoking,' said Mrs Quabarl; 'these railway companies are so careless. However, my maid can lend you things for the night,' and she led the way to her car.

During the drive to the Quabarl mansion Lady Carlotta was impressively introduced to the nature of the charge that had been thrust upon her; she learned that Claude and Wilfrid were delicate, sensitive young people, that Irene had the artistic temperament highly developed, and that Viola was something or other else of a mould equally commonplace among children of that class and type in the twentieth century.

'I wish them not only to be *taught*,' said Mrs Quabarl, 'but *interested* in what they learn. In their history lessons, for instance, you must try to make them feel that they are being introduced to the life-stories of men and women who really lived, not merely committing a mass of names and dates to memory. French, of course, I shall expect you to talk at mealtimes several days in the week.'

'I shall talk French four days of the week and Russian in the remaining three.'

'Russian? My dear Miss Hope, no one in the house speaks or understands Russian.'

'That will not embarrass me in the least,' said Lady Carlotta coldly.

Mrs Quabarl, to use a colloquial expression, was knocked off her perch. She was one of those imperfectly self-assured individuals who are magnificent and auto-cratic as long as they are not seriously opposed. The least show of unexpected resistance goes a long way towards rendering them cowed and apologetic. When the new governess failed to express wondering admiration of the large, newly purchased and expensive car, and lightly alluded to the superior advantages of one or two makes which had just been put on the market, the discomfiture of her patroness became almost abject. Her feelings were those which might have animated a general of ancient warfaring days, on beholding his heaviest battle-elephant ignominiously driven off the field by slingers and javelin throwers.

At dinner that evening, although reinforced by her husband, who usually duplicated her opinions and lent her moral support generally, Mrs Quabarl regained none of her lost ground. The governess not only helped herself well and truly to wine, but held forth with considerable show of critical knowledge on various vintage matters, concerning which the Quabarls were in no wise able to pose as authorities. Previous governesses had limited their conversation on the wine topic to a respectful and doubt-less sincere expression of a preference for water. When this one went as far as to recommend a wine firm in whose hands you could not go very far wrong Mrs Quabarl thought it time to turn the conversation into more usual channels.

'We got very satisfactory references about you from Canon Teep,' she observed; 'a very estimable man, I should think.'

'Drinks like a fish and beats his wife, otherwise a very lovable character,' said the governess imperturbably.

'My *dear* Miss Hope! I trust you are exaggerating,' exclaimed the Quabarls in unison.

'One must in justice admit that there is some provocation,' continued the romancer. 'Mrs Teep is quite the most irritating bridge-player that I have ever sat down with; her leads and declarations would condone a certain amount of brutality in her partner, but to souse her with the contents of the only soda-water syphon in the house on a Sunday afternoon, when one couldn't get another, argues an indifference to the comfort of others which I cannot altogether overlook. You may think me hasty in my judgements, but it was practically on account of the syphon incident that I left.'

'We will talk of this some other time,' said Mrs Quabarl hastily.

'I shall never allude to it again,' said the governess with decision.

Mr Quabarl made a welcome diversion by asking what studies the new instructress proposed to inaugurate on the morrow.

'History to begin with,' she informed him.

'Ah, history,' he observed sagely; 'now in teaching them history you must take care to interest them in what they learn. You must make them feel that they are being introduced to the life-stories of men and women who really lived –'

'I've told her all that,' interposed Mrs Quabarl.

'I teach history on the Schartz-Metterklume method,' said the governess loftily.

'Ah, yes,' said her listeners, thinking it expedient to assume an acquaintance at least with the name.

'What are you children doing out here?' demanded Mrs Quabarl the next morning, on finding Irene sitting rather glumly at the head of the stairs, while her sister was perched in an attitude of depressed discomfort on the window-seat behind her, with a wolf-skin rug almost covering her.

'We are having a history lesson,' came the unexpected reply. 'I am supposed to be Rome, and Viola up there is the she-wolf; not a real wolf, but the figure of one that the Romans used to set store by – I forget why. Claude and Wilfrid have gone to fetch the shabby women.'

'The shabby women?'

'Yes, they've got to carry them off. They didn't want to, but Miss Hope got one of father's fives-bats and said she'd give them a number nine spanking if they didn't, so they've gone to do it.'

A loud, angry screaming from the direction of the lawn drew Mrs Quabarl thither in hot haste, fearful lest the threatened castigation might even now be in process of infliction. The outcry, however, came principally from the two small daughters of the lodge-keeper, who were being hauled and pushed towards the house by the panting and dishevelled Claude and Wilfrid, whose task was rendered even more arduous by the incessant, if not very effectual, attacks of the captured maidens' small brother. The governess, fives-bat in hand, sat negligently on the stone balustrade, presiding over the scene with the cold impartiality of a Goddess of Battles. A furious and repeated chorus of

'I'll tell muvver' rose from the lodge children, but the lodge-mother, who was hard of hearing, was for the moment immersed in the preoccupation of her washtub. After an apprehensive glance in the direction of the lodge (the good woman was gifted with the highly militant temper which is sometimes the privilege of deafness) Mrs Quabarl flew indignantly to the rescue of the struggling captives.

'Wilfrid! Claude! Let those children go at once. Miss Hope, what on earth is the meaning of this scene?'

'Early Roman history; the Sabine women, don't you know? It's the Schartz-Metterklume method to make children understand history by acting it themselves; fixes it in their memory, you know. Of course, if, thanks to your interference, your boys go through life thinking that the Sabine women ultimately escaped, I really cannot be held responsible.'

'You may be very clever and modern, Miss Hope,' said Mrs Quabarl firmly, 'but I should like you to leave here by the next train. Your luggage will be sent after you as soon as it arrives.'

'I'm not certain exactly where I shall be for the next few days,' said the dismissed instructress of youth; 'you might keep my luggage till I wire my address. There are only a couple of trunks and some golf-clubs and a leopard cub.'

'A leopard cub!' gasped Mrs Quabarl. Even in her departure this extraordinary person seemed destined to leave a trail of embarrassment behind her.

'Well, it's rather left off being a cub; it's more than half-grown, you know. A fowl every day and a rabbit on Sundays is what it usually gets. Raw beef makes it too excitable. Don't trouble about getting the car for me, I'm rather inclined for a walk.'

And Lady Carlotta strode out of the Quabarl horizon.

The advent of the genuine Miss Hope, who had made a mistake as to the day on which she was due to arrive, caused a turmoil which that good lady was quite unused to inspiring. Obviously the Quabarl family had been woefully befooled, but a certain amount of relief came with the knowledge.

'How tiresome for you, dear Carlotta,' said her hostess, when the overdue guest ultimately arrived; 'how very tiresome losing your train and having to stop overnight in a strange place.'

'Oh, dear, no,' said Lady Carlotta; 'not at all tiresome – for me.'

The Seventh Pullet

'IT'S NOT THE daily grind that I complain of,' said Blenkinthrope resentfully; 'it's the dull grey sameness of my life outside of office hours. Nothing of interest comes my way, nothing remarkable or out of the common. Even the little things that I do try to find some interest in don't seem to interest other people. Things in my garden, for instance.'

'The potato that weighed just over two pounds,' said his friend Gorworth.

'Did I tell you about that?' said Blenkinthrope; 'I was telling the others in the train this morning. I forgot if I'd told you.'

'To be exact you told me that it weighed just under two pounds, but I took into account the fact that abnormal vegetables and freshwater fish have an after-life, in which growth is not arrested.'

'You're just like the others,' said Blenkinthrope sadly, 'you only make fun of it.'

'The fault is with the potato, not with us,' said Gorworth; 'we are not in the least interested in it because it is not in the least interesting. The men you go up in the train with every day are just in the same case as yourself; their lives are commonplace and not very interesting to themselves, and they certainly are not going to wax enthusiastic over the commonplace events in other men's lives. Tell them something startling, dramatic, piquant, that has happened to yourself or to some one in your family, and you will capture their interest at once. They will talk about you with a certain personal pride to all their acquaintances. "Man I know intimately, fellow called

Blenkinthrope, lives down my way, had two of his fingers clawed clean off by a lobster he was carrying home to supper. Doctor says entire hand may have to come off." Now that is conversation of a very high order. But imagine walking into a tennis club with the remark: "I know a man who has grown a potato weighing two and a quarter pounds."'

'But hang it all, my dear fellow,' said Blenkinthrope impatiently, 'haven't I just told you that nothing of a remarkable nature ever happens to me?'

'Invent something,' said Gorworth. Since winning a prize for excellence in Scriptural knowledge at a preparatory school he had felt licensed to be a little more unscrupulous than the circle he moved in. Much might surely be excused to one who in early life could give a list of seventeen trees mentioned in the Old Testament.

'What sort of thing?' asked Blenkinthrope, somewhat snappishly.

'A snake got into your hen-run yesterday morning and killed six out of seven pullets, first mesmerizing them with its eyes and then biting them as they stood helpless. The seventh pullet was one of that French sort, with feathers all over its eyes, so it escaped the mesmeric snare, and just flew at what it could see of the snake and pecked it to pieces.'

'Thank you,' said Blenkinthrope stiffly; 'it's a very clever invention. If such a thing had really happened in my poultry-run I admit I should have been proud and interested to tell people about it. But I'd rather stick to fact, even if it is plain fact.' All the same his mind dwelt wistfully on the story of the Seventh Pullet. He could picture himself telling it in the train amid the absorbed interest of his fellow-passengers. Unconsciously all sorts of little details and improvements began to suggest themselves.

Wistfulness was still his dominant mood when he took his seat in the railway carriage the next morning. Opposite him sat Stevenham, who had attained to a recognized brevet of importance through the fact of an uncle having dropped dead in the act of voting at a Parliamentary election. That had happened three years ago, but Stevenham was still deferred to on all questions of home and foreign politics.

'Hullo, how's the giant mushroom, or whatever it was?' was all the notice Blenkinthrope got from his fellow-travellers.

Young Duckby, whom he mildly disliked, speedily monopolized the general attention by an account of a domestic bereavement.

'Had four young pigeons carried off last night by a whacking big rat. Oh, a monster he must have been; you could tell by the size of the hole he made breaking into the loft.'

No moderate-sized rat ever seemed to carry out any predatory operations in these regions; they were all enormous in their enormity.

'Pretty hard lines that,' continued Duckby, seeing that he had secured the attention and respect of the company; 'four squeakers carried off at one swoop. You'd find it rather hard to match that in the way of unlooked-for bad luck.'

'I had six pullets out of a pen of seven killed by a snake yesterday afternoon,' said Blenkinthrope, in a voice which he hardly recognized as his own.

'By a snake?' came in excited chorus.

'It fascinated them with its deadly, glittering eyes, one

after the other, and struck them down while they stood helpless. A bedridden neighbour, who wasn't able to call for assistance, witnessed it all from her bedroom window.'

'Well, I never!' broke in the chorus, with variations.

'The interesting part of it is about the seventh pullet, the one that didn't get killed,' resumed Blenkinthrope, slowly lighting a cigarette. His diffidence had left him, and he was beginning to realize how safe and easy depravity can seem once one has the courage to begin. 'The six dead birds were Minorcas; the seventh was a Houdan with a mop of feathers all over its eyes. It could hardly see the snake at all, so of course it wasn't mesmerized like the others. It just could see something wriggling on the ground, and went for it and pecked it to death.'

'Well, I'm blessed!' exclaimed the chorus.

In the course of the next few days Blenkinthrope discovered how little the loss of one's self-respect affects one when one has gained the esteem of the world. His story found its way into one of the poultry papers, and was copied thence into a daily news-sheet as a matter of general interest. A lady wrote from the North of Scotland recounting a similar episode which she had witnessed as occurring between a stoat and a blind grouse. Somehow a lie seems so much less reprehensible when one can call it a lee.

For a while the adapter of the Seventh Pullet story enjoyed to the full his altered standing as a person of consequence, one who had had some share in the strange events of his times. Then he was thrust once again into the cold grey background by the sudden blossoming into importance of Smith-Paddon, a daily fellow-traveller, whose little girl had been knocked down and nearly hurt by a car belonging to a musical-comedy actress. The actress was not in the car at the time, but she was in numerous photographs which appeared in the illustrated papers of Zoto Dobreen inquiring after the well-being of Maisie, daughter of Edmund Smith-Paddon, Esq. With this new human interest to absorb them the travelling companions were almost rude when Blenkinthrope tried to explain his contrivance for keeping vipers and peregrine falcons out of his chicken-run.

Gorworth, to whom he unburdened himself in private, gave him the same counsel as theretofore.

'Invent something.'

'Yes, but what?'

The ready affirmative coupled with the question betrayed significant shifting of the ethical standpoint.

It was a few days later that Blenkinthrope revealed a chapter of family history to the customary gathering in the railway carriage.

'Curious thing happened to my aunt, the one who lives in Paris,' he began. He had several aunts, but they were all geographically distributed over Greater London.

'She was sitting on a seat in the Bois the other afternoon, after lunching at the Roumanian Legation.'

Whatever the story gained in picturesqueness for the dragging-in of diplomatic 'atmosphere', it ceased from that moment to command any acceptance as a record of current events. Gorworth had warned his neophyte that this would be the case, but the traditional enthusiasm of the neophyte had triumphed over discretion.

'She was feeling rather drowsy, the effect probably of the champagne, which she's not in the habit of taking in the middle of the day.'

A subdued murmur of admiration went round the company. Blenkinthrope's aunts were not used to taking champagne in the middle of the year, regarding it exclusively as a Christmas and New Year accessory.

'Presently a rather portly gentleman passed by her seat and paused an instant to light a cigar. At that moment a youngish man came up behind him, drew the blade from a swordstick, and stabbed him half a dozen times through and through. "Scoundrel," he cried to his victim, "you do not know me. My name is Henri Leturc." The elder man wiped away some of the blood that was spattering his clothes, turned to his assailant, and said: "And since when has an attempted assassination been considered an introduction?" Then he finished lighting his cigar and walked away. My aunt had intended screaming for the police, but seeing the indifference with which the principal in the affair treated the matter she felt that it would be an impertinence on her part to interfere. Of course I need hardly say she put the whole thing down to the effects of a warm, drowsy afternoon and the Legation champagne. Now comes the astonishing part of my story. A fortnight later a bank manager was stabbed to death with a swordstick in that very part of the Bois. His assassin was the son of a charwoman formerly working at the bank, who had been dismissed from her job by the manager on account of chronic intemperance. His name was Henri Leturc.'

From that moment Blenkinthrope was tacitly accepted as the Munchausen of the party. No effort was spared to draw him out from day to day in the exercise of testing their powers of credulity, and Blenkinthrope, in the false security of an assured and receptive audience, waxed industrious and ingenious in supplying the demand for marvels. Duckby's satirical story of a tame otter that had a tank in the garden to swim in, and whined restlessly whenever the water-rate was overdue, was scarcely an unfair parody of some of Blenkinthrope's wilder efforts. And then one day came Nemesis.

Returning to his villa one evening Blenkinthrope found his wife sitting in front of a pack of cards, which she was scrutinizing with unusual concentration.

'The same old patience-game?' he asked carelessly.

'No, dear; this is the Death's Head patience, the most difficult of them all. I've never got it to work out, and somehow I should be rather frightened if I did. Mother only got it out once in her life; she was afraid of it, too. Her great-aunt had done it once and fallen dead from excitement the next moment, and mother always had a feeling that she would die if she ever got it out. She died the same night that she did it. She was in bad health at the time, certainly, but it was a strange coincidence.'

'Don't do it if it frightens you,' was Blenkinthrope's practical comment as he left the room. A few minutes later his wife called to him.

'John, it gave me such a turn, I nearly got it out. Only the five of diamonds held me up at the end. I really thought I'd done it.'

'Why, you can do it,' said Blenkinthrope, who had come back to the room; 'if you shift the eight of clubs on to that open nine the five can be moved on to the six.'

His wife made the suggested move with hasty, trembling fingers, and piled the outstanding cards on to their respective packs. Then she followed the example of her mother and great-grand-aunt.

Blenkinthrope had been genuinely fond of his wife, but in the midst of his bereavement one dominant thought obtruded itself. Something sensational and real had at last come into his life; no longer was it a grey, colourless record. The headlines which might appropriately describe his domestic tragedy kept shaping themselves in his brain. 'Inherited presentiment comes true'. 'The Death's Head patience: Card-game that justified its sinister name in three generations'. He wrote out a full story of the fatal occurrence for the *Essex Vedette*, the editor of which was a friend of his, and to another friend he gave a condensed account, to be taken up to the office of one of the half-penny dailies. But in both cases his reputation as a romancer stood fatally in the way of the fulfilment of his ambitions. 'Not the right thing to be Munchausening in a time of sorrow,' agreed his friends among themselves, and a brief note of regret at the 'sudden death of the wife of our respected neighbour, Mr John Blenkinthrope, from heart failure', appearing in the news column of the local paper was the forlorn outcome of his visions of widespread publicity.

Blenkinthrope shrank from the society of his erstwhile travelling companions and took to travelling townwards by an earlier train. He sometimes tries to enlist the sympathy and attention of a chance acquaintance in details of the whistling prowess of his best canary or the dimensions of his largest beetroot; he scarcely recognizes himself as the man who was once spoken about and pointed out as the owner of the Seventh Pullet.

The Blind Spot

'YOU'VE JUST COME back from Adelaide's funeral, haven't you?' said Sir Lulworth to his nephew; 'I suppose it was very like most other funerals?'

'I'll tell you all about it at lunch,' said Egbert.

'You'll do nothing of the sort. It wouldn't be respectful either to your great-aunt's memory or to the lunch. We begin with Spanish olives, then a borsch, then more olives and a bird of some kind, and a rather enticing Rhenish wine, not at all expensive as wines go in this country, but still quite laudable in its way. Now there's absolutely nothing in that menu that harmonizes in the least with the subject of your great-aunt Adelaide or her funeral. She was a charming woman, and quite as intelligent as she had any need to be, but somehow she always reminded me of an English cook's idea of a Madras curry.'

'She used to say you were frivolous,' said Egbert. Something in his tone suggested that he rather endorsed the verdict.

'I believe I once considerably scandalized her by declaring that clear soup was a more important factor in life than a clear conscience. She had very little sense of proportion. By the way, she made you her principal heir, didn't she?'

'Yes,' said Egbert, 'and executor as well. It's in that connection that I particularly want to speak to you.'

'Business is not my strong point at any time,' said Sir Lulworth, 'and certainly not when we're on the immediate threshold of lunch.'

'It isn't exactly business,' explained Egbert, as he followed his uncle into the dining-room. 'It's something rather serious. Very serious.'

'Then we can't possibly speak about it now,' said Sir Lulworth; 'no one could talk seriously, during a borsch. A beautifully constructed borsch, such as you are going to experience presently, ought not only to banish conversation but almost to annihilate thought. Later on, when we arrive at the second stage of olives, I shall be quite ready to discuss that new book on Borrow, or, if you prefer it, the present situation in the Grand Duchy of Luxemburg. But I absolutely decline to talk anything approaching business till we have finished with the bird.'

For the greater part of the meal Egbert sat in an abstracted silence, the silence of a man whose mind is focused on one topic. When the coffee stage had been reached he launched himself suddenly athwart his uncle's reminiscences of the Court of Luxemburg.

'I think I told you that great-aunt Adelaide had made me her executor. There wasn't very much to be done in the way of legal matters, but I had to go through her papers.'

'That would be a fairly heavy task in itself. I should imagine there were reams of family letters.'

'Stacks of them, and most of them highly uninteresting. There was one packet, however, which I thought might repay a careful perusal. It was a bundle of correspondence from her brother Peter.'

'The Canon of tragic memory,' said Lulworth.

'Exactly, of tragic memory, as you say; a tragedy that has never been fathomed.'

'Probably the simplest explanation was the correct one,' said Sir Lulworth; 'he slipped on the stone staircase and fractured his skull in falling.'

Egbert shook his head. 'The medical evidence all went to prove that the blow on the head was struck by some one coming up behind him. A wound caused by violent contact with the steps could not possibly have been inflicted at that angle of the skull. They experimented with a dummy figure falling in every conceivable position.'

'But the motive?' exclaimed Sir Lulworth; 'no one had any interest in doing away with him, and the number of people who destroy Canons of the Established Church for the mere fun of killing must be extremely limited. Of course there are individuals of weak mental balance who do that sort of thing, but they seldom conceal their handiwork; they are more generally inclined to parade it.'

'His cook was under suspicion,' said Egbert shortly.

'I know he was,' said Sir Lulworth, 'simply because he was about the only person on the premises at the time of the tragedy. But could anything be sillier than trying to fasten a charge of murder on to Sebastien? He had nothing to gain, in fact, a good deal to lose, from the death of his employer. The Canon was paying him quite as good wages as I was able to offer him when I took him over into my service. I have since raised them to something a little more in accordance with his real worth, but at the time he was glad to find a new place without troubling about an increase of wages. People were fighting rather shy of him, and he had no friends in this country. No; if any one in the world was interested in the prolonged life and unimpaired digestion of the Canon it would certainly be Sebastien.'

'People don't always weigh the consequences of their rash acts,' said Egbert, 'otherwise there would be very few murders committed. Sebastien is a man of hot temper.'

'He is a southerner,' admitted Sir Lulworth; 'to be geographically exact I believe he hails from the French slopes of the Pyrenees. I took that into consideration when he nearly killed the gardener's boy the other day for bringing him a spurious substitute for sorrel. One must always make allowances for origin and locality and early environment; "Tell me your longitude and I'll know what latitude to allow you," is my motto.'

'There, you see,' said Egbert, 'he nearly killed the gardener's boy.'

'My dear Egbert, between nearly killing a gardener's boy and altogether killing a Canon there is a wide difference. No doubt you have often felt a temporary desire to kill a gardener's boy; you have never given way to it, and I respect you for your self-control. But I don't suppose you have ever wanted to kill an octogenarian Canon. Besides, as far as we know, there had never been any quarrel or disagreement between the two men. The evidence at the inquest brought that out very clearly.'

'Ah!' said Egbert, with the air of a man coming at last into a deferred inheritance of conversational importance, 'that is precisely what I want to speak to you about.'

He pushed away his coffee cup and drew a pocket-book from his inner breast-pocket. From the depths of the pocket-book he produced an envelope, and from the envelope he extracted a letter, closely written in a small, neat handwriting.

'One of the Canon's numerous letters to Aunt Adelaide,' he explained, 'written a few days before his death. Her memory was already failing when she received it, and I dare say she forgot the contents as soon as she had read it; otherwise, in the light of what subsequently happened, we should have heard something of this letter before now. If it had been produced at the inquest I fancy it would have made some difference in the course of affairs. The evidence, as you remarked just now, choked off suspicion against Sebastien by disclosing an utter absence of anything that could be considered a motive or provocation for the crime, if crime there was.'

'Oh, read the letter,' said Sir Lulworth impatiently.

'It's a long rambling affair, like most of his letters in his later years,' said Egbert. 'I'll read the part that bears immediately on the mystery.

'"I very much fear I shall have to get rid of Sebastien. He cooks divinely, but he has the temper of a fiend or an anthropoid ape, and I am really in bodily fear of him. We had a dispute the other day as to the correct sort of lunch to be served on Ash Wednesday, and I got so irritated and annoyed at his conceit and obstinacy that at last I threw a cupful of coffee in his face and called him at the same time an impudent jackanapes. Very little of the coffee went actually in his face, but I have never seen a human being show such deplorable lack of self-control. I laughed at the threat of killing me that he spluttered out in his rage, and thought the whole thing would blow over, but I have several times since caught him scowling and muttering in a highly unpleasant fashion, and lately I have fancied that he was dogging my footsteps about the grounds, particularly when I walk of an evening in the Italian Garden."

'It was on the steps in the Italian Garden that the body was found,' commented Egbert, and resumed reading.

'"I dare say the danger is imaginary; but I shall feel more at ease when he has quitted my service."'

Egbert paused for a moment at the conclusion of the extract; then, as his uncle made no remark, he added: 'If lack of motive was the only factor that saved Sebastien from prosecution I fancy this letter will put a different complexion on matters.'

'Have you shown it to any one else?' asked Sir

Lulworth, reaching out his hand for the incriminating piece of paper.

'No,' said Egbert, handing it across the table, 'I thought I would tell you about it first. Heavens, what are you doing?'

Egbert's voice rose almost to a scream. Sir Lulworth had flung the paper well and truly into the glowing centre of the grate. The small, neat handwriting shrivelled into black flaky nothingness.

'What on earth did you do that for?' gasped Egbert. 'That letter was our one piece of evidence to connect Sebastien with the crime.'

'That is why I destroyed it,' said Sir Lulworth.

'But why should you want to shield him?' cried Egbert; 'the man is a common murderer.'

'A common murderer, possibly, but a very uncommon cook.'

Dusk

NORMAN GORTSBY SAT on a bench in the Park, with his back to a strip of bush-planted sward, fenced by the park railings, and the Row fronting him across a wide stretch of carriage drive. Hyde Park Corner, with its rattle and hoot of traffic, lay immediately to his right. It was some thirty minutes past six on an early March evening, and dusk had fallen heavily over the scene, dusk mitigated by some faint moonlight and many street lamps. There was a wide emptiness over road and sidewalk, and yet there were many unconsidered figures moving silently through the half-light or dotted unobtrusively on bench and chair, scarcely to be distinguished from the shadowed gloom in which they sat.

The scene pleased Gortsby and harmonized with his present mood. Dusk, to his mind, was the hour of the defeated. Men and women, who had fought and lost, who hid their fallen fortunes and dead hopes as far as possible from the scrutiny of the curious, came forth in this hour of gloaming, when their shabby clothes and bowed shoulders and unhappy eyes might pass unnoticed, or, at any rate, unrecognized.

A king that is conquered must see strange looks,
So bitter a thing is the heart of man.

The wanderers in the dusk did not choose to have strange looks fasten on them, therefore they came out in this bat-fashion, taking their pleasure sadly in a pleasure-ground that had emptied of its rightful occupants. Beyond the sheltering screen of bushes and palings came a realm of brilliant lights and noisy, rushing traffic. A blazing, many-tiered stretch of windows shone through the dusk and almost dispersed it, marking the haunts of those other people, who held their own in life's struggle, or at any rate had not had to admit failure. So Gortsby's imagination pictured things as he sat on his bench in the almost deserted walk. He was in the mood to count himself among the defeated. Money troubles did not press on him; had he so wished he could have strolled into the thoroughfares of light and noise, and taken his place among the jostling ranks of those who enjoyed prosperity or struggled for it. He had failed in a more subtle ambition, and for the moment he was heart sore and disillusionized, and not disinclined to take a certain cynical pleasure in observing and labelling his fellow wanderers as they went their ways in the dark stretches between the lamp-lights.

On the bench by his side sat an elderly gentleman with a drooping air of defiance that was probably the remaining vestige of self-respect in an individual who had ceased to defy successfully anybody or anything. His clothes could scarcely be called shabby, at least they passed muster in the half-light, but one's imagination could not have pictured the wearer embarking on the purchase of a half-crown box of chocolates or laying out ninepence on a carnation buttonhole. He belonged unmistakably to that forlorn orchestra to whose piping no one dances; he was one of the world's lamenters who induces no responsive weeping. As he rose to go Gortsby imagined him returning to a home circle where he was snubbed and of no account, or to some bleak lodging where his ability to pay a weekly bill was the beginning and end of the interest he inspired. His retreating figure vanished slowly into the shadows, and his place on the bench was taken almost immediately by a young man, fairly well dressed but scarcely more cheerful of mien than his predecessor. As if to emphasize the fact that the world went badly with him the new-comer unburdened himself of an angry and very audible expletive as he flung himself into the seat.

'You don't seem in a very good temper,' said Gortsby, judging that he was expected to take due notice of the demonstration.

The young man turned to him with a look of disarming frankness which put him instantly on his guard.

'You wouldn't be in a good temper if you were in the fix I'm in,' he said; 'I've done the silliest thing I've ever done in my life.'

'Yes?' said Gortsby dispassionately.

'Came up this afternoon, meaning to stay at the Patagonian Hotel in Berkshire Square,' continued the young man; 'when I got there I found it had been pulled down some weeks ago and a cinema theatre run up on the site. The taxi driver recommended me to another hotel some way off and I went there. I just sent a letter to my people, giving them the address, and then I went out to buy some soap – I'd forgotten to pack any and I hate using hotel soap. Then I strolled about a bit, had a drink at a bar and looked at the shops, and when I came to turn my steps back to the hotel I suddenly realized that I didn't remember its name or even what street it was in. There's a nice predicament for a fellow who hasn't any friends or connections in London! Of course I can wire to my people for the address, but they won't have got my letter till to-morrow; meantime I'm without any money, came out with about a shilling on me, which went in buying the soap and getting the drink, and here I am, wandering about with twopence in my pocket and nowhere to go for the night.'

There was an eloquent pause after the story had been told. 'I suppose you think I've spun you rather an impossible yarn,' said the young man presently, with a suggestion of resentment in his voice.

'Not at all impossible,' said Gortsby judicially; 'I remember doing exactly the same thing once in a foreign capital, and on that occasion there were two of us, which made it more remarkable. Luckily we remembered that the hotel was on a sort of canal, and when we struck the canal we were able to find our way back to the hotel.'

The youth brightened at the reminiscence. 'In a foreign city I wouldn't mind so much,' he said; 'one could go to one's Consul and get the requisite help from him. Here in one's own land one is far more derelict if one gets into a fix. Unless I can find some decent chap to swallow my story and lend me some money I seem likely to spend the night on the Embankment. I'm glad, anyhow, that you don't think the story outrageously improbable.'

He threw a good deal of warmth into the last remark, as though perhaps to indicate his hope that Gortsby did not fall far short of the requisite decency.

'Of course,' said Gortsby slowly, 'the weak point of your story is that you can't produce the soap.'

The young man sat forward hurriedly, felt rapidly in the pockets of his overcoat, and then jumped to his feet.

'I must have lost it,' he muttered angrily.

'To lose an hotel and a cake of soap on one afternoon suggests wilful carelessness,' said Gortsby, but the young man scarcely waited to hear the end of the remark. He flitted away down the path, his head held high, with an air of somewhat jaded jauntiness.

'It was a pity,' mused Gortsby; 'the going out to get one's own soap was the one convincing touch in the whole story, and yet it was just that little detail that brought him to grief. If he had had the brilliant forethought to provide himself with a cake of soap, wrapped and sealed with all the solicitude of the chemist's counter, he would have been a genius in his particular line. In his particular line genius certainly consists of an infinite capacity for taking precautions.'

With that reflection Gortsby rose to go; as he did so an exclamation of concern escaped him. Lying on the ground by the side of the bench was a small oval packet, wrapped and sealed with the solicitude of a chemist's counter. It could be nothing else but a cake of soap, and it had evidently fallen out of the youth's overcoat pocket when he flung himself down on the seat. In another moment Gortsby was scudding along the dusk-shrouded path in anxious quest for a youthful figure in a light overcoat. He had nearly given up the search when he caught sight of the object of his pursuit standing irresolutely on the border of the carriage drive, evidently uncertain whether to strike across the Park or make for the bustling pavements of Knightsbridge. He turned round sharply with an air of defensive hostility when he found Gortsby hailing him.

'The important witness to the genuineness of your story has turned up,' said Gortsby, holding out the cake of soap; 'it must have slid out of your overcoat pocket when you sat down on the seat. I saw it on the ground after you left. You must excuse my disbelief, but appearances were really rather against you, and now, as I appealed to the testimony of the soap I think I ought to abide by its verdict. If the loan of a sovereign is any good to you –'

The young man hastily removed all doubt on the subject by pocketing the coin.

'Here is my card with my address,' continued Gortsby;

'any day this week will do for returning the money, and here is the soap – don't lose it again; it's been a good friend to you.'

'Lucky thing your finding it,' said the youth, and then, with a catch in his voice, he blurted out a word or two of thanks and fled headlong in the direction of Knightsbridge.

'Poor boy, he as nearly as possible broke down,' said Gortsby to himself. 'I don't wonder either; the relief from his quandary must have been acute. It's a lesson to me not to be too clever in judging by circumstances.'

As Gortsby retraced his steps past the seat where the little drama had taken place he saw an elderly gentleman poking and peering beneath it and on all sides of it, and recognized his earlier fellow occupant.

'Have you lost anything, sir?' he asked.

'Yes, sir, a cake of soap.'

Clovis on Parental Responsibilities

MARION EGGELBY SAT talking to Clovis on the only subject that she ever willingly talked about – her offspring and their varied perfections and accomplishments. Clovis was not in what could be called a receptive mood; the younger generation of Eggelby, depicted in the glowing improbable colours of parent impressionism, aroused in him no enthusiasm. Mrs Eggelby, on the other hand, was furnished with enthusiasm enough for two.

'You would like Eric,' she said, argumentatively rather than hopefully. Clovis had intimated very unmistakably that he was unlikely to care extravagantly for either Amy or Willie. 'Yes, I feel sure you would like Eric. Every one takes to him at once. You know, he always reminds me of that famous picture of the youthful David – I forget who it's by, but it's very well known.'

'That would be sufficient to set me against him, if I saw much of him,' said Clovis. 'Just imagine at auction bridge, for instance, when one was trying to concentrate one's mind on what one's partner's original declaration had been, and to remember what suits one's opponents had originally discarded, what it would be like to have some one persistently reminding one of a picture of the youthful David. It would be simply maddening. If Eric did that I should detest him.'

'Eric doesn't play bridge,' said Mrs Eggelby with dignity.

'Doesn't he?' asked Clovis; 'why not?'

'None of my children have been brought up to play card games,' said Mrs Eggelby; 'draughts and halma and those sorts of games I encourage. Eric is considered quite a wonderful draughts-player.'

'You are strewing dreadful risks in the path of your family,' said Clovis; 'a friend of mine who is a prison chaplain told me that among the worst criminal cases that have come under his notice, men condemned to death or to long periods of penal servitude, there was not a single bridge-player. On the other hand, he knew at least two expert draughts-players among them.'

'I really don't see what my boys have got to do with the criminal classes,' said Mrs Eggelby resentfully. 'They have been most carefully brought up, I can assure you that.'

'That shows that you were nervous as to how they would turn out,' said Clovis. 'Now, my mother never bothered about bringing me up. She just saw to it that I got whacked at decent intervals and was taught the difference between right and wrong; there is some difference, you know, but I've forgotten what it is.'

'Forgotten the difference between right and wrong!' exclaimed Mrs Eggelby.

'Well, you see, I took up natural history and a whole lot of other subjects at the same time, and one can't remember everything, can one? I used to know the difference between the Sardinian dormouse and the ordinary kind, and whether the wryneck arrives at our shores earlier than the cuckoo, or the other way round, and how long the walrus takes in growing to maturity; I dare say you knew all those sorts of things once, but I bet you've forgotten them.'

'Those things are not important,' said Mrs Eggelby, 'but –'

'The fact that we've both forgotten them proves that they *are* important,' said Clovis; 'you must have noticed that it's always the important things that one forgets, while the trivial, unnecessary facts of life stick in one's memory.

There's my cousin, Editha Clubberly, for instance; I can never forget that her birthday is on the 12th of October. It's a matter of utter indifference to me on what date her birthday falls, or whether she was born at all; either fact seems to me absolutely trivial, or unnecessary – I've heaps of other cousins to go on with. On the other hand, when I'm staying with Hildegarde Shrubley I can never remember the important circumstance whether her first husband got his unenviable reputation on the Turf or the Stock Exchange, and that uncertainty rules Sport and Finance out of the conversation at once. One can never mention travel, either, because her second husband had to live permanently abroad.'

'Mrs Shrubley and I move in very different circles,' said Mrs Eggelby stiffly.

'No one who knows Hildegarde could possibly accuse her of moving in a circle,' said Clovis; 'her view of life seems to be a non-stop run with an inexhaustible supply of petrol. If she can get some one else to pay for the petrol so much the better. I don't mind confessing to you that she has taught me more than any other woman I can think of.'

'What kind of knowledge?' demanded Mrs Eggelby, with the air a jury might collectively wear when finding a verdict without leaving the box.

'Well, among other things, she's introduced me to at least four different ways of cooking lobster,' said Clovis gratefully. 'That, of course, wouldn't appeal to you; people who abstain from the pleasures of the card-table never really appreciate the finer possibilities of the dining-table. I suppose their powers of enlightened enjoyment get atrophied from disuse.'

'An aunt of mine was very ill after eating a lobster,' said Mrs Eggelby.

'I dare say, if we knew more of her history, we should find out that she'd often been ill before eating the lobster. Aren't you concealing the fact that she'd had measles and influenza and nervous headache and hysteria, and other things that aunts do have, long before she ate the lobster? Aunts that have never known a day's illness are very rare; in fact, I don't personally know of any. Of course if she ate it as a child of two weeks old it might have been her first illness – and her last. But if that was the case I think you should have said so.'

'I must be going,' said Mrs Eggelby, in a tone which had been thoroughly sterilized of even perfunctory regret.

Clovis rose with an air of graceful reluctance.

'I have so enjoyed our little talk about Eric,' he said; 'I quite look forward to meeting him some day.'

'Good-bye,' said Mrs Eggelby frostily; the supplementary remark which she made at the back of her throat was –

'I'll take care that you never shall!'

A Holiday Task

KENELM JERTON ENTERED the dining-hall of the Golden Galleon Hotel in the full crush of the luncheon hour. Nearly every seat was occupied, and small additional tables had been brought in, where floor space permitted, to accommodate late-comers, with the result that many of the tables were almost touching each other. Jerton was beckoned by a waiter to the only vacant table that was discernible, and took his seat with the uncomfortable and wholly groundless idea that every one in the room was staring at him. He was a youngish man of ordinary appearance, quiet of dress and unobtrusive of manner, and he could never wholly rid himself of the idea that a fierce light of public scrutiny beat on him as though he had been a notability or a super-nut. After he had ordered his lunch there came the unavoidable interval of waiting, with nothing to do but to stare at the flower-vase on his table and to be stared at (in imagination) by several flappers, some maturer beings of the same sex, and a satirical-looking Jew. In order to carry off the situation with some appearance of unconcern he became spuriously interested in the contents of the flower-vase.

'What is the name of those roses, d'you know?' he asked the waiter. The waiter was ready at all times to conceal his ignorance concerning items of the wine-list or *menu*; he was frankly ignorant as to the specific name of the roses.

'*Amy Silvester Partington*,' said a voice at Jerton's elbow.

The voice came from a pleasant-faced, well-dressed young woman who was sitting at a table that almost touched Jerton's. He thanked her hurriedly and nervously for the information, and made some inconsequent remark about the flowers.

'It is a curious thing,' said the young woman, 'that I should be able to tell you the name of those roses without an effort of memory, because if you were to ask me my name I should be utterly unable to give it to you.'

Jerton had not harboured the least intention of extending his thirst for name-labels to his neighbour. After her rather remarkable announcement, however, he was obliged to say something in the way of polite inquiry.

'Yes,' answered the lady, 'I suppose it is a case of partial loss of memory. I was in the train coming down here; my ticket told me that I had come from Victoria and was bound for this place. I had a couple of five-pound notes and a sovereign on me, no visiting cards or any other means of identification, and no idea as to who I am. I can only hazily recollect that I have a title; I am Lady Somebody – beyond that my mind is a blank.'

'Hadn't you any luggage with you?' asked Jerton.

'That is what I didn't know. I knew the name of this hotel and made up my mind to come here, and when the hotel porter who meets the trains asked if I had any luggage I had to invent a dressing-bag and dress-basket; I could always pretend that they had gone astray. I gave him the name of Smith, and presently he emerged from a confused pile of luggage and passengers with a dressing-bag and dress-basket labelled Kestrel-Smith. I had to take them; I don't see what else I could have done.'

Jerton said nothing, but he rather wondered what the lawful owner of the baggage would do.

'Of course it was dreadful arriving at a strange hotel with the name of Kestrel-Smith, but it would have been worse to have arrived without luggage. Anyhow, I hate causing trouble.'

Jerton had visions of harassed railway officials and distraught Kestrel-Smiths, but he made no attempt to clothe his mental picture in words. The lady continued her story.

'Naturally, none of my keys would fit the things, but I told an intelligent page boy that I had lost my key-ring, and he had the locks forced in a twinkling. Rather too intelligent, that boy; he will probably end in Dartmoor. The Kestrel-Smith toilet tools aren't up to much, but they are better than nothing.'

'If you feel sure that you have a title,' said Jerton, 'why not get hold of a peerage and go right through it?'

'I tried that. I skimmed through the list of the House of Lords in "Whitaker", but a mere printed string of names conveys awfully little to one, you know. If you were an army officer and had lost your identity you might pore over the Army List for months without finding out who you were. I'm going on another tack; I'm trying to find out by various little tests who I am *not* – that will narrow the range of uncertainty down a bit. You may have noticed, for instance, that I'm lunching principally off lobster Newburg.'

Jerton had not ventured to notice anything of the sort.

'It's an extravagance, because it's one of the most expensive dishes on the menu, but at any rate it proves that I'm not Lady Starping; she never touches shell-fish, and poor Lady Braddleshrub has no digestion at all; if I am *her* I shall certainly die in agony in the course of the afternoon, and the duty of finding out who I am will devolve on the press and the police and those sort of people; I shall be past caring. Lady Knewford doesn't know one rose from another and she hates men, so she wouldn't have spoken to you in any case; and Lady Mousehilton flirts with every man she meets – I haven't flirted with you, have I?'

Jerton hastily gave the required assurance.

'Well, you see,' continued the lady, 'that knocks four off the list at once.'

'It'll be rather a lengthy process bringing the list down to one,' said Jerton.

'Oh, but, of course, there are heaps of them that I couldn't possibly be – women who've got grandchildren or sons old enough to have celebrated their coming of age. I've only got to consider the ones about my own age. I tell you how you might help me this afternoon, if you don't mind; go through any of the back numbers of *Country Life* and those sort of papers that you can find in the smoking-room, and see if you come across my portrait with infant son or anything of that sort. It won't take you ten minutes. I'll meet you in the lounge about tea-time. Thanks awfully.'

And the Fair Unknown, having graciously pressed Jerton into the search for her lost identity, rose and left the room. As she passed the young man's table she halted for a moment and whispered:

'Did you notice that I tipped the waiter a shilling? We can cross Lady Ulwight off the list; she would have died rather than do that.'

At five o'clock Jerton made his way to the hotel lounge; he had spent a diligent but fruitless quarter of an hour among the illustrated weeklies in the smoking-room. His new acquaintance was seated at a small tea-table, with a waiter hovering in attendance.

'China tea or Indian?' she asked as Jerton came up.

'China, please, and nothing to eat. Have you discovered anything?'

'Only negative information. I'm not Lady Befnal. She disapproves dreadfully at any form of gambling, so when I recognized a well-known book-maker in the hotel lobby I went and put a tenner on an unnamed filly by William the Third out of Mitrovitza for the three-fifteen race. I suppose the fact of the animal being nameless was what attracted me.'

'Did it win?' asked Jerton.

'No, came in fourth, the most irritating thing a horse can do when you've backed it win or place. Anyhow, I know now that I'm not Lady Befnal.'

'It seems to me that the knowledge was rather dearly bought,' commented Jerton.

'Well, yes, it has rather cleared me out,' admitted the identity-seeker; 'a florin is about all I've got left on me. The lobster Newburg made my lunch rather an expensive one, and, of course, I had to tip that boy for what he did to the Kestrel-Smith locks. I've got rather a useful idea, though. I feel certain that I belong to the Pivot Club; I'll go back to town and ask the hall porter there if there are any letters for me. He knows all the members by sight, and if there are any letters or telephone messages waiting for me, of course that will solve the problem. If he says there aren't any, I shall say: "You know who I am, don't you?" so I'll find out anyway.'

The plan seemed a sound one; a difficulty in its execution suggested itself to Jerton.

'Of course,' said the lady, when he hinted at the obstacle, 'there's my fare back to town, and my bill here and cabs and things. If you lend me three pounds that ought to see me through comfortably. Thanks ever so.

Then there is the question of that luggage: I don't want to be saddled with that for the rest of my life. I'll have it brought down to the hall and you can pretend to mount guard over it while I'm writing a letter. Then I shall just slip away to the station, and you can wander off to the smoking-room, and they can do what they like with the things. They'll advertise them after a bit and the owner can claim them.'

Jerton acquiesced in the manœuvre, and duly mounted guard over the luggage while its temporary owner slipped unobtrusively out of the hotel. Her departure was not, however, altogether unnoticed. Two gentlemen were strolling past Jerton, and one of them remarked to the other:

'Did you see that tall young woman in grey who went out just now? She is the Lady –'

His promenade carried him out of earshot at the critical moment when he was about to disclose the elusive identity. The Lady Who? Jerton could scarcely run after a total stranger, break into his conversation, and ask him for information concerning a chance passer-by. Besides, it was desirable that he should keep up the appearance of looking after the luggage. In a minute or two, however, the important personage, the man who knew, came strolling back alone. Jerton summoned up all his courage and waylaid him.

'I think I heard you say you knew the lady who went out of the hotel a few minutes ago, a tall lady, dressed in grey. Excuse me for asking if you could tell me her name; I've been talking to her for half an hour; she – er – she knows all my people and seems to know me, so I suppose I've met her somewhere before, but I'm blest if I can put a name to her. Could you –?'

'Certainly. She's a Mrs Stroope.'

'*Mrs?*' queried Jerton.

'Yes, she's the Lady Champion at golf in my part of the world. An awful good sort, and goes about a good deal in Society, but she has an awkward habit of losing her memory every now and then, and gets into all sorts of fixes. She's furious, too, if you make any allusion to it afterwards. Good day, sir.'

The stranger passed on his way, and before Jerton had had time to assimilate his information he found his whole attention centred on an angry-looking lady who was making loud and fretful-seeming inquiries of the hotel clerks.

'Has any luggage been brought here from the station by mistake, a dress-basket and dressing-case, with the name Kestrel-Smith? It can't be traced anywhere. I saw it put in at Victoria, that I'll swear. Why – there *is* my luggage! and the locks have been tampered with!'

Jerton heard no more. He fled down to the Turkish bath, and stayed there for hours.

The Story-Teller

IT WAS A hot afternoon, and the railway carriage was correspondingly sultry, and the next stop was at Templecombe, nearly an hour ahead. The occupants of the carriage were a small girl, and a smaller girl, and a small boy. An aunt belonging to the children occupied one corner seat, and the further corner seat on the opposite side was occupied by a bachelor who was a stranger to their party, but the small girls and the small boy emphatically occupied the compartment. Both the aunt and the children were conversational in a limited, persistent way, reminding one of the attentions of a housefly that refused to be discouraged. Most of the aunt's remarks seemed to begin with 'Don't', and nearly all of the children's remarks began with 'Why?' The bachelor said nothing out loud.

'Don't, Cyril, don't,' exclaimed the aunt, as the small boy began smacking the cushions of the seat, producing a cloud of dust at each blow.

'Come and look out of the window,' she added.

The child moved reluctantly to the window. 'Why are those sheep being driven out of that field?' he asked.

'I expect they are being driven to another field where there is more grass,' said the aunt weakly.

'But there is lots of grass in that field,' protested the boy; 'there's nothing else but grass there. Aunt, there's lots of grass in that field.'

'Perhaps the grass in the other field is better,' suggested the aunt fatuously.

'Why is it better?' came the swift, inevitable question.

'Oh, look at those cows!' exclaimed the aunt. Nearly every field along the line had contained cows or bullocks, but she spoke as though she were drawing attention to a rarity.

'Why is the grass in the other field better?' persisted Cyril.

The frown on the bachelor's face was deepening to a scowl. He was a hard, unsympathetic man, the aunt decided in her mind. She was utterly unable to come to any satisfactory decision about the grass in the other field.

The smaller girl created a diversion by beginning to recite 'On the Road to Mandalay'. She only knew the first line, but she put her limited knowledge to the fullest possible use. She repeated the line over and over again in a dreamy but resolute and very audible voice; it seemed to the bachelor as though some one had had a bet with her that she could not repeat the line aloud two thousand times without stopping. Whoever it was who had made the wager was likely to lose his bet.

'Come over here and listen to a story,' said the aunt, when the bachelor had looked twice at her and once at the communication cord.

The children moved listlessly towards the aunt's end of the carriage. Evidently her reputation as a story-teller did not rank high in their estimation.

In a low, confidential voice, interrupted at frequent intervals by loud, petulant questions from her listeners, she began an unenterprising and deplorably uninteresting story about a little girl who was good, and made friends with every one on account of her goodness, and was finally saved from a mad bull by a number of rescuers who admired her moral character.

'Wouldn't they have saved her if she hadn't been good?' demanded the bigger of the small girls. It was exactly the question that the bachelor had wanted to ask.

'Well, yes,' admitted the aunt lamely, 'but I don't think they would have run quite so fast to her help if they had not liked her so much.'

'It's the stupidest story I've ever heard,' said the bigger of the small girls, with immense conviction.

'I didn't listen after the first bit, it was so stupid,' said Cyril.

The smaller girl made no actual comment on the story, but she had long ago recommenced a murmured repetition of her favourite line.

'You don't seem to be a success as a story-teller,' said the bachelor suddenly from his corner.

The aunt bristled in instant defence at this unexpected attack.

'It's a very difficult thing to tell stories that children can both understand and appreciate,' she said stiffly.

'I don't agree with you,' said the bachelor.

'Perhaps *you* would like to tell them a story,' was the aunt's retort.

'Tell us a story,' demanded the bigger of the small girls.

'Once upon a time,' began the bachelor, 'there was a little girl called Bertha, who was extraordinarily good.'

The children's momentarily-aroused interest began at once to flicker; all stories seemed dreadfully alike, no matter who told them.

'She did all that she was told, she was always truthful, she kept her clothes clean, ate milk puddings as though they were jam tarts, learned her lessons perfectly, and was polite in her manners.'

'Was she pretty?' asked the bigger of the small girls.

'Not as pretty as any of you,' said the bachelor, 'but she was horribly good.'

There was a wave of reaction in favour of the story; the

word horrible in connection with goodness was a novelty that commended itself. It seemed to introduce a ring of truth that was absent from the aunt's tales of infant life.

'She was so good,' continued the bachelor, 'that she won several medals for goodness, which she always wore, pinned on to her dress. There was a medal for obedience, another medal for punctuality, and a third for good behaviour. They were large metal medals and they clicked against one another as she walked. No other child in the town where she lived had as many as three medals, so everybody knew that she must be an extra good child.'

'Horribly good,' quoted Cyril.

'Everybody talked about her goodness, and the Prince of the country got to hear about it, and he said that as she was so very good she might be allowed once a week to walk in his park, which was just outside the town. It was a beautiful park, and no children were ever allowed in it, so it was a great honour for Bertha to be allowed to go there.'

'Were there any sheep in the park?' demanded Cyril.

'No,' said the bachelor, 'there were no sheep.'

'Why weren't there any sheep?' came the inevitable question arising out of that answer.

The aunt permitted herself a smile, which might almost have been described as a grin.

'There were no sheep in the park,' said the bachelor, 'because the Prince's mother had once had a dream that her son would either be killed by a sheep or else by a clock falling on him. For that reason the Prince never kept a sheep in his park or a clock in his palace.'

The aunt suppressed a gasp of admiration.

'Was the Prince killed by a sheep or by a clock?' asked Cyril.

'He is still alive, so we can't tell whether the dream will come true,' said the bachelor unconcernedly; 'anyway, there were no sheep in the park, but there were lots of little pigs running all over the place.'

'What colour were they?'

'Black with white faces, white with black spots, black all over, grey with white patches, and some were white all over.'

The story-teller paused to let a full idea of the park's treasures sink into the children's imaginations; then he resumed:

'Bertha was rather sorry to find that there were no flowers in the park. She had promised her aunts, with tears in her eyes, that she would not pick any of the kind Prince's flowers, and she had meant to keep her promise, so of course it made her feel silly to find that there were no flowers to pick.'

'Why weren't there any flowers?'

'Because the pigs had eaten them all,' said the bachelor promptly. 'The gardeners had told the Prince that you couldn't have pigs and flowers, so he decided to have pigs and no flowers.'

There was a murmur of approval, at the excellence of the Prince's decision; so many people would have decided the other way.

'There were lots of other delightful things in the park. There were ponds with gold and blue and green fish in them, and trees with beautiful parrots that said clever things at a moment's notice, and humming birds that hummed all the popular tunes of the day. Bertha walked up and down and enjoyed herself immensely, and thought to herself: "If I were not so extraordinarily good I should not have been allowed to come into this beautiful park

233

and enjoy all that there is to be seen in it,' and her three medals clinked against one another as she walked and helped to remind her how very good she really was. Just then an enormous wolf came prowling into the park to see if it could catch a fat little pig for its supper.'

'What colour was it?' asked the children, amid an immediate quickening of interest.

'Mud-colour all over, with a black tongue and pale grey eyes that gleamed with unspeakable ferocity. The first thing that it saw in the park was Bertha; her pinafore was so spotlessly white and clean that it could be seen from a great distance. Bertha saw the wolf and saw that it was stealing towards her, and she began to wish that she had never been allowed to come into the park. She ran as hard as she could, and the wolf came after her with huge leaps and bounds. She managed to reach a shrubbery of myrtle bushes and she hid herself in one of the thickest of the bushes. The wolf came sniffing among the branches, its black tongue lolling out of its mouth and its pale grey eyes glaring with rage. Bertha was terribly frightened, and thought to herself: "If I had not been so extraordinarily good I should have been safe in the town at this moment." However, the scent of the myrtle was so strong that the wolf could not sniff out where Bertha was hiding, and the bushes were so thick that he might have hunted about in them for a long time without catching sight of her, so he thought he might as well go off and catch a little pig instead. Bertha was trembling very much at having the wolf prowling and sniffing so near her, and as she trembled the medal for obedience clinked against the medals for good conduct and punctuality. The wolf was just moving away when he heard the sound of the medals clinking and stopped to listen; they clinked again in a bush quite near

234

him. He dashed into the bush, his pale grey eyes gleaming with ferocity and triumph, and dragged Bertha out and devoured her to the last morsel. All that was left of her were her shoes, bits of clothing, and the three medals for goodness.'

'Were any of the little pigs killed?'

'No, they all escaped.'

'The story began badly,' said the smaller of the small girls, 'but it had a beautiful ending.'

'It is the most beautiful story that I ever heard,' said the bigger of the small girls, with immense decision.

'It is the *only* beautiful story I have ever heard,' said Cyril.

A dissentient opinion came from the aunt.

'A most improper story to tell young children! You have undermined the effect of years of careful teaching.'

'At any rate,' said the bachelor, collecting his belongings preparatory to leaving the carriage, 'I kept them quiet for ten minutes, which was more than you were able to do.'

'Unhappy woman!' he observed to himself as he walked down the platform of Templecombe station; 'for the next six months or so those children will assail her in public with demands for an improper story!'

The Lumber-Room

THE CHILDREN WERE to be driven, as a special treat, to the sands at Jagborough. Nicholas was not to be of the party; he was in disgrace. Only that morning he had refused to eat his wholesome bread-and-milk on the seemingly frivolous ground that there was a frog in it. Older and wiser and better people had told him that there could not possibly be a frog in his bread-and-milk and that he was not to talk nonsense; he continued, nevertheless, to talk what seemed the veriest nonsense, and described with much detail the coloration and markings of the alleged frog. The dramatic part of the incident was that there really was a frog in Nicholas' basin of bread-and- milk; he had put it there himself, so he felt entitled to know something about it. The sin of taking a frog from the garden and putting it into a bowl of wholesome bread-and-milk was enlarged on at great length, but the fact that stood out clearest in the whole affair, as it presented itself to the mind of Nicholas, was that the older, wiser and better people had been proved to be profoundly in error in matters about which they had expressed the utmost assurance.

'You said there couldn't possibly be a frog in my bread-and-milk; there *was* a frog in my bread-and-milk,' he repeated, with the insistence of a skilled tactician who does not intend to shift from favourable ground.

So his boy-cousin and girl-cousin and his quite uninteresting younger brother were to be taken to Jagborough sands that afternoon and he was to stay at home. His cousins' aunt, who insisted, by an unwarranted stretch of imagination, in styling herself his aunt also, had hastily invented the Jagborough expedition in order to impress on Nicholas the delights that he had justly forfeited by his disgraceful conduct at the breakfast-table. It was her habit, whenever one of the children fell from grace, to improvise something of a festival nature from which the offender would be rigorously debarred; if all the children sinned collectively they were suddenly informed of a circus in a neighbouring town, a circus of unrivalled merit and uncounted elephants, to which, but for their depravity, they would have been taken that very day.

A few decent tears were looked for on the part of Nicholas when the moment for the departure of the expedition arrived. As a matter of fact, however, all the crying was done by his girl-cousin, who scraped her knee rather painfully against the step of the carriage as she was scrambling in.

'How she did howl,' said Nicholas cheerfully, as the party drove off without any of the elation of high spirits that should have characterized it.

'She'll soon get over that,' said the *soi-disant* aunt; 'it will be a glorious afternoon for racing about over those beautiful sands. How they will enjoy themselves!'

'Bobby won't enjoy himself much, and he won't race much either,' said Nicholas with a grim chuckle; 'his boots are hurting him. They're too tight.'

'Why didn't he tell me they were hurting?' asked the aunt with some asperity.

'He told you twice, but you weren't listening. You often don't listen when we tell you important things.'

'You are not to go into the gooseberry garden,' said the aunt, changing the subject.

'Why not?' demanded Nicholas.

'Because you are in disgrace,' said the aunt loftily.

Nicholas did not admit the flawlessness of the reasoning; he felt perfectly capable of being in disgrace and in a gooseberry garden at the same moment. His face took on an expression of considerable obstinacy. It was clear to his aunt that he was determined to get into the gooseberry garden, 'only', as she remarked to herself, 'because I have told him he is not to'.

Now the gooseberry garden had two doors by which it might be entered, and once a small person like Nicholas could slip in there he could effectually disappear from view amid the masking growth of artichokes, raspberry canes, and fruit bushes. The aunt had many other things to do that afternoon, but she spent an hour or two in trivial gardening operations among flower beds and shrubberies, whence she could keep a watchful eye on the two doors that led to the forbidden paradise. She was a woman of few ideas, with immense powers of concentration.

Nicholas made one or two sorties into the front garden, wriggling his way with obvious stealth of purpose towards one or other of the doors, but never able for a moment to evade the aunt's watchful eye. As a matter of fact, he had no intention of trying to get into the gooseberry garden, but it was extremely convenient for him that his aunt should believe that he had; it was a belief that would keep her on self-imposed sentry-duty for the greater part of the afternoon. Having thoroughly confirmed and fortified her suspicions, Nicholas slipped back into the house and rapidly put into execution a plan of action that had long germinated in his brain. By standing on a chair in the library one could reach a shelf on which reposed a fat, important-looking key. The key was as important as it looked; it was the instrument which kept the mysteries of the lumber-room secure from unauthorized intrusion, which opened a way only for aunts and such-like privileged persons. Nicholas had not much experience of the art of fitting keys into keyholes and turning locks, but for some days past he had practised with the key of the schoolroom door; he did not believe in trusting too much to luck and accident. The key turned stiffly in the lock, but it turned. The door opened, and Nicholas was in an unknown land, compared with which the gooseberry garden was a stale delight, a mere material pleasure.

Often and often Nicholas had pictured to himself what the lumber-room might be like, that region that was so carefully sealed from youthful eyes and concerning which no questions were ever answered. It came up to his expectations. In the first place it was large and dimly lit, one high window opening on to the forbidden garden being its only source of illumination. In the second place it was a storehouse of unimagined treasures. The aunt-by-assertion was one of those people who think that things spoil by use and consign them to dust and damp by way of preserving them. Such parts of the house as Nicholas knew best were rather bare and cheerless, but here there were wonderful things for the eye to feast on. First and foremost there was a piece of framed tapestry that was evidently meant to be a fire-screen. To Nicholas it was a living, breathing story; he sat down on a roll of Indian hangings, glowing in wonderful colours beneath a layer of dust, and took in all the details of the tapestry picture. A man, dressed in the hunting costume of some remote period, had just transfixed a stag with an arrow; it could not have been a difficult shot because the stag was only one or two paces away from him; in the thickly growing vegetation that the picture suggested it would not have been difficult to creep up to a feeding stag, and the two spotted dogs that were springing forward to join in the chase had evidently been trained to keep to heel till the arrow was discharged. That part of the picture was simple, if interesting, but did the huntsman see, what Nicholas saw, that four galloping wolves were coming in his direction through the wood? There might be more than four of them hidden behind the trees, and in any case would the man and his dogs be able to cope with the four wolves if they made an attack? The man had only two arrows left in his quiver, and he might miss with one or both of them; all one knew about his skill in shooting was that he could hit a large stag at a ridiculously short range. Nicholas sat for many golden minutes revolving the possibilities of the scene; he was inclined to think that there were more than four wolves and that the man and his dogs were in a tight corner.

But there were other objects of delight and interest claiming his instant attention: here were quaint twisted candlesticks in the shape of snakes, and a teapot fashioned like a china duck, out of whose open beak the tea was supposed to come. How dull and shapeless the nursery teapot seemed in comparison! And there was a carved sandalwood box packed tight with aromatic cotton-wool, and between the layers of cotton-wool were little brass figures, hump-necked bulls, and peacocks and goblins, delightful to see and to handle. Less promising in appearance was a large square book with plain black covers; Nicholas peeped into it, and, behold, it was full of coloured pictures of birds. And such birds! In the garden, and in the lanes when he went for a walk, Nicholas came across a few birds, of which the largest were an occasional magpie or woodpigeon; here were herons and bustards, kites, toucans, tiger-bitterns, brush turkeys, ibises, golden pheasants, a whole portrait gallery of undreamed-of creatures. And as he was admiring the colouring of the mandarin duck and assigning a life-history to it the voice of his aunt in shrill vociferation of his name came from the gooseberry garden without. She had grown suspicious at his long disappearance, and had leapt to the conclusion that he had climbed over the wall behind the sheltering screen of the lilac bushes; she was now engaged in energetic and rather hopeless search for him among the artichokes and raspberry canes.

'Nicholas, Nicholas!' she screamed, 'you are to come out of this at once. It's no use trying to hide there; I can see you all the time.'

It was probably the first time for twenty years that any one had smiled in that lumber-room.

Presently the angry repetitions of Nicholas' name gave way to a shriek, and a cry for somebody to come quickly. Nicholas shut the book, restored it carefully to its place in a corner, and shook some dust from a neighbouring pile of newspapers over it. Then he crept from the room, locked the door, and replaced the key exactly where he had found it. His aunt was still calling his name when he sauntered into the front garden.

'Who's calling?' he asked.

'Me,' came the answer from the other side of the wall; 'didn't you hear me? I've been looking for you in the gooseberry garden, and I've slipped into the rain-water tank. Luckily there's no water in it, but the sides are slippery and I can't get out. Fetch the little ladder from under the cherry tree –'

'I was told I wasn't to go into the gooseberry garden,' said Nicholas promptly.

'I told you not to, and now I tell you that you may,'

came the voice from the rain-water tank, rather impatiently.

'Your voice doesn't sound like aunt's,' objected Nicholas; 'you may be the Evil One tempting me to be disobedient. Aunt often tells me that the Evil One tempts me and that I always yield. This time I'm not going to yield.'

'Don't talk nonsense,' said the prisoner in the tank; 'go and fetch the ladder.'

'Will there be strawberry jam for tea?' asked Nicholas innocently.

'Certainly there will be,' said the aunt, privately resolving that Nicholas should have none of it.

'Now I know that you are the Evil One and not aunt,' shouted Nicholas gleefully; 'when we asked aunt for strawberry jam yesterday she said there wasn't any. I know there are four jars of it in the store cupboard, because I looked, and of course you know it's there, but *she* doesn't, because she said there wasn't any. Oh, Devil, you *have* sold yourself!'

There was an unusual sense of luxury in being able to talk to an aunt as though one was talking to the Evil One, but Nicholas knew, with childish discernment, that such luxuries were not to be over-indulged in. He walked noisily away, and it was a kitchenmaid, in search of parsley, who eventually rescued the aunt from the rain-water tank.

Tea that evening was partaken of in a fearsome silence. The tide had been at its highest when the children had arrived at Jagborough Cove, so there had been no sands to play on – a circumstance that the aunt had overlooked in the haste of organizing her punitive expedition. The tightness of Bobby's boots had had disastrous effect on his temper the whole of the afternoon, and altogether the children could not have been said to have enjoyed themselves. The aunt maintained the frozen muteness of one who has suffered undignified and unmerited detention in a rain-water tank for thirty-five minutes. As for Nicholas, he, too, was silent, in the absorption of one who has much to think about; it was just possible, he considered, that the huntsman would escape with his hounds while the wolves feasted on the stricken stag.

Fur

'YOU LOOK WORRIED, dear,' said Eleanor.

'I am worried,' admitted Suzanne; 'not worried exactly, but anxious. You see, my birthday happens next week —'

'You lucky person,' interrupted Eleanor; 'my birthday doesn't come till the end of March.'

'Well, old Bertram Kneyght is over in England just now from the Argentine. He's a kind of distant cousin of my mother's, and so enormously rich that we've never let the relationship drop out of sight. Even if we don't see him or hear from him for years he is always Cousin Bertram when he does turn up. I can't say he's ever been of much solid use to us, but yesterday the subject of my birthday cropped up, and he asked me to let him know what I wanted for a present.'

'Now I understand the anxiety,' observed Eleanor.

'As a rule when one is confronted with a problem like that,' said Suzanne, 'all one's ideas vanish; one doesn't seem to have a desire in the world. Now it so happens that I have been very keen on a little Dresden figure that I saw somewhere in Kensington; about thirty-six shillings, quite beyond my means. I was very nearly describing the figure, and giving Bertram the address of the shop. And then it suddenly struck me that thirty-six shillings was such a ridiculously inadequate sum for a man of his immense wealth to spend on a birthday present. He could give thirty-six pounds as easily as you or I could buy a bunch of violets. I don't want to be greedy, of course, but I don't like being wasteful.'

'The question is,' said Eleanor, 'what are his ideas as to present-giving? Some of the wealthiest people have curiously cramped views on that subject. When people grow gradually rich their requirements and standard of living expand in proportion, while their present-giving instincts often remain in the undeveloped condition of their earlier days. Something showy and not-too-expensive in a shop is their only conception of the ideal gift. That is why even quite good shops have their counters and windows crowded with things worth about four shillings that look as if they might be worth seven-and-six, and are priced at ten shillings and labelled "seasonable gifts".'

'I know,' said Suzanne; 'that is why it is so risky to be vague when one is giving indications of one's wants. Now if I say to him: "I am going out to Davos this winter, so anything in the travelling line would be acceptable," he *might* give me a dressing-bag with gold-mounted fittings, but, on the other hand, he might give me Baedeker's *Switzerland*, or *Ski-ing without Tears*, or something of that sort.'

'He would be more likely to say: "She'll be going to lots of dances, a fan will be sure to be useful."'

'Yes, and I've got tons of fans, so you see where the danger and anxiety lies. Now if there is one thing more than another that I really urgently want it is furs. I simply haven't any. I'm told that Davos is full of Russians, and they are sure to wear the most lovely sables and things. To be among people who are smothered in furs when one hasn't any oneself makes one want to break most of the Commandments.'

'If it's furs that you're out for,' said Eleanor, 'you will have to superintend the choice of them in person. You can't be sure that your cousin knows the difference between silver-fox and ordinary squirrel.'

'There are some heavenly silver-fox stoles at Goliath and Mastodon's,' said Suzanne, with a sigh; 'if I could only inveigle Bertram into their building and take him for a stroll through the fur department!'

'He lives somewhere near there, doesn't he?' said Eleanor. 'Do you know what his habits are? Does he take a walk at any particular time of day?'

'He usually walks down to his club about three o'clock, if it's a fine day. That takes him right past Goliath and Mastodon's.'

'Let us two meet him accidentally at the street corner tomorrow,' said Eleanor; 'we can walk a little way with him, and with luck we ought to be able to side-track him into the shop. You can say you want to get a hair-net or something. When we're safely there I can say: "I wish you'd tell me what you want for your birthday." Then you'll have everything ready to hand – the rich cousin, the fur department, and the topic of birthday presents.'

'It's a great idea,' said Suzanne; 'you really are a brick. Come round tomorrow at twenty to three; don't be late, we must carry out our ambush to the minute.'

At a few minutes to three the next afternoon the fur-trappers walked warily towards the selected corner. In the near distance rose the colossal pile of Messrs Goliath and Mastodon's famed establishment. The afternoon was brilliantly fine, exactly the sort of weather to tempt a gentleman of advancing years into the discreet exercise of a leisurely walk.

'I say, dear, I wish you'd do something for me this evening,' said Eleanor to her companion; 'just drop in after dinner on some pretext or other, and stay on to make a fourth at bridge with Adela and the aunts. Otherwise I shall have to play, and Harry Scarisbrooke is going to come in unexpectedly about nine-fifteen, and I particularly wanted to be free to talk to him while the others are playing.'

'Sorry, my dear, no can do,' said Suzanne; 'ordinary bridge at threepence a hundred, with such dreadfully slow players as your aunts, bores me to tears. I nearly go to sleep over it.'

'But I most particularly want an opportunity to talk with Harry,' urged Eleanor, an angry glint coming into her eyes.

'Sorry, anything to oblige, but not that,' said Suzanne cheerfully; the sacrifices of friendship were beautiful in her eyes as long as she was not asked to make them.

Eleanor said nothing further on the subject, but the corners of her mouth rearranged themselves.

'There's our man!' exclaimed Suzanne suddenly; 'hurry!'

Mr Bertram Kneyght greeted his cousin and her friend with genuine heartiness, and readily accepted their invitation to explore the crowded mart that stood temptingly at their elbow. The plate-glass doors swung open and the trio plunged bravely into the jostling throng of buyers and loiterers.

'Is it always as full as this?' asked Bertram of Eleanor.

'More or less, and autumn sales are on just now,' she replied.

Suzanne, in her anxiety to pilot her cousin to the desired haven of the fur department, was usually a few paces ahead of the others, coming back to them now and then if they lingered for a moment at some attractive counter, with the nervous solicitude of a parent rook encouraging its young ones on their first flying expedition.

'It's Suzanne's birthday on Wednesday next,' confided Eleanor to Bertram Kneyght at a moment when Suzanne had left them unusually far behind; 'my birthday comes the day before, so we are both on the look-out for something to give each other.'

'Ah,' said Bertram. 'Now, perhaps you can advise me on that very point. I want to give Suzanne something, and I haven't the least idea what she wants.'

'She's rather a problem,' said Eleanor. 'She seems to have everything one can think of, lucky girl. A fan is always useful; she'll be going to a lot of dances at Davos this winter. Yes, I should think a fan would please her more than anything. After our birthdays are over we inspect each other's muster of presents, and I always feel dreadfully humble. She gets such nice things, and I never have anything worth showing. You see, none of my relations or any of the people who give me presents are at all well off, so I can't expect them to do anything more than just remember the day with some little trifle. Two years ago an uncle on my mother's side of the family, who had come into a small legacy, promised me a silver-fox stole for my birthday. I can't tell you how excited I was about it, how I pictured myself showing it off to all my friends and enemies. Then just at that moment his wife died, and, of course, poor man, he could not be expected to think of birthday presents at such a time. He has lived abroad ever since, and I never got my fur. Do you know, to this day I can scarcely look at a silver-fox pelt in a shop window or round any one's neck without feeling ready to burst into tears. I suppose if I hadn't had the prospect of getting one I shouldn't feel that way. Look, there is the fan counter, on your left; you can easily slip away in the crowd. Get her as nice a one as you can see – she is such a dear, dear girl.'

'Hullo, I thought I had lost you,' said Suzanne, making her way through an obstructive knot of shoppers. 'Where is Bertram?'

'I got separated from him long ago. I thought he was on ahead with you,' said Eleanor. 'We shall never find him in this crush.'

Which turned out to be a true prediction.

'All our trouble and forethought thrown away,' said Suzanne sulkily, when they had pushed their way fruitlessly through half a dozen departments.

'I can't think why you didn't grab him by the arm,' said Eleanor; 'I would have if I'd known him longer, but I'd only just been introduced. It's nearly four now, we'd better have tea.'

Some days later Suzanne rang Eleanor up on the telephone.

'Thank you very much for the photograph frame. It was just what I wanted. Very good of you. I say, do you know what that Kneyght person has given me? Just what you said he would – a wretched fan. What? Oh, yes, quite a good enough fan in its way, but still . . .'

'You must come and see what he's given me,' came in Eleanor's voice over the 'phone.

'You! Why should he give you anything?'

'Your cousin appears to be one of those rare people of wealth who take a pleasure in giving good presents,' came the reply.

'I wondered why he was so anxious to know where she lived,' snapped Suzanne to herself as she rang off.

A cloud has arisen between the friendships of the two young women; as far as Eleanor is concerned the cloud has a silver-fox lining.

On Approval

OF ALL THE genuine Bohemians who strayed from time to time into the would-be-Bohemian circle of the Restaurant Nuremberg, Owl Street, Soho, none was more interesting and more elusive than Gebhard Knopfschrank. He had no friends, and though he treated all the restaurant frequenters as acquaintances he never seemed to wish to carry the acquaintanceship beyond the door that led into Owl Street and the outer world. He dealt with them all rather as a market woman might deal with chance passers-by, exhibiting her wares and chattering about the weather and the slackness of business, occasionally about rheumatism, but never showing a desire to penetrate into their daily lives or to dissect their ambitions.

He was understood to belong to a family of peasant farmers, somewhere in Pomerania; some two years ago, according to all that was known of him, he had abandoned the labours and responsibilities of swine tending and goose rearing to try his fortune as an artist in London.

'Why London and not Paris or Munich?' he had been asked by the curious.

Well, there was a ship that left Stolpmünde for London twice a month, that carried few passengers, but carried them cheaply; the railway fares to Munich or Paris were not cheap. Thus it was that he came to select London as the scene of his great adventure.

The question that had long and seriously agitated the frequenters of the Nuremberg was whether this goose-boy migrant was really a soul-driven genius, spreading his wings to the light, or merely an enterprising young man who fancied he could paint and was pardonably anxious to escape from the monotony of rye bread diet and the sandy, swine-bestrewn plains of Pomerania. There was reasonable ground for doubt and caution; the artistic groups that foregathered at the little restaurant contained so many young women with short hair and so many young men with long hair, who supposed themselves to be abnormally gifted in the domain of music, poetry, painting, or stagecraft, with little or nothing to support the supposition, that a self-announced genius of any sort in their midst was inevitably suspect. On the other hand, there was the ever-imminent danger of entertaining, and snubbing, an angel unawares. There had been the lamentable case of Sledonti, the dramatic poet, who had been belittled and cold-shouldered in the Owl Street hall of judgment, and had been afterwards hailed as a master singer by the Grand Duke Constantine Constantinovitch – 'the most educated of the Romanoffs', according to Sylvia Strubble, who spoke rather as one who knew every individual member of the Russian imperial family; as a matter of fact, she knew a newspaper correspondent, a young man who ate borsch with the air of having invented it. Sledonti's *Poems of Death and Passion* were now being sold by the thousand in seven European languages, and were about to be translated into Syrian, a circumstance which made the discerning critics of the Nuremberg rather shy of maturing their future judgments too rapidly and too irrevocably.

As regards Knopfschrank's work, they did not lack opportunity for inspecting and appraising it. However resolutely he might hold himself aloof from the social life of his restaurant acquaintances, he was not minded to hide his artistic performances from their inquiring gaze. Every evening, or nearly every evening, at about seven o'clock, he would make his appearance, sit himself down at his accustomed table, throw a bulky black portfolio on to the chair opposite him, nod round indiscriminately at his fellow-guests, and commence the serious business of eating and drinking. When the coffee stage was reached he would light a cigarette, draw the portfolio over to him, and begin to rummage among its contents. With slow deliberation he would select a few of his more recent studies and sketches, and silently pass them round from table to table, paying especial attention to any new diners who might be present. On the back of each sketch was marked in plain figures the announcement 'Price ten shillings'.

If his work was not obviously stamped with the hall-mark of genius, at any rate it was remarkable for its choice of an unusual and unvarying theme. His pictures always represented some well-known street or public place in London, fallen into decay and denuded of its human population, in the place of which there roamed a wild fauna, which, from its wealth of exotic species, must have originally escaped from Zoological Gardens and travelling beast shows. 'Giraffes drinking at the fountain pools, Trafalgar Square', was one of the most notable and characteristic of his studies, while even more sensational was the gruesome picture of 'Vultures attacking dying camel in Upper Berkeley Street'. There were also photographs of the large canvas on which he had been engaged for some months, and which he was now endeavouring to sell to some enterprising dealer or adventurous amateur. The subject was 'Hyænas asleep in Euston Station', a composition that left nothing to be desired in the way of suggesting unfathomed depths of desolation.

'Of course it may be immensely clever, it may be something epoch-making in the realm of art,' said Sylvia

Strubble to her own particular circle of listeners, 'but, on the other hand, it may be merely mad. One mustn't pay too much attention to the commercial aspect of the case, of course, but still, if some dealer would make a bid for that hyæna picture, or even for some of the sketches, we should know better how to place the man and his work.'

'We may all be cursing ourselves one of these days,' said Mrs Nougat-Jones, 'for not having bought up his entire portfolio of sketches. At the same time, when there is so much real talent going about, one does not feel like planking down ten shillings for what looks like a bit of whimsical oddity. Now that picture that he showed us last week, "Sand-grouse roosting on the Albert Memorial", was very impressive, and of course I could see there was good workmanship in it and breadth of treatment; but it didn't in the least convey the Albert Memorial to me, and Sir James Beanquest tells me that sand-grouse don't roost, they sleep on the ground.'

Whatever talent or genius the Pomeranian artist might possess, it certainly failed to receive commercial sanction. The portfolio remained bulky with unsold sketches, and the 'Euston Siesta', as the wits of the Nuremberg nicknamed the large canvas, was still in the market. The outward and visible signs of financial embarrassment began to be noticeable; the half-bottle of cheap claret at dinnertime gave way to a small glass of lager, and this in turn was displaced by water. The one-and-sixpenny set dinner receded from an everyday event to a Sunday extravagance; on ordinary days the artist contented himself with a sevenpenny omelette and some bread and cheese, and there were evenings when he did not put in an appearance at all. On the rare occasions when he spoke of his own affairs it was observed that he began to talk more about Pomerania and less about the great world of art.

'It is a busy time there now with us,' he said wistfully; 'the schwines are driven out into the fields after harvest, and must be looked after. I could be helping to look after if I was there. Here it is difficult to live; art is not appreciate.'

'Why don't you go home on a visit?' some one asked tactfully.

'Ah, it cost money! There is the ship passage to Stolpmünde, and there is money that I owe at my lodgings. Even here I owe a few schillings. If I could sell some of my sketches –'

'Perhaps,' suggested Mrs Nougat-Jones, 'if you were to offer them for a little less, some of us would be glad to buy a few. Ten shillings is always a consideration, you know, to people who are not over well off. Perhaps if you were to ask six or seven shillings –'

Once a peasant, always a peasant. The mere suggestion of a bargain to be struck brought a twinkle of awakened alertness into the artist's eyes, and hardened the lines of his mouth.

'Nine schilling, nine pence each,' he snapped, and seemed disappointed that Mrs Nougat-Jones did not pursue the subject further. He had evidently expected her to offer seven-and-fourpence.

The weeks sped by, and Knopfschrank came more rarely to the restaurant in Owl Street, while his meals on those occasions became more and more meagre. And then came a triumphal day, when he appeared early in the evening in a high state of elation, and ordered an elaborate meal that scarcely stopped short of being a banquet. The ordinary resources of the kitchen were supplemented by an imported dish of smoked goosebreast, a Pomeranian delicacy that was luckily procurable at a firm of *delikatessen* merchants in Coventry Street, while a long-necked bottle of Rhine wine gave a finishing touch of festivity and good cheer to the crowded table.

'He has evidently sold his masterpiece,' whispered Sylvia Strubble to Mrs Nougat-Jones, who had come in late.

'Who has bought it?' she whispered back.

'Don't know; he hasn't said anything yet, but it must be some American. Do you see, he has got a little American flag on the dessert dish, and he has put pennies in the music box three times, once to play the "Star-spangled Banner", then a Sousa march, and then the "Star-spangled Banner" again. It must be an American millionaire, and he's evidently got a big price for it; he's just beaming and chuckling with satisfaction.'

'We must ask him who has bought it,' said Mrs Nougat-Jones.

'Hush! no, don't. Let's buy some of his sketches, quick, before we are supposed to know that he's famous; otherwise he'll be doubling the prices. I *am* so glad he's had a success at last. I always believed in him, you know.'

For the sum of ten shillings each Miss Strubble acquired the drawings of the camel dying in Upper Berkeley Street and of the giraffes quenching their thirst in Trafalgar Square; at the same price Mrs Nougat-Jones secured the study of roosting sand-grouse. A more ambitious picture, 'Wolves and wapiti fighting on the steps of the Athenæum Club', found a purchaser at fifteen shillings.

'And now what are your plans?' asked a young man who contributed occasional paragraphs to an artistic weekly.

'I go back to Stolpmünde as soon as the ship sails,' said the artist, 'and I do not return. Never.'

'But your work? Your career as painter?'

'Ah, there is nossing in it. One starves. Till today I have sold not one of my sketches. Tonight you have bought a few, because I am going away from you, but at other times, not one.'

'But has not some American –?'

'Ah, the rich American,' chuckled the artist. 'God be thanked. He dash his car right into our herd of schwines as they were being driven out to the fields. Many of our best schwines he killed, but he paid all damages. He paid perhaps more than they were worth, many times more than they would have fetched in the market after a month of fattening, but he was in a hurry to get on to Danzig. When one is in a hurry one must pay what one is asked. God be thanked for rich Americans, who are always in a hurry to get somewhere else. My father and mother, they have now so plenty of money; they send me some to pay my debts and come home. I start on Monday for Stolpmünde and I do not come back. Never.'

'But your picture, the hyænas?'

'No good. It is too big to carry to Stolpmünde. I burn it.'

In time he will be forgotten, but at present Knopfschrank is almost as sore a subject as Sledonti with some of the frequenters of the Nuremberg Restaurant, Owl Street, Soho.

THE TOYS OF
PEACE (1919)

The Toys of Peace

'HARVEY,' SAID ELEANOR Bope, handing her brother a cutting from a London morning paper[1] of the 19th of March, 'just read this about children's toys, please; it exactly carries out some of our ideas about influence and upbringing.'

'In the view of the National Peace Council,' ran the extract, 'there are grave objections to presenting our boys with regiments of fighting men, batteries of guns, and squadrons of "Dreadnoughts". Boys, the Council admits, naturally love fighting and all the panoply of war ... but that is no reason for encouraging, and perhaps giving permanent form to, their primitive instincts. At the Children's Welfare Exhibition, which opens at Olympia in three weeks' time, the Peace Council will make an alternative suggestion to parents in the shape of an exhibition of "peace toys". In front of a specially painted representation of the Peace Palace at The Hague will be grouped, not miniature soldiers but miniature civilians, not guns but ploughs and the tools of industry ... It is hoped that manufacturers may take a hint from the exhibit, which will bear fruit in the toy shops.'

'The idea is certainly an interesting and very well-meaning one,' said Harvey; 'whether it would succeed well in practice –'

'We must try,' interrupted his sister; 'you are coming down to us at Easter, and you always bring the boys some toys, so that will be an excellent opportunity for you to inaugurate the new experiment. Go about in the shops

[1] An actual extract from a London paper of March 1914.

and buy any little toys and models that have special bearing on civilian life in its more peaceful aspects. Of course you must explain the toys to the children and interest them in the new idea. I regret to say that the "Siege of Adrianople" toy, that their Aunt Susan sent them, didn't need any explanation; they knew all the uniforms and flags, and even the names of the respective commanders, and when I heard them one day using what seemed to be the most objectionable language they said it was Bulgarian words of command; of course it *may* have been, but at any rate I took the toy away from them. Now I shall expect your Easter gifts to give quite a new impulse and direction to the children's minds; Eric is not eleven yet, and Bertie is only nine-and-a-half, so they are really at a most impressionable age.'

'There is primitive instinct to be taken into consideration, you know,' said Harvey doubtfully, 'and hereditary tendencies as well. One of their great-uncles fought in the most intolerant fashion at Inkerman – he was specially mentioned in dispatches, I believe – and their great-grandfather smashed all his Whig neighbours' hothouses when the great Reform Bill was passed. Still, as you say, they are at an impressionable age. I will do my best.'

On Easter Saturday Harvey Bope unpacked a large, promising-looking red cardboard box under the expectant eyes of his nephews. 'Your uncle has brought you the newest thing in toys,' Eleanor had said impressively, and youthful anticipation had been anxiously divided between Albanian soldiery and a Somali camel-corps. Eric was hotly in favour of the latter contingency. 'There would be Arabs on horseback,' he whispered; 'the Albanians have got jolly uniforms, and they fight all day long, and all night too, when there's a moon, but the country's rocky, so they've got no cavalry.'

A quantity of crinkly paper shavings was the first thing that met the view when the lid was removed; the most exciting toys always began like that. Harvey pushed back the top layer and drew forth a square, rather featureless building.

'It's a fort!' exclaimed Bertie.

'It isn't, it's the palace of the Mpret of Albania,' said Eric, immensely proud of his knowledge of the exotic title; 'it's got no windows, you see, so that passers-by can't fire in at the Royal Family.'

'It's a municipal dust-bin,' said Harvey hurriedly; 'you see all the refuse and litter of a town is collected there, instead of lying about and injuring the health of the citizens.'

In an awful silence he disinterred a little lead figure of a man in black clothes.

'That,' he said, 'is a distinguished civilian, John Stuart Mill. He was an authority on political economy.'

'Why?' asked Bertie.

'Well, he wanted to be; he thought it was a useful thing to be.'

Bertie gave an expressive grunt, which conveyed his opinion that there was no accounting for tastes.

Another square building came out, this time with windows and chimneys.

'A model of the Manchester branch of the Young Women's Christian Association,' said Harvey.

'Are there any lions?' asked Eric hopefully. He had been reading Roman history and thought that where you found Christians you might reasonably expect to find a few lions.

'There are no lions,' said Harvey. 'Here is another civilian, Robert Raikes, the founder of Sunday schools, and here is a model of a municipal wash-house. These little round things are loaves baked in a sanitary bake-house. That lead figure is a sanitary inspector, this one is a district councillor, and this one is an official of the Local Government Board.'

'What does he do?' asked Eric wearily.

'He sees to things connected with his Department,' said Harvey. 'This box with a slit in it is a ballot-box. Votes are put into it at election times.'

'What is put into it at other times?' asked Bertie.

'Nothing. And here are some tools of industry, a wheel-barrow and a hoe, and I think these are meant for hop-poles. This is a model beehive, and that is a ventilator, for ventilating sewers. This seems to be another municipal dust-bin – no, it is a model of a school of art and a public library. This little lead figure is Mrs Hemans, a poetess, and this is Rowland Hill, who introduced the system of penny postage. This is Sir John Herschel, the eminent astrologer.'

'Are we to play with these civilian figures?' asked Eric.

'Of course,' said Harvey, 'these are toys; they are meant to be played with.'

'But how?'

It was rather a poser. 'You might make two of them contest a seat in Parliament,' said Harvey, 'and have an election –'

'With rotten eggs, and free fights, and ever so many broken heads!' exclaimed Eric.

'And noses all bleeding and everybody drunk as can be,' echoed Bertie, who had carefully studied one of Hogarth's pictures.

'Nothing of the kind,' said Harvey, 'nothing in the least like that. Votes will be put in the ballot-box, and the Mayor will count them – the district councillor will do for the Mayor – and he will say which has received the most votes, and then the two candidates will thank him for presiding, and each will say that the contest has been conducted throughout in the pleasantest and most straightforward fashion, and they part with expressions of mutual esteem. There's a jolly game for you boys to play. I never had such toys when I was young.'

'I don't think we'll play with them just now,' said Eric, with an entire absence of the enthusiasm that his uncle had shown; 'I think perhaps we ought to do a little of our holiday task. It's history this time; we've got to learn up something about the Bourbon period in France.'

'The Bourbon period,' said Harvey, with some disapproval in his voice.

'We've got to know something about Louis the Fourteenth,' continued Eric; 'I've learnt the names of all the principal battles already.'

This would never do. 'There were, of course, some battles fought during his reign,' said Harvey, 'but I fancy the accounts of them were much exaggerated; news was very unreliable in those days, and there were practically no war correspondents, so generals and commanders could magnify every little skirmish they engaged in till they reached the proportions of decisive battles. Louis was really famous, now, as a landscape gardener; the way he laid out Versailles was so much admired that it was copied all over Europe.'

'Do you know anything about Madame Du Barry?' asked Eric; 'didn't she have her head chopped off?'

'She was another great lover of gardening,' said Harvey

evasively; 'in fact, I believe the well-known rose Du Barry was named after her, and now I think you had better – play for a little and leave your lessons till later.'

Harvey retreated to the library and spent some thirty or forty minutes in wondering whether it would be possible to compile a history, for use in elementary schools, in which there should be no prominent mention of battles, massacres, murderous intrigues, and violent deaths. The York and Lancaster period and the Napoleonic era would, he admitted to himself, present considerable difficulties, and the Thirty Years' War would entail something of a gap if you left it out altogether. Still, it would be something gained if, at a highly impressionable age, children could be got to fix their attention on the invention of calico printing instead of the Spanish Armada or the Battle of Waterloo.

It was time, he thought, to go back to the boys' room, and see how they were getting on with their peace toys. As he stood outside the door he could hear Eric's voice raised in command; Bertie chimed in now and again with a helpful suggestion.

'That is Louis the Fourteenth,' Eric was saying, 'that one in knee-breeches, that Uncle said invented Sunday schools. It isn't a bit like him, but it'll have to do.'

'We'll give him a purple coat from my paintbox by and by,' said Bertie.

'Yes, an' red heels. That is Madame de Maintenon, that one he called Mrs Hemans. She begs Louis not to go on this expedition, but he turns a deaf ear. He takes Marshal Saxe with him, and we must pretend that they have thousands of men with them. The watchword is *Qui vive?* and the answer is *L'état c'est moi* – that was one of his favourite remarks, you know. They land at Manchester in the dead of night, and a Jacobite conspirator gives them the keys of the fortress.'

Peeping in through the doorway Harvey observed that the municipal dust-bin had been pierced with holes to accommodate the muzzles of imaginary cannon, and now represented the principal fortified position in Manchester; John Stuart Mill had been dipped in red ink, and apparently stood for Marshal Saxe.

'Louis orders his troops to surround the Young Women's Christian Association and seize the lot of them. "Once back at the Louvre and the girls are mine," he exclaims. We must use Mrs Hemans again for one of the girls; she says "Never," and stabs Marshal Saxe to the heart.'

'He bleeds dreadfully,' exclaimed Bertie, splashing red ink liberally over the façade of the Association building.

'The soldiers rush in and avenge his death with the utmost savagery. A hundred girls are killed' – here Bertie emptied the remainder of the red ink over the devoted building – 'and the surviving five hundred are dragged off to the French ships. "I have lost a Marshal," says Louis, "but I do not go back empty-handed."'

Harvey stole away from the room, and sought out his sister.

'Eleanor,' he said, 'the experiment –'

'Yes?'

'Has failed. We have begun too late.'

Louise

'THE TEA WILL be quite cold, you'd better ring for some more,' said the Dowager Lady Beanford.

Susan Lady Beanford was a vigorous old woman who had coquetted with imaginary ill-health for the greater part of a lifetime; Clovis Sangrail irreverently declared that she had caught a chill at the Coronation of Queen Victoria and had never let it go again. Her sister, Jane Thropplestance, who was some years her junior, was chiefly remarkable for being the most absent-minded woman in Middlesex.

'I've really been unusually clever this afternoon,' she remarked gaily, as she rang for the tea. 'I've called on all the people I meant to call on, and I've done all the shopping that I set out to do. I even remembered to try and match that silk for you at Harrod's, but I'd forgotten to bring the pattern with me, so it was no use. I really think that was the only important thing I forgot during the whole afternoon. Quite wonderful for me, isn't it?'

'What have you done with Louise?' asked her sister. 'Didn't you take her out with you? You said you were going to.'

'Good gracious,' exclaimed Jane, 'what *have* I done with Louise? I must have left her somewhere.'

'But where?'

'That's just it. Where have I left her? I can't remember if the Carrywoods were at home or if I just left cards. If they were at home I may have left Louise there to play bridge. I'll go and telephone to Lord Carrywood and find out.'

'Is that you, Lord Carrywood?' she queried over the

telephone; 'it's me, Jane Thropplestance. I want to know, have you seen Louise?'

'"Louise",' came the answer, 'it's been my fate to see it three times. At first, I must admit, I wasn't impressed by it, but the music grows on one after a bit. Still, I don't think I want to see it again just at present. Were you going to offer me a seat in your box?'

'Not the opera "Louise" – my niece, Louise Thropplestance. I thought I might have left her at your house.'

'You left cards on us this afternoon, I understand, but I don't think you left a niece. The footman would have been sure to have mentioned it if you had. Is it going to be a fashion to leave nieces on people as well as cards? I hope not; some of these houses in Berkeley Square have practically no accommodation for that sort of thing.'

'She's not at the Carrywoods',' announced Jane, returning to her tea; 'now I come to think of it, perhaps I left her at the silk counter at Selfridge's. I may have told her to wait there a moment while I went to look at the silks in a better light, and I may easily have forgotten about her when I found I hadn't your pattern with me. In that case she's still sitting there. She wouldn't move unless she was told to; Louise has no initiative.'

'You said you tried to match the silk at Harrod's,' interjected the dowager.

'Did I? Perhaps it was Harrod's. I really don't remember. It was one of those places where every one is so kind and sympathetic and devoted that one almost hates to take even a reel of cotton away from such pleasant surroundings.'

'I think you might have taken Louise away. I don't like the idea of her being there among a lot of strangers.

Supposing some unprincipled person was to get into conversation with her.'

'Impossible. Louise has no conversation. I've never discovered a single topic on which she'd anything to say beyond "Do you think so? I dare say you're right." I really thought her reticence about the fall of the Ribot Ministry was ridiculous, considering how much her dear mother used to visit Paris. This bread and butter is cut far too thin; it crumbles away long before you can get it to your mouth. One feels so absurd, snapping at one's food in mid-air, like a trout leaping at may-fly.'

'I am rather surprised,' said the dowager, 'that you can sit there making a hearty tea when you've just lost a favourite niece.'

'You talk as if I'd lost her in a churchyard sense, instead of having temporarily mislaid her. I'm sure to remember presently where I left her.'

'You didn't visit any place of devotion, did you? If you've left her mooning about Westminster Abbey or St Peter's, Eaton Square, without being able to give any satisfactory reason why she's there, she'll be seized under the Cat and Mouse Act and sent to Reginald McKenna.'

'That would be extremely awkward,' said Jane, meeting an irresolute piece of bread and butter halfway; 'we hardly know the McKennas, and it would be very tiresome having to telephone to some unsympathetic private secretary, describing Louise to him and asking to have her sent back in time for dinner. Fortunately, I didn't go to any place of devotion, though I did get mixed up with a Salvation Army procession. It was quite interesting to be at close quarters with them, they're so absolutely different to what they used to be when I first remember them in the 'eighties. They used to go about then unkempt and dishevelled, in a sort of smiling rage with the world, and now they're spruce and jaunty and flamboyantly decorative, like a geranium bed with religious convictions. Laura Kettleway was going on about them in the lift of the Dover Street Tube the other day, saying what a lot of good work they did, and what a loss it would have been if they'd never existed. "If they had never existed," I said, "Granville Barker would have been certain to have invented something that looked exactly like them." If you say things like that, quite loud, in a Tube lift, they always sound like epigrams.'

'I think you ought to do something about Louise,' said the dowager.

'I'm trying to think whether she was with me when I called on Ada Spelvexit. I rather enjoyed myself there. Ada was trying, as usual, to ram that odious Koriatoffski woman down my throat, knowing perfectly well that I detest her, and in an unguarded moment she said: "She's leaving her present house and going to Lower Seymour Street." "I dare say she will, if she stays there long enough," I said. Ada didn't see it for about three minutes, and then she was positively uncivil. No, I am certain I didn't leave Louise there.'

'If you could manage to remember where you *did* leave her, it would be more to the point than these negative assurances,' said Lady Beanford; 'so far, all that we know is that she is not at the Carrywoods', or Ada Spelvexit's, or Westminster Abbey.'

'That narrows the search down a bit,' said Jane hopefully; 'I rather fancy she must have been with me when I went to Mornay's. I know I went to Mornay's, because I remember meeting that delightful Malcolm What's-his-name there – you know whom I mean. That's the great advantage of people having unusual first names, you needn't try and remember what their other name is. Of course I know one or two other Malcolms, but none that could possibly be described as delightful. He gave me two tickets for the Happy Sunday Evenings in Sloane Square. I've probably left them at Mornay's, but still it was awfully kind of him to give them to me.'

'Do you think you left Louise there?'

'I might telephone and ask. Oh, Robert, before you clean the tea-things away I wish you'd ring up Mornay's, in Regent Street, and ask if I left two theatre tickets and one niece in their shop this afternoon.'

'A niece, ma'am?' asked the footman.

'Yes, Miss Louise didn't come home with me, and I'm not sure where I left her.'

'Miss Louise has been upstairs all the afternoon, ma'am, reading to the second kitchenmaid, who has the neuralgia. I took up tea to Miss Louise at a quarter to five o'clock, ma'am.'

'Of course, how silly of me. I remember now, I asked her to read the *Faërie Queene* to poor Emma, to try to send her to sleep. I always get some one to read the *Faërie Queene* to me when I have neuralgia, and it usually sends me to sleep. Louise doesn't seem to have been successful, but one can't say she hasn't tried. I expect after the first hour or so the kitchenmaid would rather have been left alone with her neuralgia, but of course Louise wouldn't leave off till some one told her to. Anyhow, you can ring up Mornay's, Robert, and ask whether I left two theatre tickets there. Except for your silk, Susan, those seem to be the only things I've forgotten this afternoon. Quite wonderful for me.'

Tea

JAMES CUSHAT-PRINKLY was a young man who had always had a settled conviction that one of these days he would marry; up to the age of thirty-four he had done nothing to justify that conviction. He liked and admired a great many women collectively and dispassionately without singling out one for especial matrimonial consideration, just as one might admire the Alps without feeling that one wanted any particular peak as one's own private property. His lack of initiative in this matter aroused a certain amount of impatience among the sentimentally minded women-folk of his home circle; his mother, his sisters, an aunt-in-residence, and two or three intimate matronly friends regarded his dilatory approach to the married state with a disapproval that was far from being inarticulate. His most innocent flirtations were watched with the straining eagerness which a group of unexercised terriers concentrates on the slightest movements of a human being who may be reasonably considered likely to take them for a walk. No decent-souled mortal can long resist the pleading of several pairs of walk-beseeching dog-eyes; James Cushat-Prinkly was not sufficiently obstinate or indifferent to home influences to disregard the obviously expressed wish of his family that he should become enamoured of some nice marriageable girl, and when his Uncle Jules departed this life and bequeathed him a comfortable little legacy it really seemed the correct thing to do to set about discovering some one to share it with him. The process of discovery was carried on more by the force of suggestion and the weight of public opinion than by any initiative of his own; a clear working majority of his female relatives and the aforesaid matronly friends had pitched on Joan Sebastable as the most suitable young woman in his range of acquaintance to whom he might propose marriage, and James became gradually accustomed to the idea that he and Joan would go together through the prescribed stages of congratulations, present-receiving, Norwegian or Mediterranean hotels, and eventual domesticity. It was necessary, however, to ask the lady what she thought about the matter; the family had so far conducted and directed the flirtation with ability and discretion, but the actual proposal would have to be an individual effort.

Cushat-Prinkly walked across the Park towards the Sebastable residence in a frame of mind that was moderately complacent. As the thing was going to be done he was glad to feel that he was going to get it settled and off his mind that afternoon. Proposing marriage, even to a nice girl like Joan, was a rather irksome business, but one could not have a honeymoon in Minorca and a subsequent life of married happiness without such preliminary. He wondered what Minorca was really like as a place to stop in; in his mind's eye it was an island in perpetual half-mourning, with black or white Minorca hens running all over it. Probably it would not be a bit like that when one came to examine it. People who had been in Russia had told him that they did not remember having seen any Muscovy ducks there, so it was possible that there would be no Minorca fowls on the island.

His Mediterranean musings were interrupted by the sound of a clock striking the half-hour. Half-past four. A frown of dissatisfaction settled on his face. He would arrive at the Sebastable mansion just at the hour of afternoon tea. Joan would be seated at a low table, spread with an array of silver kettles and cream-jugs and delicate porcelain teacups, behind which her voice would tinkle pleasantly in a series of little friendly questions about weak or strong tea, how much, if any, sugar, milk, cream, and so forth. 'Is it one lump? I forgot. You do take milk, don't you? Would you like some more hot water, if it's too strong?'

Cushat-Prinkly had read of such things in scores of novels, and hundreds of actual experiences had told him that they were true to life. Thousands of women, at this solemn afternoon hour, were sitting behind dainty porcelain and silver fittings, with their voices tinkling pleasantly in a cascade of solicitous little questions. Cushat-Prinkly detested the whole system of afternoon tea. According to his theory of life a woman should lie on a divan or couch, talking with incomparable charm or looking unutterable thoughts, or merely silent as a thing to be looked on, and from behind a silken curtain a small Nubian page should silently bring in a tray with cups and dainties, to be accepted silently, as a matter of course, without drawn-out chatter about cream and sugar and hot water. If one's soul was really enslaved at one's mistress's feet, how could one talk coherently about weakened tea? Cushat-Prinkly had never expounded his views on the subject to his mother; all her life she had been accustomed to tinkle pleasantly at tea-time behind dainty porcelain and silver, and if he had spoken to her about divans and Nubian pages she would have urged him to take a week's holiday at the seaside. Now, as he passed through a tangle of small streets that led indirectly to the elegant Mayfair terrace for which he was bound, a horror at the idea of confronting Joan Sebastable at her tea-table seized on him. A momentary deliverance presented itself; on one floor of a narrow little house at the noisier end of Esquimault Street lived Rhoda Ellam, a sort of remote cousin, who made a living by creating hats out of costly materials. The hats really looked as if they had come from Paris; the cheques she got for them unfortunately never looked as if they were going to Paris. However, Rhoda appeared to find life amusing and to have a fairly good time in spite of her straitened circumstances. Cushat-Prinkly decided to climb up to her floor and defer by half-an-hour or so the important business which lay before him; by spinning out his visit he could contrive to reach the Sebastable mansion after the last vestiges of dainty porcelain had been cleared away.

Rhoda welcomed him into a room that seemed to do duty as workshop, sitting-room, and kitchen combined, and to be wonderfully clean and comfortable at the same time.

'I'm having a picnic meal,' she announced. 'There's caviare in that jar at your elbow. Begin on that brown bread-and-butter while I cut some more. Find yourself a cup; the teapot is behind you. Now tell me about hundreds of things.'

She made no other allusion to food, but talked amusingly and made her visitor talk amusingly too. At the same time she cut the bread-and-butter with a masterly skill and produced red pepper, and sliced lemon, where so many women would merely have produced reasons and regrets for not having any. Cushat-Prinkly found that he was enjoying an excellent tea without having to answer as many questions about it as a Minister for Agriculture might be called on to reply to during an outbreak of cattle plague.

'And now tell me why you have come to see me,' said Rhoda suddenly. 'You arouse not merely my curiosity but my business instincts. I hope you've come about hats. I heard that you had come into a legacy the other day, and, of course, it struck me that it would be a beautiful and desirable thing for you to celebrate the event by buying brilliantly expensive hats for all your sisters. They may not have said anything about it, but I feel sure the same idea has occurred to them. Of course, with Goodwood on us, I am rather rushed just now, but in my business we're accustomed to that; we live in a series of rushes – like the infant Moses.'

'I didn't come about hats,' said her visitor. 'In fact, I don't think I really came about anything. I was passing and I just thought I'd look in and see you. Since I've been sitting talking to you, however, a rather important idea has occurred to me. If you'll forget Goodwood for a moment and listen to me, I'll tell you what it is.'

Some forty minutes later James Cushat-Prinkly returned to the bosom of his family, bearing an important piece of news.

'I'm engaged to be married,' he announced.

A rapturous outbreak of congratulation and self-applause broke out.

'Ah, we knew! We saw it coming! We foretold it weeks ago!'

'I'll bet you didn't,' said Cushat-Prinkly. 'If any one had told me at lunch-time today that I was going to ask Rhoda Ellam to marry me and that she was going to accept me, I would have laughed at the idea.'

The romantic suddenness of the affair in some measure compensated James's women-folk for the ruthless negation of all their patient effort and skilled diplomacy. It was rather trying to have to deflect their enthusiasm at a moment's notice from Joan Sebastable to Rhoda Ellam;

but, after all, it was James's wife who was in question, and his tastes had some claim to be considered.

On a September afternoon of the same year, after the honeymoon in Minorca had ended, Cushat-Prinkly came into the drawing-room of his new house in Granchester Square. Rhoda was seated at a low table, behind a service of dainty porcelain and gleaming silver. There was a pleasant tinkling note in her voice as she handed him a cup.

'You like it weaker than that, don't you? Shall I put some more hot water to it? No?'

The Disappearance of Crispina Umberleigh

IN A FIRST-CLASS carriage of a train speeding Balkan-
ward across the flat, green Hungarian plain, two Britons
sat in friendly, fitful converse. They had first foregathered in the cold grey dawn at the frontier line, where
the presiding eagle takes on an extra head and Teuton
lands pass from Hohenzollern to Habsburg keeping –
and where a probing official beak requires to delve in
polite and perhaps perfunctory, but always tiresome,
manner into the baggage of sleep-hungry passengers.
After a day's break of their journey at Vienna the
travellers had again foregathered at the trainside and
paid one another the compliment of settling instinctively
into the same carriage. The elder of the two had the
appearance and manner of a diplomat; in point of
fact he was the well-connected foster-brother of a wine
business. The other was certainly a journalist. Neither
man was talkative and each was grateful to the other for
not being talkative. That is why from time to time they
talked.

One topic of conversation naturally thrust itself forward in front of all others. In Vienna the previous day
they had learned of the mysterious vanishing of a world-
famous picture from the walls of the Louvre.

'A dramatic disappearance of that sort is sure to produce
a crop of imitations,' said the Journalist.

'It has had a lot of anticipations, for the matter of that,'
said the Wine-brother.

'Oh, of course there have been thefts from the Louvre
before.'

'I was thinking of the spiriting away of human

277

beings rather than pictures. In particular I was thinking of the case of my aunt, Crispina Umberleigh.'

'I remember hearing something of the affair,' said the Journalist, 'but I was away from England at the time. I never quite knew what was supposed to have happened.'

'You may hear what really happened if you will respect it as a confidence,' said the Wine Merchant. 'In the first place I may say that the disappearance of Mrs Umberleigh was not regarded by the family entirely as a bereavement. My uncle, Edward Umberleigh, was not by any means a weak-kneed individual, in fact in the world of politics he had to be reckoned with more or less as a strong man, but he was unmistakably dominated by Crispina; indeed I never met any human being who was not frozen into subjection when brought into prolonged contact with her. Some people are born to command; Crispina Mrs Umberleigh was born to legislate, codify, administrate, censor, license, ban, execute, and sit in judgment generally. If she was not born with that destiny she adopted it at an early age. From the kitchen regions upwards every one in the household came under her despotic sway and stayed there with the submissiveness of molluscs involved in a glacial epoch. As a nephew on a footing of only occasional visits she affected me merely as an epidemic, disagreeable while it lasted, but without any permanent effect; but her own sons and daughters stood in mortal awe of her; their studies, friendships, diet, amusements, religious observances, and way of doing their hair were all regulated and ordained according to the august lady's will and pleasure. This will help you to understand the sensation of stupefaction which was caused in the family when she unobtrusively and inexplicably vanished. It was as though St Paul's Cathedral or the Piccadilly Hotel had disappeared in the night, leaving nothing but an open space to mark where it had stood. As far as was known nothing was troubling her; in fact there was much before her to make life particularly well worth living. The young-est boy had come back from school with an unsatisfactory report, and she was to have sat in judgment on him the very afternoon of the day she disappeared – if it had been he who had vanished in a hurry one could have supplied the motive. Then she was in the middle of a newspaper correspondence with a rural dean in which she had already proved him guilty of heresy, inconsistency, and unworthy quibbling, and no ordinary consideration would have induced her to discontinue the controversy. Of course the matter was put in the hands of the police, but as far as possible it was kept out of the papers, and the generally accepted explanation of her withdrawal from her social circle was that she had gone into a nursing home.'

'And what was the immediate effect on the home circle?' asked the Journalist.

'All the girls bought themselves bicycles; the feminine cycling craze was still in existence, and Crispina had rigidly vetoed any participation in it among the members of her household. The youngest boy let himself go to such an extent during his next term that it had to be his last as far as that particular establishment was concerned. The elder boys propounded a theory that their mother might be wandering somewhere abroad, and searched for her as-siduously, chiefly, it must be admitted, in a class of Montmartre resort where it was extremely improbable that she would be found.'

'And all this while couldn't your uncle get hold of the least clue?'

'As a matter of fact he had received some information,

though of course I did not know of it at the time. He got a message one day telling him that his wife had been kidnapped and smuggled out of the country; she was said to be hidden away, in one of the islands off the coast of Norway I think it was, in comfortable surroundings and well cared for. And with the information came a demand for money; a lump sum was to be handed over to her kidnappers and a further sum of £2,000 was to be paid yearly. Failing this she would be immediately restored to her family.'

The Journalist was silent for a moment, and then began to laugh quietly.

'It was certainly an inverted form of holding to ransom,' he said.

'If you had known my aunt,' said the Wine Merchant, 'you would have wondered that they didn't put the figure higher.'

'I realize the temptation. Did your uncle succumb to it?'

'Well, you see, he had to think of others as well as himself. For the family to have gone back into the Crispina thraldom after having tasted the delights of liberty would have been a tragedy, and there were even wider considerations to be taken into account. Since his bereavement he had unconsciously taken up a far bolder and more initiatory line in public affairs, and his popularity and influence had increased correspondingly. From being merely a strong man in the political world he began to be spoken of as *the* strong man. All this he knew would be jeopardized if he once more dropped into the social position of the husband of Mrs Umberleigh. He was a rich man, and the £2,000 a year, though not exactly a fleabite, did not seem an extravagant price to pay for the boarding-out of

Crispina. Of course, he had severe qualms of conscience about the arrangement. Later on, when he took me into his confidence, he told me that in paying the ransom, or hush-money as I should have called it, he was partly influenced by the fear that if he refused it the kidnappers might have vented their rage and disappointment on their captive. It was better, he said, to think of her being well cared for as a highly valued paying-guest in one of the Lofoden Islands than to have her struggling miserably home in a maimed and mutilated condition. Anyway he paid the yearly instalment as punctually as one pays a fire insurance, and with equal promptitude there would come an acknowledgement of the money and a brief statement to the effect that Crispina was in good health and fairly cheerful spirits. One report even mentioned that she was busying herself with a scheme for proposed reforms in Church management to be pressed on the local pastorate. Another spoke of a rheumatic attack and a journey to a "cure" on the mainland, and on that occasion an additional eighty pounds was demanded and conceded. Of course it was to the interest of the kidnappers to keep their charge in good health, but the secrecy with which they managed to shroud their arrangements argued a really wonderful organization. If my uncle was paying a rather high price, at least he could console himself with the reflection that he was paying specialists' fees.'

'Meanwhile had the police given up all attempts to track the missing lady?' asked the Journalist.

'Not entirely; they came to my uncle from time to time to report on clues which they thought might yield some elucidation as to her fate or whereabouts, but I think they had their suspicions that he was possessed of more information than he had put at their disposal. And then, after a disappearance of more than eight years, Crispina returned with dramatic suddenness to the home she had left so mysteriously.'

'She had given her captors the slip?'

'She had never been captured. Her wandering away had been caused by a sudden and complete loss of memory. She usually dressed in the style of a superior kind of char-woman, and it was not so very surprising that she should have imagined that she was one, and still less that people should accept her statement and help her to get work. She had wandered as far afield as Birmingham, and found fairly steady employment there, her energy and enthusi-asm in putting people's rooms in order counter-balancing her obstinate and domineering characteristics. It was the shock of being patronizingly addressed as "my good woman" by a curate, who was disputing with her where the stove should be placed in a parish concert hall, that led to the sudden restoration of her memory. "I think you forget who you are speaking to," she observed crushingly, which was rather unduly severe, considering she had only just remembered it herself.'

'But,' exclaimed the Journalist, 'the Lofoden Island people! Who had they got hold of?'

'A purely mythical prisoner. It was an attempt in the first place by some one who knew something of the domestic situation, probably a discharged valet, to bluff a lump sum out of Edward Umberleigh before the missing woman turned up; the subsequent yearly instalments were an unlooked-for increment to the original haul.

'Crispina found that the eight years' interregnum had materially weakened her ascendency over her now grown-up offspring. Her husband, however, never accomplished anything great in the political world after her return; the strain of trying to account satisfactorily for an unspecified expenditure of sixteen thousand pounds spread over eight years sufficiently occupied his mental energies. Here is Belgrade and another custom house.'

The Wolves of Cernogratz

'ARE THERE ANY old legends attached to the castle?' asked Conrad of his sister. Conrad was a prosperous Hamburg merchant, but he was the one poetically-dispositioned member of an eminently practical family.

The Baroness Gruebel shrugged her plump shoulders.

'There are always legends hanging about these old places. They are not difficult to invent and they cost nothing. In this case there is a story that when any one dies in the castle all the dogs in the village and the wild beasts in the forest howl the night long. It would not be pleasant to listen to, would it?'

'It would be weird and romantic,' said the Hamburg merchant.

'Anyhow, it isn't true,' said the Baroness complacently; 'since we bought the place we have had proof that nothing of the sort happens. When the old mother-in-law died last spring-time we all listened, but there was no howling. It is just a story that lends dignity to the place without costing anything.'

'The story is not as you have told it,' said Amalie, the grey old governess. Every one turned and looked at her in astonishment. She was wont to sit silent and prim and faded in her place at table, never speaking unless some one spoke to her, and there were few who troubled themselves to make conversation with her. Today a sudden volubility had descended on her; she continued to talk, rapidly and nervously, looking straight in front of her and seeming to address no one in particular.

'It is not when *any one* dies in the castle that the howling is heard. It was when one of the Cernogratz family died here that the wolves came from far and near and howled at the edge of the forest just before the death hour. There were only a few couple of wolves that had their lairs in this part of the forest, but at such a time the keepers say there would be scores of them, gliding about in the shadows and howling in chorus, and the dogs of the castle and the village and all the farms round would bay and howl in fear and anger at the wolf chorus, and as the soul of the dying one left its body a tree would crash down in the park. That is what happened when a Cernogratz died in his family castle. But for a stranger dying here, of course no wolf would howl and no tree would fall. Oh, no.'

There was a note of defiance, almost of contempt, in her voice as she said the last words. The well-fed, much-too-well-dressed Baroness stared angrily at the dowdy old woman who had come forth from her usual and seemly position of effacement to speak so disrespectfully.

'You seem to know quite a lot about the von Cernogratz legends, Fräulein Schmidt,' she said sharply; 'I did not know that family histories were among the subjects you are supposed to be proficient in.'

The answer to her taunt was even more unexpected and astonishing than the conversational outbreak which had provoked it.

'I am a von Cernogratz myself,' said the old woman, 'that is why I know the family history.'

'You a von Cernogratz? You!' came in an incredulous chorus.

'When we became very poor,' she explained, 'and I had to go out and give teaching lessons, I took another name; I thought it would be more in keeping. But my grandfather spent much of his time as a boy in this castle, and my father used to tell me many stories about it, and, of course, I knew all the family legends and stories. When one has nothing left to one but memories, one guards and dusts them with especial care. I little thought when I took service with you that I should one day come with you to the old home of my family. I could wish it had been anywhere else.'

There was silence when she finished speaking, and then the Baroness turned the conversation to a less embarrassing topic than family histories. But afterwards, when the old governess had slipped away quietly to her duties, there arose a clamour of derision and disbelief.

'It was an impertinence,' snapped out the Baron, his protruding eyes taking on a scandalized expression; 'fancy the woman talking like that at our table. She almost told us we were nobodies, and I don't believe a word of it. She is just Schmidt and nothing more. She has been talking to some of the peasants about the old Cernogratz family, and raked up their history and their stories.'

'She wants to make herself out of some consequence,' said the Baroness; 'she knows she will soon be past work and she wants to appeal to our sympathies. Her grandfather, indeed!'

The Baroness had the usual number of grandfathers, but she never, never boasted about them.

'I dare say her grandfather was a pantry boy or something of the sort in the castle,' sniggered the Baron; 'that part of the story may be true.'

The merchant from Hamburg said nothing; he had seen tears in the old woman's eyes when she spoke of guarding her memories – or, being of an imaginative disposition, he thought he had.

'I shall give her notice to go as soon as the New Year festivities are over,' said the Baroness; 'till then I shall be too busy to manage without her.'

But she had to manage without her all the same, for in the cold biting weather after Christmas, the old governess fell ill and kept to her room.

'It is most provoking,' said the Baroness, as her guests sat round the fire on one of the last evenings of the dying year; 'all the time that she has been with us I cannot remember that she was ever seriously ill, too ill to go about and do her work, I mean. And now, when I have the house full, and she could be useful in so many ways, she goes and breaks down. One is sorry for her, of course, she looks so withered and shrunken, but it is intensely annoying all the same.'

'Most annoying,' agreed the banker's wife sympathetically; 'it is the intense cold, I expect, it breaks the old people up. It has been unusually cold this year.'

'The frost is the sharpest that has been known in December for many years,' said the Baron.

'And, of course, she is quite old,' said the Baroness; 'I wish I had given her notice some weeks ago, then she would have left before this happened to her. Why, Wappi, what is the matter with you?'

The small, woolly lapdog had leapt suddenly down from its cushion and crept shivering under the sofa. At the same moment an outburst of angry barking came from the dogs in the castle-yard, and other dogs could be heard yapping and barking in the distance.

'What is disturbing the animals?' asked the Baron.

And then the humans, listening intently, heard the sound that had roused the dogs to their demonstrations of fear and rage; heard a long-drawn whining howl, rising and falling, seeming at one moment leagues away, at others sweeping across the snow until it appeared to come from the foot of the castle walls. All the starved, cold misery of a frozen world, all the relentless hunger-fury of the wild, blended with other forlorn and haunting melodies to which one could give no name, seemed concentrated in that wailing cry.

'Wolves!' cried the Baron.

Their music broke forth in one raging burst, seeming to come from everywhere.

'Hundreds of wolves,' said the Hamburg merchant, who was a man of strong imagination.

Moved by some impulse which she could not have explained, the Baroness left her guests and made her way to the narrow, cheerless room where the old governess lay watching the hours of the dying year slip by. In spite of the biting cold of the winter night, the window stood open. With a scandalized exclamation on her lips, the Baroness rushed forward to close it.

'Leave it open,' said the old woman in a voice that for all its weakness carried an air of command such as the Baroness had never heard before from her lips.

'But you will die of cold!' she expostulated.

'I am dying in any case,' said the voice, 'and I want to hear their music. They have come from far and wide to sing the death-music of my family. It is beautiful that they have come; I am the last von Cernogratz that will die in our old castle, and they have come to sing to me. Hark, how loud they are calling!'

The cry of the wolves rose on the still winter air and floated round the castle walls in long-drawn piercing wails; the old woman lay back on her couch with a look of long-delayed happiness on her face.

'Go away,' she said to the Baroness; 'I am not lonely any more. I am one of a great old family. ....'

'I think she is dying,' said the Baroness when she had rejoined her guests; 'I suppose we must send for a doctor. And that terrible howling! Not for much money would I have such death-music.'

'That music is not to be bought for any amount of money,' said Conrad.

'Hark! What is that other sound?' asked the Baron, as a noise of splitting and crashing was heard.

It was a tree falling in the park.

There was a moment of constrained silence, and then the banker's wife spoke.

'It is the intense cold that is splitting the trees. It is also the cold that has brought the wolves out in such numbers. It is many years since we have had such a cold winter.'

The Baroness eagerly agreed that the cold was responsible for these things. It was the cold of the open window, too, which caused the heart failure that made the doctor's ministrations unnecessary for the old Fräulein. But the notice in the newspapers looked very well –

'On December 29th, at Schloss Cernogratz, Amalie von Cernogratz, for many years the valued friend of Baron and Baroness Gruebel.'

The Guests

'THE LANDSCAPE SEEN from our windows is certainly charming,' said Annabel; 'those cherry orchards and green meadows, and the river winding along the valley, and the church tower peeping out among the elms, they all make a most effective picture. There's something dreadfully sleepy and languorous about it, though; stagnation seems to be the dominant note. Nothing ever happens here; seedtime and harvest, an occasional outbreak of measles or a mildly destructive thunderstorm, and a little election excitement about once in five years, that is all that we have to modify the monotony of our existence. Rather dreadful, isn't it?'

'On the contrary,' said Matilda, 'I find it soothing and restful; but then, you see, I've lived in countries where things do happen, ever so many at a time, when you're not ready for them happening all at once.'

'That, of course, makes a difference,' said Annabel.

'I have never forgotten,' said Matilda, 'the occasion when the Bishop of Bequar paid us an unexpected visit; he was on his way to lay the foundation-stone of a mission-house or something of the sort.'

'I thought that out there you were always prepared for emergency guests turning up,' said Annabel.

'I was quite prepared for half a dozen bishops,' said Matilda, 'but it was rather disconcerting to find out after a little conversation that this particular one was a distant cousin of mine, belonging to a branch of the family that had quarrelled bitterly and offensively with our branch about a Crown Derby dessert service; they got it, and we ought to have got it, in some legacy, or else we got it and they thought they ought to have it, I forget which; anyhow, I know they behaved disgracefully. Now here was one of them turning up in the odour of sanctity, so to speak, and claiming the traditional hospitality of the East.'

'It was rather trying, but you could have left your husband to do most of the entertaining.'

'My husband was fifty miles up-country, talking sense, or what he imagined to be sense, to a village community that fancied one of their leading men was a were-tiger.'

'A what tiger?'

'A were-tiger; you've heard of were-wolves, haven't you, a mixture of wolf and human being and demon? Well, in those parts they have were-tigers, or think they have, and I must say that in this case, so far as sworn and uncontested evidence went, they had every ground for thinking so. However, as we gave up witchcraft prosecutions about three hundred years ago, we don't like to have other people keeping on our discarded practices; it doesn't seem respectful to our mental and moral position.'

'I hope you weren't unkind to the Bishop,' said Annabel.

'Well, of course he was my guest, so I had to be outwardly polite to him, but he was tactless enough to rake up the incidents of the old quarrel, and to try to make out that there was something to be said for the way his side of the family had behaved; even if there was, which I don't for a moment admit, my house was not the place in which to say it. I didn't argue the matter, but I gave my cook a holiday to go and visit his aged parents some ninety miles away. The emergency cook was not a specialist in curries; in fact, I don't think cooking in any shape or form could have been one of his strong points. I believe he originally came to us in the guise of a gardener, but as we never

291

pretended to have anything that could be considered a garden he was utilized as assistant goatherd, in which capacity, I understand, he gave every satisfaction. When the Bishop heard that I had sent away the cook on a special and unnecessary holiday, he saw the inwardness of the manœuvre, and from that moment we were scarcely on speaking terms. If you have ever had a Bishop with whom you were not on speaking terms staying in your house, you will appreciate the situation.'

Annabel confessed that her life-story had never included such a disturbing experience.

'Then,' continued Matilda, 'to make matters more complicated, the Gwadlipichee overflowed its banks, a thing it did every now and then when the rains were unduly prolonged, and the lower part of the house and all the out-buildings were submerged. We managed to get the ponies loose in time, and the syce swam the whole lot of them off to the nearest rising ground. A goat or two, the chief goatherd, the chief goatherd's wife, and several of their babies came to anchorage in the verandah. All the rest of the available space was filled up with wet, bedraggled-looking hens and chickens; one never really knows how many fowls one possesses till the servants' quarters are flooded out. Of course, I had been through something of the sort in previous floods, but never before had I had a houseful of goats and babies and half-drowned hens, supplemented by a Bishop with whom I was hardly on speaking terms.'

'It must have been a trying experience,' commented Annabel.

'More embarrassments were to follow. I wasn't going to let a mere ordinary flood wash out the memory of that Crown Derby dessert service, and I intimated to the

Bishop that his large bedroom, with a writing table in it, and his small bathroom, with a sufficiency of cold-water jars in it, was his share of the premises, and that space was rather congested under the existing circumstances. However, at about three o'clock in the afternoon, when he had awakened from his midday sleep, he made a sudden incursion into the room that was normally the drawing-room, but was now dining-room, storehouse, saddle-room, and half a dozen other temporary premises as well. From the condition of my guest's costume he seemed to think it might also serve as his dressing-room.

'"I'm afraid there is nowhere for you to sit," I said coldly; "the verandah is full of goats."

'"There is a goat in my bedroom," he observed with equal coldness, and more than a suspicion of sardonic reproach.

'"Really," I said, "another survivor! I thought all the other goats were done for."

'"This particular goat is quite done for," he said; "it is being devoured by a leopard at the present moment. That is why I left the room; some animals resent being watched while they are eating."

'The leopard, of course, was easily explained; it had been hanging round the goat-sheds when the flood came, and had clambered up by the outside staircase leading to the Bishop's bath-room, thoughtfully bringing a goat with it. Probably it found the bath-room too damp and shut-in for its taste, and transferred its banqueting operations to the bedroom while the Bishop was having his nap.'

'What a frightful situation!' exclaimed Annabel; 'fancy having a ravening leopard in the house, with a flood all round you.'

'Not in the least ravening,' said Matilda; 'it was full of

goat, had any amount of water at its disposal if it felt thirsty, and probably had no more immediate wish than a desire for uninterrupted sleep. Still, I think any one will admit that it was an embarrassing predicament to have your only available guest-room occupied by a leopard, the verandah choked up with goats and babies and wet hens, and a Bishop with whom you were scarcely on speaking terms planted down in your only sitting-room. I really don't know how I got through those crawling hours, and of course meal-times only made matters worse. The emergency cook had every excuse for sending in watery soup and sloppy rice, and as neither the chief goatherd nor his wife were expert divers, the cellar could not be reached. Fortunately the Gwadlipichee subsides as rapidly as it rises, and just before dawn the syce came splashing back, with the ponies only fetlock deep in water. Then there arose some awkwardness from the fact that the Bishop wished to leave sooner than the leopard did, and as the latter was ensconced in the midst of the former's personal possessions there was an obvious difficulty in altering the order of departure. I pointed out to the Bishop that a leopard's habits and tastes are not those of an otter, and that it naturally preferred walking to wading, and that in any case a meal of entire goat, washed down with tub-water, justified a certain amount of repose; if I had had guns fired to frighten the animal away, as the Bishop suggested, it would probably merely have left the bedroom to come into the already overcrowded drawing-room. Altogether it was rather a relief when they both left. Now, perhaps, you can understand my appreciation of a sleepy country-side where things don't happen.'

Bertie's Christmas Eve

IT WAS CHRISTMAS EVE, and the family circle of Luke Steffink, Esq., was aglow with the amiability and random mirth which the occasion demanded. A long and lavish dinner had been partaken of, waits had been round and sung carols, the house-party had regaled itself with more carolling on its own account, and there had been romping which, even in a pulpit reference, could not have been condemned as ragging. In the midst of the general glow, however, there was one black unkindled cinder.

Bertie Steffink, nephew of the aforementioned Luke, had early in life adopted the profession of ne'er-do-weel; his father had been something of the kind before him. At the age of eighteen Bertie had commenced that round of visits to our Colonial possessions, so seemly and desirable in the case of a Prince of the Blood, so suggestive of insincerity in a young man of the middle-class. He had gone to grow tea in Ceylon and fruit in British Columbia, and to help sheep to grow wool in Australia. At the age of twenty he had just returned from some similar errand in Canada, from which it may be gathered that the trial he gave to these various experiments was of the summary drum-head nature. Luke Steffink, who fulfilled the troubled rôle of guardian and deputy-parent to Bertie, deplored the persistent manifestation of the homing instinct on his nephew's part, and his solemn thanks earlier in the day for the blessing of reporting a united family had no reference to Bertie's return.

Arrangements had been promptly made for packing the youth off to a distant corner of Rhodesia, whence return would be a difficult matter; the journey to this uninviting destination was imminent, in fact a more careful and willing traveller would have already begun to think about his packing. Hence Bertie was in no mood to share in the festive spirit which displayed itself around him, and resentment smouldered within him at the eager, self-absorbed discussion of social plans for the coming months which he heard on all sides. Beyond depressing his uncle and the family circle, generally by singing 'Say au revoir, and not good-bye', he had taken no part in the evening's conviviality.

Eleven o'clock had struck some half-hour ago, and the elder Steffinks began to throw out suggestions leading up to that process which they called retiring for the night.

'Come, Teddie, it's time you were in your little bed, you know,' said Luke Steffink to his thirteen-year-old son.

'That's where we all ought to be,' said Mrs Steffink.

'There wouldn't be room,' said Bertie.

The remark was considered to border on the scandalous; everybody ate raisins and almonds with the nervous industry of sheep feeding during threatening weather.

'In Russia,' said Horace Bordenby, who was staying in the house as a Christmas guest, 'I've read that the peasants believe that if you go into a cow-house or stable at midnight on Christmas Eve you will hear the animals talk. They're supposed to have the gift of speech at that one moment of the year.'

'Oh, *do* let's *all* go down to the cow-house and listen to what they've got to say?' exclaimed Beryl, to whom anything was thrilling and amusing if you did it in a troop.

Mrs Steffink made a laughing protest, but gave a virtual consent by saying, 'We must all wrap up well then.' The idea seemed a scatterbrained one to her, and almost heathenish, but it afforded an opportunity for 'throwing the young people together', and as such, she welcomed it. Mr Horace Bordenby was a young man with quite substantial prospects, and he had danced with Beryl at a local subscription ball a sufficient number of times to warrant the authorized inquiry on the part of the neighbours whether 'there was anything in it'. Though Mrs Steffink would not have put it in so many words, she shared the idea of the Russian peasantry that on this night the beast might speak.

The cow-house stood at the junction of the garden with a small paddock, an isolated survival, in a suburban neighbourhood, of what had once been a small farm. Luke Steffink was complacently proud of his cow-house and his two cows; he felt that they gave him a stamp of solidity which no number of Wyandottes or Orpingtons could impart. They even seemed to link him in a sort of inconsequent way with those patriarchs who derived importance from their floating capital of flocks and herds, he-asses and she-asses. It had been an anxious and momentous occasion when he had had to decide definitely between 'the Byre' and 'the Ranch' for the naming of his villa residence. A December midnight was hardly the moment he would have chosen for showing his farm-building to visitors, but since it was a fine night, and the young people were anxious for an excuse for a mild frolic, Luke consented to chaperon the expedition. The servants had long since gone to bed, so the house was left in charge of Bertie, who scornfully declined to stir out on the pretext of listening to bovine conversation.

'We must go quietly,' said Luke, as he headed the procession of giggling young folk, brought up in the rear by the shawled and hooded figure of Mrs Steffink; 'I've always laid stress on keeping this a quiet and orderly neighbourhood.'

It was a few minutes to midnight when the party reached the cow-house and made its way in by the light of Luke's stable lantern. For a moment every one stood in silence, almost with a feeling of being in church.

'Daisy – the one lying down – is by a shorthorn bull out of a Guernsey cow,' announced Luke in a hushed voice, which was in keeping with the foregoing impression.

'Is she?' said Bordenby, rather as if he had expected her to be by Rembrandt.

'Myrtle is –'

Myrtle's family history was cut short by a little scream from the women of the party.

The cow-house door had closed noiselessly behind them and the key had turned gratingly in the lock; then they heard Bertie's voice pleasantly wishing them good night and his footsteps retreating along the garden path.

Luke Steffink strode to the window; it was a small square opening of the old-fashioned sort, with iron bars let into the stonework.

'Unlock the door this instant,' he shouted, with as much air of menacing authority as a hen might assume when screaming through the bars of a coop at a marauding hawk. In reply to his summons the hall-door closed with a defiant bang.

A neighbouring clock struck the hour of midnight. If the cows had received the gift of human speech at that moment they would not have been able to make themselves heard. Seven or eight other voices were engaged in describing Bertie's present conduct and his general character at a high pressure of excitement and indignation.

In the course of half an hour or so everything that it was permissible to say about Bertie had been said some dozens of times, and other topics began to come to the front – the extreme mustiness of the cow-house, the possibility of it catching fire, and the probability of it being a Rowton House for the vagrant rats of the neighbourhood. And still no sign of deliverance came to the unwilling vigil-keepers.

Towards one o'clock the sound of rather boisterous and undisciplined carol-singing approached rapidly, and came to a sudden anchorage, apparently just outside the garden-gate. A motor-load of youthful 'bloods', in a high state of conviviality, had made a temporary halt for repairs; the stoppage, however, did not extend to the vocal efforts of the party, and the watchers in the cow-shed were treated to a highly unauthorized rendering of 'Good King Wenceslas', in which the adjective 'good' appeared to be very carelessly applied.

The noise had the effect of bringing Bertie out into the garden, but he utterly ignored the pale angry faces peering out at the cow-house window, and concentrated his attention on the revellers outside the gate.

'Wassail, you chaps!' he shouted.

'Wassail, old sport!' they shouted back; 'we'd jolly well drink y'r health, only we've nothing to drink it in.'

'Come and wassail inside,' said Bertie hospitably; 'I'm all alone, and there's heaps of "wet".'

They were total strangers, but his touch of kindness made them instantly his kin. In another moment the unauthorized version of King Wenceslas, which, like many other scandals, grew worse on repetition, went echoing up the garden path; two of the revellers gave an impromptu performance on the way by executing the staircase waltz up the terraces of what Luke Steffink, hitherto with some justification, called his rock-garden. The rock part of it was still there when the waltz had been accorded its third encore. Luke, more than ever like a cooped hen behind the cow-house bars, was in a position to realize the feelings of concert-goers unable to countermand the call for an encore which they neither desire nor deserve.

The hall door closed with a bang on Bertie's guests, and the sounds of merriment became faint and muffled to the weary watchers at the other end of the garden. Presently two ominous pops, in quick succession, made themselves distinctly heard.

'They've got at the champagne!' exclaimed Mrs Steffink.

'Perhaps it's the sparkling Moselle,' said Luke hopefully.

Three or four more pops were heard.

'The champagne *and* the sparkling Moselle,' said Mrs Steffink.

Luke uncorked an expletive which, like brandy in a temperance household, was only used on rare emergencies. Mr Horace Bordenby had been making use of similar expressions under his breath for a considerable time past. The experiment of 'throwing the young people together' had been prolonged beyond a point when it was likely to produce any romantic result.

Some forty minutes later the hall door opened and disgorged a crowd that had thrown off any restraint of shyness that might have influenced its earlier actions. Its vocal efforts in the direction of carol-singing were now supplemented by instrumental music; a Christmas-tree that had been prepared for the children of the gardener and other household retainers had yielded a rich spoil of tin trumpets, rattles, and drums. The life-story of King Wenceslas had been dropped, Luke was thankful to notice, but it was intensely irritating for the chilled prisoners in the cow-house to be told that it was 'a hot time in the old town tonight', together with some accurate but entirely superfluous information as to the imminence of Christmas morning. Judging by the protests which began to be shouted from the upper windows of neighbouring houses, the sentiments prevailing in the cowhouse were heartily echoed in other quarters.

The revellers found their car, and, what was more remarkable, managed to drive off in it, with a parting fanfare of tin trumpets. The lively beat of a drum disclosed the fact that the master of the revels remained on the scene.

'Bertie!' came in an angry, imploring chorus of shouts and screams from the cow-house window.

'Hullo,' cried the owner of the name, turning his rather errant steps in the direction of the summons; 'are you people still there? Must have heard everything cows got to say by this time. If you haven't, no use waiting. After all, it's a Russian legend, and Russian Chrismush Eve not due for 'nother fortnight. Better come out.'

After one or two ineffectual attempts he managed to pitch the key of the cow-house door in through the window. Then, lifting his voice in the strains of 'I'm afraid to go home in the dark', with a lusty drum accompaniment, he led the way back to the house. The hurried procession of the released that followed in his steps came in for a good deal of the adverse comment that his exuberant display had evoked.

It was the happiest Christmas Eve he had ever spent. To quote his own words, he had a rotten Christmas.

Mark

AUGUSTUS MELLOWKENT WAS a novelist with a future; that is to say, a limited but increasing number of people read his books, and there seemed good reason to suppose that if he steadily continued to turn out novels year by year a progressively increasing circle of readers would acquire the Mellowkent habit, and demand his works from the libraries and bookstalls. At the instigation of his publisher he had discarded the baptismal Augustus and taken the front name of Mark.

'Women like a name that suggests some one strong and silent, able but unwilling to answer questions. Augustus merely suggests idle splendour, but such a name as Mark Mellowkent, besides being alliterative, conjures up a vision of some one strong and beautiful and good, a sort of blend of Georges Carpentier and the Reverend What's-his-name.'

One morning in December Augustus sat in his writing-room, at work on the third chapter of his eighth novel. He had described at some length, for the benefit of those who could not imagine it, what a rectory garden looks like in July; he was now engaged in describing at greater length the feelings of a young girl, daughter of a long line of rectors and archdeacons, when she discovers for the first time that the postman is attractive.

'Their eyes met, for a brief moment, as he handed her two circulars, and the fat wrapper-bound bulk of the *East Essex News*. Their eyes met, for the merest fraction of a second, yet nothing could ever be quite the same again. Cost what it might she felt that she must speak, must break the intolerable, unreal silence that had fallen on them. "How is your mother's rheumatism?" she said.'

The author's labours were cut short by the sudden intrusion of a maidservant.

'A gentleman to see you, sir,' said the maid, handing a card with the name Caiaphas Dwelf inscribed on it; 'says it's important.'

Mellowkent hesitated and yielded; the importance of the visitor's mission was probably illusory, but he had never met any one with the name Caiaphas before. It would be at least a new experience.

Mr Dwelf was a man of indefinite age; his high, narrow forehead, cold grey eyes, and determined manner bespoke an unflinching purpose. He had a large book under his arm, and there seemed every probability that he had left a package of similar volumes in the hall. He took a seat before it had been offered him, placed the book on the table, and began to address Mellowkent in the manner of an 'open letter'.

'You are a literary man, the author of several well-known books –'

'I am engaged on a book at the present moment – rather busily engaged,' said Mellowkent pointedly.

'Exactly,' said the intruder; 'time with you is a commodity of considerable importance. Minutes, even, have their value.'

'They have,' agreed Mellowkent, looking at his watch.

'That,' said Caiaphas, 'is why this book that I am introducing to your notice is not a book that you can afford to be without. *Right Here* is indispensable for the writing man; it is no ordinary encyclopædia, or I should not trouble to show it to you. It is an inexhaustible mine of concise information –'

'On a shelf at my elbow,' said the author, 'I have a row of reference books that supply me with all the information I am likely to require.'

'Here,' persisted the would-be salesman, 'you have it all in one compact volume. No matter what the subject may be which you wish to look up, or the fact you desire to verify, *Right Here* gives you all that you want to know in the briefest and most enlightening form. Historical reference, for instance; career of John Huss, let us say. Here we are: "Huss, John, celebrated religious reformer. Born: 1369, burned at Constance 1415. The Emperor Sigismund universally blamed."'

'If he had been burnt in these days every one would have suspected the Suffragettes,' observed Mellowkent.

'Poultry-keeping, now,' resumed Caiaphas, 'that's a subject that might crop up in a novel dealing with English country life. Here we have all about it: "The Leghorn as egg-producer. Lack of maternal instinct in the Minorca. Gapes in chickens, its cause and cure. Ducklings for the early market, how fattened." There, you see, there it all is, nothing lacking.'

'Except the maternal instinct in the Minorca, and that you could hardly be expected to supply.'

'Sporting records, that's important too; now how many men, sporting men even, are there who can say off-hand what horse won the Derby in any particular year? Now it's just a little thing of that sort –'

'My dear sir,' interrupted Mellowkent, 'there are at least four men in my club who can not only tell me what horse won in any given year, but what horse ought to have won and why it didn't. If your book could supply a method for protecting one from information of that sort, it would do more than anything you have yet claimed for it.'

'Geography,' said Caiaphas imperturbably; 'that's a thing that a busy man, writing at high pressure, may easily make a slip over. Only the other day a well-known author made the Volga flow into the Black Sea instead of the Caspian; now, with this book –'

'On a polished rose-wood stand behind you there reposes a reliable and up-to-date atlas,' said Mellowkent; 'and now I must really ask you to be going.'

'An atlas,' said Caiaphas, 'gives merely the chart of the river's course, and indicates the principal towns that it passes. Now *Right Here* gives you the scenery, traffic, ferry-boat charges, the prevalent types of fish, boatmen's slang terms, and hours of sailing of the principal river steamers. It gives you –'

Mellowkent sat and watched the hard-featured, resolute, pitiless salesman, as he sat doggedly in the chair wherein he had installed himself, unflinchingly extolling the merits of his undesired wares. A spirit of wistful emulation took possession of the author. Why could he not live up to the cold stern name he had adopted? Why must he sit here weakly and listen to this weary, unconvincing tirade? Why could he not be Mark Mellowkent for a few brief moments, and meet this man on level terms?

A sudden inspiration flashed across him.

'Have you read my last book, *The Cageless Linnet*?' he asked.

'I don't read novels,' said Caiaphas tersely.

'Oh, but you ought to read this one, every one ought to,' exclaimed Mellowkent, fishing the book down from a shelf; 'published at six shillings, you can have it at four-and-six. There is a bit in chapter five that I feel sure you would like, where Emma is alone in the birch copse waiting for Harold Huntingdon – that is the man her family want her to marry. She really wants to marry him too, but she does not discover that till chapter fifteen. Listen: "Far as the eye could stretch rolled the mauve and purple billows of heather, lit up here and there with the glowing yellow of gorse and broom, and edged round with the delicate greys and silver and green of the young birch trees. Tiny blue and brown butterflies fluttered above the fronds of heather, revelling in the sunlight, and overhead the larks were singing as only larks can sing. It was a day when all Nature –"'

'In *Right Here* you have full information on all branches of Nature study,' broke in the book-agent, with a tired note sounding in his voice for the first time; 'forestry, insect life, bird migration, reclamation of waste lands. As I was saying, no man who has to deal with the varied interests of life –'

'I wonder if you would care for one of my earlier books, *The Reluctance of Lady Cullumpton*,' said Mellowkent, hunting again through the bookshelf; 'some people consider it my best novel. Ah, here it is. I see there are one or two spots on the cover, so I won't ask more than three-and-ninepence for it. Do let me read you how it opens:

'"Beatrice Lady Cullumpton entered the long, dimly lit drawing-room, her eyes blazing with a hope that she guessed to be groundless, her lips trembling with a fear that she could not disguise. In her hand she carried a small fan, a fragile toy of lace and satinwood. Something snapped as she entered the room; she had crushed the fan into a dozen pieces."

'There, what do you think of that for an opening? It tells you at once that there's something afoot.'

'I don't read novels,' said Caiaphas sullenly.

'But just think what a resource they are,' exclaimed the

author, 'on long winter evenings, or perhaps when you are laid up with a strained ankle – a thing that might happen to any one; or if you were staying in a house-party with persistent wet weather and a stupid hostess and insufferably dull fellow-guests, you would just make an excuse that you had letters to write, go to your room, light a cigarette, and for three-and-ninepence you could plunge into the society of Beatrice Lady Cullumpton and her set. No one ought to travel without one or two of my novels in their luggage as a stand-by. A friend of mine said only the other day that he would as soon think of going into the tropics without quinine as of going on a visit without a couple of Mark Mellowkents in his kit-bag. Perhaps sensation is more in your line. I wonder if I've got a copy of *The Python's Kiss*.'

Caiaphas did not wait to be tempted with selections from that thrilling work of fiction. With a muttered remark about having no time to waste on monkey-talk, he gathered up his slighted volume and departed. He made no audible reply to Mellowkent's cheerful 'Good morning,' but the latter fancied that a look of respectful hatred flickered in the cold, grey eyes.

The Mappined Life

'THESE MAPPIN TERRACES at the Zoological Gardens are a great improvement on the old style of wild-beast cage,' said Mrs James Gurtleberry, putting down an illustrated paper; 'they give one the illusion of seeing the animals in their natural surroundings. I wonder how much of the illusion is passed on to the animals?'

'That would depend on the animal,' said her niece; 'a jungle-fowl, for instance, would no doubt think its lawful jungle surroundings were faithfully reproduced if you gave it a sufficiency of wives, a goodly variety of seed food and ants' eggs, a commodious bank of loose earth to dust itself in, a convenient roosting tree, and a rival or two to make matters interesting. Of course there ought to be jungle-cats and birds of prey and other agencies of sudden death to add to the illusion of liberty, but the bird's own imagination is capable of inventing those – look how a domestic fowl will squawk an alarm note if a rook or wood-pigeon passes over its run when it has chickens.'

'You think, then, they really do have a sort of illusion, if you give them space enough –'

'In a few cases only. Nothing will make me believe that an acre or so of concrete enclosure will make up to a wolf or a tiger-cat for the range of night prowling that would belong to it in a wild state. Think of the dictionary of sound and scent and recollection that unfolds before a real wild beast as it comes out from its lair every evening, with the knowledge that in a few minutes it will be hieing along to some distant hunting ground where all the joy and fury of the chase awaits it; think of the crowded sensations of the brain when every rustle, every cry, every bent twig, and every whiff across the nostrils means something, something to do with life and death and dinner. Imagine the satisfaction of stealing down to your own particular drinking spot, choosing your own particular tree to scrape your claws on, finding your own particular bed of dried grass to roll on. Then, in the place of all that, put a concrete promenade, which will be of exactly the same dimensions whether you race or crawl across it, coated with stale, unvarying scents and surrounded with cries and noises that have ceased to have the least meaning or interest. As a substitute for a narrow cage the new enclosures are excellent, but I should think they are a poor imitation of a life of liberty.'

'It's rather depressing to think that,' said Mrs Gurtleberry; 'they look so spacious and so natural, but I suppose a good deal of what seems natural to us would be meaningless to a wild animal.'

'That is where our superior powers of self-deception come in,' said the niece; 'we are able to live our unreal, stupid little lives on our particular Mappin terrace, and persuade ourselves that we really are untrammelled men and women leading a reasonable existence in a reasonable sphere.'

'But good gracious,' exclaimed the aunt, bouncing into an attitude of scandalized defence, 'we *are* leading reasonable existences! What on earth do you mean by trammels? We are merely trammelled by the ordinary decent conventions of civilized society.'

'We are trammelled,' said the niece, calmly and pitilessly, 'by restrictions of income and opportunity, and above all by lack of initiative. To some people a restricted income doesn't matter a bit, in fact it often seems to help as a means for getting a lot of reality out of life; I am sure there are men and women who do their shopping in little back streets of Paris, buying four carrots and a shred of beef for their daily sustenance, who lead a perfectly real and eventful existence. Lack of initiative is the thing that really cripples one, and that is where you and I and Uncle James are so hopelessly shut in. We are just so many animals stuck down on a Mappin terrace, with this difference in our disfavour, that the animals are there to be looked at, while nobody wants to look at us. As a matter of fact there would be nothing to look at. We get colds in winter and hay-fever in summer, and if a wasp happens to sting one of us, well, that is the wasp's initiative, not ours; all we do is to wait for the swelling to go down. Whenever we do climb into local fame and notice, it is by indirect methods; if it happens to be a good flowering year for magnolias the neighbourhood observes, "Have you seen the Gurtleberrys' magnolia? It is a perfect mass of flowers," and we go about telling people that there are fifty-seven blossoms as against thirty-nine the previous year.'

'In Coronation year there were as many as sixty,' put in the aunt; 'your uncle has kept a record for the last eight years.'

'Doesn't it ever strike you,' continued the niece relent-lessly, 'that if we moved away from here or were blotted out of existence our local claim to fame would pass on automatically to whoever happened to take the house and garden? People would say to one another, "Have you seen the Smith-Jenkins' magnolia? It is a perfect mass of flowers," or else, "Smith-Jenkins tells me there won't be a single blossom on their magnolia this year; the east winds have turned all the buds black." Now if, when we had gone, people still associated our names with the magnolia tree, no matter who temporarily possessed it, if they said, "Ah, that's the tree on which the Gurtleberrys hung their cook because she sent up the wrong kind of sauce with the asparagus," that would be something really due to our own initiative, apart from anything east winds or magnolia vitality might have to say in the matter.'

'We should never do such a thing,' said the aunt. The niece gave a reluctant sigh.

'I can't imagine it,' she admitted. 'Of course,' she continued, 'there are heaps of ways of leading a real existence without committing sensational deeds of violence. It's the dreadful little everyday acts of pretended importance that give the Mappin stamp to our life. It would be entertaining, if it wasn't so pathetically tragic, to hear Uncle James fuss in here in the morning and announce, "I must just go down into the town and find out what the men there are saying about Mexico. Matters are beginning to look serious there." Then he patters away into the town, and talks in a highly serious voice to the tobacconist, incidentally buying an ounce of tobacco; perhaps he meets one or two others of the world's thinkers and talks to them in a highly serious voice, then he patters back here and announces with increased importance, "I've just been talking to some men in the town about the condition of affairs in Mexico. They agree with the view that I have formed, that things there will have to get worse before they get better." Of course nobody in the town cared in the least little bit what his views about Mexico were or whether he had any. The tobacconist wasn't even fluttered at his buying the ounce of tobacco; he knows that he purchases the same quantity of the same sort of tobacco every week. Uncle James might just as well have lain on his back in the garden and chattered to the lilac tree about the habits of caterpillars.'

'I really will not listen to such things about your uncle,' protested Mrs James Gurtleberry angrily.

'My own case is just as bad and just as tragic,' said the niece dispassionately; 'nearly everything about me is conventional make-believe. I'm not a good dancer, and no one could honestly call me good-looking, but when I go to one of our dull little local dances I'm conventionally supposed to "have a heavenly time", to attract the ardent homage of the local cavaliers, and to go home with my head awhirl with pleasurable recollections. As a matter of fact, I've merely put in some hours of indifferent dancing, drunk some badly made claret cup, and listened to an enormous amount of laborious light conversation. A moonlight hen-stealing raid with the merry-eyed curate would be infinitely more exciting; imagine the pleasure of carrying off all those white Minorcas that the Chibfords are always bragging about. When we had disposed of them we could give the proceeds to a charity, so there would be nothing really wrong about it. But nothing of that sort lies within the Mappined limits of my life. One of these days somebody dull and decorous and undistinguished will "make himself agreeable" to me at a tennis party, as the saying is, and all the dull old gossips of the neighbourhood will begin to ask when we are to be engaged, and at last we shall be engaged, and people will give us butter-dishes and blotting-cases and framed pictures of young women feeding swans. Hullo, Uncle, are you going out?'

'I'm just going down to the town,' announced Mr James Gurtleberry, with an air of some importance: 'I want to hear what people are saying about Albania. Affairs there are beginning to take on a very serious look.

It's my opinion that we haven't seen the worst of things yet.'

In this he was probably right, but there was nothing in the immediate or prospective condition of Albania to warrant Mrs Gurtleberry in bursting into tears.

Fate

REX DILLOT WAS nearly twenty-four, almost good-looking and quite penniless. His mother was supposed to make him some sort of an allowance out of what her creditors allowed her, and Rex occasionally strayed into the ranks of those who earn fitful salaries as secretaries or companions to people who are unable to cope unaided with their correspondence or their leisure. For a few months he had been assistant editor and business manager of a paper devoted to fancy mice, but the devotion had been all on one side, and the paper disappeared with a certain abruptness from club reading-rooms and other haunts where it had made a gratuitous appearance. Still, Rex lived with some air of comfort and well-being, as one can live if one is born with a genius for that sort of thing, and a kindly Providence usually arranged that his week-end invitations coincided with the dates on which his one white dinner-waistcoat was in a laundry-returned condition of dazzling cleanness. He played most games badly, and was shrewd enough to recognize the fact, but he had developed a marvellously accurate judgement in estimating the play and chances of other people, whether in a golf match, billiard handicap, or croquet tournament. By dint of parading his opinion of such and such a player's superiority with a sufficient degree of youthful assertiveness he usually succeeded in provoking a wager at liberal odds, and he looked to his week-end winnings to carry him through the financial embarrassments of his mid-week existence. The trouble was, as he confided to Clovis Sangrail, that he never had enough available or even prospective cash at his command to

314

enable him to fix the wager at a figure really worth winning.

'Some day,' he said, 'I shall come across a really safe thing, a bet that simply can't go astray, and then I shall put it up for all I'm worth, or rather for a good deal more than I'm worth if you sold me up to the last button.'

'It would be awkward if it didn't happen to come off,' said Clovis.

'It would be more than awkward,' said Rex; 'it would be a tragedy. All the same, it would be extremely amusing to bring it off. Fancy awaking in the morning with about three hundred pounds standing to one's credit. I should go and clear out my hostess's pigeon-loft before breakfast out of sheer good-temper.'

'Your hostess of the moment mightn't have a pigeon-loft,' said Clovis.

'I always choose hostesses that have,' said Rex; 'a pigeon-loft is indicative of a careless, extravagant, genial disposition, such as I like to see around me. People who strew corn broadcast for a lot of feathered inanities that just sit about cooing and giving each other the glad eye in a Louis Quatorze manner are pretty certain to do you well.'

'Young Strinnit is coming down this afternoon,' said Clovis reflectively; 'I dare say you won't find it difficult to get him to back himself at billiards. He plays a pretty useful game, but he's not quite as good as he fancies he is.'

'I know one member of the party who can walk round him,' said Rex softly, an alert look coming into his eyes; 'that cadaverous-looking Major who arrived last night. I've seen him play at St Moritz. If I could get Strinnit to lay odds on himself against the Major the money would be safe in my pocket. This looks like the good thing I've been watching and praying for.'

'Don't be rash,' counselled Clovis, 'Strinnit may play up to his self-imagined form once in a blue moon.'

'I intend to be rash,' said Rex quietly, and the look on his face corroborated his words.

'Are you all going to flock to the billiard-room?' asked Teresa Thundleford, after dinner, with an air of some disapproval and a good deal of annoyance. 'I can't see what particular amusement you find in watching two men prodding little ivory balls about on a table.'

'Oh, well,' said her hostess, 'it's a way of passing the time, you know.'

'A very poor way, to my mind,' said Mrs Thundleford; 'now I was going to have shown all of you the photographs I took in Venice last summer.'

'You showed them to us last night,' said Mrs Cuvering hastily.

'Those were the ones I took in Florence. These are quite a different lot.'

'Oh, well, some time tomorrow we can look at them. You can leave them down in the drawing-room, and then every one can have a look.'

'I should prefer to show them when you are all gathered together, as I have quite a lot of explanatory remarks to make, about Venetian art and architecture, on the same lines as my remarks last night on the Florentine galleries. Also, there are some verses of mine that I should like to read you, on the rebuilding of the Campanile. But, of course, if you all prefer to watch Major Latton and Mr Strinnit knocking balls about on a table –'

'They are both supposed to be first-rate players,' said the hostess.

'I have yet to learn that my verses and my art *causerie* are of second-rate quality,' said Mrs Thundleford with

316

acerbity. 'However, as you all seem bent on watching a silly game, there's no more to be said. I shall go upstairs and finish some writing. Later on, perhaps, I will come down and join you.'

To one, at least, of the onlookers the game was anything but silly. It was absorbing, exciting, exasperating, nerve-stretching, and finally it grew to be tragic. The Major with the St Moritz reputation was playing a long way below his form, young Strinnit was playing slightly above his, and had all the luck of the game as well. From the very start the balls seemed possessed by a demon of contrariness; they trundled about complacently for one player, they would go nowhere for the other.

'A hundred and seventy, seventy-four,' sang out the youth who was marking. In a game of two hundred and fifty up it was an enormous lead to hold. Clovis watched the flush of excitement die away from Dillot's face, and a hard white look take its place.

'How much have you got on?' whispered Clovis. The other whispered the sum through dry, shaking lips. It was more than he or any one connected with him could pay; he had done what he had said he would do. He had been rash.

'Two hundred and six, ninety-eight.'

Rex heard a clock strike ten somewhere in the hall, then another somewhere else, and another, and another; the house seemed full of striking clocks. Then in the distance the stable clock chimed in. In another hour they would all be striking eleven, and he would be listening to them as a disgraced outcast, unable to pay, even in part, the wager he had challenged.

'Two hundred and eighteen, a hundred and three.' The game was as good as over. Rex was as good as done for. He longed desperately for the ceiling to fall in, for the house to catch fire, for anything to happen that would put an end to that horrible rolling to and fro of red and white ivory that was jostling him nearer and nearer to his doom.

'Two hundred and twenty-eight, a hundred and seven.'

Rex opened his cigarette-case; it was empty. That at least gave him a pretext to slip away from the room for the purpose of refilling it; he would spare himself the drawn-out torture of watching that hopeless game played out to the bitter end. He backed away from the circle of absorbed watchers and made his way up a short stairway to a long, silent corridor of bedrooms, each with a guest's name written in a little square on the door. In the hush that reigned in this part of the house he could still hear the hateful click-click of the balls; if he waited for a few minutes longer he would hear the little outbreak of clapping and buzz of congratulation that would hail Strinnit's victory. On the alert tension of his nerves there broke another sound, the aggressive, wrath-inducing breathing of one who sleeps in heavy after-dinner slumber. The sound came from a room just at his elbow; the card on the door bore the announcement: 'Mrs Thundleford'. The door was just slightly ajar; Rex pushed it open an inch or two more and looked in. The august Teresa had fallen asleep over an illustrated guide to Florentine art-galleries; at her side, somewhat dangerously near the edge of the table, was a reading-lamp. If Fate had been decently kind to him, thought Rex, bitterly, that lamp would have been knocked over by the sleeper and would have given them something to think of besides billiard matches.

There are occasions when one must take one's Fate in one's hands. Rex took the lamp in his.

'Two hundred and thirty-seven, one hundred and

318

fifteen.' Strinnit was at the table, and the balls lay in good position for him; he had a choice of two fairly easy shots, a choice which he was never to decide. A sudden hurricane of shrieks and a rush of stumbling feet sent every one flocking to the door. The Dillot boy crashed into the room, carrying in his arms the vociferous and somewhat dishevelled Teresa Thundleford; her clothing was certainly not a mass of flames, as the more excitable members of the party afterwards declared, but the edge of her skirt and part of the table-cover in which she had been hastily wrapped were alight in a flickering, half-hearted manner. Rex flung his struggling burden on to the billiard table, and for one breathless minute the work of beating out the sparks with rugs and cushions and playing on them with soda-water syphons engrossed the energies of the entire company.

'It was lucky I was passing when it happened,' panted Rex; 'some one had better see to the room. I think the carpet is alight.'

As a matter of fact the promptitude and energy of the rescuer had prevented any great damage being done, either to the victim or her surroundings. The billiard table had suffered most, and had to be laid up for repairs; perhaps it was not the best place to have chosen for the scene of salvage operations; but then, as Clovis remarked, when one is rushing about with a blazing woman in one's arms one can't stop to think out exactly where one is going to put her.

The Bull

TOM YORKFIELD HAD always regarded his half-brother, Laurence, with a lazy instinct of dislike, toned down, as years went on, to a tolerant feeling of indifference. There was nothing very tangible to dislike him for; he was just a blood-relation, with whom Tom had no single taste or interest in common, and with whom, at the same time, he had had no occasion for quarrel. Laurence had left the farm early in life, and had lived for a few years on a small sum of money left him by his mother; he had taken up painting as a profession, and was reported to be doing fairly well at it, well enough, at any rate, to keep body and soul together. He specialized in painting animals, and he was successful in finding a certain number of people to buy his pictures. Tom felt a comforting sense of assured superiority in contrasting his position with that of his half-brother; Laurence was an artist-chap, just that and nothing more, though you might make it sound more important by calling him an animal painter; Tom was a farmer, not in a very big way, it was true, but the Helsery farm had been in the family for some generations, and it had a good reputation for the stock raised on it. Tom had done his best, with the little capital at his command, to maintain and improve the standard of his small herd of cattle, and in Clover Fairy he had bred a bull which was something rather better than any that his immediate neighbours could show. It would not have made a sensation in the judging-ring at an important cattle show, but it was as vigorous, shapely, and healthy a young animal as any small practical farmer could wish to possess. At the King's Head on market days Clover Fairy was very highly spoken of, and Yorkfield used to declare that he would not part with him for a hundred pounds; a hundred pounds is a lot of money in the small farming line, and probably anything over eighty would have tempted him.

It was with some especial pleasure that Tom took advantage of one of Laurence's rare visits to the farm to lead him down to the enclosure where Clover Fairy kept solitary state – the grass widower of a grazing harem. Tom felt some of his old dislike for his half-brother reviving; the artist was becoming more languid in his manner, more unsuitably turned-out in attire, and he seemed inclined to impart a slightly patronizing tone to his conversation. He took no heed of a flourishing potato crop, but waxed enthusiastic over a clump of yellow-flowering weed that stood in a corner by a gateway, which was rather galling to the owner of a really very well weeded farm; again, when he might have been duly complimentary about a group of fat, black-faced lambs, that simply cried aloud for admiration, he became eloquent over the foliage tints of an oak copse on the hill opposite. But now he was being taken to inspect the crowning pride and glory of Helsery; however grudging he might be in his praises, however backward and niggardly with his congratulations, he would have to see and acknowledge the many excellencies of that redoubtable animal. Some weeks ago, while on a business journey to Taunton, Tom had been invited by his half-brother to visit a studio in that town, where Laurence was exhibiting one of his pictures, a large canvas representing a bull standing knee-deep in some marshy ground; it had been good of its kind, no doubt, and Laurence had seemed inordinately pleased with it; 'the best thing I've done yet', he had said over and over again, and Tom had generously agreed that it was fairly life-like. Now, the man of pigments was going to be shown a real picture, a living model of strength and comeliness, a thing to feast the eyes on, a picture that exhibited new pose and action with every shifting minute, instead of standing glued into one unvarying attitude between the four walls of a frame. Tom unfastened a stout wooden door and led the way into a straw-bedded yard.

'Is he quiet?' asked the artist, as a young bull with a curly red coat came inquiringly towards them.

'He's playful at times,' said Tom, leaving his half-brother to wonder whether the bull's ideas of play were of the catch-as-catch-can order. Laurence made one or two perfunctory comments on the animal's appearance and asked a question or so as to his age and such-like details; then he coolly turned the talk into another channel.

'Do you remember the picture I showed you at Taunton?' he asked.

'Yes,' grunted Tom; 'a white-faced bull standing in some slush. Don't admire those Herefords much myself; bulky-looking brutes, don't seem to have much life in them. Daresay they're easier to paint that way; now, this young beggar is on the move all the time, aren't you, Fairy?'

'I've sold that picture,' said Laurence, with considerable complacency in his voice.

'Have you?' said Tom; 'glad to hear it, I'm sure. Hope you're pleased with what you've got for it.'

'I got three hundred pounds for it,' said Laurence.

Tom turned towards him with a slowly rising flush of anger in his face. Three hundred pounds! Under the most favourable market conditions that he could imagine his prized Clover Fairy would hardly fetch a hundred, yet here was a piece of varnished canvas, painted by his half-brother, selling for three times that sum. It was a cruel insult that went home with all the more force because it emphasized the triumph of the patronizing, self-satisfied Laurence. The young farmer had meant to put his relative just a little out of conceit with himself by displaying the jewel of his possessions, and now the tables were turned, and his valued beast was made to look cheap and insignificant beside the price paid for a mere picture. It was so monstrously unjust; the painting would never be anything more than a dexterous piece of counterfeit life, while Clover Fairy was the real thing, a monarch in his little world, a personality in the countryside. After he was dead, even, he would still be something of a personality; his descendants would graze in those valley meadows and hillside pastures, they would fill stall and byre and milking-shed, their good red coats would speckle the landscape and crowd the market-place; men would note a promising heifer or a well-proportioned steer, and say: 'Ah, that one comes of good old Clover Fairy's stock.' All that time the picture would be hanging, lifeless and unchanging, beneath its dust and varnish, a chattel that ceased to mean anything if you chose to turn it with its back to the wall. These thoughts chased themselves angrily through Tom Yorkfield's mind, but he could not put them into words. When he gave tongue to his feelings he put matters bluntly and harshly.

'Some soft-witted fools may like to throw away three hundred pounds on a bit of paintwork; can't say as I envy them their taste. I'd rather have the real thing than a picture of it.'

He nodded towards the young bull, that was alternately staring at them with nose held high and lowering its horns with a half-playful, half-impatient shake of the head.

Laurence laughed a laugh of irritating, indulgent amusement.

'I don't think the purchaser of my bit of paintwork, as you call it, need worry about having thrown his money away. As I get to be better known and recognized my pictures will go up in value. That particular one will probably fetch four hundred in a sale-room five or six years hence; pictures aren't a bad investment if you know enough to pick out the work of the right men. Now you can't say your precious bull is going to get more valuable the longer you keep him; he'll have his little day, and then, if you go on keeping him, he'll come down at last to a few shillings-worth of hoofs and hide, just at a time, perhaps, when *my* bull is being bought for a big sum for some important picture gallery.'

It was too much. The united force of truth and slander and insult put over heavy a strain on Tom Yorkfield's powers of restraint. In his right hand he held a useful oak cudgel, with his left he made a grab at the loose collar of Laurence's canary-coloured silk shirt. Laurence was not a fighting man; the fear of physical violence threw him off his balance as completely as overmastering indignation had thrown Tom off his, and thus it came to pass that Clover Fairy was regaled with the unprecedented sight of a human being scudding and squawking across the enclosure, like the hen that would persist in trying to establish a nesting-place in the manger. In another crowded happy moment the bull was trying to jerk Laurence over his left shoulder, to prod him in the ribs while still in the air, and to kneel on him when he reached the ground. It was only the vigorous intervention of Tom that induced him to relinquish the last item of his programme.

Tom devotedly and ungrudgingly nursed his half-brother to a complete recovery from his injuries, which consisted of nothing more serious than a dislocated shoulder, a broken rib or two, and a little nervous prostration. After all, there was no further occasion for rancour in the young farmer's mind; Laurence's bull might sell for three hundred, or for six hundred, and be admired by thousands in some big picture gallery, but it would never toss a man over one shoulder and catch him a jab in the ribs before he had fallen on the other side. That was Clover Fairy's noteworthy achievement, which could never be taken away from him.

Laurence continues to be popular as an animal artist, but his subjects are always kittens or fawns or lambkins – never bulls.

Shock Tactics

ON A LATE spring afternoon Ella McCarthy sat on a green-painted chair in Kensington Gardens, staring listlessly at an uninteresting stretch of park landscape, that blossomed suddenly into tropical radiance as an expected figure appeared in the middle distance.

'Hullo, Bertie!' she exclaimed sedately, when the figure arrived at the painted chair that was the nearest neighbour to her own, and dropped into it eagerly, yet with a certain due regard for the set of its trousers; 'hasn't it been a perfect spring afternoon?'

The statement was a distinct untruth as far as Ella's own feelings were concerned; until the arrival of Bertie the afternoon had been anything but perfect.

Bertie made a suitable reply, in which a questioning note seemed to hover.

'Thank you ever so much for those lovely handkerchiefs,' said Ella, answering the unspoken question; 'they were just what I've been wanting. There's only one thing spoilt my pleasure in your gift,' she added, with a pout.

'What was that?' asked Bertie anxiously, fearful that perhaps he had chosen a size of handkerchief that was not within the correct feminine limit.

'I should have liked to have written and thanked you for them as soon as I got them,' said Ella, and Bertie's sky clouded at once.

'You know what mother is,' he protested; 'she opens all my letters, and if she found I'd been giving presents to any one there'd have been something to talk about for the next fortnight.'

'Surely, at the age of twenty –' began Ella.

'I'm not twenty till September,' interrupted Bertie.

'At the age of nineteen years and eight months,' persisted Ella, 'you might be allowed to keep your correspondence private to yourself.'

'I ought to be, but things aren't always what they ought to be. Mother opens every letter that comes into the house, whoever it's for. My sisters and I have made rows about it time and again, but she goes on doing it.'

'I'd find some way to stop her if I were in your place,' said Ella valiantly, and Bertie felt that the glamour of his anxiously deliberated present had faded away in the disagreeable restriction that hedged round its acknowledgement.

'Is anything the matter?' asked Bertie's friend Clovis when they met that evening at the swimming-bath.

'Why do you ask?' said Bertie.

'When you wear a look of tragic gloom in a swimming-bath,' said Clovis, 'it's especially noticeable from the fact that you're wearing very little else. Didn't she like the handkerchiefs?'

Bertie explained the situation.

'It is rather galling, you know,' he added, 'when a girl has a lot of things she wants to write to you and can't send a letter except by some roundabout, underhand way.'

'One never realizes one's blessings while one enjoys them,' said Clovis; 'now I have to spend a considerable amount of ingenuity inventing excuses for not having written to people.'

'It's not a joking matter,' said Bertie resentfully: 'you wouldn't find it funny if your mother opened all your letters.'

'The funny thing to me is that you should let her do it.'

'I can't stop it. I've argued about it –'

'You haven't used the right kind of argument, I expect. Now, if every time one of your letters was opened you lay on your back on the dining-table during dinner and had a fit, or roused the entire family in the middle of the night to hear you recite one of Blake's "Poems of Innocence", you would get a far more respectful hearing for future protests. People yield more consideration to a mutilated mealtime or a broken night's rest, than ever they would to a broken heart.'

'Oh, dry up,' said Bertie crossly, inconsistently splashing Clovis from head to foot as he plunged into the water.

It was a day or two after the conversation in the swimming-bath that a letter addressed to Bertie Heasant slid into the letter-box at his home, and thence into the hands of his mother. Mrs Heasant was one of those empty-minded individuals to whom other people's affairs are perpetually interesting. The more private they are intended to be the more acute is the interest they arouse. She would have opened this particular letter in any case; the fact that it was marked 'private', and diffused a delicate but penetrating aroma, merely caused her to open it with headlong haste rather than matter-of-course deliberation. The harvest of sensation that rewarded her was beyond all expectations.

'Bertie, carissimo,' it began, 'I wonder if you will have the nerve to do it; it will take some nerve, too. Don't forget the jewels. They are a detail, but details interest me.
'Yours as ever,
'CLOTILDE.

'Your mother must not know of my existence. If questioned swear you never heard of me.'

328

For years Mrs Heasant had searched Bertie's corres-pondence diligently for traces of possible dissipation or youthful entanglements, and at last the suspicions that had stimulated her inquisitorial zeal were justified by this one splendid haul. That any one wearing the exotic name 'Clotilde' should write to Bertie under the incriminating announcement 'as ever' was sufficiently electrifying, with-out the astounding allusion to the jewels. Mrs Heasant could recall novels and dramas wherein jewels played an exciting and commanding rôle, and here, under her own roof, before her very eyes as it were, her own son was carrying on an intrigue in which jewels were merely an interesting detail. Bertie was not due home for another hour, but his sisters were available for the immediate unburdening of a scandal-laden mind.

'Bertie is in the toils of an adventuress,' she screamed; 'her name is Clotilde,' she added, as if she thought they had better know the worst at once. There are occasions when more harm than good is done by shielding young girls from a knowledge of the more deplorable realities of life.

By the time Bertie arrived his mother had discussed every possible and improbable conjecture as to his guilty secret; the girls limited themselves to the opinion that their brother had been weak rather than wicked.

'Who is Clotilde?' was the question that confronted Bertie almost before he had got into the hall. His denial of any knowledge of such a person was met with an out-burst of bitter laughter.

'How well you have learned your lesson!' exclaimed Mrs Heasant. But satire gave way to furious indignation when she realized that Bertie did not intend to throw any further light on her discovery.

'You shan't have any dinner till you've confessed everything,' she stormed.

Bertie's reply took the form of hastily collecting material for an impromptu banquet from the larder and locking himself into his bedroom. His mother made frequent visits to the locked door and shouted a succession of interrogations with the persistence of one who thinks that if you ask a question often enough an answer will eventually result. Bertie did nothing to encourage the supposition. An hour had passed in fruitless one-sided palaver when another letter addressed to Bertie and marked 'private' made its appearance in the letter-box. Mrs Heasant pounced on it with the enthusiasm of a cat that has missed its mouse and to whom a second has been unexpectedly vouchsafed. If she hoped for further disclosures assuredly she was not disappointed.

'So you have really done it!' the letter abruptly commenced; 'Poor Dagmar. Now she is done for I almost pity her. You did it very well, you wicked boy, the servants all think it was suicide, and there will be no fuss. Better not touch the jewels till after the inquest. 'CLOTILDE.'

Anything that Mrs Heasant had previously done in the way of outcry was easily surpassed as she raced upstairs and beat frantically at her son's door.

'Miserable boy, what have you done to Dagmar?'

'It's Dagmar now, is it?' he snapped; 'it will be Geraldine next.'

'That it should come to this after all my efforts to keep you at home of an evening,' sobbed Mrs Heasant; 'it's no use you trying to hide things from me; Clotilde's letter betrays everything.'

'Does it betray who she is?' asked Bertie. 'I've heard so much about her, I should like to know something about her home-life. Seriously, if you go on like this I shall fetch a doctor; I've often enough been preached at about nothing, but I've never had an imaginary harem dragged into the discussion.'

'Are these letters imaginary?' screamed Mrs Heasant. 'What about the jewels, and Dagmar, and the theory of suicide?'

No solution of these problems was forthcoming through the bedroom door, but the last post of the evening produced another letter for Bertie, and its contents brought Mrs Heasant that enlightenment which had already dawned on her son.

'DEAR BERTIE,' it ran; 'I hope I haven't distracted your brain with the spoof letters I've been sending in the name of a fictitious Clotilde. You told me the other day that the servants, or somebody at your home, tampered with your letters, so I thought I would give any one that opened them something exciting to read. The shock might do them good.

'Yours,
'CLOVIS SANGRAIL.'

Mrs Heasant knew Clovis slightly, and was rather afraid of him. It was not difficult to read between the lines of his successful hoax. In a chastened mood she rapped once more at Bertie's door.

'A letter from Mr Sangrail. It's all been a stupid hoax. He wrote those other letters. Why, where are you going?'

Bertie had opened the door; he had on his hat and overcoat.

'I'm going for a doctor to come and see if anything's the

matter with you. Of course it was all a hoax, but no person in his right mind could have believed all that rubbish about murder and suicide and jewels. You've been making enough noise to bring the house down for the last hour or two.'

'But what was I to think of those letters?' whimpered Mrs Heasant.

'I should have known what to think of them,' said Bertie; 'if you choose to excite yourself over other people's correspondence it's your own fault. Anyhow, I'm going for a doctor.'

It was Bertie's great opportunity, and he knew it. His mother was conscious of the fact that she would look rather ridiculous if the story got about. She was willing to pay hush-money.

'I'll never open your letters again,' she promised.

And Clovis has no more devoted slave than Bertie Heasant.

The Seven Cream Jugs

'I SUPPOSE WE shall never see Wilfrid Pigeoncote here now that he has become heir to the baronetcy and to a lot of money,' observed Mrs Peter Pigeoncote regretfully to her husband.

'Well, we can hardly expect to,' he replied, 'seeing that we always choked him off from coming to see us when he was a prospective nobody. I don't think I've set eyes on him since he was a boy of twelve.'

'There was a reason for not wanting to encourage his acquaintanceship,' said Mrs Peter. 'With that notorious failing of his he was not the sort of person one wanted in one's house.'

'Well, the failing still exists, doesn't it?' said her husband; 'or do you suppose a reform of character is entailed along with the estate?'

'Oh, of course, there is still that drawback,' admitted the wife, 'but one would like to make the acquaintance of the future head of the family, if only out of mere curiosity. Besides, cynicism apart, his being rich *will* make a difference in the way people will look at his failing. When a man is absolutely wealthy, not merely well-to-do, all suspicion of sordid motive naturally disappears; the thing becomes merely a tiresome malady.'

Wilfrid Pigeoncote had suddenly become heir to his uncle, Sir Wilfrid Pigeoncote, on the death of his cousin, Major Wilfrid Pigeoncote, who had succumbed to the after-effects of a polo accident. (A Wilfrid Pigeoncote had covered himself with honours in the course of Marlborough's campaigns, and the name Wilfrid had been a baptismal weakness in the family ever since.) The new heir to the family dignity and estates was a young man of about five-and-twenty, who was known more by reputation than by person to a wide circle of cousins and kinsfolk. And the reputation was an unpleasant one. The numerous other Wilfrids in the family were distinguished one from another chiefly by the names of their residences or professions, as Wilfrid of Hubbledown, and young Wilfrid the Gunner, but this particular scion was known by the ignominious and expressive label of Wilfrid the Snatcher. From his late schooldays onward he had been possessed by an acute and obstinate form of kleptomania; he had the acquisitive instinct of the collector without any of the collector's discrimination. Anything that was smaller and more portable than a sideboard, and above the value of ninepence, had an irresistible attraction for him, provided that it fulfilled the necessary condition of belonging to some one else. On the rare occasions when he was included in a country-house party, it was usual and almost necessary for his host, or some member of the family, to make a friendly inquisition through his baggage on the eve of his departure, to see if he had packed up 'by mistake' any one else's property. The search usually produced a large and varied yield.

'This is funny,' said Peter Pigeoncote to his wife, some half-hour after their conversation; 'here's a telegram from Wilfrid, saying he's passing through here in his motor, and would like to stop and pay us his respects. Can stay for the night if it doesn't inconvenience us. Signed "Wilfrid Pigeoncote". Must be the Snatcher; none of the others have a motor. I suppose he's bringing us a present for the silver wedding.'

'Good gracious!' said Mrs Peter, as a thought struck her; 'this is rather an awkward time to have a person with his failing in the house. All those silver presents set out in the drawing-room, and others coming by every post; I hardly know what we've got and what are still to come. We can't lock them all up; he's sure to want to see them.'

'We must keep a sharp look-out, that's all,' said Peter reassuringly.

'But these practised kleptomaniacs are so clever,' said his wife apprehensively, 'and it will be so awkward if he suspects that we are watching him.'

Awkwardness was indeed the prevailing note that evening when the passing traveller was being entertained. The talk flitted nervously and hurriedly from one impersonal topic to another. The guest had none of the furtive, half-apologetic air that his cousins had rather expected to find; he was polite, well-assured, and, perhaps, just a little inclined to 'put on side'. His hosts, on the other hand, wore an uneasy manner that might have been the hall-mark of conscious depravity. In the drawing-room, after dinner, their nervousness and awkwardness increased.

'Oh, we haven't shown you the silver-wedding presents,' said Mrs Peter suddenly, as though struck by a brilliant idea for entertaining the guest; 'here they all are. Such nice, useful gifts. A few duplicates, of course.'

'Seven cream jugs,' put in Peter.

'Yes, isn't it annoying,' went on Mrs Peter; 'seven of them. We feel that we must live on cream for the rest of our lives. Of course, some of them can be changed.'

Wilfrid occupied himself chiefly with such of the gifts as were of antique interest, carrying one or two of them over to the lamp to examine their marks. The anxiety of his hosts at these moments resembled the solicitude of a cat whose newly born kittens are being handed round for inspection.

'Let me see; did you give me back the mustard-pot? This is its place here,' piped Mrs Peter.

'Sorry. I put it down by the claret-jug,' said Wilfrid, busy with another object.

'Oh, just let me have that sugar-sifter again,' asked Mrs Peter, dogged determination showing through her nervousness. 'I must label it who it comes from before I forget.'

Vigilance was not completely crowned with a sense of victory. After they had said 'Good night' to their visitor, Mrs Peter expressed her conviction that he had taken something.

'I fancy, by his manner, that there was something up,' corroborated her husband. 'Do you miss anything?'

Mrs Peter hastily counted the array of gifts.

'I can only make it thirty-four, and I think it should be thirty-five,' she announced. 'I can't remember if thirty-five includes the Archdeacon's cruet-stand that hasn't arrived yet.'

'How on earth are we to know?' said Peter. 'The mean pig hasn't brought us a present, and I'm hanged if he shall carry one off.'

'Tomorrow, when he's having his bath,' said Mrs Peter excitedly, 'he's sure to leave his keys somewhere, and we can go through his portmanteau. It's the only thing to do.'

On the morrow an alert watch was kept by the conspirators behind half-closed doors, and when Wilfrid, clad in a gorgeous bathrobe, had made his way to the bath-room, there was a swift and furtive rush by two excited individuals towards the principal guest-chamber. Mrs Peter kept guard outside, while her husband first made a hurried and successful search for the keys, and then plunged at the portmanteau with the air of a disagreeably conscientious

336

Customs official. The quest was a brief one; a silver cream jug lay embedded in the folds of some zephyr shirts.

'The cunning brute,' said Mrs Peter; 'he took a cream jug because there were so many; he thought one wouldn't be missed. Quick, fly down with it and put it back among the others.'

Wilfrid was late in coming down to breakfast, and his manner showed plainly that something was amiss.

'It's an unpleasant thing to have to say,' he blurted out presently, 'but I'm afraid you must have a thief among your servants. Something's been taken out of my portmanteau. It was a little present from my mother and myself for your silver wedding. I should have given it to you last night after dinner, only it happened to be a cream jug, and you seemed annoyed at having so many duplicates, so I felt rather awkward about giving you another. I thought I'd get it changed for something else, and now it's gone.'

'Did you say it was from your *mother* and yourself?' asked Mr and Mrs Peter almost in unison. The Snatcher had been an orphan these many years.

'Yes, my mother's at Cairo just now, and she wrote to me at Dresden to try and get you something quaint and pretty in the old silver line, and I pitched on this cream jug.'

Both the Pigeoncotes had turned deadly pale. The mention of Dresden had thrown a sudden light on the situation. It was Wilfrid the Attaché, a very superior young man, who rarely came within their social horizon, whom they had been entertaining unawares in the supposed character of Wilfrid the Snatcher. Lady Ernestine Pigeoncote, his mother, moved in circles which were entirely beyond their compass or ambitions, and the son

337

would probably one day be an Ambassador. And they had rifled and despoiled his portmanteau! Husband and wife looked blankly and desperately at one another. It was Mrs Peter who arrived first at an inspiration.

'How dreadful to think there are thieves in the house! We keep the drawing-room locked up at night, of course, but anything might be carried off while we are at breakfast.'

She rose and went out hurriedly, as though to assure herself that the drawing-room was not being stripped of its silverware, and returned a moment later, bearing a cream jug in her hands.

'There are eight cream jugs now, instead of seven,' she cried; 'this one wasn't there before. What a curious trick of memory, Mr Wilfrid! You must have slipped downstairs with it last night and put it there before we locked up, and forgotten all about having done it in the morning.'

'One's mind often plays one little tricks like that,' said Mr Peter, with desperate heartiness. 'Only the other day I went into the town to pay a bill, and went in again next day, having clean forgotten that I'd –'

'It is certainly the jug that I brought for you,' said Wilfrid, looking closely at it; 'it was in my portmanteau when I got my bathrobe out this morning, before going to my bath, and it was not there when I unlocked the portmanteau on my return. Some one had taken it while I was away from the room.'

The Pigeoncotes had turned paler than ever. Mrs Peter had a final inspiration.

'Get me my smelling-salts, dear,' she said to her husband; 'I think they're in the dressing-room.'

Peter dashed out of the room with glad relief; he had

lived so long during the last few minutes that a golden wedding seemed within measurable distance.

Mrs Peter turned to her guest with confidential coyness.

'A diplomat like you will know how to treat this as if it hadn't happened. Peter's little weakness; it runs in the family.'

'Good Lord! Do you mean to say he's a kleptomaniac, like Cousin Snatcher?'

'Oh, not exactly,' said Mrs Peter, anxious to whitewash her husband a little greyer than she was painting him. 'He would never touch anything he found lying about, but he can't resist making a raid on things that are locked up. The doctors have a special name for it. He must have pounced on your portmanteau the moment you went to your bath, and taken the first thing he came across. Of course, he had no motive for taking a cream jug; we've already got *seven*, as you know – not, of course, that we don't value the kind gift you and your mother – Hush, here's Peter coming.'

Mrs Peter broke off in some confusion, and tripped out to meet her husband in the hall.

'It's all right,' she whispered to him; 'I've explained everything. Don't say anything more about it.'

'Brave little woman,' said Peter, with a gasp of relief; 'I could never have done it.'

Diplomatic reticence does not necessarily extend to family affairs. Peter Pigeoncote was never able to understand why Mrs Consuelo van Bullyon, who stayed with them in the spring, always carried two very obvious jewel-cases with her to the bath-room, explaining them to any one she chanced to meet in the corridor as her manicure and face-massage set.

339

The Occasional Garden

'DON'T TALK TO me about town gardens,' said Elinor
Rapsley; 'which means, of course, that I want you to
listen to me for an hour or so while I talk about nothing
else. "What a nice-sized garden you've got," people said
to us when we first moved here. What I suppose they
meant to say was what a nice-sized site for a garden we'd
got. As a matter of fact, the size is all against it; it's too
large to be ignored altogether and treated as a yard, and
it's too small to keep giraffes in. You see, if we could keep
giraffes or reindeer or some other species of browsing
animal there we could explain the general absence of
vegetation by a reference to the fauna of the garden:
"You can't have wapiti *and* Darwin tulips, you know,
so we didn't put down any bulbs last year." As it is, we
haven't got the wapiti, and the Darwin tulips haven't sur-
vived the fact that most of the cats of the neighbourhood
hold a parliament in the centre of the tulip bed; that
rather forlorn-looking strip that we intended to be a border of alternating geranium and spiræa has been utilized
by the cat-parliament as a division lobby. Snap divisions
seem to have been rather frequent of late, far more frequent than the geranium blooms are likely to be. I
shouldn't object so much to ordinary cats, but I do complain of having a congress of vegetarian cats in my garden;
they must be vegetarians, my dear, because, whatever rav-
ages they may commit among the sweet-pea seedlings,
they never seem to touch the sparrows; there are always
just as many adult sparrows in the garden on Saturday as
there were on Monday, not to mention newly fledged
additions. There seems to have been an irreconcilable

difference of opinion between sparrows and Providence since the beginning of time as to whether a crocus looks best standing upright with its roots in the earth or in a recumbent posture with its stem neatly severed; the sparrows always have the last word in the matter, at least in our garden they do. I fancy that Providence must have originally intended to bring in an amending Act, or whatever it's called, providing either for a less destructive sparrow or a more indestructible crocus. The one consoling point about our garden is that it's not visible from the drawing-room or the smoking-room, so unless people are dining or lunching with us they can't spy out the nakedness of the land. That is why I am so furious with Gwenda Pottingdon, who has practically forced herself on me for lunch on Wednesday next; she heard me offer the Paulcote girl lunch if she was up shopping on that day, and, of course, she asked if she might come too. She is only coming to gloat over my bedraggled and flowerless borders and to sing the praises of her own detestably over-cultivated garden. I'm sick of being told that it's the envy of the neighbourhood; it's like everything else that belongs to her – her car, her dinner-parties, even her headaches, they are all superlative; no one else ever had anything like them. When her eldest child was confirmed it was such a sensational event, according to her account of it, that one almost expected questions to be asked about it in the House of Commons, and now she's coming on purpose to stare at my few miserable pansies and the gaps in my sweet-pea border, and to give me a glowing, full-length description of the rare and sumptuous blooms in her rose-garden.'

'My dear Elinor,' said the Baroness, 'you would save yourself all this heart-burning and a lot of gardener's bills, not to mention sparrow anxieties, simply by paying an annual subscription to the O.O.S.A.'

'Never heard of it,' said Elinor; 'what is it?'

'The Occasional-Oasis Supply Association,' said the Baroness; 'it exists to meet cases exactly like yours, cases of backyards that are of no practical use for gardening purposes, but are required to blossom into decorative scenic backgrounds at stated intervals, when a luncheon or dinner-party is contemplated. Supposing, for instance, you have people coming to lunch at one-thirty; you just ring up the Association at about ten o'clock the same morning, and say, "Lunch garden." That is all the trouble you have to take. By twelve forty-five your yard is carpeted with a strip of velvety turf, with a hedge of lilac or red may, or whatever happens to be in season, as a background, one or two cherry trees in blossom, and clumps of heavily flowered rhododendrons filling in the odd corners; in the foreground you have a blaze of carnations or Shirley poppies, or tiger lilies in full bloom. As soon as the lunch is over and your guests have departed the garden departs also, and all the cats in Christendom can sit in council in your yard without causing you a moment's anxiety. If you have a bishop or an antiquary or something of that sort coming to lunch you just mention the fact when you are ordering the garden, and you get an old-world pleasaunce, with clipped yew hedges and a sun-dial and hollyhocks, and perhaps a mulberry tree, and borders of sweet-williams and Canterbury bells, and an old-fashioned beehive or two tucked away in a corner. Those are the ordinary lines of supply that the Oasis Association undertakes, but by paying a few guineas a year extra you are entitled to its emergency E.O.N. service.'

'What on earth is an E.O.N. service?'

'It's just like a conventional signal to indicate special cases like the incursion of Gwenda Pottingdon. It means you've got some one coming to lunch or dinner whose garden is alleged to be "the envy of the neighbourhood".'

'Yes,' exclaimed Elinor, with some excitement, 'and what happens then?'

'Something that sounds like a miracle out of the Arabian Nights. Your backyard becomes voluptuous with pomegranate and almond trees, lemon groves, and hedges of flowering cactus, dazzling banks of azaleas, marble-basined fountains, in which chestnut-and-white pond-herons step daintily amid exotic water-lilies, while golden pheasants strut about on alabaster terraces. The whole effect rather suggests the idea that Providence and Norman Wilkinson have dropped mutual jealousies and collaborated to produce a background for an open-air Russian Ballet; in point of fact, it is merely the background to your luncheon party. If there is any kick left in Gwenda Pottingdon, or whoever your E.O.N. guest of the moment may be, just mention carelessly that your climbing putella is the only one in England, since the one at Chatsworth died last winter. There isn't such a thing as a climbing putella, but Gwenda Pottingdon and her kind don't usually know one flower from another without prompting.'

'Quick,' said Elinor, 'the address of the Association.'

Gwenda Pottingdon did not enjoy her lunch. It was a simple yet elegant meal, excellently cooked and daintily served, but the piquant sauce of her own conversation was notably lacking. She had prepared a long succession of eulogistic comments on the wonders of her town garden, with its unrivalled effects of horticultural magnificence, and, behold, her theme was shut in on every side by the luxuriant hedge of Siberian berberis that formed a glowing background to Elinor's bewildering fragment of fairyland. The pomegranate and lemon trees, the terraced fountain, where golden carp slithered and wriggled amid the roots of gorgeous-hued irises, the banked masses of exotic blooms, the pagoda-like enclosure, where Japanese sand-badgers disported themselves, all these contributed to take away Gwenda's appetite and moderate her desire to talk about gardening matters.

'I can't say I admire the climbing putella,' she observed shortly, 'and anyway it's not the only one of its kind in England; I happen to know of one in Hampshire. How gardening is going out of fashion. I suppose people haven't the time for it nowadays.'

Altogether it was quite one of Elinor's most successful luncheon parties.

It was distinctly an unforeseen catastrophe that Gwenda should have burst in on the household four days later at lunch-time and made her way unbidden into the dining-room.

'I thought I must tell you that my Elaine has had a water-colour sketch accepted by the Latent Talent Art Guild; it's to be exhibited at their summer exhibition at the Hackney Gallery. It will be the sensation of the moment in the art world – Hullo, what on earth has happened to your garden? It's not there!'

'Suffragettes,' said Elinor promptly; 'didn't you hear about it? They broke in and made hay of the whole thing in about ten minutes. I was so heartbroken at the havoc that I had the whole place cleared out; I shall have it laid out again on rather more elaborate lines.'

'That,' she said to the Baroness afterwards, 'is what I call having an emergency brain.'

THE SQUARE
EGG (1924)

The Square Egg

ASSUREDLY A BADGER is the animal that one most resembles in this trench warfare, that drab-coated creature of the twilight and darkness, digging, burrowing, listening; keeping itself as clean as possible under unfavourable circumstances, fighting tooth and nail on occasion for possession of a few yards of honeycombed earth.

What the badger thinks about life we shall never know, which is a pity, but cannot be helped; it is difficult enough to know what one thinks about, oneself, in the trenches. Parliament, taxes, social gatherings, economies, and expenditure, and all the thousand and one horrors of civilization seem immeasurably remote, and the war itself seems almost as distant and unreal. A couple of hundred yards away, separated from you by a stretch of dismal untidy-looking ground and some strips of rusty wire-entanglement, lies a vigilant, bullet-splitting enemy; lurking and watching in those opposing trenches are foemen who might stir the imagination of the most sluggish brain, descendants of the men who went to battle under Moltke, Blücher, Frederick the Great, and the Great Elector, Wallenstein, Maurice of Saxony, Barbarossa, Albert the Bear, Henry the Lion, Witekind the Saxon. They are matched against you there, man for man and gun for gun, in what is perhaps the most stupendous struggle that modern history has known, and yet one thinks remarkably little about them. It would not be advisable to forget for the fraction of a second that they are there, but one's mind does not dwell on their existence; one speculates little as to whether they are drinking warm soup and eating sausage, or going cold and hungry, whether they are well supplied with copies of the *Meggendorfer Blätter* and other light literature or bored with unutterable weariness.

Much more to be thought about than the enemy over yonder or the war all over Europe is the mud of the moment, the mud that at times engulfs you as cheese engulfs a cheesemite. In Zoological Gardens one has gazed at an elk or bison loitering at its pleasure more than knee-deep in a quagmire of greasy mud, and one has wondered what it would feel like to be soused and plastered, hour long, in such a muck-bath. One knows now. In narrow-dug support-trenches, when thaw and heavy rain have come suddenly atop of a frost, when everything is pitch-dark around you, and you can only stumble about and feel your way against streaming mud walls, when you have to go down on hands and knees in several inches of soup-like mud to creep into a dug-out, when you stand deep in mud, lean against mud, grasp mud-slimed objects with mud-caked fingers, wink mud away from your eyes, and shake it out of your ears, bite muddy biscuits with muddy teeth, then at least you are in a position to understand thoroughly what it feels like to wallow – on the other hand the bison's idea of pleasure becomes more and more incomprehensible.

When one is not thinking about mud one is probably thinking about *estaminets*. An *estaminet* is a haven that one finds in agreeable plenty in most of the surrounding townships and villages, flourishing still amid roofless and deserted houses, patched up where necessary in rough-and-ready fashion, and finding a new and profitable tide of customers from among the soldiers who have replaced the bulk of the civil population. An *estaminet* is a sort of compound between a wine-shop and a coffee-house, having a tiny bar in one corner, a few long tables and benches, a prominent cooking stove, generally a small grocery store tucked away in the back premises, and always two or three children running and bumping about at inconvenient angles to one's feet. It seems to be a fixed rule that *estaminet* children should be big enough to run about and small enough to get between one's legs. There must, by the way, be one considerable advantage in being a child in a war-zone village; no one can attempt to teach it tidiness. The wearisome maxim, 'A place for everything and everything in its proper place', can never be insisted on when a considerable part of the roof is lying in the backyard, when a bedstead from a neighbour's demolished bedroom is half buried in the beetroot pile, and the chickens are roosting in a derelict meat-safe because a shell has removed the top and sides and front of the chicken-house.

Perhaps there is nothing in the foregoing description to suggest that a village wine-shop, frequently a shell-nibbled building in a shell-gnawed street, is a paradise to dream about, but when one has lived in a dripping wilderness of unrelieved mud and sodden sandbags for any length of time one's mind dwells on the plain-furnished parlour with its hot coffee and *vin ordinaire* as some thing warm and snug and comforting in a wet and slushy world. To the soldier on his trench-to-billets migration the wine-shop is what the tavern rest-house is to the caravan nomad of the East. One comes and goes in a crowd of chance-foregathered men, noticed or unnoticed as one wishes; amid the khaki-clad, be-putteed throng of one's own kind one can be as unobtrusive as a green caterpillar on a green cabbage leaf; one can sit undisturbed, alone or with one's own friends, or if one wishes to be talkative and talked to one can readily find a place in a circle where men of divers variety of cap badges are exchanging experiences, real or improvised.

Besides the changing throng of mud-stained khaki there is a drifting leaven of local civilians, uniformed interpreters, and men in varying types of foreign military garb, from privates in the Regular Army to Heaven-knows-what in some intermediate corps that only an expert in such matters could put a name to, and, of course, here and there are representatives of that great army of adventurer purse-sappers, that carries on its operations uninterruptedly in time of peace or war alike, over the greater part of the earth's surface. You meet them in England and France, in Russia and Constantinople; probably they are to be met with also in Iceland, though on that point I have no direct evidence.

In the *estaminet* of the Fortunate Rabbit I found myself sitting next to an individual of indefinite age and nondescript uniform, who was obviously determined to make the borrowing of a match serve as a formal introduction and a banker's reference. He had the air of jaded jauntiness, the equipment of temporary amiability, the aspect of a foraging crow, taught by experience to be wary and prompted by necessity to be bold; he had the contemplative downward droop of nose and moustache and the furtive sidelong range of eye – he had all those things that are the ordinary outfit of the purse-sapper the world over.

'I am a victim of the war,' he exclaimed after a little preliminary conversation.

'One cannot make an omelette without breaking eggs,' I answered, with the appropriate callousness of a man who had seen some dozens of square miles of devastated country-side and roofless homes.

'Eggs!' he vociferated, 'but it is precisely of eggs that I am about to speak. Have you ever considered what is the great drawback in the excellent and most useful egg – the ordinary, everyday egg of commerce and cookery?'

'Its tendency to age rapidly is sometimes against it,' I hazarded; 'unlike the United States of North America, which grow more respectable and self-respecting the longer they last, an egg gains nothing by persistence; it resembles your Louis the Fifteenth, who declined in popular favour with every year he lived – unless the historians have entirely misrepresented his record.'

'No,' replied the Tavern Acquaintance seriously, 'it is not a question of age. It is the shape, the roundness. Consider how easily it rolls. On a table, a shelf, a shop counter, perhaps, one little push, and it may roll to the floor and be destroyed. What catastrophe for the poor, the frugal!'

I gave a sympathetic shudder at the idea; eggs here cost 6 sous apiece.

'Monsieur,' he continued, 'it is a subject I had often pondered and turned over in my mind, this economical malformation of the household egg. In our little village of Verchey-les-Torteaux, in the Department of the Tarn, my aunt has a small dairy and poultry farm, from which we drew a modest income. We were not poor, but there was always the necessity to labour, to contrive, to be sparing. One day I chanced to notice that one of my aunt's hens, a hen of the mop-headed Houdan breed, had laid an egg that was not altogether so round-shaped as the eggs of other hens; it could not be called square, but it had well-defined angles. I found out that this particular bird always laid eggs of this particular shape. The discovery gave a new stimulus to my ideas. If one collected all the hens that one could find with a tendency to lay a slightly angular egg and bred chickens only from those hens, and went on selecting and selecting, always choosing those that laid the squarest egg, at last, with patience and enterprise, one would produce a breed of fowls that laid only square eggs.'

'In the course of several hundred years one might arrive at such a result,' I said; 'it would more probably take several thousands.'

'With your cold Northern conservative slow-moving hens that might be the case,' said the Acquaintance impatiently and rather angrily; 'with our vivacious Southern poultry it is different. Listen. I searched, I experimented, I explored the poultry-yards of our neighbours, I ransacked the markets of the surrounding towns, wherever I found a hen laying an angular egg I bought her; I collected in time a vast concourse of fowls all sharing the same tendency; from their progeny I selected only those pullets whose eggs showed the most marked deviation from the normal roundness. I continued, I persevered. Monsieur, I produced a breed of hens that laid an egg which could not roll, however much you might push or jostle it. My experiment was more than a success; it was one of the romances of modern industry.'

Of that I had not the least doubt, but I did not say so.

'My eggs became known,' continued the *soi-disant* poultry-farmer; 'at first they were sought after as a novelty, something curious, bizarre. Then merchants and house-wives began to see that they were a utility, an improvement, an advantage over the ordinary kind. I was able to command a sale for my wares at a price considerably above market rates. I began to make money. I had a monopoly.

I refused to sell any of my "square-layers", and the eggs that went to market were carefully sterilized, so that no chickens should be hatched from them. I was in the way to become rich, comfortably rich. Then this war broke out, which has brought misery to so many. I was obliged to leave my hens and my customers and go to the Front. My aunt carried on the business as usual, sold the square eggs, the eggs that I had devised and created and perfected, and received the profits; can you imagine it, she refuses to send me one centime of the takings! She says that she looks after the hens, and pays for their corn, and sends the eggs to market, and that the money is hers. Legally, of course, it is mine; if I could afford to bring a process in the Courts I could recover all the money that the eggs have brought in since the war commenced, many thousands of francs. To bring a process would only need a small sum; I have a lawyer friend who would arrange matters cheaply for me. Unfortunately I have not sufficient funds in hand; I need still about eighty francs. In war-time, alas! it is difficult to borrow.'

I had always imagined that it was a habit that was especially indulged in during war-time, and said so.

'On a big scale, yes, but I am talking of a very small matter. It is easier to arrange a loan of millions than of a trifle of eighty or ninety francs.'

The would-be financier paused for a few tense moments. Then he recommenced in a more confidential strain.

'Some of you English soldiers, I have heard, are men with private means: is it not so? It is perhaps possible that among your comrades there might be some one willing to advance a small sum – you yourself, perhaps – it would be a secure and profitable investment, quickly repaid –'

'If I get a few days' leave I will go down to Verchey-les-Torteaux and inspect the square-egg hen-farm,' I said gravely, 'and question the local egg-merchants as to the position and prospects of the business.'

The Tavern Acquaintance gave an almost impercept-ible shrug to his shoulders, shifted in his seat, and began moodily to roll a cigarette. His interest in me had suddenly died out, but for the sake of appearances he was bound to make a perfunctory show of winding up the conversation he had so laboriously started.

'Ah, you will go to Verchey-les-Torteaux and make inquiries about our farm. And if you find that what I have told you about the square eggs is true, Monsieur, what then?'

'I shall marry your aunt.'